About the Author

John Dempsey lives in a dormitory town near Salford. He
doesn't enjoy very much.

I'm All Smiles

John Dempsey

I'm All Smiles

Olympia Publishers
London

www.olympiapublishers.com
OLYMPIA PAPERBACK EDITION

A CIP catalogue record for this title is
available from the British Library.

ISBN: 978-1-80074-629-9

First Published in 2023

Olympia Publishers
Tallis House
2 Tallis Street
London
EC4Y 0AB

Printed in Great Britain

Dedication

To those who dare to dream? Don't. It saves time.

THURSDAY

In the car adjacent, the giant tattooed infant glared at Brian with mad, porcine eyes. Brian returned the glare, quailed inwardly, and then pretended to retune the car radio. He had avoided nodding off in the traffic jam by trying to recall as many euphemisms for death as he could muster. He'd done well considering his low mood. He'd recollected the epigrams kiffed it, carked it, kicked the bucket, shuffled off this mortal coil, snuffed it, departed to the bliss eternal, cashed in one's chips and gone to the great hereafter. Whilst pondering the implication of an afterlife contained in the phrase, "Crossed over to the other side", the giant tattooed infant's eyes again affixed him. His hate-filled stare inferred that he desperately wanted to kill someone and Brian was closest to hand. In his turn, Brian was struck by the strange confluence of the speculative with the horribly immediate.

The giant tattooed infant momentarily swivelled his bulbous head back to the road and then resumed glaring at him. Brian had no clue why this creature exuded such hostility towards him but he wasn't in the least surprised. Britain and the people in it had been hateful for so long that he had forgotten what life had been like before The Great Mess. Following the near-collapse of the global financial system four years previously, he was convinced that Earth had suffered an alien invasion. The males of the human species had been supplanted by a race of bald grotesques, clad in loud training shoes and shirts worn with the tails out to conceal their enormous bellies. These creatures grew huger every day, gorging fast food and grazing on pornography relayed to their mobile phones. Male *Homo sapiens* seemed to be in hiding from their usurpers as these grotesque doppelgangers stalked the earth. Even policemen and postmen were now grunting, pop-eyed, coked-up hominids bereft of any of any common courtesy.

The giant tattooed infant bared his bleached fangs whilst aggressively gunning his engine. Brian shivered and slunk further into his seat, his muscles contracting in response to the cold. The heater in his aging saloon had failed months ago but, as with every other issue of major importance, he'd ignored it. He had been too wounded by his split with Helen to focus on practicalities. As spring elided into summer and the heater remained unfixed, he had speculated that the weather might not be too unkind until his finances improved, at which point he would have the heater repaired. As it transpired, neither the weather nor his finances had enjoyed even a glimmer of an upturn. Driving to work was an endurance test as the all-day darkness of winter had supplanted autumn. Today he was late for his last appointment, he was freezing and had only narrowly avoided being murdered. He was also flat broke. He had recently read that England was the best country in which to die. Every cloud et cetera.

The traffic began to inch along, there was a break in the seething rain, and the single functional windscreen wiper provided a clearer view of the road ahead. The creature from another world could now be safely ignored and there was also a carrier bag full of small change on the back seat of the car to be taken to the hypermarket. Previous experience of exchanging a cache of small denomination coins suggested that the carrier bag might contain as much as seventy quid. Having seventy quid on any Thursday evening would be a rare and welcome fillip. He also recalled that tomorrow would be the start of the weekend. The shambolic state of his car, murder at the hands of an extra-terrestrial and the parlous state of his finances could be misremembered for another forty-eight hours. Or forever, if things didn't work out satisfactorily tomorrow.

Even the most unobservant of people can usually spot a residential home accommodating the elderly and disabled. Such properties are almost invariably bungalows and accoutred with ramps, handrails and other gubbins at the front entrance. Substantial vehicles with roller bars containing complicated steel apparatus litter the driveways. The gardens are sometimes bedecked with juvenilia. Tubby garden gnomes and signs importuning "Santa to Please Stop Here" bedeck the front garden, even in the middle of June. Brian parked, trudged up the drive, eased past a tank-like SUV and rang the doorbell. It was usual to spend up to a minute waiting for an effusively apologetic care assistant who would splutter that she was, "Just seeing to so and so", or some other barely plausible alibi. He had never yet heard an apology from a care assistant that she was tardy in answering the door because she'd fallen asleep, but over the years this must have been the case. Not that he would have cared too much as long as the residents were safe and well. He himself had been a care assistant before undertaking training as a social worker and was sympathetic towards the eternally exhausted, underpaid drones who at the end of their working day returned home rank with the stench of human excreta.

'What time d'you call this? I thought you said you were coming at half past two?'

'Traffic, Pam. It's murder out there today.'

'Oh aye? Traffic? I'll give you bleedin' traffic. Idle sod you're nowt else.'

11

Brian had long been aware that Pam was someone who delighted in getting her retaliation in first, particularly if Brian himself was in her crosshairs. She displayed the contempt that all care assistants reserve for social workers, but Brian seemed to arouse in her an almost elemental ire. Pam and her team were lions whilst Brian and his ilk were preening donkeys, forever rescheduling appointments and issuing impractical diktats from brutalist local authority buildings. Today Pam was even tetchier than usual, which didn't bode well for her long-suffering though slavishly loyal colleagues. And if her opening remarks were any yardstick it didn't bode too well for Brian either.

Brian smiled warily into Pam's faux-designer spectacles and saw someone ready to capsize. The billowing bags under her eyes suggested that she hadn't slept for some thirty-eight hours. He wondered if when she was younger, she could have envisioned her seventh decade to be so devoid of solace. In the previous century she might have envisaged her autumn years to be at least tolerable and shared with someone she could abide, or even cherish. That this had not transpired was probably due to the decisions she'd taken when young and incautious. It seemed that only a select few are armed with the knowledge that it might all end in tears and take precautions to avoid the abyss. Brian himself had almost invariably taken the wrong turning when arriving at life's crossroads and was now suffering the consequences. The only surprise to him was how comfortless later life actually was. It certainly was for Pam.

'He's still not bloody well y'know.'

'That might be because he's terminally ill, Pam. What did the district nurse say? Is he going into hospital or what?'

'She said he's all right with us at the minute. But I told her. We're just bloody care assistants we are. We're not qualified bloody nurses are we? What if he teks really bad? We can't help him straight away if he gets into difficulties. And what do you want to drink? Tea? We've got tea on.'

'Here's what you do if there's a crisis. You ring nine nine nine. Then you wait until an ambulance turns up. If it turns up, and that's a big if, you hand over Arthur's notes to the paramedic. Then you ring his sister and tell her that Arthur's been admitted. Then wait a bit. And then ring Arthur's sister again.'

'Why? I don't want to be mithering his sister every two bleedin' minutes. She's got enough on her plate as it is.'

'Because she's his next of kin, not you. Well I don't think you are. So you ring his sister to find out how he's doing. Then you ring me. Can I have coffee instead?'

'You'll have tea and bloody like it.'

'Right-ho.'

'That snotty cow of a community nurse said just keep him comfortable till Monday. What does she mean by keep him comfortable? He's been more comfortable since he moved in here than he's ever been in his life, the cheeky twat.'

Brian prudently forbore from explaining that, "Keeping someone comfortable till Monday" was a clinical euphemism and loaded with terminal consequence. Arthur had already lived out his last Monday and Pam and her staff would be merely helpmeets in his final hours. This was not news he thought he should impart at this time. Pam seemed to have enough to contend with, not least an imminent buckling from exhaustion and a new tattoo that was scabbing over into something science fictional. It might be an alien life form implanted into the forearm of its unsuspecting host and growing stronger each day by feeding on the flesh of the minimum waged. It might gestate into a giant tattooed infant, yet another hairless psychotic

13

extraterrestrial terrifying users of the East Lancashire Road.

Brian studied Pam as she busied herself preparing the tea with a gusto usually reserved for an armed confrontation. Pam's volubility, particularly when presented with an opportunity to traduce a social worker, was failing her. This was both unusual and disturbing. Her motto repeated to inanition was: I say what I mean and I mean what I say. This roughly translated as: I'm incredibly rude, but just try and pull me up for it and I'll tear your bleedin' face off.

And this was no idle threat. Two years ago at her company's Christmas party she'd dismantled a new male member of staff who had foolishly sniggered at her singular attire. She was dressed in a Black Sabbath T-shirt circa 1979, a short skirt, high heels and fishnet stockings that gave her stout legs the appearance of two family-sized black puddings. This young man had made the category mistake of thinking that the obese were jolly, a misapprehension that cost him two teeth. He took a month's sick leave during which he penned an outraged letter of resignation and threatened litigation against his assailant. He was covertly counselled against taking action by his former colleagues who warned him of Pam's two sons. Both were enthusiastic psychopaths who would have no compunction in depositing his mutilated body in the Manchester Ship Canal. That was the end of the matter.

Pam's visible decline was a worrying inconvenience. Brian needed her to be fit enough to cope with the rigours of this coming weekend as she was the only member of staff in whom he felt truly confident. When Pam cared for anyone, they were cosseted as though the very survival of the human species depended upon it. He nodded his thanks, took the cup of scalding tea into the lounge, sat on the couch and desultorily flicked through the notes taken by the support staff since his last visit.

Arthur's bundle was unusually comprehensive, extending as far back as his thirteenth birthday. There were ancient communications from Arthur's general practitioner hammered out on a sturdy Remington typewriter. The family doctor had been emphatic in his view that a mentally subnormal adolescent would become even more burdensome as he made the transition to adulthood. In the best interests of his family, Arthur would be placed in a special hospital. In this therapeutic environment he would doubtlessly thrive, thus allowing his mother to concentrate her energies on her abler and less demanding offspring.

That was 1952. Arthur was finally discharged almost forty years later. In the intervening years his mother, father and four of his siblings passed away without his knowledge as, from the moment he was admitted to hospital, he had received no visitors. With a deference common to that period his parents immediately acceded to the doctor's injunction to sever all ties. The medic opined that Arthur's sense of abandonment would be only amplified by their occasional visits and, in view of Arthur's increasingly unmanageable behaviours, it was for the good of all concerned. It was inconceivable to Arthur's father that a directive from someone with a posh accent could be queried. Arthur was admitted to hospital and was never to be spoken of under his roof again.

Arthur remained behind the walls of the special hospital whilst rationing came to an end, a football team perished in the snows of Munich, a redneck from Tupelo, Mississippi became the bete noire of the Establishment, the Berlin Wall was constructed, four young Liverpudlians catalysed a social revolution, England won the World Cup, a young boxer from Kentucky became the most recognisable figure on the planet, a

British experiment in workers' democracy resulted in nationwide strikes, a South African lawyer was incarcerated on Robben Island, the Irish war raged on the British mainland and then a grocer's daughter from Grantham decided to inculcate the nation with her ideas of how things should be done. By any yardstick Arthur had been hospitalised for a very long time.

When he was fourteen, Arthur's teeth were removed. This suggested that he had been a biter whilst in hospital. Patients who used their teeth on others, particularly the hospital staff, were subjected to the peremptory removal of all of their dentition and usually without recourse to anaesthetic. Whilst reading Arthur's chequered history, Brian again reflected how horrific Arthur would have found the experience of being snatched away from everything familiar to him. How impossible he would have found it to adjust to his new circumstances, still less ventilate his terror. At the age of seventy-four his command of language still extended to only a few words.

The agony of separation from his family kindled an outrage that quickly translated into aggression. Brian could only imagine the brutal restraints Arthur had endured at the hands of hospital staff only too ready to subdue oppositional behaviours by force. In his notes there was no explanation for the pronounced limp Arthur disported upon his discharge, neither was there any evidence to suggest Arthur had experienced gait problems prior to his admission to hospital. Disturbing in the extreme. Brian reflected that if the walls of the institution in which Arthur spent forty years could talk, they'd probably scream.

Many years later, amidst the chaos of decanting people from special hospitals into community settings, an enterprising nurse decided to pursue the possibility of Arthur having relatives of whom no one was unaware. She figured that the tradition of women producing as many children as possible as insurance against a penurious old age rendered inconceivable the possibility of Arthur being an only child. Following his discharge from hospital into temporary accommodation, the tenacious nurse persisted with her investigations. It was still possible back then for people to live anonymously, undisturbed by the baleful omniscience of the Internet. Anonymity, particularly if one was immured behind the walls of a special hospital, was virtually guaranteed. After several years of fruitless toiling, the nurse finally located Dorothy, a lady of pensionable age who lived in an opulent bungalow in Cheshire with her retired husband. Meanwhile Arthur had been moved into his current residence along with two other aged and severely disabled residents. Pam was appointed as Arthur's key worker and Brian as his social worker. The nurse apprised Brian of her investigation into Arthur's family tree and the revelation of a surviving sister. Brian then telephoned Dorothy and informed her that she may need to prepare herself for a shock. Arthur was of course oblivious to the superhuman efforts the nurse had made on his behalf.

Brian acted as an intermediary at the introductory meeting of Dorothy and a brother she never knew she had. Arthur was impassive, glancing suspiciously at his sister whilst raising his beaker to request another cup of tea. Dorothy sat opposite and dabbed at the tears rolling down her veined nose. She too was silent except for occasional utterances such as, 'I can see me dad in him', or 'He's got a look of our Alan'. For his part Brian spent a great deal of the encounter smoking furiously in the garden, close to tears himself. Since that meeting on a chilly February morning, the redoubtable Dorothy and her pleasantly confused husband had made twice weekly visits to Arthur. He was treated to album after album of family photographs by which he was visibly unmoved. He was taken to North Wales for day trips. He made regular visits to Jodrell Bank to stare in puzzlement at the Lovell telescope. He was propelled into gastropubs in a gleaming power-assisted wheelchair purchased by his brother-in-law. The only restaurant Arthur had ever previously visited was the hospital canteen.

For the last five years of his life Arthur was no longer alone, vilified, assaulted and left to howl in an isolation room. Some people had discovered him, discovered they loved him, and devoted all of their free time introducing Arthur to both himself and the wider world. He was the child of a miner and a tannery worker and once shared a home with four older siblings. Dorothy, his younger sister, was born after he was admitted to hospital. He was the brother of a renowned professional rugby league player and a female songstress who became the owner of a string of nightclubs. In their own modest and understated way, all of Arthur's siblings had been successes and Dorothy was anxious that Arthur should understand this. He didn't of course. And by Monday he would be dead.

Pam wiped the drool from the chin of another resident, flicked her purple fringe in the direction of Arthur's bedroom and affixed Brian with a meaningful grimace. He sighed, rose from the couch, padded through the pool of weak sunlight suffusing the lounge carpet and entered the bedroom. The familiar but ineffable odour of a human hours from death seeped into every niche of the only private space Arthur had ever known. He slept deeply, his laboured breaths rattling noisily like marbles rolling in a shoebox. Pam whispered that he'd been sleeping for nineteen hours at a time. Brian nodded and mused that ceasing to exist was an exhausting business, a fact worth storing for future reference. Arthur's tissue-paper skin had curdled to a nauseous taupe and

18

striated with rivulets of broken veins. Although his swallowing reflex was still functional, Brian intuited that his refusal to take nourishment and fluids was the precursor to a busy weekend for everyone involved in his care. He gazed morosely at the unconscious septuagenarian whilst making a mental calculation of the paperwork required to close his case.

Pam held Arthur's hand, mewling incoherences whilst glancing through the window at the rear garden. She then lowered her gaze and swivelled her head around to transfix Brian with a gorgonic stare. Her eyes brimmed and her lips quivered. Brian remained impassive. Life had been incontestably cruel to Pam but a glimpse of the endgame, a dread peer into the abyss, had left her enervated by terror. She had no words to describe her desolation. Her fear was a testament to the fact that however much people are tired of life, the prospect of unbeing was unendurable. Senescence, decay, unconsciousness and then the void. The unfunny punchline to a cosmic joke that took decades in the telling.

Brian was surprised to find himself sympathetic towards someone who had regularly berated him in the most explicit terms, to the point that if she referred to him as a, "Useless streak of piss" he took it as a compliment. He hated to watch her buckling under the deadweight of misery but found it strange that people were never prepared for the intensity of emotions accompanying a death. There had been seventy-four years' notice of Arthur's departure but Brian knew that his end would be as flabbergasting as snow in the Sahara. Eyeing the tiny festive tree in Arthur's room he reflected that Christmas was meticulously prepared for each year by millions of people; but this once-in-a-lifetime event always seemed to blindside them.

'Right then. I'll be off. Ring me if anything happens over the weekend. I want to know what I'm walking into on Monday morning.'

'Will you be coming tomorrow or Saturday?'

'I can't come tomorrow. And you know I don't work weekends.'

'All right for some, innit? You can see yourself out you can. Idle pig you're nothing else.'

'Look Pam…'

'Before you start, I'm not leaving him.'

'Let's get you home so you can get some sleep. You can come back in when you're a bit fresher. I'm not even sure it's safe for you to carry on here.'

'If you don't want my toe up your useless arse get yourself through that front door.'

'If you're sure.'

'Course I'm bloody sure.'

'When the night staff come on get down on that settee for a bit.'

'Useless streak of piss you're nothin' else.'

An hour later Brian was wading through the detritus strewn across the hypermarket car park whilst cursing his stupidity at forgetting his umbrella. A knife-sharp wind spat volleys of hail into the faces of customers lingering outside the store. They stood in clutches of twos and threes, seemingly at a loss at what to do next. At least the hypermarket facade provided a lee from the wind sufficient for them to roll a fag before struggling through the freezing murk. A Santa Claus with the pared physique of a marathon runner stole a drag from a cigarette under his beard, gave Brian an amicable nod and muttered, Fuckin' cold, innit? Whilst desultorily ringing a bell with his left hand. Brian curtly returned the nod, entered the hypermarket and strode towards the

20

automated exchange machine, its flickering lights a salvatory beacon to the financially embarrassed.

If Brian needed any further confirmation of how low his stock had fallen, then tipping his collected spare change into the tray of the machine would probably suffice. He was, however, wearing a chain-store suit, thus controverting the usual assumption that he was a drug-addled benefits claimant completely on his uppers. He had learned that although clothes may not maketh the man they certainly colour people's perception of the man they contain. Breathless until the device computed a total of sixty-two quid, Brian stood as nonchalantly as his elation would allow as the payment slip was disgorged from the machine. He approached the service counter and offered the slip to one of the assistants with the sangfroid of a successful businessman collecting a donation for his favourite charity; the favourite charity in this instance being himself. He suspected that the assistant understood his real situation and was silently deriding his pretensions, but he couldn't have cared less. In a mere forty minutes he would have a drink in his hand and she would be just someone else to forget about.

Thank you and good day madam. I'm away to purchase foodstuffs and strong waters for the indigent and mentally unwell. Me, in other words.

Buoyed by the softness of six ten pound notes nestling in his trouser pocket, Brian practically sashayed across the car park. The downpour had declined to spots, the cumulus had broken and a sallow sun was taking its leave for the day. The rush hour of snake traffic was immobile but becoming thinner. He opened the driver's side door and heaved himself in. Brian never locked the car as he had rightly figured that no self-respecting gangbanger would be seen dead in such a jalopy.

A strident female voice on the car radio demanded that he focus his attention on Something Important. Brian's radio was constantly attuned to Radio Four, but in recent months he had found himself swearing at well-intentioned people demanding free contraceptives for Paralympians or the exposure of three year olds to the plays of Harold Pinter to aid cognitive development. These desperately sincere people seemed to use the word "need" a great deal without seeming to fully understand its darker meaning. The preceding four years of The Great Mess had brought into sharp relief exactly who was and who not was in need. Meanwhile the villains responsible for The Great Mess had thundered on, unhindered by either pricks of conscience or censure by the courts. The elites continued their hegemony of the public realm but life continued to be as unfair as ever for the frowned-upon and overlooked. It seemed that things could only get worse, particularly for Brian himself if the fates were unkind tomorrow.

On the radio an actress, whose speaking voice was almost certainly cultivated in a fee-paying school, trilled that she was, "Taking so many risks" in her role as a sexually promiscuous android in the latest CGI-fest. In her rarefied world dressing up and pretending to be someone else for a while was a hazardous occupation. Meanwhile, in this twilit and increasingly nasty country, people were running the risk of eviction if they were more than a day late with their rent. Brian turned off the irksome risk taker and listened to a scratchy CD of The Hot Club de France. Django's *esprit de jeu* always lightened even the bleakest of moods.

The car was almost dry of petrol. Brian drove into the petrol station around the corner from his home and replenished the tank with enough fuel to avoid another embarrassing breakdown on the way to work. One nightmarish Friday a fortnight ago, he was penniless and the needle on the petrol gauge was fixed at E as though it had been glued there. The car was also making intermittent coughing noises that in human beings prefigured serious illness; but, galvanised by the possibility of being paid that afternoon, Brian gambled on a shorter though potentially fraught route via the motorway. Predictably he gambled and lost, the engine being parched of both fuel and cooling water. He also lost a full day's pay as the problems with the car meant he was stranded on one of the nation's busiest motorways until two o'clock that afternoon. He also incurred the crippling cost of having his vehicle towed home, having mistakenly figured that being stranded on a motorway would be an occurrence so rare as to warrant the cancellation of his breakdown cover. He had grown used to being humiliated by lack of funds but having to implore his acidly sarcastic father to collect him from the hard shoulder and meet the cost of the car's removal was akin to walking the length of the motorway stark naked. The drive home with his father was a familiar but uncomfortable experience.

'Jesus, Brian. I don't how you do it, I'm not kidding you. How bleeding old are you?'

Brian knew better than to answer this enquiry as his father would tell him anyway.

'You're bloody fifty, you. Fifty. D'you hear me? You need a motor for work and you let your breakdown cover run out? Are you completely bloody daft?'

Aware that his father had already drawn his own conclusions regarding his intellectual powers, Brian remained silent and stared at the end-of-the world weather outside. He waited for his father's sermon upon how miserable his life would be when he and his mother were no longer around to protect him from his own idiocy, but on this occasion it was oddly unforthcoming. In less than a week, however, his father was presented with another opportunity to offer a bleak prognosis of Brian's future. And this time his powers of rhetoric didn't fail him.

A miscalculation of how much money he had in his current account led to Brian's aghast discovery that his debit card was about as useful in purchasing the petrol he'd sluiced into his fuel tank as Monopoly money. The granite-faced female counter staff were unmoved by his tirade against the larcenous bank, surreptitiously removing his remaining thirty quid as a penalty for exceeding his overdraft by eighty pence.

'Someone should go to jail for what these greedy bastards have done. They've lived high on the hog for years and then us taxpayers have had to bail them out. Bloody billions we've handed over to them and we still don't know if that's the end of it yet. This isn't petty theft this, you know. This isn't pinching a Mars bar from Woollies. This is bankrupting a country to line your own pockets. Where's the justice?'

'If you don't give us fifteen quid for that petrol, you're in dead lumber you are.'

The expressions of the counter assistants were impassive, but their body language suggested that they'd be quite happy to club Brian to death in full view of an elderly lady who had popped in for a packet of mints.

'Well I haven't got fifteen quid. I haven't got anything. What do I do?'

'Shift out of the bloody road for a minute while we serve this lady. And drive that skip on wheels over near the car wash. It's on CCTV. That'll stop you having any funny ideas.'

'Are you implying that I'd just drive off without paying?'

'I'm not implying nowt. I'm just telling you to shift it. That car's not going nowhere until we've had fifteen nicker out of you.'

Brian stood with hands in trouser pockets, vacillating between either remaining to remonstrate with the saleswomen or removing the car from its berth by the pump. The increasing queue of cars made the decision for him, but not before the elderly lady had shot him a glance so larded with contempt he practically shrivelled. Her gnomic remark stung Brian to the core.

'You in a suit and all. You're all the bloody same you lot. You crack on that you're summat special, but you've not got a pot to piss in or a window to throw it out of. My husband was a Desert Rat. He fought for the likes of you. I don't know why he fuckin' bothered.'

After relocating the car, Brian was left with no alternative other than to telephone his parents. When he enquired if his father was in possession of fifteen pounds the reply was characteristically terse.

'I should bloody hope so. Me and your mam would be buggered if we hadn't wun't we?'

Having determined his father's relative liquidity, Brian then posited the question that he knew would cost him more than the price of a dribble of petrol. He explained his plight and the reason for the loan. His father laughed with the glee of an executioner despatching a child murderer, exulting in his son's penury and humiliation. He guffawed into the phone whilst enumerating an extensive inventory of Brian's intellectual, financial and personal shortcomings. Brian envisioned his mother shaking her head in sorrow between drags on a cigarette.

'Oh bloody hell. You've done it again you, haven't you? Not a week goes by without you doing summat daft. Even your mother's saying you're a right dozy bugger. She's not wrong either, for a bloody change.'

'Well can I have it or not?'

'Walk round to our house. Be quick though. Your mam's programme's on in a bit. She won't want any mithering when that's on and I want my tea early. I've got a snooker match on tonight so bleedin' shift yourself.'

He entered the kitchen by the back door. His mother barely acknowledged him whilst savaging a piece of steak with a knife and eyeing the portable television shelved in one corner. The house was equipped with three televisions. There was a set in the lounge, one in the kitchen and a flat-screen device in the master bedroom, all of which were usually on at the same time. His mother had debated having one installed in the bathroom but had decided against it. That, she had opined, would be a bit common. His father was lounging on the couch glaring evilly at the television. The darts match was poised at three games to two. Upon seeing his hapless offspring he sighed, listlessly pulled two crushed ten pound notes from his pocket and laid them on the vacant space on the couch.

'I don't know how you manage to get from one bloody day to the next I don't. When me and your mam cark it you'll be buggered, I'm not kidding you. Who's going to help you out when we're gone? Our bloody Elaine won't. She wouldn't part with wind her, never mind owt else. She doesn't take after me and your mam you know.'

Whether due to fatigue or the stress induced by his latest brush with the forces of Mammon, Brian was flummoxed by his father's musings. What was he on about? Was he referring to Elaine's parsimony or her reluctance to pass wind? If she displayed any disinclination in that regard then she was definitely not her father's daughter. His father could teach flatulence as a first language to economic migrants. He picked up the repellently warm tenners from the couch and mumbled that he'd pay back the loan in full the following payday.

'Don't bleedin' bother. You'll only be asking for it again the day after.'

'Right-ho. Ta.'

'Have you had your tea yet?'

'I haven't been home yet. My car's still stuck in the petrol station. Why?'

'I'm on steak tonight. That means your mother's after summat.'

'Another telly?'

'Prob'ly.'

But that was then. Now, his petrol tank was a third full thanks to the largess of the automated change machine. Brian sauntered back to the car whistling a snatch from a Philip Glass string quartet. Quite why he had brought such funereal music to mind he had no clue, but then again there are limits to anyone's sanguinity. As he drove from the forecourt he noted that the car was listing slightly to the left due to a slow puncture on a rear tyre, but tonight that was of little consequence. If spent wisely, forty-five quid bought a lot of forgetting. He hardly noticed that it had begun to rain again as he pulled up outside his home.

He inserted a key into the lock of the scum-coloured front door. Desperate to escape another cannonade of rain he gave the key a savage twist and almost snapped it in the barrel. He withdrew the key gingerly from the lock and debated whether to try again and risk the possibility of being locked out of the house all night. Worse than that, having to walk the two hundred yards to his parents' house to beg shelter whilst enduring their usual derision. They would also conveniently overlook that being locked out of his own home was directly attributable to his father and his ham-fisted repair work.

Why? Why me? Why now? Why this fucking rain, this fucking lock, my fucking dad, his fucking toolbag, why?

The lock had been faulty for some weeks. Despite his son's protestations that he was happy to wait until it was repaired by someone competent, Derek Paget wouldn't hear of it. There was of course a degree of ulteriority behind Derek's insistence on fixing the device. It was a handy pretext to grant him another hour's respite from his wife, Jean, who, since her husband's retirement was constantly berating him for making the house look untidy. Derek had worked for thirty-eight years in a local factory manufacturing a range of alloys for the car industry. In the past Brian himself had also worked at the factory, albeit on shifts and in another department.

In common with many men of his generation, the factory and its extra-curricular activities had been at the centre of Derek's life. He was a member of the committee of the club affiliated to the factory and devoted most his leisure time to promoting its continuing success. He was the captain of the dominoes team, a member of the pigeon fanciers' club, the first reserve for the snooker team and the secretary of the crown green bowls team. This was Derek's idea of public service, but few parliamentarians displayed his zeal when lobbying for an improvement in the quality of the mild. One of Brian's few enduring childhood memories was of his father wolfing down an evening meal consisting of chips, fried eggs, baked beans or pork chops on paydays, having a quick swill and then stumbling out of the front door of their three-bedroomed council semi. His mother and sister, Elaine, would stare catatonically at the new colour

28

television whilst breaking off chunks from a chocolate bar and washing down the confectionery with Lucozade. Without taking her eyes from the television his mother would intone:

'I think that bloody club would shut if your dad didn't go there every night. The bloody brewery would shut and all. What would they do with all that ale if your dad didn't sup it?'

This would usually be the last thing she said before retiring to bed at ten o'clock sharp. Jean had been a cleaner at the municipal bus station, rising at four o'clock each morning before cycling to work for a five o'clock start. One of the few things she had in common with her husband was an appetite for regular but unstimulating labour with the promise of an occupational pension. She had applied herself for forty long years. Free health care courtesy of the National Health Service (Brian's mother was the grateful recipient of dentures at the age of nineteen), secure employment, cheap beer and inside lavatories were the stuff of dreams for those whom the thirties were a dark folk memory. A tough job is only for eight hours a day whereas poverty is for life.

Upon their retirement Brian's parents realised that they didn't really know one another very well and what little they did know was not to their taste. As a consequence each found creative outlets to pursue singly, whilst maintaining an uneasy detente. Brian's mother assiduously cultivated a periodic depression she referred to as "poorly nerves". This unpredictable mental disorder was a cue for Derek to make himself scarce all day until he could re-immerse himself in the comfort and familiarity of the working men's club. His wife palliated her poorly nerves by lying on the living room couch, fortifying herself with hot chocolate and chain-smoking furiously whilst flicking through television channels like the pages of a dull magazine. Derek regarded afternoon television as aesthetically offensive and a waste of

29

what precious time he had left on earth. And he was nothing if not a man of action.

Many retirees are bereft of an absorbing pastime at the very time of their lives they need it most. When younger they neglected to cultivate a hinterland of reading or playing the tuba, so retirement renders them not only economically inactive but deprived of any social utility. In their prime they endured physically draining days at the grind followed by weekends that scuttered by in a blur of beer, sport, visits to the bookies, colossal Sunday lunches and teatime television to aid post-prandial naps. Weekends were concluded with an early night on Sunday to briskly expedite the task of sexual intercourse before returning to the clamour and heat of the workplace. Following their retirement all this was consigned to the past. Days were long, leisure time was valueless and the continuing dramas of ordinary life were enacted without them. But Derek Paget was not a man to submit willingly to the isolation and enforced idleness endured by so many of his peers. His sense of injustice at being old, married and the father of two disappointing children ensured that he would rage against the dying of the light, and swearing horribly as he did so.

In the course of the last few years Derek had devised an itinerary taking in the betting shop, the local convenience store, at least one pub and a visit to a care home to console a former workmate who had developed Alzheimer's. His peregrinations across Least, the housing estate he had called home all his adult life, easily ran the clock down until late afternoon. Brian's return to Least in June following the collapse of his relationship with Helen was an unexpected boon. Derek had been presented with another scheduled stop on his itinerary. He insisted that Brian give him a spare key as being such a dozy bugger he would lock himself out more times than soft Mick. This was a fiat with which Brian reluctantly complied, and a decision that in time he would come to regard as a howling mistake.

On numberless occasions Brian had returned home from work with a bursting bladder, only to discover that ingress to the ground-floor bathroom was prevented by his father's occupancy. A muttered entreaty to, "Just use the bloody sink" rumbled from beyond the bathroom door, followed by a timorous enquiry if it was indeed Brian attempting to avail himself of the lavatory. Brian would affirm his identity whilst hosing down the previous evening's soiled crockery. He would then enquire if Derek was expecting anyone else. A local dignitary perhaps, or a member of Her Majesty's Constabulary. Or perhaps Nicole Kidman was in town, found herself indisposed and had dropped by to use the lavatory and to sample a mug of Derek's tea, a brew capable of inducing anaphylactic shock in the unwary. Derek's silence suggested that he was preoccupied by other matters. When in his own home Derek was known to take a raft of newspapers, a cup of tea and two rounds of jam on toast into the smallest room. He had long cleaved to the notion that a bathroom was multi-functional: a library, a restaurant and a space for silent contemplation. His wife thought he had either gone completely doolally or was building something in there.

Some weeks previously Brian had discovered that the front door lock was faulty and speculated that this would be a perfect opportunity to deny his father unwarranted access to his home. The old lock would be replaced by the landlord, thus rendering the key held by Derek redundant. When his father demanded to know why he was unable to let himself in Brian would casually report that the landlord had replaced the lock, thereby necessitating new keys. When his father demanded a new key

Brian would then stonewall the issue until it was no longer a subject for discussion. Or so he hoped. With a dread predictability his father thwarted him again.

Derek prosecuted home improvements with the artisanal skill of a nightclub doorman braining a drunk. It was a constant source of surprise to Mrs. Paget that she'd survived her husband's domestic projects without sustaining permanent physical injury. An incident with the hot water in the shower had induced a protracted bout of poorly nerves and the prescription of stronger antidepressants. When Brian suggested that she was merely attention seeking and being over-medicated by a quack, she hit him on the arm with the flat side of a hot iron. She was a martyr to myriad ailments but hypochondria was not one of them.

Dismissive of his wife's accusations that he was trying to murder her for the insurance money, Derek continued to perform periodic refurbishments in cheerful defiance of the local authority's protocols on such matters. No supporting wall or gable end was off limits on his watch. When Brian returned to the orbit of his parents, Derek had long ruminated upon how to improve his son's new domestic environment.

As he was congenitally incapable of keeping his own counsel at crucial moments, Brian had alerted his father to a possible DIY intervention by way of a question. Derek was in the bathroom devoting all of his divinatory powers to the racing page, whilst Brian revivified himself with a large vodka and orange juice. Suitably irrigated and feeling uncharacteristically raffish, Brian casually enquired if his father had encountered any difficulty in opening the front door. His father's silence prefigured the inevitable and Brian thrust his face in his hands. This was yet another of the innumerable occasions he had shot himself squarely in the foot.

The following morning whilst Brian was at work, his father had dismantled, removed and reinstated the lock. Of course the locksmith manque had imprinted the device with his usual hallmark of cack-handed incompetence, so from then on it was by luck alone that Brian was able to enter his own home. Breathlessly he again slowly slid the key into the barrel, praying for the reassuring confirmatory clicks. For once his supplications to a higher power were answered.

Bingo. Oh get in, you bastard. How come everything is going right today? This won't bloody last. It can't. It's against the natural order.

Brian carefully retrieved the key from the door, entered and dripped filthy rain onto the pile of flyers scattered across the laminate flooring. There was also a large number of white envelopes that doubtlessly contained more bad news. He added them to the burgeoning pile on the occasional table. The envelopes seemed to throb with menace, but for tonight at least rumination upon his dire financial health could be postponed. He would devote his time to the rather more pleasurable pursuit of getting drunk. There was also the possibility that tomorrow the bank might offer some respite from his immiseration, but if no relief was available then he'd already made provision for that eventuality.

He reflected that if he did elect to humanely destroy himself, his passing would not be universally mourned. Saddening perhaps, but no less true for all that. There was also some consolation to be derived from the ferocity of the suicide note he'd been mentally composing in advance of his possible self-destruction. In this valediction he excoriated his parents for his conception and subsequent condemnation to an existence devoid of meaning and consequence. Had they forbore from copulation then he wouldn't have been born at all, thereby saving him an awful lot of unnecessary anguish. He hoped that after his passing they would be convulsed by guilt for rest of their lives. It would be nice to get his own back for once.

He slung his briefcase onto the ancient settee, patted his overcoat to ensure he was equipped with keys and wallet, slammed the front door and headed towards the unkempt esplanade consisting of a single convenience store, several takeaways, two bookies and a charity outlet. This down-at-heel boulevard was referred to by locals as The Gaza Strip. The Strip also contained what was now the only pub in Least, The Long Pig. This daunting hostelry was a recent addition to the Strip, its purely functional decor redolent of a remand centre; and for very good reasons.

Numerous pubs had suffered unsustainable losses as a result of the twin evils of declining incomes and the smoking ban. Previously vibrant establishments were forced to close, thus leaving the field open for The Long Pig to absorb the custom of these now defunct hostelries. A children's charity had acquired the usage of The Bull and Dog and had converted it into a tea shop staffed by people with a learning disability. They exhorted the passing trade of The Gaza Strip to sample the wares within, but the residents of Least had always preferred something more bracing than a cuppa and a vanilla slice. The beleaguered hostess of The Long Pig who ministered to the social and pastoral needs of her expanded client base had long ago waved a sad but fond farewell to her sanity.

Over the decades, Least had earned and retained an unenviable reputation. The estate had produced more than a few hard men, lunatics, drug fiends, wife beaters, adulterers, petty thieves and career criminals. Incorrigibility seemed to be stitched into the genetic fabric of the males of Least. Admissions to secure mental hospitals, drug-related fatalities and suicides were regular and unremarkable occurrences. But curiously, the residents of Least resolutely refused to live anywhere else. A crude though tangible sense of community had been hewn from hedonism, hard times and a tacit recognition of their low social caste. Least had engendered an inexplicable pride in its inhabitants. Brian's father had declared it to be God's own country whereas Brian believed that all who were raised in Least, including himself, suffered a form of Stockholm Syndrome. Least was the devil you knew and it owned you. A psychiatric nurse of Brian's acquaintance once confided that if she ever became deranged, she would immediately relocate to Least. The stigma of mental illness would be avoided as she would be regarded as just someone else from Least, where everyone is mad. Brian found himself swelling with proprietorial pride. There was a point to Least after all.

The Long Pig was an addition to The Gaza Strip courtesy of a huckster from Manchattan. He was anxious to deflect attention from his more nefarious activities in the North-West's largest metropolis by investing in a legitimate business a few miles distant. The interior of this cavernous beer hall was furnished with skeletal chairs and laminated tables from which alcohol and bodily fluids were easily dispersed. A whiteboard displaying the names of those who had been barred for violence, drug dealing, sexual intercourse in the latrines or other socially opprobrious activities was within the eyeline of the bar staff, who were ever vigilant for the arrival of a current offender.

The penal code was largely complied with by The Pig's regular patrons. Condemnation to a temporary purdah was the favoured punitive measure and appeared to have the desired effect. The period of exile was supposedly consistent with the severity of the offence. Dealing class A narcotics was the most serious infraction, although this did not necessarily lead to a lifetime ban from the establishment. The loss of revenue sustained when a drug dealer and his enforcers took their custom elsewhere would hit any licensee squarely where it hurt, and after several weeks an agreement between the pub management and the dealer would usually be brokered. There was also an element of back-channel diplomacy involved in this negotiation, as the manageress was anxious to avoid the attentions of people with firearms. There were consequences to inflaming the ire of some of the residents of Least.

Brian never frequented The Long Pig after dark, preferring to call in at lunchtime when the regulars tended to invoke a less menacing ambience. The afternoon patrons were also older than the congeries of giant tattooed infants, yammering girls in T-shirts, sociopaths yelling threats into mobile phones and rancid melanalcoholics trying to importune a free drink. The afternoon drinkers were also more garrulous but still exuded the guardedness and cynicism characteristic of the average Least male. Some would occasionally welcome him into their conversations, but Brian was aware that he would always be an outsider. His office attire marked him as Other and therefore suspicious. Under usual circumstances, the only occasions upon which a Least male would ever wear a shirt and tie were either funerals or court hearings. Even a man from Least couldn't attend so many funerals and trials, therefore, it was safe to assume that Brian had a posh job. Men with posh jobs who frequented The Pig might have a hidden agenda and were therefore not to be trusted.

Brian slipped quietly into The Pig. The cluster of daytime

regulars was seated close to the plate glass entrance as though trying to absorb the remaining daylight. Jimmy the Bike held a tabloid newspaper up to the window behind him, whistling a tuneless catch as he studied the racing form. Jimmy was an organic machine emitting white noise, whistles, ruminative whines, gnomic utterances and catchphrases comprehensible only to Wesley, his son, housemate and factotum. Wesley punctuated his father's aural blizzards with an occasional monosyllabic mutter or a pensive nod. Jimmy's irruptions were a constant irritant to other customers, but it was strangely touching that his bletherings went unchecked by a snarl or physical assault. Following the untimely death of his wife Jimmy had unravelled, to the point of being eased into a regional mental health facility and then eased out of his job. Sympathy was scant in Least but Jimmy the Bike appeared to be a deserving case.

Wesley, a somnolent island of flab and cold sores, studied the back pages of the tabloids with the fervid piety of a biblical scholar. He added a new and disconcerting dimension to the term taciturn, but this was understandable given the girlish squeal he extruded from his vocal chords in lieu of normal speech. Brian liked him. Whenever he entered the bar Wesley would always catch Brian's eye and proffer a wink or a perfunctory wave. If Wesley came to the bar whilst he was buying a drink, Wesley would offer a whispered enquiry of how Brian was keeping. This betokened a gentlemanliness rare in Least.

In the eighties and nineties Brian had worked alongside many Wesleys. The Wesleys of this world were unburdened by a lively intellect or even a point of view. They were softly spoken, punctual and endued with an almost bovine dispassion. In the days when England made things to sell, Wesley would have been referred to by his factory workmates as a steady lad. Although a mere cipher when compared to the more mercurial characters on the shop floor, Wesley would be the go-to man if someone needed to borrow a few bob, a spare cigarette, or a pornographic magazine for a visit to the lavatory. But as obliging as lads like Wesley were, one learned little about their lives away from the factory. They were hermetically sealed. On occasions, someone would come into work and reveal that they'd spotted Wesley in a town centre pub with a female. Cruel jokes and speculations would fly around the locker room like angry gnats, but Wesley would remain impervious to his workmate's salacious curiosity.

In their dogged, unobtrusive way, Wesley and his lady friend would scratch up the deposit for a terraced house, marry, and sire a couple of children. The direction of their lives would be in a slow but upwards trajectory. Their weeknights would be spent in front of the television and their weekends spent in garden centres. Unremarkable people, beavering away in unglamorous professions in the hope that regular work would bring its own reward and even a caravan at Rhyl. But now, in a post-industrial meritocracy in which a master's degree is required for a job as a barista, Wesley and young men like him would never know a tough but honest week on the assembly line, a reasonable wage, a sense of purpose and a new fitted kitchen. Wesley would probably continue to live with his father, continue to be a statistic on the unemployment register and continue to grasp the odd shift in the black economy in between visits to the bookie. In a life as transient as that of a tinker, Wesley's only certainties were death, the dole and *Strictly Come Dancing*. And he wasn't even twenty-five.

On occasions Brian had sat in The Pig and studied Wesley as intently as Wesley himself studied the sports pages. He concluded that with the demise of the Wesleys of this world something had been lost to Britain. If this nation had ever possessed a soul then young men like Wesley were it. The quiescent and uncomplaining who require little from life and now not granted even that much. These days everyone needed a status of some description. A pointless job title, a Facebook following, a Linkedin profile, regular posts on Twitter, a smartphone and a lot going on. What about the undynamic, the non-movers and no-shakers, those happy to be on the periphery? Brian's eyes had been pricked by mawkish tears and he hurried to the ghastly pub lavatory to hide his embarrassment. He grieved for the loss of a native species once populous but now lost to antiquity. The unremarkable steady lad. Wesley deserved more than this. In fact, he deserved a cenotaph and a documentary on national television.

Spex was even drunker than usual, suggesting that he'd either had a winner at the bookies or sold some of his medication. Spex was short, compact, belligerent and vociferous. From observations conducted at a judicious distance, Brian had concluded that there was a correlation between the volume of alcohol Spex had consumed and the depth of his contempt for the political classes, the middle classes, the upper classes, the royal family, anyone foreign, Channel 5, popular music, cat lovers, baseball caps, young men, women of any age and the nation's addiction to communications technology. Some years previously, a brouhaha in Spex's personal life had induced a temporary mental disintegration. Whilst almost fully recovered Spex had yet to completely regain the volatility that made him kryptonite to the world at large; but despite his relative equanimity, the people around him knew not to poke a sleeping snake.

In common with many men over forty Spex had spent many hours in the kitchen, idly browsing an array of pornographic websites whilst his wife stared catatonically at the television in the living room. He happened upon a snippet of footage depicting his wife of fifteen years gorging on several male pudenda in a car park and seeming to enjoy the gustatory experience. In a move perhaps prejudicial to his best interests he reviewed the footage again. Having satisfied himself that it was indeed the woman in the room adjacent, his ire was amplified to an uncontrollable magnitude. He was bloated by the toxins of outrage, nausea, cuckoldry and untameable aggression.

He leapt from the kitchen chair and charged into the living room. The Jezebel he had so foolishly married was sprawled on the couch, cutting her scarlet toenails whilst gazing vacantly at a quiz programme. Spex grabbed the first thing that entered his line of vision. Unaware of her husband's intentions, his wife had no time to react as Spex hit her squarely in the face with Simba, the Jack Russell terrier dozing by the skirting board. Two premolars were immediately dislodged and her nose was splintered as Spex cudgelled her with the howling, drool-flecked cur. An observer of this cameo of domestic horror would have been torn in deciding who was in greatest pain and anguish, but perhaps the smart money might have been on the dog. Roars, screams, yowls, appallingly crude epithets and the uniquely sickening sound of canine flesh contusing human flesh shredded the air. Neighbours banged indignantly on the wall, not from humane concern but because of a plot twist in the television serial they were viewing. The dialogue was inaudible over the clamour issuing from next door.

The carnage was over in less than a minute. Breathing heavily, Spex surveyed the aftermath of his blitzkrieg. He collected himself, stared around the previously neat living room and was then suffused with a remorse endured only by the truly penitent. His beloved Simba was wild-eyed, drooling and scratching at the skirting board as though trying to burrow her way out of this house of horrors. Excruciated by regret, Spex bent low and timorously offered a consoling hand to the dog whilst cooing conciliatory noises. Simba howled in dread anticipation of further violence and drooled even more. Spex stood and appraised the stricken animal. He deduced that the only creature in the world that had ever really loved him was now completely radio rental and of no further useful purpose. Her rabbiting days were over.

Spex gathered Simba in his arms and strode past the couch upon which his stuporous wife lay bleeding. He strode into the garden, laid Simba gently on the lawn, extracted a hefty shovel from the shed and euthanized the dog with two smart blows. He then removed his spectacles and sank to his knees, in thrall to the agonies of bereavement. Of all of the travails in his fifty-one years, the task of despatching Simba to the hereafter was the least endurable. He would have to reach deep within himself to accept the rightness of his decision and hope that Simba wouldn't judge him too harshly in the canine afterlife. He then replaced his spectacles, wiped his brow and returned to the house to address less distressing matters. He rang the police and requested to be put through to the local duty desk.

'Is that the dibble?'

'This is the police, yes. Can I take your name please?'

'Trevor.'

'Okay, Trevor, that's fine. And do you have a second name?'

'I've just give my missus a good hiding because the cheeky cunt was having it off with loads of blokes behind my back.'

There was a brief pause before the urbane officer responded to Trevor's staccato disclosure.

'Okay Trevor, that's fine. And where is your wife now?'

41

'She's in the front room. Where d'you think she'd be? There's not many people who could fuck off after a good hiding is there? I thought you'd know that, being a dibble and that. Are you sure you're a dibble? I want to talk to the organ grinder not his bastard monkey.'

'Okay, Trevor, that's fine.'

'I've had to kill our dog as well. She's gone off on one so I've put her out of her misery. Best thing for her really. She'd be fuck all use for going rabbiting any more. I'll have to sell my air rifles as well. They're fuck all use now.'

'Okay, Trevor, that's fine. Am I given to believe that you're in possession of firearms?'

'Not really, no. They're just air rifles, not proper guns like. For shooting rats and rabbits. Or ducks if there's any knocking about. Mind you. If I shot YOU with one it'd put your fuckin' eye out. They're not toys, are they?'

'Okay, Trevor, that's fine. Now, Trevor, are you able to give me your current location?'

'Eh?'

'Can you tell me where you are?'

'Our house. Where do you think I'd be? I'm not in a fuckin' phone box if that's what you're thinking. You don't see phone boxes any more do you? I don't know what they did with 'em. Probably in a warehouse or summat.'

'Okay, Trevor, that's fine. Now can you tell me if you're on any medication of any description?'

'I've got summat for athlete's foot. Does that count? And why're YOU bothered?'

Spex stood by the phone in befuddlement as the silence on the line extended beyond two minutes. He was about to replace the receiver and make a cheese and piccalilli sandwich when the

42

honeyed tones of the police officer insinuated themselves once more into the receiver.

'Okay, Trevor, that's fine. Now in your own time Trevor. Could you please give me your exact address?'

'I live in Least, me.'

'Least? Oh Jesus Christ. Don't you move a fucking muscle you, you barmy fucker.'

A commendably short response time saw a fleet of police cars, two ambulances and ancillary support staff jamming the cul-de-sac in which Spex and his wife resided. Two muscular German shepherd dogs strained at leashes gripped by their equally muscular handlers. A psychiatrist and a social worker knocked timorously at the front door of Spex's property whilst police marksmen stole into the back garden via the next door neighbour's kitchen. The episode of the programme they had been watching had ended by the time the police had arrived, so they were not unduly inconvenienced by the arrival of a team of trained assassins. The marksmen politely declined the offer of a glass of lemon barley water or pale ale if they preferred.

As with all operations of this stripe, many of the emergency response team needn't have been there. On hearing the knock at the door, Spex opened it, peered into the evening darkness, noted the son et lumière of the assembled vehicles and invited the mental health specialists in whilst enjoining them to wipe their feet on the mat. The police marksmen were already in the kitchen and, heedless of the social worker's protests against unnecessary force, swiftly incapacitated the hapless Spex. In less than thirty seconds the entire operation was over. Spex was on his way to a custody suite whilst his wife was heading to hospital. It was piquant to note that not a single resident of the cul-de-sac had ventured outside to witness these dramatic events. This was Least after all.

Following exhaustive investigations, assessments, reports and testimonies, the trial judge concluded that in this instance a custodial sentence would be inappropriate. Having heard the evidence of a psychiatrist, the judge recommended that Spex be referred to a medium secure mental health facility to receive therapeutic interventions. The ferocity of the assault upon his wife alone would have guaranteed a prison term. If this was an indicator of his potential for violence when in fugue then he posed a significant risk to both himself and the public. The judge also observed that the defendant had displayed not a scintilla of insight or remorse into the nature and gravity of his crime. In view of his wife's serial infidelities, Spex regarded his appalling assault as completely justifiable. He was indeed a suitable case for treatment.

Spex didn't protest, figuring that anything was better than sharing a cell with a fucking shirt-lifter. Homosexuals were to Spex as rats were to Winston Smith. In hindsight, the court's decision to commute the sentence may have averted the murder of any prisoner harbouring carnal intentions towards the newly detained. Spex was admitted to a facility in greenbelt land some twenty miles from his home and remained there for a considerable period. Being far from unintelligent, upon his arrival at the hospital Spex immediately began devising strategies to secure his future when he was discharged from this sinkhole of nutters, kiddie fiddlers and druggies.

Finagling a discharge from a secure mental health facility is merely a war of attrition, and one in which Spex was happy to engage. He became a model patient, figuring correctly that all detainees were under constant surveillance. Even a glimmer of anomalous behaviour would be subject to endless and usually inaccurate analysis. Spex performed the role of the sufferer of a psychotic episode with the elan of a National Theatre veteran. He swallowed medication with alacrity, he was the epitome of civility when dealing with clinical staff, expressed tearful remorse for the harm inflicted upon both his wife and cur and was the first to volunteer for any therapeutic activities. On occasions he had also been an informal conduit to the nurses, discreetly apprising them of the to-doings of his fellow patients when staff supervision was relaxed. A grass, in other words.

Some years later, a tribunal was presented with an unblemished history of his period in hospital and had no other recourse than to recommend a conditional discharge with community support. Apart from anything else, beds in secure accommodation are expensive and Spex was just taking up room. In anticipation of his discharge an obliging social worker had secured Spex a single person's flat in Least, organised a range of welfare benefits and also access to a day centre. In the day centre he could commune with fellow survivors of a mental disorder in a non-judgemental environment, together with free usage of a pool table and tea retailing for only twenty pence per cup. Spex was having none of that. He had other, more pressing matters to attend to.

Prior to his admission to hospital, Spex had never patronised The Long Pig, opining that its habitues were nothing less than the dregs of a terminally decadent society. Neither had he any previous experience of narcotics, but upon his return to the wider world he figured that his pharmacopeia of antidepressants and sedatives would find plenty of takers. He resolved to test the marketplace, aware that The Long Pig was a magnet for junk lovers of every persuasion. Spex was also aware that The Pig also served as an ad hoc recruitment agency for the black economy.

As an experienced electrician and competent plumber he was confident he could secure a great many off-the-books contracts, particularly if he made it known that he was happy to install a shower for half the price of a legitimate craftsman. He was newly single, in receipt of welfare benefits and ready to rejoin the world of work. Some small revenge would be visited upon them fuckin' cheeky Polack bastards who were hoovering up all the tradesmen's contracts in the area. He was also expecting a windfall from the sale of the former family home, his erstwhile spouse having moved to Scotland with a white reggae musician called Jah Smellie. Frequenting The Long Pig was an unedifying prospect but he had steeled himself to do so. He had always considered benefits claimants to be bone-idle fuckers and he wasn't about to join their number at this particular juncture. Emoluments from the state were merely a bulwark against brief periods of unemployment. Not that he expected any.

The social worker and community psychiatric nurse visited sporadically in the months following his discharge. They were anxious to ensure that he avoided social isolation as this was a proven trigger in the recurrence of psychoses. Spex averred that he was compliant with medication, he accessed the community every day, he self-cared with competence and his household bills were promptly paid. He forbore from mentioning that he oscillated between the bookies and The Long Pig most days and had already sold a range of medication to schoolchildren who dawdled by the convenience store adjacent to the pub. Spex had deduced that disclosure of such news could disadvantage him and was, therefore, circumspect about his private enterprises. His subterfuge worked perfectly. Within four months both the nurse and social worker had withdrawn their support and offered an array of telephone numbers in case of any difficulties in the future. Spex was confident that he would have no further need of their valuable services and declared that he'd never felt better. Six months after their final visit he was slouched in The Long Pig brandishing a middle-market tabloid and glowering at Brian.

Ever the rhetorician, Spex enquired if Brian was happy to watch his country going down the shitter. Brian was reluctant to respond as even thinking about it made him tired. Like everyone else he was enervated by the carnage wreaked by The Great Mess, but like everyone else he had no grand prescriptions for depolluting the public realm of feral financial institutions, preening plutocrats and right-wing lunatics. All major political parties seemed to embrace the same simplistic and punitive thinking. The deficit must come down and the poor, the young and the sick must bear the brunt for the damage inflicted by financial gluttons. The only certainty was that after this crisis something worse was bound to happen. Brian had no idea what it would be or when it would occur, but given the downward trajectory of the new century then more bad news was only around the next corner. He sighed and summoned the least provocative response he could muster.

'I know what you mean, but what can we do? No one cares. Certainly not the greedy bastards who nearly killed off the world's economy. They knew what they were doing. They were making a packet knowing full well that it'd all go tits up. They've fucked us, but all we do is shut our gobs. That's so British, that. We kiss the arse of people beating the shit out of us but kick one of our own when he's down. We're beating up lads with Down's syndrome. We're pushing people in wheelchairs in front of traffic. Why? Because the bastards in power say they're shirkers and we're dozy enough to believe them. But we won't string up the bastards who took us to the brink will we? It stinks and it's

47

going to get worse.'

Although nonplussed by Brian's peroration, to everyone's relief Spex was animated but pacific. The anticipated explosion of rage from the fissile element in soiled jeans and overly large spectacles was unforthcoming. Spex nodded emphatically and raised his thumbs in woozy approbation.

'Too fuckin' right pal. We can't even be arsed to be fuckin' arsed, can we? It's too much bastard effort. Innit? Innit? Fuckin' bastards. You know what me and you's trouble is pal?'

'What?'

'We know how this'll turn out. It's going to be the biggest pile of shite you've ever seen. I'd kill myself if I had any sense, me. Austerity? Fuck off. We're fucked no matter which way you look at it.'

'The suicide rate for young males is going through the roof. There's a reason for that.'

'I'll bet there fuckin' is.'

Jimmy the Bike grunted, moued his lips, slapped his cheek to produce a whop-whop sound and then whistled a couple bars of 'Somewhere' from *West Side Story*. Wesley scratched his crotch as his eyes strayed towards the sports news channel on the television. Spex rose to leave but not before he bought a drink for Harry, a silent, ossified octogenarian who in all weathers tottered every day to The Long Pig to take two pints and a whisky before returning to his sheltered accommodation. In the loud voice young people reserve for anyone over forty, Spex enquired whether Harry would like a pint. The old man slowly nodded his lizardic head, the nubs of his cheekbones pressing for release from his leathery face. Brian noted that Harry was always meticulously dressed, a habit he had probably cultivated in the armed forces. He never divested himself of his cap and coat, remaining fully swathed as though expecting a mayday call to which he must immediately respond.

Brian intuited that the remaining years of Harry's life were now very few. He was dying a very public death but somehow still managing to be in the world, wearing the mask of pained remoteness characteristic of men of his age. If people of Brian's generation were bewildered by the new century then Harry must wake up every morning wondering if he was in a different universe. Brian recalled that his grandfather wore the same expression for a number of months before finally succumbing to unbeing. His gurn of querulous puzzlement suggested that he had something distasteful in his mouth that was impossible to spit out. Like Harry he was generally silent and impassive, but in a rare instance of familial intimacy he once grabbed Brian by the arm, stared hard at him and whispered:

'I'm bastard tired all the time, Brian. But when I get to bed I can't sleep. And I don't like it here any more. I'm fed up. What's wrong with me? What should I do?'

Gifted with a literal-mindedness that ensured he always overlooked the wood for the trees, Brian recommended his grandfather make an appointment with his doctor to discuss this chronic lethargy. A course of sedatives would aid restful sleep and perhaps alleviate the low mood by which he seemed afflicted. Of course his grandfather wasn't referring to his disturbed sleep patterns and misery, he was simply looking for someone to endorse the taking of his own life. He had avoided making an enemy of Brian in spite of the enmity he had fostered among the rest of his family. Any counsel he received from his grandson would be heeded. In the event Brian's utterly useless advice was irrelevant. His grandfather went to bed promptly following a tea-time visit from his home help and simply forgot to wake up.

Whilst studying Harry, Brian recalled the satisfaction he had derived from the denouement to his grandfather's life. He was the epitome of parsimony, tyranny and detestable in almost every aspect, but at the last he had managed to avoid the presumed deserts for a lifetime of cruelty to his unfortunate family. The absence of pain and humiliation in his passing seemed to be a riposte to karma. Brian's mother was less charitably disposed towards her father and was incensed that had he escaped a painful end. She declared that if anyone deserved a rotten death then it was that miserable old bleeder. But Brian had long suspected that good things no more happen to good people than bad things happen to bad people. Things just happen and destiny is morally neutral. One may as well lead a dissolute but pleasurable life as one virtuous but undistinguished, as in the end it all wrote up the same. Dead is dead. It had begun to rain again and Brian wondered when Harry's taxi would arrive. He could catch his death in this weather.

The pub was in almost total darkness when Spex nodded curt adieus to Jimmy, Wes and Harry before charging through the exit door. The spectral glow of the television flickered on the stippled ceiling and the pool table was bathed in a rectangle of muted light. A wiry young man dressed as Father Christmas played alone, viciously smashing balls across the baize with an unlit cigarette dangling from his mouth. Other than the crackpot ramblings of the television presenter, all was silence. Brian peered at the garishly lit hardware store across the road, its facade garlanded with Christmas lights imported from countries victimised by globalisation. Nativity scenes in which the fauna resembled angry bears were pointed at by toddlers strapped in sodden baby buggies. Their scantily clad mothers swore, gossiped and stabbed at mobile phones with skeletal forefingers.

The sussurus of cars driving though kerbside puddles chivvied the dawdlers to go home. Brian remembered that he'd forgotten his umbrella again, but as his luck was holding today perhaps he might avoid being soaked on the way home. Or he might not. Destiny is morally neutral.

The early evening seemed like three o'clock in the morning. He shivered like a wind chime in a gale as he hurried towards the convenience store. The cloying air of the store was punctured by the monotone voice of a female sales assistant extolling the virtues of breads and pastries approaching their sell-by date.

'Tonight, why not treat the special one in your life to a couple of our delicious steak pies, washed down with a bottle of our new selection of dry white or full-bodied red wines from Chile. Whooh, I bet it's warmer there than it is here. Also, liquorice allsorts are on offer for this week only... Darren, what you playin' at? Will you stop fuckin' mitherin' me while I'm talkin'? I'm on the fuckin' mic here. Are you mad or what?'

Brian drifted aimlessly through the aisles, befogged by the beers and vodkas he'd consumed. A globular infant excruciated by the arrival of new teeth declaimed his agony in an ear-splitting caterwaul. His mother deftly filched jars of coffee and sanitary products, secreting them inside a voluminous zebra-striped onesie whilst exhorting her progeny to, 'Bleedin' shut it, Kyle, I've had enough now.' Two heroin addicts with lank hair and kamikaze eyes stood motionless in the tinned goods aisle gazing at one another in desolation. The few coins held in the hand of the toothless male were clearly inadequate for the weekly shop. An ancient Eurovision hit screeched from the store's loudspeakers whilst a redoubtable female store assistant, Amazonian in pink leggings and unseasonal fake tan, swore horribly at schoolchildren she suspected of thievery.

51

'Bugger off out of it you lot or I'll be telling your bleedin' mams on you.'

Brian studied the nutritional contents of a low-fat vegetarian lasagne as though they were the companion notes to 'The Waste Land'. He had been uncomfortably aware of his expanding waistline for a number of months now and post-Helen he'd rediscovered his appetite for flesh. His clothes were tighter and catching sight of himself naked was as mildly shocking as a jolt from a battery. Physically he was beginning to resemble a beige beanbag. A novelist had once observed that forty was the age when mirrors begin to lie, duping viewers of their own image into believing that they are less decrepit than they really are. Brian had never made any claims to comeliness, but these days he would be content merely to be recognised as a member of his own species. He resolved to ignore the Indian set meal for two he inwardly craved. Small steps in the right direction were better than none at all, or at least that was the received wisdom. Harm reduction is the key to a better life. Laden with pitta bread, hummus, a low-fat vegetarian lasagne and the cheapest bottle of wine available, he trudged towards the tills.

Kelly-Leanne sported a button badge emblazoned with the phrase, "Here to Help!" but for the queue of tutting, cursing customers who snaked from her till she was doing anything but. She had commenced employment at the store that very morning and it had become quickly apparent that till operation was not her field of expertise. She had also learned that the customers were as surly and uncivil as she herself; but she was not without mental fortitude and had been the best fighter in her school, a useful attribute in her new profession. Confrontation with the public was an occupational hazard when working in the retail sector in Least, and Kelly-Leanne was confident that she was equal to her new role. Each sigh of impatience or muttered oath was met with a stare that could freeze a lava fountain. Kelly-Leanne was not a young woman to take aspersions regarding her professional competence lightly, nor waste time pandering to the trivial concerns of paying customers. The constant warring with her mother's new boyfriend, coupled with her own partner being practically comatose by daily cannabis usage, meant that she already had a full plate. In Kelly-Leanne's world every morning was Monday morning. And she didn't care who knew it.

Brian queued for twenty minutes behind a thick-set car mechanic who sporadically spat profanities into his mobile telephone at someone Brian assumed to be his fiancée, although it may well have been his wife. The mechanic repeated his aversion to spending an evening with, 'Your fucking Mam and Dad,' whilst rolling his eyes and absently booting a bollard warning customers of a wet floor. The mechanic purchased an evening paper and a packet of chewing gum with a debit card, a habit prevalent amongst the young and quietly dementing to Brian. Using any debit card in this store invariably led to a transaction taking longer than the completion of a crossword in a Sunday supplement. The young were often accused by their seniors of being ignorant of the value of money. As far as Brian was concerned they knew perfectly well the value of money but hazier when it came to the value of time.

When Kelly-Leanne's resigned grimace signalled that the mechanic's debit card had been rejected for a fourth time, Brian considered looking around for something with which to self-harm. The mechanic mooched around in his pockets and produced almost the exact change to pay for his purchases, but sadly not enough. This scenario may have led to some unpleasantness but Kelly-Leanne's filthy mood influenced her decision to waive the requisite seven pence. She couldn't be arsed about seven pissin' pence or indeed anything pissin' else. She refused to meet Brian's gaze when he finally deposited his shopping basket on the counter.

When she had finished checking Brian's purchases Kelly-Leanne silently held out her hand in request for payment. Brian nodded to the shelf behind her, pointed to a half-litre of vodka and requested she add this to his list of purchases. She did so without demur. In more prosperous neighbourhoods a middle-aged man purchasing spirits on a weeknight may have provoked raised eyebrows, but in Least this was as unremarkable as dog mess in the street.

From the early-morning shufflers who sought out newsagents selling extra-strength lager, to the lunchtime tipplers in public parks sharing a bottle whilst discussing their various ailments, Least was a colony of habitual and unsocial drinkers. Brian knew that they were sedating themselves against the vicious banality of their lives, and he himself had recently been panged by anxieties regarding his intake. He knew he was drinking too much, drinking to silence dark musings upon his seemingly intractable financial problems and the terror of a comfortless future. Following his scission from Helen he had become centreless and unmoored. She would never have countenanced such sloth and self-indulgence. He had vowed that if tomorrow's appointment with the bank proved providential he would arrest the decline. A bailout from the bank that had endured his custom for some thirty years would provide a fresh start and an opportunity to enter the final straight of his life with an easier mind, a more resolute outlook and a renascence of self-discipline. If not? Then an alternative solution upon which he had been labouring for some eleven weeks would provide the panacea. He nodded his thanks to Kelly-Leanne, who seemed abstracted by thoughts of murder.

Upon arriving home Brian turned on both the radio and the television. Voices, however disembodied, palliated the sense of isolation endured by those who return to a house empty of anyone but themselves. The received pronunciation of the Radio Four presenter rose like steam in the air of the kitchen whilst more regional accents burred from the television in the living room. Brian delved into the bag of shopping, tore the packaging from the frozen lasagne, stabbed the polythene cover of the block of pallid mush and tossed it into the microwave oven. The hummus and pitta bread were shelved in the refrigerator next to a solitary jar of pasta sauce whilst the red wine remained unopened on a worktop. The half-litre of vodka was quickly cracked open and he mixed a generous measure with orange juice and tap water. He swallowed half of the contents of the glass, waited for the afterglow, and then switched the beatbox from radio to CD. Debussy smeared a soothing balsam on his mind as he began his nightly decompression, swimming slowly up from the swirling depths of anxiety into the placid waters of tipsiness. He stared at a cold fat moon through the kitchen window as he absorbed Debussy's preludes through his pores.

Although drawn to music since adolescence, Brian had never envisaged a time in his life when classical music would be preferable to the vibrancy of rock or jazz. Perhaps it was less a sign of a honed artistic sensibility than of his advancing years and a yen for order in an increasingly incomprehensible world. Unlike human life, with its unpredictable tempos and digressions, classical music organised time into chronological sense and almost all of the pieces were satisfactorily resolved. Although still heart-sore at Helen's peremptory dismissal of him, in more reflective moods he would admit his gratitude for her tutelage in music sometimes centuries old but so fresh that it could have been composed yesterday. Debussy's imagistic chords painted seascapes as Brian recharged his glass and entered the living room.

He switched on a table lamp, lit two squat scented candles, slumped onto the couch, spilled his drink down his tie and gazed at the television. He was drawn to the regional news these days, if only to boggle at the increasing number of violent crimes committed across the region. It had been trumpeted that despite The Great Mess and austerian cuts to law enforcement funding, crime was supposedly decreasing. Criminal justice pundits were scratching their heads as the trend was contrary to their predictions of anarchy in times of financial hardship. Perhaps Spex was right. People really couldn't be arsed to be arsed these days, too beaten down and too disinterested to commit even casual larcenies, but Brian wasn't convinced. The opportunism, brutality and callousness of some of the assaults perpetrated against innocents was something new and malign. Acid attacks on young women and the elderly appalled him. Brian had been alive long enough to recognise a new and disturbing demographic. This was an anger against the elites turning in on itself, a whipped dog biting off its own leg instead of the hand of its tormentor.

The regional news segued into the national bulletin, with its usual melange of the horrific and the banal. The unmemorable faces of the male and female broadcasters were recomposed into a rictus of solemnity as they prepared themselves to impart Something Important. Apparently the government was to tackle the problem of forced marriages among what the female broadcaster referred to with a slight catch in her voice as ethnic minorities. A task force had been appointed to investigate this latest exigency.

Brian laughed so much he almost choked on his drink. Aside from the idiocy of referring to tens of billions of people as a minority he also wondered what item of real importance was sneaking under the radar whilst this latest canard exercised the public. This could only mean that government mandarins were up to something they'd rather not announce any time soon. Brian had no clue what it was, but given the shocks of the last four years then it was bound to be something unpleasant. Apart from anything else he couldn't see anything intrinsically wrong in arranged marriages. There was simply too much choice in life, therefore too many opportunities to make the wrong decisions. An arranged marriage reminded him of being a boy, demanding to know what was for tea and being tersely informed that it was either fish fingers or bugger all. It seemed that contentment was the absence of choice and perhaps these communities were on to something. An arranged marriage was like fish fingers. It would suffice if there was nothing else.

More disturbing was a brief interview with a distraught middle-aged man whose daughter had disappeared. She had posted messages on the Web that she was joining the struggle for the establishment of a caliphate in a country not usually a holiday destination for the sane. The weeping father claimed that his daughter was merely an impressionable young girl, although his definition of an impressionable young girl didn't chime with Brian's. His idea of an impressionable young girl was his sister Elaine, who, prior to becoming a dreadful nouveau riche tawpie, would pin snaps of vacuous pop stars to her bedroom wall and blow kisses at them. A girl who would wail horribly along with her latest gormless pop record. A girl who spent hours on the telephone and swooned at a glimpse of George Michael on the television. A young female seeking vistas of genocide, bombings and beheadings didn't strike Brian as a hormonal simperer finding her feet in the adult world. Her teenage rites of passage were unlikely to be discussed in the problem pages of teen magazines.

Dear Margy. I have been seeing my boyfriend for a long time and I like him a very lot. I think I am ready to have sex with him but all he thinks about is shooting infidels, blowing things up and cutting people's heads off. Do you think we have a future together?

In the future this lost girl would be a case study for ologists of all stripes and discussed by pundits in the field of aberrant behaviours. When all of the authoritative tracts had been published in scholarly journals, no one would be any the wiser but at least someone would get to appear on the telly. Brian applauded the morose father's attempts to efface his daughter's behaviours, but he couldn't help thinking that there were times when a spade really ought to be called a shovel.

It was unlikely that this poor man's appeal for forbearance would elicit much sympathy, and it was obvious that his understanding of normal adolescent behaviours was a little skew-whiff. He seemed to be the kind of man that under duress might admit that Pol Pot could be a bit off with people now and again. As a parent he was definitely a work in progress. If Brian's mother was watching this she'd sniffily remark that her parents should have put more sugar in the girl's tea. Sugary tea was both a sedative and a laxative and this dozy mare was probably in need of both. Brian was thankful that his mother had never aspired to public service beyond working in busmen's washrooms.

The efficacy of sugary tea as an effective prophylactic against genocidal mayhem had yet to be proven. He peered into his glass and frowned. It was empty again.

Debussy's *Jeux* arrived to its enigmatic conclusion as he delved in the refrigerator for the remaining dregs of the orange juice. He remembered he'd stored an emergency can of diet cola in the cupboard in which his cache of stolen medication was stored. He opened the cupboard, grabbed the can of diet cola and then took a tobacco tin from the shelf. He prised off the lid and examined the assortment of tablets he'd been steadily appropriating from hospitals and care homes. People were notoriously lax in keeping tabs on their medication and in recent months Brian had taken full advantage. And yet whilst he had illicitly accrued a respectable cache of hypnotics, anxiolytics and strong analgesics, he had yet to realise his ambition of stealing The Grail. An annihilator which, when combined with alcohol, offered a copper-bottomed painless exit from the world. Good old Sister Morphine. In one of her reflective moods Helen was fond of remarking that death was but an after-dinner sleep. If eternal sleep was required then morphine would pretty much guarantee it, but even without the ne plus ultra of pain relief Brian was comforted by his stash. The contents of his tobacco tin were more than enough to kill him. Life would have no dominion once he'd swallowed this lot.

As he worried at the tablets with his forefinger, he reflected that had he himself observed someone stealing medication he would have immediately alerted the police and mental health services, but in his own case he really couldn't be bothered. He was vexed beyond reason by the constant hectoring of the bank, the utilities companies, the credit card company and the mobile phone company. He was exhausted by the constant terror of finding money for the rent or answering the telephone to yet another faceless witchfinder chasing yet another failed direct debit. In tandem with all of this was the inevitability of losing his job in the next two months resulting from his redistribution of local authority monies. He was ready to cede defeat unless the bank exercised a little clemency tomorrow. If the bank elected to reschedule his debts and offer him a clean slate then that would be all right. If it didn't, there was always the contents of the tobacco tin. And that would be all right. And at least he was enjoying himself this evening.

He returned to the couch and eyed the pile of mail on the occasional table. Taking a long pull on his glass, he reluctantly reached for an envelope and tore it open. He learned that the energy company required three monthly payments due to two failed direct debits. He need not do anything as the energy company would simply extract the deferred payments along with his usual monthly remission from his bank account, thereby bringing his account up to date. Direct debits were the simplest way to pay but Brian was to contact the energy company immediately if he found difficulty in making the payments. Brian mused that finding difficulty in making the payments was easy enough, but contacting the energy company would be an act of supreme folly. Can't make a payment? Finding it difficult to keep on top of your bills? No problem. We'll simply cut you off. Have a pleasant evening freezing to death in the dark, loser. We are an equal opportunities employer.

Brian had calculated that maintaining a dignified silence in response to the demands of his creditors was the most prudent course of action. The energy suppliers would be vacillating between whether he had merely overlooked the debt or whether he really was in financial trouble. If he declared his penury then punitive action such as a swingeing increase in his tariff would surely be invoked. This was a nonsensical approach to debt management. After all, if Brian couldn't meet the cost of the original tariff then odds of meeting an increase in payments were as insuparable as playing centre forward for England, or copping off with a supermodel. Or indeed copping off with anyone. But if he maintained the pretence that his life was such a giddy social whirl that he'd overlooked such trivial concerns as keeping the lights on, then surely it would be illegal to cut him off. There was probably something about this in the small print of the contract that Brian, in common with millions of others, had chosen to ignore.

With grim satisfaction he noted that he was only one payment late for his water rates. His council tax was in credit but the rent was due tomorrow. Overdraft charges would, as usual, be filched from his account whilst he was asleep. He calculated that as of three o'clock tomorrow afternoon he would be left with approximately fifteen quid to purchase diesel for the car, food and tobacco. His outstanding debts to the bank, the energy company, the water company, the credit card company and his Internet and phone provider amounted to something in the region of eight thousand pounds, the equivalent of something like five monthly take-home salaries. As Brian was unaware of any dispensation for an increase on the Gregorian calendar to allow him another three hundred and fifty hours of paid work he was completely hamstrung. His financial well-being rested squarely in the hands of the bank, that avaricious risk-taking monster recently recapitalised by an arcane financial tool called quantitative easing. It was awash with taxpayer's money and could easily afford eight grand or so. It wasn't as if he was asking

61

for a several hundred billion as the banks had. But, if he wasn't offered a lifeline tomorrow, then the contents of the tobacco tin would become more alluring by the hour.

Brian had read somewhere that the government paid a death grant for those so poor that meeting the costs of interment was impossible. This was useful to know as he doubted his parents would leap at the opportunity to provide the funds necessary to bankroll his final journey. His father would simply shake his head and point the mortician in the direction of the nearest skip. His sister Elaine probably wouldn't even bother to attend his dispatch to futurity, particularly if it clashed with an appointment with her nail technician or a session of transcendental zumba. On the television a weather woman with very large teeth pointed at the city of Chester and enjoined viewers to take an umbrella if they were out and about the following day. Brian sighed. If the weather was an augur of how he would fare at the bank tomorrow, he may as well reach for the tobacco tin now. Then his eyes alighted upon a soiled piece of paper wedged between two flyers advertising the opening of yet another fast food emporium. The leaf of paper had been torn from the pages of what seemed to be a children's exercise book. By the light of a guttering candle he read the terse missive written in red biro:

YOUR CUNTISHNESS APPALS ME. SEE YOU TOMORROW NIGHT. BRING DRINK.

Brian had forgotten about Friday night. He'd forgotten about Splatch. He resolved to pick up a consignment of wine and a bottle of strong alcohol before he taxied over to Splatch's flat the following evening. It was unlikely that Splatch would have purchased any strong waters for either himself or his guest. He exchanged Debussy for an album by the uncategorisable Thelonious Monk. The contents of the vodka bottle had dwindled to dregs, the carton of orange juice was empty and there was no more than a smidgeon of coke left in the can.

His whiffled equanimity was fading and he became uncomfortably aware of his reclusion. Solitude sometimes hurt. Even Brian occasionally felt a keening desire to commune with others, and in such moods his sense of isolation rocketed. Monk's dissonant chords evoked the murmurous tumult of a fight happening out of sight but just within earshot. Brian was bored with himself and craved diversion. His armour of detachment had been pierced by an excess of alcohol and self-pity. He ached for human adjacency, a relief from his miserable selfhood. A faint stirring in his groin also reminded him that he was still chained to an idiot. He closed the living room curtains and crossed to the creaking table bearing an ancient laptop that Splatch had thoughtfully stolen for him. He donned the headphones trailing from the side of the device and with a couple of mouse clicks entered the flesh labyrinth.

Brian's occasional usage of Internet pornography to relieve transient carnal urges was, as with everything else he enjoyed, tinged with guilt and anxiety. He also worried that freely available access to such material was poisoning human minds, particularly his. These days it seemed almost de rigeur for adults to blithely declare their penchant for regular consumption of two-backed beastliness in high definition picture quality and surround sound. The liberal press was awash with articles by women proclaiming the inherent healthiness of jerking off to images deemed illegal only thirty years earlier. Female novelists were monopolising the market with romps featuring males slaking their thirst for physical subjugation of the opposite sex. The world of desire had become very strange.

Brian had arrived to sexual maturity in the late 1970s, the period in which a trannie was a portable radio and emotional and sexual continence were the modus vivendi. Prior to the cults of the self and possessive individualism championed by the New Right, pornography was as it should be: ugly, tawdry and shameful. In the nineteen seventies a regular consumer of top-shelf magazines would be disparaged for being either physically repugnant or in need of psychiatric help. The inveterate self-abuser would be reviled as a social inadequate, derided by his peers and always regarded with suspicion. It was another mysterious concomitant of the new century that the worst epithet one human being could level at another was that he or she was a smoker, whereas masturbating oneself into mental derangement was a signifier of bracingly mature adulthood. Fewer people smoked these days but everyone seemed more jittery and quicker to take offence.

He alighted upon a group of middle-aged bon viveurs who conversed in Germanic voices rasped by decades of strong tobacco. They were engaged in a dismal pastiche of an orgy with the alacrity of people who had just been informed that it was their turn to put the bins out. Their embarrassment was almost palpable as they muttered, ja, ja, or padded clumsily across the indifferently furnished lounge to attend to another carnal duty of care. This vista of excruciation was underpinned by dreadful Krautrock, and it was plain that the participants weren't much cop at reckless debauchery. Polishing horse brasses would have been preferable to spending an afternoon with others so denuded of allure. Their very ordinariness was aphrodisiacal, the absence of sculpted pectorals or pneumatic curves arousing not prurience but tender concern. There was something indefinably stimulating

64

about nondescript people usually seen in a bus queue feigning shameless decadence. They embodied a piteous humanity that grasped at Brian's heart as he sensed their inward pleading for it all to soon be over. And for Brian, it soon was. He closed his eyes, gritted his teeth, sighed and voided himself. That was that.

Although towards the end of their relationship Helen had been tireless in berating him for his chronic shambolism, when it came to the disposal of slivers of genetic material Brian was a model of cold-eyed efficiency. The rapidly disintegrating sheets of Best Buy toilet paper containing the requisite ingredients to manufacture a mini-Brian was held at arm's length as he marched towards the kitchen. He thrust the wad of toilet paper to the very bottom of the swing bin, deep into the miasma of reeking tuna tins, soiled newspapers and those unnameable vile fluids seemingly generated by the swing bin itself. He then strode resolutely to the bathroom to wash his hands. Out, damn'd spot.

The ubiquity of CCTVs, smartphones, laptops and other instruments of surveillance was profoundly disquieting to him. His occasional angst-ridden forays into the world of Internet smut frightened him as he speculated that persons unknown might be harvesting evidence of his improprieties to use them as leverage. He was, after all, a public servant, paid by the gubernatorial purse. The public were right to expect unimpeachable probity from its employees, despite being daily bombarded with evidence pointing to the contrary. He was also irrationally hagridden by a nightmare scenario in which he was implicated in a macabre crime by a failure to safely dispose of his ejaculate.

He envisioned a situation in which a murder had been committed locally. Prior to the ghastly event a sharp-eyed waste management technician, or whatever binmen were called these days, had spotted evidence of Brian's emissions. The police were at a loss to identify the murderer and requested members of the public to come forward if they had noted any suspicious behaviour among local residents. The acutely observant binman then immediately reported his concerns regarding a single, white middle-aged recluse who seemed to spend most of his time in a lonely sexual frenzy. The mere inference of louche behaviour tended to result in trial by tabloid followed by a life led under a cloud of suspicion. In a world shorn of personal privacy a little assiduity in erasing evidence of recreational onanism went a long way.

As the adrenaline rush of sexual release dissipated Brian was surprised by a stabbing pang of hunger. He'd been home for hours and forgotten to eat. He checked his watch and was horrified to discover it was just past ten. He needed to eat, retire to bed and be ready for what promised to be a challenging day tomorrow. Whilst he awaited the microwave to sear the mucoid lump masquerading as lasagne, there was a peremptory rap on the front door. Brian's heart thumped in alarm. He received no visitors at all, or least any that were welcome. His father didn't count as he was a locum squatter. As he approached the door his stomach churned. He wondered if his mother had finally succumbed to the stroke she'd been so sedulously cultivating all these years. Upon opening the door Brian was immediately perplexed. A woman in her forties with an eruption of dark curls framing an ovate face grinned evilly at him. In one hand she was carrying a polythene bag containing bottles of wine and in the other an unlit cigarette. She swayed in time to an internal rhythm and was obviously one over the eight. Brian had no idea who this woman was, but at least she wasn't a Mormon.

'Hiya, Brian.'

'Er… yeah. Hiya.'

'I went to school with your Elaine, me. I saw your dad in the pie shop. He said you'd moved back round here.'

'Did you? That's… nice.'

Why was that of any relevance? And why come at this time of night to tell me this? What did she want for going to school with my sister? A Duke of Edinburgh award? Do I owe her money?

'I've been in The Pig. I won this lot in a raffle. I'm absolutely choking for a wee. I won't make it home without pissing myself. Can I use your bog a minute?'

If he hadn't been a son of this parish Brian would have been disquieted by such an importunity, but unusual requests at strange hours were common in Least. The contingent lives led by the people of Least defied analysis, therefore a woman arriving at his door late at night to use the lavatory was unsurprising. He was thankful that at least it wasn't his father bringing news of either his mother's demise or his bloody toolbag. He invited her in and pointed towards the bathroom. She muttered her gratitude and stumbled past him, depositing her payload of cheap wine on a kitchen worktop. Brian squinted into the street, sniffed the cold, checked his watch again and closed the door against the December chill. When the woman emerged from the bathroom she lingered in the kitchen and gawped at her surroundings as though visiting a black museum. She called Brian into the kitchen.

'All right in here, innit? Are you buying it?'

'No, just renting. It's owned by a bloke who lives in Lanzarote. His mate picks the rent up in cash every Friday or Saturday.'

'Right. Have you got a glass?'

'Er... yeah. Do you want a glass of water?'

'What, with this lot here? You're fucking kidding aren't you? Come on Brian. Have one with us. It's not even closing time yet.'

Brian vacillated. He didn't wish to be rude to whoever she was but he also wanted to eat and go to bed. The woman sensed his indecision, rolled her eyes coquettishly and began searching the cupboards. She produced two plastic beer glasses and unscrewed a bottle of red wine. Her curls bounced on her head as though on springs as she swayed to what seemed a bossa nova via Madchester. She decanted the contents of the bottle into two glasses. Brian checked his watch again.

'You can't remember my name can you?'

Brian was certain he hadn't known it in the first place. She eyed him with an interrogatory gaze.

'I used to come to your house and play with your Elaine years ago. You were on shifts with my dad. D'you remember?'

Brian immediately remembered who she was, although he hadn't set eyes on her since she was, what? Fifteen? Her father was originally from Hungary, fetching up in northern England as a fugitive from the Soviet Union. He was accused of conspiring with the forces of reaction and had he lingered in Budapest his life wouldn't have been worth tuppence. He was one of the most physically durable men Brian had ever met. He married a local woman and sired two slab-like sons who had drifted into the netherworld of nightclub security and narcotics. And then, belatedly, a daughter arrived.

Late additions to a family were always subject to scurrilous speculation. It was rumoured that she was the progeny of a truck driver who delivered bottles of discounted soft drinks. This woman's father had died from a massive heart attack shortly after retirement, having developed a gargantuan appetite for the local delicacies of fried food and pies. His daughter had regularly

68

visited Brian's family home many years ago but back then she had barely registered on his radar. She was just another one of Elaine's idiot friends. Nowadays it was unlikely that Elaine and this woman would be companions as Elaine would deem her rather declasse, and perhaps given what Brian had heard on the grapevine over the years that would be a fair assessment. If she was who Brian thought she was, she had grown up to be something of a handful. Tracey, the Dame of Disorder.

'Are you Tracey?'

'Bloody hell, give that lad a gold star and a tick. Here. Get that down you.'

Brian sipped timorously at his glass whilst Tracey imbibed more thirstily. Without consulting her host Tracy investigated her new environment, perusing the novels and textbooks on the bookshelves and deriding his supposedly discerning taste. She pulled out CDs at random from a fragile storage cabinet, scrutinised the covers and then shook her head in resignation. In common with her erstwhile playmate Elaine, she was evidently not a fan of niche music. She stalked, sniffed, pawed and stretched like a stray cat eager to familiarise herself with her new surroundings. Her presence had conjured an unsettling ambience in Brian's usually quiet and candle-shadowed home. Discounting the occasional visit of his mother, who only called only to complain about his father, no female had ever crossed his threshold. He couldn't decide if he was irritated or diverted by the intrusion but it was undeniably interesting. He inwardly agonised that Tracey might have scented his ejaculate putrefying in the swing bin. If the local gossip was to be believed she had a nose for that sort of thing.

Tracey quickly polished off the contents of her glass and reached to open another bottle. Whilst wrenching the screw top she glanced at Brian concernedly, as though he was a child suffering a nasty cough or an unexplained limp. Brian was struck by how in mere minutes their acquaintance had developed from the strained into something more convivial, although this elision was common among the residents of Least. A reservoir of shared history meant that individuals and families were integers in a Venn diagram, all of them interlinked by tenuous kinships over time. Tracy depressed the play button on the CD. 'Round Midnight' hung like ether in the air of the kitchen. Her retroussé nose wrinkled in disapproval but she ignored Monk's fractured harmonies to focus on Brian instead. She wanted to know how things were with him and the family. Brian was unnerved. He was unused to anyone expressing interest in anything he had to say.

He dilated upon his parents' state of health and how Elaine was faring with her fiancé, Dave, although he forbore from mentioning that he rarely spoke to either of them. Their money-obsession, materialism and Elaine's arrant snobbery were repellent to him, although Brian sometimes envied his sister's parsimony. Elaine had always known the price of a shilling and unlikely to be terrified by the arrival of a final reminder. Dave was also an estate agent, similarly cautious with money and the stripe of man who became tumescent at the thought of the compound interest accrued on a fifteen-year fixed term savings plan. He also ascribed the adjective "cool" to everything, from his job to the food he consumed. Brian was incensed by this, secure in his conviction that no white Anglo-Saxon male should ever use the terms "cool" or "man" at any time or in any context. He would rather be fellated by a crocodile than spend more than five minutes in Dave's excruciating company. His mother liked Dave as he always brought cake when he and Elaine made one of their increasingly rare visits to Least, whereas his father's opinion of his daughter's fiancé was rather more nuanced. Derek always made himself scarce upon Dave's arrival as the gobby bleeder could talk a glass eye to sleep.

All of this was merely a preamble to Tracey making

70

enquiries about matters of a more personal nature, and she was piercingly direct in her enquiries. She demanded to know why Brian had returned to Least, the identity of the woman with whom he had co-habited, and what Brian had done to upset her. Among the women of Least the presumption of guilt on the part of the male in the breakdown of a relationship was a given. Brian blinked, swallowed and checked his watch again. He was uncomfortably conscious that he had never discussed his break with Helen with anyone, not even Splatch. It would have been pointless to broach the matter with his family as their modus operandi where emotional turmoil was concerned was to suffer in silence. Disappointment was the natural concomitant to being alive and one should never be surprised by failure. Ventilating, reaching out, sharing or whatever argot one used to describe bloody moaning was inimical to their unsmiling stoicism. Leave it alone. Don't pick it or it'll bleed. Maxims that could be engraved on the headstone of any member of the Paget tribe, including Brian's.

Brian prevaricated whilst mentally browsing a catalogue of witless alibis to satisfy someone wishing to rake over the embers. We'd reached the end of the road. We'd outgrown one another (or rather she, him). She didn't want children (he didn't either). He plumped for the hardy perennial of there was nothing between them any more, figuring that this smidgeon of drivel would satisfy Tracy's forensic curiosity. She did not let the matter rest. With a brute remorselessness that would have made her father proud, she stuck to the task of extruding the truth from an increasingly embattled Brian. Tracy's eye of Horus stare, punctuated by the occasional acute apercu, undid Brian's compacted emotions and inspired a Vesuvian discharge.

He raged, declaimed, rued, regretted, self-flagellated and practically pawed the ground in frustration at the waste of over a decade and a half of life that he could never retrieve. Had he never met Helen in the first place he might have taken more care to provide for the future. Instead, he had vaguely supposed that at some point in their relationship they would begin building a nest egg for an interesting and fulfilling retirement. Of course, this hadn't happened because in common with many childless couples they had lived to, and frequently beyond, their means. They had enjoyed the moment rather than save for emergencies that might never happen. Which of course did. Worse than that, he knew that Helen would continue to prosper as the legatee of her parents' considerable estate, go on to meet a man of a similar social stratum and then breeze on into a late middle age of financial security and foreign holidays. He would be reduced to begging for spare change outside bus stations. It just wasn't bloody fair, was it?

Tracey continued to stare, her occasional twitching betraying intense cerebral activity. She looked like she was vividly dreaming whilst still awake. As Brian approached a crescendo of self-reproach and despair her shoulders drooped and she began to weep. Brian was mystified as to why she was so moved by his plight. Derision and *Schadenfreude* was the natural response of all Least inhabitants to the travails of others. She really should have collapsed into derisive laughter at his despondency.

'I'm sorry for upsetting you Tracey, but that's how it is for me at the minute.'

'I couldn't give a shit about you Brian. You're all right really. You just need summat to fuckin' whinge about, you do.'

'Oh. Yeah. You're probably right. So what's up with you then?'

'My stepson keeps shagging me.'

'Come again?'

'I said, my stepson keeps shagging me.'

'Oh. And you don't want him to, am I right?'

'Fucking hell, Brian. Are you Mystic bleedin' Meg or what?

72

Course I bleedin' don't. His dad would murder me if he finds out. I mean literally kill me stone dead. The little bastard's blackmailing me. He's threatening to tell his dad about summat I did years ago. Summat to do with a car smash and a shitload of weed.'

'How old is he, this lad?'

'Fifteen.'

'Well tell his dad then. Let him sort it out. Or go to the police. This sounds like rape if you ask me, if rape is defined as a sexual act against one's will. He sounds oversexualised and dangerous to others. This needs to be reported.'

'Are you're telling me to go to the bobbies and tell 'em I'm having it off my partner's lad?'

'Definitely. This boy needs help.'

'Oh HE needs help. Right, Brian, got that. And when I go to the cop shop you expect them to believe me when I say it's not my fault?'

'Absolutely. Just put it out there and let things take their course.'

'Do you not read the bleedin' papers? I'm a paedo Brian. A kiddie-fiddler. The dibble will lock me up as soon as they look at me. And when him at home finds out? I'm dead. Dead, Brian. D'you get me?'

At this, Brian fell silent. Tracey's previous history of riotous promiscuity, drug-fuelled bohemianism and her frowsy, just-out-of-bed insouciance would scandalise any officer of the law. As soon as she opened her mouth to speak, his lips would purse and condemn her as a slattern who deserved every ounce of obloquy heaped upon her. Brian knew her life to be as byzantine as any encountered in popular novels but there would be no compassion shown by the court of public opinion. Buttoned-up mortgage-paying citizens viewed Tracey and her ilk as a threat to the British way of doing things. She was a candidate for television shows lampooning welfare claimants and the mentally disordered. Although fifteen centuries had elapsed since the departure of the Romans, the natives of these islands still enjoyed a public crucifixion. Tracey would be unmissable viewing for the silent majority who nevertheless never seemed to shut up vilifying the unlucky and unlikeable. Brian didn't need to ask her if she wished to talk about her latest mishap as he knew she would anyway. To his horror, he learned that after many unsuccessful dalliances with permanent relationships, she had taken up with Zorb.

Zorb. A legendary face-ripper who in adolescence was tipped for stardom as a rugby league player, until he broke the jaws of a referee and two touch judges in the local park. Zorb, who then tried his hand at boxing and again shone in his chosen sport until one night he was caught breaking into a local warehouse. Zorb, who then knocked out cold two policemen who were foolish enough to attempt his apprehension. Zorb, who when subsequently confronted by police officers at his home grappled an attack dog to the ground and tried to bite out its throat. Zorb the vampire, the murrain, the gouger, the puncher, the thief, the terrifier. And how typical of Tracey to end up living with him and one of his vile spawn.

It was pointless to conciliate with Tracey. If time was reversible she may have stayed sober long enough to reflect upon the repercussions of cohabiting with a dangerous raptor like Zorb. She may have rebuffed his demand to move in with him if a spill of good sense had kindled in her mind. But she did not, and at some point Zorb would discover Tracey's crypto-incestuous infidelity. Retribution would mean hospitalisation and invasive surgery for at least two members of this scarcely believable *ménage à trois*. Brian enquired if Tracey had anywhere to go if she decided to decamp from the family home, but Tracey silently shrugged her shoulders as though the question was too ridiculous to answer. Women's refuges take a dim view of those implicated in paedophilia. Zorb's vengeance would be inevitable, pitiless and sanguinary.

'Right then. I'm going to get off. He'll be wondering where I am. Thanks for letting me use the bog.'

'Right-oh. Thanks for the wine. Will you be all right walking home on your own? It's nearly one o'clock.'

'Jesus, Brian. You know who I live with. Who's going to go near me if they like having teeth?'

'Good point.'

'Right then, Einstein. I'm off. It's quite a big place for a terraced is this. Two good sized bedrooms. Have you started seeing anyone since you split up with the other piece?'

'Nah. Having a break from all that. Anyway, it'd be a bit expensive for me at the minute. It's hard enough taking myself out for a drink never mind anyone else.'

'Fucking hell. Six months without a legover? I bet you're wanking yourself daft in here. Haven't you got a fuck buddy? Everyone's got one of them these days.'

'I've no desire for a buddy, fuck or otherwise.'

'Suit yourself. See you.'

Brian leaned his head against the front door and listened to cadence of Tracey's departing footsteps. He cringed with the shameful realisation that by dint of her reference to his miserable personal life, Tracey had indeed scented him. The swing bin had to be emptied as matter of urgency.

FRIDAY

In the morning Brian awoke with a hangover so wretched he felt like he'd joined the ranks of the undead. Whilst he lay in bed scratching at his inexplicably itchy lower legs, he woozily recalled an article theorising that sleep therapy could be a useful tool in the detoxification of drug addicts. They could dream their way through withdrawal instead of enduring gut-splitting indignities and pain whilst conscious. He needed that now, to sleep for days and wake into a world where Tracey and the previous night hadn't happened. He ached all over and even his mind was sprained. He eased his lower half gingerly from under the duvet and waited for his head to stop swimming before standing upright. In the full-length mirror opposite he was glared at by a red-eyed wild-haired demon, a bloated fugitive from a Hieronymus Bosch painting. Saliva dribbled from both sides of its maw as it scratched a bulbous hirsute belly. Last night must have been really eventful if a gargoyle had broken into the house whilst he was asleep.

He found his dressing gown and lurched downstairs. He turned on the radio, lent an ear and then immediately turned it off again. A male news presenter was in truculent humour, disparaging a cabinet minister unlucky enough to be landed with explaining away the government's latest lies and missteps. Brian wasn't ready for the foulness of the world yet. He glanced at his watch and blearily calculated that he was already twenty minutes late for work. Swift remedial action was required. He reached for his ancient mobile phone and called Rona. She echoed Brian's mutterings with her usual speaking-clock monotone. Brian would be in the office by eleven (by eleven. Right Brian). He had forgotten to pick up a carer's assessment from a nursing home (nursing home. Right Brian). He would be leaving the office shortly afterwards for a home visit to Ted and Mavis (Ted and Mavis. Right Brian). Before taking the afternoon off (Off. Right Brian). He'd been given permission for the time off by Kali (got permission. Right Brian). He was an agency worker so he wasn't paid for any time off (not paid. Right Brian). No adjustment to the weekly timesheet was necessary (no adjustment. Right Brian).

The telephone call to Rona had enfeebled him so much that he needed to return to the horizontal. He slumped lengthways on the couch and aimed the remote control at the television. On-screen a woman with a rictus grin babbled monkeyshine. Brian supposed that her usual audience comprised of the long-term unemployed, the elderly and night-shift workers considering a morning nightcap before heading bedwards. She gibbered her glee at the arrival of a minor celebrity declaring his intention to ride a pig bareback in aid of a Christmas charity. Listening to her fatuous irruptions Brian was even more convinced that the twenty-first century was a dangerous place for sensible people. Morning television was a weapon, a relentless bombardment of banality, trivia as an instrument of sadistic violence. Five consecutive days of morning television could render a sentient human being catatonic within less than a week. His face contorted as though he'd tasted something unexpectedly sour.

It was pointless to consider leaving the house until the rush hour traffic had died away. Brian eased himself from the couch, reached inside the refrigerator and swore horribly upon realising that he'd forgotten to purchase milk the previous evening. He

77

went to the front door, glanced furtively up and down the street and then swiftly removed a bottle of milk from an adjacent doorstep. The tenant of the house, with whom Brian had never exchanged so much as a word, never stirred until at least ten o'clock each morning. She would doubtless place the blame for the theft on one of Least's malignant children. He chastised himself for the thievery but on this day of all days, black coffee would be useless in kick-starting his injured sensibilities. He needed his faculties locked and loaded if he was to win even a hollow victory.

He almost fell asleep again whilst evacuating a thin stream the colour of porphyry into the lavatory bowl. The piss-prophet in him diagnosed that he was either dangerously dehydrated or suffering end-stage kidney failure. Judging by the way he felt it was probably the latter. Rancid pockets of gas escaped from his mouth as he sluiced away last night's patina of grog and cigarette smoke under the shower. The stench of the perfumed body wash made him nauseous to the point of vomiting. In recent months Brian had been purchasing his toiletries in bulk from a pound shop in the centre of town, but the bouquet of this algae-like goo could knock out a polecat. If negotiations with the bank today were successful he resolved to purchase self-care products costing a bit more than a second-hand paperback. The misted image of an ogre glared at him from the bathroom mirror as the disposable razor dragged at his face like the claws of a witch. Having noticed that the towel he had used to dry himself was already sodden, he refused to speculate to what use Tracey had put the faded rectangle of flannel the night before. This might set the tone for an unrewarding day. He had never heard of men embarked upon missions of epochal significance worrying about wet towels.

He dressed, poured another cup of coffee, glanced through the window and concluded that the weather was likely to remain gloomy. In seven days it would be Christmas Eve, heralding two consecutive bank holidays at the time of the year least conducive to relaxation. Whilst lolling on the couch some weeks ago he had been diverted by a television theologian who posited the notion that Christ was actually born in May, a month which afforded the opportunity of a walk to the pub with only a marginal threat of hypothermia. Quite why the birthday of the son of God had been rescheduled to coincide with the most abominable time of the year remained a sacred mystery. Perhaps not even God, should he/she/it exist, could control the perversity of humans. In all likelihood he/she/it had already abandoned humankind to climate change, neo-liberalism and permanent internecine conflict in a fit of disgust. It certainly felt like that, and Brian had to concede that he/she/it probably had a point. If we couldn't even get the date of His boy's birthday right, what good were we?

Given a choice, Brian would have been happy to spend his first Christmas without Helen in a medically induced coma. Even when he and Helen were together he recoiled from the mawkishness and phony bonhomie of the season. No relief was afforded to those who prefer to retreat from the madness, not even in the usually sparsely populated gastropubs. In Advent these oases of calm were inundated by once-a-year revellers on seasonal outings, guffawing at humourless in-jokes and looking silly in the paper hats provided by Sheila from Human Resources. The prurience of their exchanges increased proportionally to the amount of alcohol they had imbibed until inevitably someone took offence. Tears, recriminations and year-long *froideurs* ensued. If these people were children, their guardians would have been quietly advised to either get a grip of the little bastards or take their custom elsewhere. Little wonder that young people seemed permanently aggrieved these days. In addition to being denied free tertiary education, secure employment and an affordable home, their traditional social role of being insufferable pains in the arse had been supplanted by their parents. Life really wasn't fair.

Following his third cup of coffee Brian was sufficiently oriented to focus on the day ahead, but he was immediately discouraged when he recalled that he had a supervision session with Kali before lunch. Despite being an agency worker, and therefore a vassal whose services were dispensable at any time, Brian's longevity within the department had led to his appointment as the de facto deputy team manager. Whilst his promotion obviously didn't include a pay rise he was expected to accept more complex casework and deputise for his superior during her many unexplained absences. His supervision would be a pointless but thankfully brief encounter as Kali had devised a strategy by which she could disappear every Friday afternoon. If anyone bothered to check her diary it would usually contain a curt directive that she would be in meetings, although the whereabouts of these meetings and their purpose was never made clear. Brian was aware that speculation among his colleagues upon Kali's absences ranged from an appointment with a psychotherapist to visiting a swingers' club but, as professional etiquette demanded, Brian maintained a seignurial detachment. His colleagues were unaware that his history with Kali, née Brenda Cartwright, was rather more extensive than he let on. Previous experience had taught him that where Kali was concerned a degree of circumspection was obligatory.

Brian had encountered Kali in another local authority some years previously and became quickly aware that nothing was beyond her except professional competence. He became inured to her penchant for self-dramatisation, her embroilment with unsuitable men and her many leaves of absence for depression resulting from yet another failed romantic interlude. Her episodic absences provoked wrathful curiosity among council mandarins but Kali was astute enough to know that no one can hit a moving target. When it seemed that she might have to answer for her relaxed approach to regular attendance at work she would deftly decamp from one local authority to another.

When he arrived for the interview for his current post, he was aghast to discover that Kali had been appointed as team manager. He rightly assumed that as a social worker she had been a disaster, therefore the local authority had been left with no other recourse than to promote her. Without any preamble Kali had offered him the vacant post. Brian understood that his silence regarding her turbid personal life was a condition of employment. In a true meritocracy, people like Kali simply couldn't happen.

Her cluelessness had been to Brian's advantage. All year he had been clandestinely increasing his department's expenditure on the care packages of certain individuals in the client base. The regime of austerity had demanded that public service expenditure be slashed and burned. Free access to libraries, a decent bus service and regular access to day centres were now considered superfluities. In Brian's view austerity was simply a smokescreen behind which to shrink the state and a blunt instrument with which to bludgeon those whom the government deemed dotards, promiscuous and workshy into an awareness that the safety net of state assistance would not be available in perpetuity. Self-reliance and the largess of loved ones would be the only defences against the indignities of poverty, but of course tax cuts and tax avoidance schemes would continue to be available to the

81

wealthiest.

Brian could envisage a future in which the welfare state would be regarded as an anachronism, the hubristic creation of a nation far too pleased with itself. He believed that the current radical surgery had been ordered to restore the natural order of things. The old, the frail, the poor, the mad and the weak would eventually be excised from decent society by the scalpel of governmental parsimony. In a not too distant future Britain would be a nation unfettered from giving a toss. Endemic despair and an astronomical suicide rate would be prices worth paying for a glittering, free-market future unsullied by concerns about those at the bottom. Brian wasn't happy about this.

Irrespective of the funding ceilings imposed, Brian had been covertly finagling additional spending on care packages. It was his job to evaluate the care assessments conducted by his junior colleagues and decide the level of funding required. He was expected to be creative or, more accurately, miserly with assigning funding to the care packages whilst also ensuring that they would be sufficiently robust to avoid a legal challenge. In many cases Brian had discreetly levelled up the financial resources, but Kali was ultimately responsible for signing off the release of the requisite funding.

As he had anticipated, Kali never so much as glanced at the documents he had placed before her. Her scrawl had unwittingly assigned more monies than the bean counters would ever be willing to disburse. Brian had relied upon the auditor's ignorance of his subterfuge, but detection of the overspend was only a matter of time. A rough calculation suggested an overspend of at least forty thousand pounds, a figure that was increasing with each passing week. Following the next quarterly audit Kali would be dragged before the star chamber and defenestrated for her

82

recklessness, but Brian believed his guerrilla war to be morally defensible. That his own career might also soon be over as a result of his role in this imbroglio mattered little. He was simply past caring about the next disaster to befall him. And, if his plea for relief at the bank today was successful, he would actually look forward to his dismissal. He could spend some of his free time mooching around the black economy, picking up manual work for thirty quid a shift and being the scourge of employment advisors anxious to remove him from their books.

The possibility of employment advisors reintroducing Brian to the world of work was completely infeasible. His age, and his role in the misappropriation of public funds, would render him a permanent burden on the state. He could look forward to visits to the Job Centre, regularly turning up late for appointments, berating the whey-faced drones for their ignorance of how the benefits system really worked and threatening legal action for their failure to inform him of his rights. As someone versed in the complexities of welfare provision he would ensure that he was in receipt of all his entitlements and would be happy to pursue a claim via the courts if necessary. He had even toyed with applying for the allowance payable to those with an enduring psychiatric disorder. He had spent a great deal of his professional life in proximity to the mentally unwell and he was also a resident of Least. He figured that it shouldn't be too difficult to persuade the authorities of palpable lunacy. Whilst harbouring a smidgeon of sympathy for Kali's certain removal from office because of his back chanel philanthropy, at least a competent team manager would then be appointed. It's always darkest before the dawn.

He then groaned in recollection that today was the team Christmas lunch, but was immediately relieved when he remembered the afternoon visit to Ted and Mavis. In more prosperous times social services departments had stumped up monies to fund a modest Christmas lunch and allowed most of the team to disappear for the afternoon. This had suited Brian's purposes perfectly. His status as a mere agency worker demanded that he remained behind to manage the office alone, thus disobliging him from expending precious drinking time upon people with whom he had nothing in common. As an appreciation of Brian's selflessness, his colleagues would invariably present him with two bottles of wine whilst effusively cooing their gratitude. Brian would then spend the afternoon in tranquil repose. He'd uncork a bottle of wine, raid the team fridge for uneaten sandwiches, mull over the *Guardian* quick crossword and occasionally answer the telephone. In these evil days of The Great Mess, however, such fripperies as Christmas lunches were inconsistent with the spirit of corporate parsimony. The leaders of the country had declared that we were all in this together and avoidance of frivolous expenditure would be sending the right message. Employees were encouraged to either forgo a get-together completely or stage it in their offices, bringing in soft drinks and home-cooked fare for the delectation of their colleagues. Predictably these indoor picnics were a culinary disaster. Despite his best efforts Brian couldn't avoid ingesting something tasting like the insole of a marathon runner's training shoe. It is difficult to feign enjoyment of a well-meaning colleague's recipe for ratatouille and mushroom bake when projectile diarrhoea is a very real possibility. He was still considering legal action for last year's vol-au-vents.

Once again he had drawn Elouise in the annual travesty of secret Santa, a woman so fatuous that Brian could imagine her believing in unicorns. She had named her oldest child Bilbo. The previous Christmas she had presented him with a folk music CD so unspeakably awful that it could have only been purchased at a car boot sale. She had handed it to Brian as though bestowing upon him the gift of eternal life, hovering to await the kudos that would surely follow. Brian tore off the packaging, glanced at the portrait of a bearded zither-playing hobo on the cover, smiled thinly, offered his exiguous thanks and immediately began plotting vengeance. To compound this woman's repellence she was also a maniacal health fanatic. A teetotal, pedometer-wearing, vegetarian, yoga class attendee for whom joyless abstemiousness is as intrinsic as heat is to the sun. Brian wondered how adept the hatchet-faced counter assistants in the local garage were at gift wrapping ten cigarettes. Revenge is a dish best served with a smoker's cough and a terminal illness. He smiled as he imagined Elouise's aghast grimace as she undid her little package of harm. A visit to the garage this morning was essential.

His mind then wandered to the vexatious issue of Christmas itself. The usual alibi he used to avoid his parents at this time of the year was now defunct. As he was detached from Helen his parents would expect him for lunch and to accompany his father for a lunchtime drink prior to the breaking of bread. If his previous experiences of family festive repasts were any yardstick, this Christmas promised to be about as convivial as hepatitis C.

On the few occasions he had accompanied his father to the social club on Christmas Day he had sat among his father's friends in morose and resentful silence. In the underlit club lounge, with the clack of snooker balls and the clangour of slot machines underpinning the residual hum of male voices, the gnarled oldsters embarked upon a symphonic bellyache. They opened with an overture about bloody immigrants stealing from

85

washing lines and concluded with a crescendo of graphic narratives concerning their latest medical disorders. Ingrowing toenails, bowel disorders and diabetes were the vogue ailments of the senior citizens of Least, although for some unfathomable reason Brian's father remained impervious to illness of any kind. On numberless occasions Brian had speculated that his father was either immortal or a mutagen swiftly adapting to new environmental challenges. That the tenor of the dialogues of these aging curmudgeons was not in keeping with the spirit of Christmas, or even the contemporary world, was largely irrelevant. All of them were veterans of over seventy Christmases so one more was hardly likely to provoke even mild excitement. In fact, Christmas was a bleedin' inconvenience, as when the lunchtime session was over the social club closed its doors for the rest of the day. They were condemned to spending Christmas night with their children and grandchildren, overfed banshees who hogged the TV remote and trod chocolate into carpets purchased on interest-free credit. A bottle of egg flip and a Richard Curtis film were scant consolations for this unwonted assault upon their drinking time. National Service had been preferable to this.

They had once been a young, Brylcreemed, short-back-and-sided army of eleven-plus failures who were decanted into industrial charnel houses before the age of consent. They were untouched by the swinging sixties, the era cited as the seedbed of modern, socially liberal Britain. Political correctness was voting Labour. Pink Floyd was something the wife might whip up when she didn't have the stuff in to make a trifle. Pot was always prefixed by the word chamber. Sex, drugs, radical politics and interminable concept albums were for dozy buggers with too much time on their hands. These bastions of unregenerate masculinity had circumvented youth completely. From early adulthood they had shouldered the burdens of marriage and children with the stoicism of Buddhist monks. Imbued with a perverse rectitude, they had assiduously cultivated a contempt for such modernist conceits as the Liberal Democrats, sexual diversity, multiculturalism and slip-on shoes. Brian found them deplorable.

When Brian had finally managed to prise the glass of complimentary whisky from his aggressively drunk father and escorted him home, they were greeted by silence and the Lady Macbeth stare of his mother. She was a fireball of malign energy, emitting heat and sparks, ready to destroy everything in her orbit. Brian maintained a tactful silence as he guided his tottering father to a seat at the drop-leaf table on which two candles guttered. When platefuls of cold vegetation and hanks of dead bird were slammed onto the table, Derek gazed intently at his wife as though seeing her for the first time. He then leaned back and studied the ceiling before listing to the left and falling to the floor. Brian and his mother ate in silence as Derek slept on the carpet. When the excruciation of the meal was over, Brian helped his father to the master bedroom whilst being sworn at in the vilest terms. The soiled plates and cutlery remained on the dinner table as Brian's mother retired to the settee to smoke, dip into a tin of chocolates and to make stabbing motions at the television with the TV remote control. As Brian's mother rarely drank and Derek drank only beer and spirits, the Christmas wine remained untouched. Brian retired to the kitchen to wash the dishes in a Blue Nun-induced haze before joining his mother in staring at the television. Not a word passed between them until Brian awoke on the couch the following morning.

Refreshed by sixteen hours of sleep, on Boxing Day Derek

breezed into the living room and announced that he was off to the bookie's and then on to the club. Brian's mother maintained her gelid silence until New Year's Day. Such was a typical Paget family Christmas. Brian was consoled by the possibility that he could be dead by next week and thereby avoid the festivities, but if that didn't transpire then a contingency plan would need to be devised. He then lit upon an idea so obvious that he cursed himself for not thinking of it sooner. If no real female companion was currently around with whom to spend Christmas then the obvious solution was to invent one. Brian screwed his eyes in rapt concentration. The choice of a suitably prosaic name for the fictional lady in question was crucial. If the name of his new partner seemed inauthentic then the deception would assuredly fail and he would again be the target of his parent's corrosive derision.

Patricia? Pat? Patty? Pats? Patso? Pats the way ah-ha ah-ha I like it, ah-ha ah-ha?

Patricia. An age-appropriate name. A name as reassuring as white bread. If Patricia was a man she'd be called Brian. Patricia could be truncated to Pat, implying that she was a warm and unserious person. Pat was someone that everyone liked. Brian liked her already and wondered what she was doing that weekend. She'd probably be out with friends as she's such a people magnet. She's thinking of buying a new car. Nothing extravagant of course. It's mid-range and very reliable. Just like Pat herself.

Pat. She's so great.

When he eased himself into the driving seat he was astonished to find that the car started at the first time of asking. In colder weather it usually required defibrillation. From unpromising beginnings today was looking propitious. His wages would be in the ATM at just past twelve o'clock and there was the appointment with the bank that might just prove transformative. He'd managed to avoid the annual Christmas lunch due to an appointment elsewhere, he'd acquired an engaging and popular new girlfriend and following his trip to the hypermarket was still ten quid to the good. When he bought a newspaper and a cheese sandwich before heading off to the M6 he was happier than he could remember. This was the extent to which his life had deteriorated.

Brian ghosted into the office and appeared at his desk unnoticed by colleagues slunk low in ergonomically sound chairs, gibbering into telephone receivers and peering myopically at computer monitors. The office thrummed to a febrile tempo. Fingers hammered maniacally at keyboards, telephones rang and then abruptly stopped, foul-tempered customer service officers bawled at social workers to answer their bleedin' phones, and Rona swore horribly at a filing cabinet whilst attempting to close the top drawer. When Brian joined the team five years ago he'd immediately felt at home. His colleagues were commonsensical, smart, sweary and refreshingly free of the bureaucratese mouthed by social workers uncertain of their professional competence. They still set about their work with a creditable dedication, but these days the usually amiable atmosphere of the office was poisoned by brittleness and fear.

A few weeks ago the chief executive had circulated an email to all council employees. It made for unpleasant reading, imparting the bombshell that to comply with central government edicts the council had been "tasked" to trim its workforce by over half of its existing staff. The shadow of the axe hovered over the salariat of this tough, decent and unfashionable former mining town. The effect of these proposed redundancies would ramify like a tsunami. When four thousand people are rendered economically inactive, then local businesses would undoubtedly suffer. Boarded shopfronts on the high street and the death of aspiration were inevitable adjuncts to such retrenchment. For a town remaining viable only because of the efforts of local government and the civic pride of its inhabitants, this could well be the death knell.

A great many women in the office were the primary breadwinners of their families. They had lived in the town all their lives and married to local men whose unskilled and semi-skilled labour was of no further use in a heavily financialised economy. Some of the men had thrown in their lot with employment agencies, gratefully seizing a succession of short-term contracts for risible hourly rates. Other men had been medically retired and received a supplement to their income from disability allowances. Denise, a resourceful and practical thirty-something, had married Johnno, a former marine injured in the second Iraq war. Johnno took care of their pre-school children whilst Denise continued her tenure in the local authority. More than a few rows had ensued between the otherwise happy couple as Johnno had ventilated his frustration at feeling diminished by his role of househusband. If the departmental axe fell on Denise then there were undoubtedly more marital spats in the pipeline.

Denise faced the vagaries of parenthood, uncertain job security and caring for an emotionally canted husband with a fortitude that Brian knew himself not to possess. Watching her on the telephone calmly conciliating with an elderly client, he was dispirited that in the wake of the most profligate financial orgy in modern history it would be families like hers who would suffer the worst. In recent years the media had been swamped by legions of analysts charged with the task of providing clarity to neologisms describing limitless greed and criminal recklessness. Sub-prime, collateralised debt obligations, derivatives, futures, bank runs. A cold, monetised nomenclature of the unfathomable. Brian was embarrassed by his inability to understand these models of financial legerdemain and suspected that many others were too. It seemed that reptiles in the City had been gambling with other people's money, and when they'd cashed out they simply asked governments across the world to refill their piggy banks. Which they duly did. Brian had been disturbed by the simplicity of this explanation. It couldn't be so elementary, otherwise responsible people would have stepped in and brought these maniacs to book. And if it was simply a case of a clique of wide boys gulling the public, where were the warnings from pundits alerting the world that it was just a heartbeat away from a complete meltdown? These days it was impossible to shut experts up, but when they needed to speak out they had stayed silent. Brian had resolved never to read another economics page in the press ever again.

He switched on his computer and glanced around the office. Whilst eyeing the slew of emails in his inbox he quickly cast an eye over the team, searching for furrowed brows or vacant stares. He was pleasantly surprised to note that all of them were abstracted but seemingly untroubled by their work. Kevin caught his eye with a languorous wave of a pudgy hand.

'All right there, Kev?'

'Not so bad Brian. I'm going the shop for a paper. D'you need owt?'

'How about a reason to live?'

'I'll see if they've got one. I'm not promising, mind.'

'Do your best.'

If there was any justice in the world then Kevin would be the team manager. He was only thirty-five but his height and bulk gave him an aldermanic authority. When Kevin spoke, his pronounced regional accent evoked folk memories of kinder, less frenetic times. Invariably dressed in a pristine white shirt, black slacks and plain knitted tie he reminded Brian of a primped and comforting pillow. He was impossible to dislike, a plaudit afforded to few people who worked in the caring professions. People felt somehow better about themselves when he was around.

'Are you up for the Christmas do, Brian?'

'Sorry, Kev. Things to do and people to see.'

'The wife's made a trifle. I'm thinking of having it sectioned.'

'Why's that?'

'It's got delusions of being edible.'

'I'm sure it'll go down a treat with these gannets.'

'Not with me it won't. I'll be off to the chipper as soon as no one's looking.'

'Those pies won't eat themselves, Kev.'

'You're dead right there pal.'

Brian stared at messages on the computer screen whilst mentally arranging them in order of priority. A suspicious red mark on the leg of a female service user sustained in a day centre required investigation. Kevin would be assigned that later. A reminder to review a service user in a secure mental health unit. Pencil that in for someone next Tuesday. There was querulous response from a physiotherapist to Brian's request for a home assessment of an elderly lady. The respondent was a typical young physio, newly qualified and believing herself to be god-gifted. From the tone of her message, imperium tinged with hysteria, Brian intuited that within six months she'd be yet another candidate for a stress-related absence from work and a course of antidepressants. Welcome to the pleasure dome, oh sister of mercy.

There was encouraging news on the dog-wank front. Jane, a detective constable, was the investigating officer of an incident concerning a moderately learning disabled service user. The young man in question had grappled with his girlfriend's Alsatian dog and then proceeded to masturbate the hound to ejaculation. Footage of the incident had been posted on the Internet and a police investigation launched following a complaint by the owner of the hound. Brian had attended several meetings in which the capacity of a service user to understand the implications of jerking off an Alsatian were weighed against the possibility of a charge of bestiality. At one point it was difficult to determine whose best interests the police were trying to serve. It was finally agreed that they were safeguarding the Alsatian against further abuse whilst also protecting a learning disabled adult from a potentially lethal attack by an outraged canine.

Brian endured a nausea akin to altitude sickness as discussions with the police ranged from the physical challenges presented by the masturbation of an Alsatian, then to more abstruse ruminations upon whether it could be legally classifiable as bestiality if the dog had enjoyed it. A junior female police officer was adamant in her belief that the dog had taken pleasure in the act. Speaking as a dog owner herself, she claimed a degree of expertise in reading the expressions of dogs. After careful study of the footage she had concluded that the Alsatian was smiling throughout the encounter. In any case, if the dog hadn't been enjoying it then he would have certainly put up more of a struggle. That the dog did not resist could be construed as

93

consent. Brian gently requested that her contribution was withdrawn from the minutes. This was a purely subjective viewpoint unsubstantiated by empirical evidence. DI Jane disclosed that at this juncture she was unable to offer a legal definition of bestiality and promised to return when she had consulted with experts in jurisprudence.

DI Jane's latest email proved enlightening. There were no legal grounds for prosecution as bestiality was currently defined as an act of penetration. As for culpability, whilst the dog had not given informed consent to manual stimulation, it had at no time evinced any desire for the act to be discontinued. There had been some debate about whether an Alsatian possessed the capacity to offer informed consent, it being a dog and therefore unable to talk, but it was pertinent to note that the dog had failed to manifest its displeasure by savaging its assailant. This could be deemed circumstantial evidence of consent. DI Jane had reported that no further action was needed, except to counsel the service user of the ill-advisedness of wanking off a dangerous dog. No victim impact statement would be available as the Alsatian, being a dog, was functionally illiterate. It could be deemed oppressive to request a written testimony of events from a member of the non-literate community.

Brian was relieved that this tawdry affair could be finally put to bed and hopefully out of his mind forever. This case would definitely not be an agenda item when he met with Kali later. The paperwork might also provoke difficulties as the department's computerised archive demanded the ethnicity of the persons involved. The white British ethnic origin of the perpetrator was obvious, but the ethnicity of the dog was a little more ticklish. He settled upon German as the dog's nationality as he recalled that Alsatians were also called German shepherds. Name? Justin.

Ethnicity? Moulting Teutonic. That might be enough to feed the ravenous local authority mainframe.

In more extravagant times it was common practice for the local authority to appoint a champion of special interest groups within the borough. A champion of the street homeless, survivors of domestic violence or those struggling with alcohol abuse. These czars were appointed from the ranks of social workers and were offered a small emolument in recognition of this new responsibility. They were occasionally pressed into lobbying at council meetings or to make Powerpoint presentations highlighting the plight of an oppressed social group. Brian speculated upon what the role of a local authority dog-wank czar might entail. A special hotline perhaps. Posters around the town featuring the visage of a mutt clearly in some discomfort:

Don't let this happen to your favourite companion. Call our hotline now and speak in confidence to Brian Paget, your local authority canine sexual abuse czar. The Council: Working Towards A Dog-Wank Free Community.

Brian's reverie was interrupted by Rona, who had teleported from across the room to alight by his left shoulder. He started as she poked him in the ear with her regulation blue biro and demanded he check his diary for available space in the busy Christmas week. Day centres expected a visit from senior social care staff, and Brian was usually dragooned into making numerous appearances. He was used to nodding appreciatively at the handiwork of the craft group, posing for pictures with service users, and then dripping the filling of an egg mayonnaise sandwich onto his suit. Brian enjoyed these functions as it reminded him of the incalculable worth of day centres and the hard work of the staff, all of which would soon come to a dead stop. By end of next year all day centres in the town would close their doors forever. By way of justification for the closures, the bean counters had claimed that day centres "ghettoised" the service users. They were effectively sub-communities hidden from plain sight. Day centres denied "valued" but "differently abled" members of society social intercourse with their "normatively abled" fellow citizens.

Local authority media managers were third dan black belts in the art of egregious bollocks, but this was an unsurpassable example of managerese. The primary but unspoken function of a day centre was to provide respite for families exhausted by caring for relatives. Packing off the "valued although differently abled" member of the community onto the morning bus allowed the carers to catch up with their sleep, their sex lives, their laundry and their shopping. If day centres continued to close, brian could foresee a future in which an army of bleary-eyed carers telephoned the local authority to report that they couldn't cope any more and the council would have to look after their relatives instead. The provision of care and accommodation for these differently abled but valued members of the community would bankrupt councils nationwide. Another brilliant example of governmental fiscal prudence and forward thinking.

Rona, tremulous with adrenaline and strong coffee, oscillated as she feverishly scribbled Brian's dates of availability for the coming week. She then reeled off a number of tasks she expected Brian to address within three days, primarily signing documents that her small administration team had to process within a stringent time frame. They were currently failing their performance quality indicators because Brian was falling behind on his back-office duties and he needed to bleedin' well shape himself. Then she produced a Christmas card and held it two inches from Brian's nose.

'Sign it.'

'Oh come on, Rona. I don't even like speech therapists. They're oxygen thieves if you ask me.'

'I haven't got time for this, Brian. Who's holding a biro here?'

'You are.'

'Well if you don't sign this card I'll bleedin' stab you with it. Now come on. And be quick about it.'

Brian sighed, signed the card and enquired how Rona's husband was faring in the job market following his redundancy. Rona's angular face hardened as she sibilated her ire at her husband's lassitude and self-pity. He was staying up later at night, spending longer in bed, and being increasingly uncommunicative. His drinking had also markedly increased. Brian nodded sympathetically. The struggles of Rona's husband mirrored those of some of his old workmates expunged by the inexorable outsourcing of smokestack industries. He had never forgotten the tears rolling down the face of Francey when he was given the boot. He was a father of five kids and so financially stretched that instead of making a monthly visit to the barber he would submit his unruly thatch to be cut for free by apprentices at the local college. In two years of their attendance at college the apprentices had only mastered the tonsorial disaster that Francey's workmates had dubbed The Drive-By Shooting. However, Francey's avoidance of a professional barber saved him three quid. Three quid was a lot of money to Francey and his brood.

Following a series of supposedly simple psychometric tests and a review of each individual's value to the company, it was concluded that Francey's intelligence and problem-solving skills would be better deployed in a less demanding environment. His final pay packet was four weeks' wages and ten days of accrued holiday pay. Mindful of Francey's testing domestic circumstances, the shop floor hard man had ordered everyone contribute a fiver to a whip-round. Any failure to contribute would lead to a fucking good hiding. A respectable two hundred quid was raised, but there were no valedictory speeches or official presentation. Francey might have perceived the money as charity and an affront to his already bruised masculine pride.

Brian persuaded the security officer of the factory to loan him the master key to the changing room. Whilst his workmates played touch rugby in the car park, Brian opened Francey's locker and carefully placed a plain white envelope atop a riffle of soft porn magazines. Francey made no mention of the gift and neither did his workmates. As was the tradition, when a workmate departed he was forbidden to buy a round on his farewell night out. At two o'clock in the morning his erstwhile workmates bundled Francey into a taxi whilst singing, "Fuck off you cunt", to the melody of 'Amazing Grace'. Twenty hopelessly drunk men then stood in the middle of the high street and threw V-signs at the retreating cab. Francey hung himself five months later.

In the passing of some twenty-odd years, Brian still couldn't decide if Francey was a victim or a symptom of the transition to a world managed for the benefit of only one per cent of the population. Progress is irresistible and deaf to the trifling concerns of individuals, but the chasm created by the extinction of reasonably paid manual labour had claimed too many men like Francey. Rona's husband was another candidate for the abyss.

Consolatory afternoon drinking sessions ineluctably

98

extended into the early hours. Bitter domestic spats culminated in a police escort away from the family home. Divorce proceedings and then an injunction to stay away from the wife and kids was usually followed by kipping down in shop doorways and underpasses, wheezing and coughing, swaddled in thrift-shop parkas and urinous undergarments. Cheap vodka, toxic medication and screaming at the shifting skies. Soiled rags on a railway embankment. Death by misadventure. Rona's husband was one of many men cored of their utility by dint of their maladaption to sedentary occupations requiring skills they didn't possess. Men without emotional intelligence or a reservoir of social capital. If this was progress then a return to simpler times wouldn't seem too bad an option, unless of course the giant tattooed infants staged their anticipated coup and converted the long-term unemployed into food. Brian was about to whisper a few words of conciliation to Rona when she became ramrod stiff and ominously silent. Her bird-of-prey eyes stared unblinkingly across the expanse of the office and then at the entrance to the office.

'Brian?'

'Hmm?'

'What's the bride of bleedin' Frankenstein doing on the shop floor?'

Brian's eyes followed the wavelet of amused curiosity breaking over each member of the team. Only Kevin remained impassive at the sight of what appeared to be a bag lady, bedizened in too large sunglasses and waving desperately in Brian's direction. Rona was unimpressed by this unwonted incursion into her dominion.

'I'm telling you now Brian. If she comes over here mithering me she can fuck the fuck off.'

99

'It's me she wants Rona, not you.'

'Look at her. The scruffy article. Her arse is that bleedin' big it's got membership of the European Union. Old slapper she's nowt else.'

'Can't we just once respect the badge of office, Rona? She is the manager you know.'

'Shut it, Brian.'

Brian stood, grabbed his folder of supervision notes and trudged in Kali's wake. When he arrived in Kali's office she was already seated and rubbing her forehead, a sign that her temperament was even more unstable than usual. A minute passed before she removed her sunglasses. Her eyes were set deep within caverns of kohl flecked with azure glitter. Brian returned her gaze impassively and remained deliberately silent. He wasn't in the mood to open the conversation. For a change it would be she who would initiate the exchanges. Another minute passed and Kali continued to stare at Brian, seemingly narcotized. He sighed in capitulation, opened his folder and steeled himself for another bout of Kali's emotional incontinence. Doubtless the first tranche of this encounter would be a rumination upon why men are such bastards. On this occasion, however, he couldn't have been more astonished if she had pulled a gun from beneath her skirt and shot him in the kneecap.

'You look like you've got something on your mind.'

'It's you who should have something on your mind, Brian, not me.'

'Eh? Such as?'

'Well. You don't work here any more for a start-off.'

'What?'

'Here. Have a look at this email. I've learned how to print

100

them off now.'

Brian snatched the document from Kali's talons and scanned the terse missive. All team managers were directed to suspend the employment of all agency workers with immediate effect. This was a cost-cutting exercise to relieve pressure on drastically reduced departmental budgets and a response to diminishing consumer demand.

'Eh? Reduced consumer demand? We're beyond capacity at the minute.'

'Are we? Oh. Well. Carry on reading.'

Brian gaped in disbelief at his superior. He hadn't figured on this at all. For her part, Kali was visibly unnerved by being the harbinger of unwelcome news. That was usually Brian's job. She rubbed her forehead again and then stared dolorously out of the window behind her. As he read the missive Brian was suffused by a peculiar and not unpleasant sense of detachment, feeling like a spectator rather than a participant in this tableau. Logic suggested that he was in shock and this new development would take several drinks to process. Being privy to the news first, Kali had been afforded more time to ponder the impact of this thunderbolt. Not upon Brian, of course, but on her.

'I don't know I'm going to manage that lot out there without a deputy, Brian. I'm snowed under as it is. With you going it'll just send me over the edge.'

'It'd help if you were a bit more visible. Get among them a bit more, keep an eye on them. Take my desk a couple of days a week. Kevin will help you out managing the team. He's really capable.'

'Who's Kevin?'

'The big lad who sits facing me.'

'I wondered who he was.'

101

Another silence ensued as Brian struggled to conjure some coherent plan of action from the half-ideas ricocheting from the walls of his skull. Kali's train of thought was concentrated purely upon the upshot of being forced to display her singular professional skills in plain sight of upper management. She feared that without the bastion of Brian to cower behind she would once again be forced to look for other opportunities. Whilst Kali contemplated her uncertain future, Brian cogitated the possibility of persuading Kali to sign next week's timesheet whilst overlooking the fact that he wouldn't be at work. In actuality this would be easy as she never read anything he put before her anyway.

'Can I have a reference to pass onto the agency? They'll need one when they start looking around for my next assignment.'

'Can't you write it Brian? I'm too traumatised to think straight at the minute.'

'Tell you what. I'll go back in the office and write it now. You sign it and I'll email it to the agency today. You can sign my timesheet as well if you would. I'm out on a visit this afternoon, then I've got an appointment at the bank so I'm a bit pressed.'

'Do what you like. I'll sign anything you want. You'll have to be quick though. I'm in meetings all afternoon. I can't seem to catch my breath these days.'

'Leave it with me.'

Brian strode from Kali's office and feverishly typed an encomium to his professional skills that stopped just short of his possession of X-ray vision and the power of flight. As an adept of composing references for both himself and others, Brian could rattle off two paragraphs of vacuous jargonese in the time it took most people to knock up a shopping list. As well as being an experienced practitioner of conflict resolution, a self-starter, a facilitator (whatever that was) and an initiator of creative solutions to real-time dilemmas, he was also attuned to the needs and aspirations of oppressed social groupings, including the currently vogue gender-fluid community.

When he had completed the screed Brian leaned back in satisfaction. In his experience no departmental manager could resist a taxonomy of the absurd. Although he might never work again following the quarterly audit of his department, he would continue to practice his profession in what little remained of his working life. Kevin looked on with interest whilst worrying at earwax with a felt tip pen.

'Bloody hell, Brian. You look busy there. What's to do?'

'A bit of preparation for next week. I've just been given the white fiver. All agency workers are out from today.'

'Ooh. Hard luck pal. D'you want a pie?'

'Not really.'

'Shout up if you change your mind.'

Brian ambled over to Rona and requested a cardboard box into which to store detritus accumulated over the previous five years. In common with most social workers Brian had difficulty in throwing anything away. Assessment documents he used as templates and articles from various journals he'd failed to get around to reading spilled from his overstuffed desk. All of them would now be despatched to the dustbin. When he imparted the news of his departure to Rona's team, they froze as though afflicted by rigor mortis. Their body language intimated not sorrow but anger and they seemed ready to give voice to their ire. Unlike the social workers they were unencumbered by the stultifying obligation to be cordial. Their candour could be both acute and withering. On more than one occasion Kevin had remarked that he'd rather be flayed with light flex than have the admin ladies on his case.

Rona scored her desk with the tip of her biro and set her jaw to attack mode. Lexi tossed her blonde mane and made an obscene gesture with her right hand in the direction of Kali's office. Suzanne wept tears of barely contained frustration whilst muttering the names of social workers she'd be quite happily murder, never mind relieve of their duties in lieu of Brian. Brian attempted to mollify them with a casual wave of his hand as though refusing a second helping of dessert. He also intuited that their wrath was underpinned by the justifiable fear that they might also be next for the heave-ho. If the junior officers could be cashiered then the grunts were easily disposed of. Rona handed Brian a cardboard box whilst her eyes bored into him. He strolled back to his desk and began packing the flotsam of five years whilst the office rumour mill groaned into life.

Brian became so engrossed in his task that he failed to notice the small but meticulously wrapped package nestling on his chair. When he did finally notice it he picked it up, examined it and then shot Kevin an enquiring glance. Kevin grinned broadly and then shrugged his shoulders in feigned ignorance. Brian then closed his eyes, pained by pricks of conscience. He had forgotten to buy a Secret Santa gift for Elouise and knew the package to be from her. He placed the package on his desk and then stared at the pristine copy of his morning newspaper. He beckoned Rona over.

'Rona? Here's my timesheets. Get Kali to sign and then email them to the agency. Get her to sign this reference as well. Send that to my private email address.'

'Right Brian.'

'And do you think you could gift wrap this for me?'

'What? A bleedin' newspaper? Are you having me on?'

'No I'm not. It's for Elouise. I'm her Secret Santa. We're not allowed to spend more than a fiver in any case.'

'And that's the best you could do? A bleedin' newspaper? Jesus, Brian. If you gave that to me I'd kick your arse that hard you wouldn't shit for a week.'

'But can you do it? I want revenge for last year. She gave me a CD so bloody awful that even charity shops won't take it. It's payback time.'

Rona regarded him evilly for a moment and then snatched the newspaper from the desk.

'Give it here. I can't stand that barmy bitch in any case. But don't you go telling her I did it. She'll go crying to the bloody management, she will. We're in enough lumber as it is.'

Rona aimed a recriminatory headshake at Brian and then scuttered back to her desk. Brian completed boxing away his papers, sat down and gazed around the office. This was the last time he would look at these surroundings. The occasion should have been informed with a regretful finality analogous to finishing an enjoyable novel, but his prevalent emotion was relief tinged with an intoxicating giddiness. He would also need to find a jumbo bin in which to dump the relics of his working life, and sod client confidentiality. He watched with wry fascination as Rona tramped over to Elouise's desk, pointed in Brian's direction and casually handed her a scrupulously wrapped package. Brian returned Elouise's guileless smile, waved and then walked out of the office without so much as a backward glance.

He drove slowly through the most affluent purlieu of the town until he stopped outside a detached bungalow he referred to as The Hurt Locker. Its well-tended lawn and shabby gentility was a facade behind which nameless depravities were enacted

105

and bloody conflicts played out. Passers-by would have no inkling of the pointless mini-wars that were daily prosecuted behind the front door he was approaching. Ted and Mavis had been married for over fifty years and their loathing of one another had grown exponentially with each passing decade. Their two children, legal professionals who avoided living in even the same hemisphere as their parents, occasionally telephoned Brian to tersely enquire after their parent's health. It was safe to assume that this was not a close family.

Ted and Mavis experienced few health problems and were relatively strapping when compared to many people their age, enjoying a septuagenarian opulence courtesy of a very healthy financial situation. Neither of them were going to go gently into that good night. A community care worker called twice weekly to assist Mavis with her ablutions and a privately hired cleaner named Jackie laundered, cleaned and discreetly disposed of the empty bottles of wine, gin and whisky drained of their contents by her employers.

In his working life Ted had been a petrochemical engineer whose expertise had been in almost universal demand following the discovery of oil gluts in developing nations. The eye-watering employment packages offered by oil companies ensured not only spectacular financial rewards but also free private education for his progeny. The children were abandoned to stern public schools in which their leadership skills, coupled with an abiding loathing of their mercurial parents, were assiduously cultivated. The incarceration of their children in two of the better schools in England liberated Ted and Mavis from the fetters of parenthood. They roamed the world posturing as the Richard and Liz of petrochemical engineering, hobbling drunkenly around the croquet lawns and tennis courts of exclusive British clubs, guffawing with blazered alickadoos, smashing back concussive cocktails and bemoaning the crushing weight of the white man's burden.

Expatriate life suited the ill-starred couple. Mavis could indulge her fondness for lunchtime eye-openers in the hotel bar whilst Ted held court, spifflicated by wine-drenched meals courtesy of a generous expense account. His entertainment allowance equalled the weekly take-home pay of most workers in his home country, therefore the couple's social calendar was predictably full. Ted was gifted with a thirst for strong drink allied to a work ethic that would shame a pit pony. The only bleak spot in their year was the flight back to Britain to collect their increasingly resentful children for the annual seaside holiday. The children sat forlornly on freezing Welsh beaches, huddled together like the bastard offspring of Neptune whilst their parents played gin rummy in pubs fragrant with the stench of farmhands and fairground roustabouts.

Material wealth and an incautious approach to alcohol are effective prophylactics against the tedious realities of life. Their children's maturity to adulthood went largely unnoticed by Ted and Mavis. Although both were mercifully absent from their children's graduation from Russell Group universities, pupillage in reputable chambers, marriages and the arrival of grand-children, Ted cheerfully divested himself of as much financial support as his offspring demanded. Ted was barely aware of his provision for engagement parties, weddings, German cars, deposits for homes in Australia and generous trust funds for grandchildren he knew only from occasional telephone calls. Ted had once likened his bank balance to an egg timer. A volume of sand slowly leaked and depleted to nothing, but when the device was inverted the sand was miraculously restored to its previous volume. The volume of sand remained the same irrespective of preceding events. The companies benefitting from his expertise continued to shower Ted with rewards beyond the imagining of even the most avaricious. Even the cost of restoring his treasured Mercedes, following Mavis's submersion of the vehicle in a swimming pool, did little to impair Ted's financial health. There was always another contract, in another interesting location, and always more lucrative than the last. His gilded existence continued until his sixty-eighth year when retirement beckoned and the party had to stop.

Enriched by a plethora of non-contributory pension funds, the couple retired to a handsomely appointed bungalow in north-west England. This was to prove a mistake. Without the diversions of work and the company of other dissolutes, Ted and Mavis were forced to confront the irrefutable truth that each had married the wrong person and it was too late for an annulment. In previous decades their acrimony had been salved by abundant ingestions of alcohol, but increasing infirmity and being forced to live out their remaining years with only each another for company presaged prolonged hostilities. Physical violence was a regular occurrence, each of them as culpable as the other in these superannuated dust-ups, but when police involvement was invoked each averred the innocence of the other. They were a wearisome drain on Brian's time but the local authority's duty of care extended to all of its citizens, not only those who actually merited it. Apart from anything else it would be meat and drink to the national media if one of them should suffer either a serious injury or expire in unusual circumstances. The adverse publicity engendered by such an incident was to be avoided. Surveillance of the couple was the obvious remedy. Brian was coerced into making episodic visits on the implausible premise of reviewing their care needs. As he tramped towards the front door Brian again wondered if he should have worn a candy-striped shirt and a dickie bow. Let's get ready to rumble.

Ted answered Brian's knock. Abnormally tall, florid-faced, shock-haired and with a handshake that could crack walnuts, brio issued from Ted like the vapours emitted by an ancient though still serviceable steam engine. Brian quietly marvelled at his refusal to bow to the miseries of old age despite suffering a debilitating stroke three years previously. His brisk and intimidating demeanour was reflective of a man used to having things done his way or not at all. Over the years he and Brian had fostered a relationship of cordiality admixed with disdain. There was a silent compact between them. Brian forbore from mentioning that Ted's dictatorial tendencies had made the lives of his family unbearable, and that far from being a bluff old cove he was a repellent, foul-smelling alcoholic. In his turn Ted refrained from expressing his view that Brian should be ashamed of himself for pursuing such a pinko nancy-boy profession as social work. Each of them recognised that it was too late for either of them to change their paths in life and both were resigned to their fates.

As he traipsed behind Ted into the spacious living room Brian discreetly sniffed the air, his nose primed to detect the stench of urine. As Mavis suffered emphysema and acute oedema in her legs, mobility difficulties were inevitable. Her problems had led to numerous occasions when she was unable to make it to the bathroom in time. Brian had suggested the possibility of a commode but both Ted and Mavis had railed at the idea, declaring that a lavatory in the living room was a furnishing fit only for the Irish and the manual labouring classes. Ted was also prone to bouts of incontinence, although his difficulties were attributable to over-indulgence in the hooligan soup rather than a physiological complaint. In defiance of client confidentiality, Brian had maintained a back-channel of communication with the couple's cleaner, Jackie, who was only too ready to recount her disgust at finding evidence of Ted, "Going to the toilet properly", whilst unconscious in bed.

In addition to witnessing all manner of indecorums Jackie had also been the target of their vituperation when the couple were in their cups, but as she was handsomely rewarded she retained her composure before venting her spleen in a weekly telephone call to Brian. Brian would close his eyes whilst Jackie recounted the latest incidents of drunken aggression the couple had visited upon both her and each other. Brian would then express his heartfelt gratitude for her efforts and wish her all the best for the coming week. It was a mutually satisfactory arrangement. Brian was able to maintain a long-arm supervision of the couple whilst Jackie could voice her dearest wish that they would die slow and agonising deaths. Such are the advantages of effective partnership working.

Brian entered the living room and received a haughty nod from the owlish Mavis. She was embayed in her usual chair and brandished her metal walking aid as though it was a talisman against malign supernatural forces. Brian immediately noted her new wig, an aquamarine hairpiece that only served to amplify her sinister eccentricity. She resembled a bibulous Lady Bracknell and was seemingly in a truculent mood. She fumed on a cheroot like a bad-hat in a vintage Western, and loured at Brian through the fug. It appeared that Mavis had something on her mind.

'How are you today, Mavis? Has there been any more swelling in the legs?'

'Of course there has. Why are you here?'

110

From the corner of his eye Brian espied Ted hovering like a crow ready to swoop on roadkill. He swallowed and prepared himself for the crossfire between the couple that would inevitably ensue.

'Just to make sure you're okay. See if there's anything else we can do to make you safer and more comfortable.'

'Have you by any chance an assassin in your employ? Or at least a number I can call?'

'Erm… no. Employing assassins is against local authority policy really. Why do you ask that, Mavis?'

'I'd like him killed as soon as possible. And I'd welcome the assistance of social services in this endeavour.'

'Ted you mean. You want Ted killed?'

'Of course I mean him. To whom did you think I was referring, you gibbering halfwit?'

'Am I right in thinking that you two haven't been getting on too well recently?'

Upon Brian's innocuous query Ted unleashed an elemental roar, a pre-human sound, the berserk vocalisation of a vowel yet to find its way into the alphabet. He hopped from one leg to another and pointed an accusatory finger at his spouse whilst Mavis smiled malevolently and brandished her walking aid at him.

'Okay. Right. I think we need to lower the temperature a little bit here.'

'I want to decapitate him. What do you think of that Mr Paget?'

'But why, Mavis?'

Mavis recomposed her ravaged features to convey polite disgust and injured sensibilities.

'He's been coming into my bedroom at night and trying to

insert himself.'

'Sorry? Come again?'

'Insert himself. Into me. Is that acceptable behaviour Mr Paget?'

Brian's sharp intake of breath betrayed his horror at a mental image that would be difficult to erase. Ted and Mavis in nightwear and surgical stockings, odorous with embrocation, unhinged by alcohol and in the throes of sexual congress. He immediately began to regret the previous night with Tracey as the foul and unmistakeable taste of vomit suffused his mouth.

'Well it isn't acceptable if one of the partners doesn't want to participate. And by the sounds of it, Mavis, you're opposed to it.'

'I'm not opposed to fucking, Mr Paget, not at all. I'd just like to be fucked by someone younger and a lot less smelly. Worse than that, when I repel him by hitting him with my stick he abuses himself until he makes a mess on the duvet. Then he goes back to his own room and soils himself in bed. Perfectly disgusting. This really can't go on. On top of all that he's making more laundry for the cleaner and we pay her enough as it is. Do you understand me Mr Paget?'

Brian was momentarily distracted by Ted growling behind him, and for one heart-stopping moment he thought that the old man would pounce and tear both he and Mavis to shreds. This situation was plainly out of hand. Brian's short breaths and moist brow suggested that either a seizure or a cardiac infarction was in train. Even after years of working with people at their worst, human beings always found new and creative methods to confound him. Conciliating with a disabled hag and a degenerate septuagenarian with late-onset satyromania was something he'd never attempted before. But Brian was nothing if not a trier.

112

'Okay. Now then, Ted. It's obvious that you're still sexually active and you still desire your wife. That's admirable in a couple that's been married for as long as you two, don't you think?'

'I don't like her. She's just the nearest to hand, that's all.'

'Well... okay. But we've got a problem here, in that Mavis really doesn't wish to engage in relations. Which is understandable given her health problems.'

'Don't put words in my mouth, Mr Paget. It's relations with HIM I don't wish to engage in.'

'Right. Okay. Now, Ted. You see the problem here. It's the problem of consent. I know she's your wife, and I know that there are certain expectations within a marriage, but if consent isn't given then it could be deemed coercion. Sexual assault if you like. And that means police involvement. Not a road either of you want to go down, am I right?

'It's her making a fuss about it. I just want to get the dirty water off my chest and go to sleep.'

'Why aren't you dead yet? And why are you behaving like an adolescent at your age? It's utterly nauseating. You're abnormal. You should die.'

'Don't be ridiculous woman. It's perfectly natural. I bet Brian's pulling his plonker at all times of the day and night, aren't you Brian? '

'I think we're getting a bit off-topic here, Ted...

Following fifteen minutes of accusations, counter-accusations and recriminatory silences, Brian managed to convince the couple of the value of a behavioural contract. The contract would lay out the rules of engagement by which they should abide. Mavis could either permit or demur copulation without recourse to beating Ted senseless with her walking stick, whilst in her turn Mavis should strive to exercise greater understanding of her husband's emotional needs. Brian suggested that Ted's bellicosity may be born of shame, and if she was reluctant to engage in intercourse then Mavis should direct Ted to find other outlets for his desire whilst avoiding censure. To Brian's astonishment, both parties slowly nodded their heads in agreement and raised their glasses to this new memorandum of understanding. Brian wasn't offered so much as a glass of water, but he was satisfied with the temporary armistice. His satisfaction was cut short when Mavis raised the issue of the television.

In common with millions of older people, Ted and Mavis squandered what little remained of their lives watching the telly. Brian had observed within his own family the incalculable benefits of adults being able to ignore each other for hours on end and submerse themselves in whatever was being screened. Television was probably responsible for the preservation of thousands of marriages. For many couples it was their only remaining touchstone, something they could do together without their companionship declining into acrimony. The relatively unchallenging activity of watching telly also allowed multi-tasking. Brian's mother smoked, cooked, cleaned, ironed and took numerous naps whilst the televisual window on the world remained was open, thus allowing his father to wreak his peculiar mischief elsewhere. Ted and Mavis could lounge around whiffled on whisky whilst focusing upon the fictional worlds of miserable Londoners or northerners who spent most of their time in the pub. Such was the utility of television that it was a wonder that John Logie Baird had not been canonised for his contribution to preserving the unions of couples whose interest in one another had dissipated long ago. But in The Hurt Locker, sovereignty over the square god was yet another casus belli.

'Okay, Mavis. If I'm correct, you want to watch *How Clean Is Your Gran?* every weeknight and then a quiz show. Am I right?'

'They are the only two programmes I stay alive for, Mr Paget. If I'm unable to watch them you will have blood on your hands.'

'And Ted? You want to watch the news.'

'Of course I bloody do. Who doesn't? Except her, the ignorant sow.'

'Well this is easy. You've got a huge kitchen. All you do is buy a flat-screen telly, mount it on the kitchen wall and then both of you can watch whatever you want. My mam and dad have the same set-up. No arguments, no fallouts. Dead simple.'

This suggestion was greeted with a glacial silence.

'Mr Paget. Are you seriously suggesting we spend our remaining savings upon acquiring another television?'

'Well lots of people do. It works for them.'

'I think you've got a bloody cheek asking pensioners to lash out on something as dear as a telly, Brian. Do you think we're made of bloody money?'

'Mr Paget. I am a sick woman not long for this world and my husband is deranged. Don't you think it's rather high-handed of you to dictate exactly how we should be spending what remaining money we have?'

'As I say, it's only a suggestion.'

'And what will social services provide in the way of assistance, Mr. Paget?'

'Well nothing really. You just go out and buy a telly, that's all.'

'Well that's bloody typical that is. I've worked all my life and never asked for a penny from the state but when we need a bit of help there's none available. You'd rather spend it on Kosovans and single bloody parents you lot. Bloody poofter do-gooder communists, that's all you lot are.'

'No, Ted, that's not the case at all…'

'I'm disappointed in you, Mr Paget. I thought you were here to help us, not instruct us upon how to spend our dwindling nest-egg.

'I'm sorry, but I really haven't got any other solution.'

'Brian? I think it's time you cleared off, my lad. You're bloody pointless.'

'Right-oh, Ted. All the fucking best for Christmas.'

'Eh?'

'Go out and buy a fucking telly you cheap bastards. You've got more money than sense but you expect the council to fork out cash on rubbish you could afford yourself? There are people out there with real problems and they're not millionaires either. You pair of sad old winos can go and fuck yourselves.'

'I don't like your tone my lad.'

'Well make a bleedin' complaint then. My boss will be all ears. Ta-ra now.'

Brian retrieved his briefcase from the sofa and made his way to the front door. He was aware that Ted was hovering behind him speechless with disconcertion, but he couldn't have cared less. He was used to being sport for these aging disparates, someone else in their strange little world to inveigh against, but unlike them he was armed with the knowledge that his dealings with them were now concluded. Ted would undoubtedly pick up the telephone and demand to speak to the chief executive regarding Brian's outburst, but retrospective disciplinary action against former employees was rare. Brian was also confident that the chief executive's personal assistant, who regularly fielded

116

Ted's calls, would curtail his invective by simply cutting him off. Without even so much as a farewell nod Brian drove away from The Hurt Locker. It was almost twelve o'clock and he needed to find an ATM.

Outwitting an automated telling machine is an art requiring guile, forward planning and finely honed time management skills. Through trial and error Brian had discovered that there was a window of seven minutes during which his weekly wages lay in his account untouched by the attentions of his creditors. At twelve noon each Friday his employment agency forwarded his wages into his account, meaning that at one minute to twelve it was imperative to be standing at an ATM with cash card at the ready. If he was not then the money was immediately leached from his account, leaving him to face another week of grubbing through his cache of coinage for petrol money and begging the odd tenner from his parents in order to eat. He had drawn up a mental map of ATMs in the town. If he was unexpectedly diverted then salvation was only a street or two away.

He drove three hundred yards and parked the car on the forecourt of a convenience store. This was the suburb in which bankers, legal professionals, college lecturers and businessmen resided, making the daily commute to Manchattan, therefore people of working age were actually working. The convenience store and the car park were blessedly free of people.

Brian checked his watch. He had five minutes to extract whatever was left in his account following the debit of an overdraft charge whilst he was asleep. He inserted his card and was dizzy with joy to discover that three hundred and fifty pounds was available. In seconds a wad of notes protruded from the machine like a rude polychromatic tongue. Thrusting the amount required to meet his rent into his left trouser pocket,

117

Brian bought cigarettes and then drove onto the slip road of the M6 for the journey home. He barely noticed the cold as he calculated that he had time for a quick drink prior to throwing himself at the mercy of the bank. Two large vodkas would certainly suffice as lunch.

Brian parked the car and entered a pub that had once been a cinema. This hostelry, one of a chain that engirdled almost every town and city in Britain, opened early to welcome the patronage of the unemployed, the insane and just-out-of-bed alcoholics. The stench of body odour had impregnated the carpeting, but this was no time for Brian to hold his nose in disdain. It would suffice as somewhere to while away half an hour until his appointment.

He returned the languorous wave of Nicko, a former enforcer for a notorious drug dealer in the town. Nicko had been the scourge of bagheads, weed-heads, pill-heads and coke-noses who had been remiss in paying their debts. A darkling creature who stalked the night with a fire-axe, reducing the doors of council flats to kindling and demanding the occupants to pay their dues or be ready to lose a limb. Beyond the law and without any of the common decencies uniting all humanity, Nicko had visited hell upon the strung-out and toothless indebted to his employer. One evening Brian had found Nicko naked and bleeding from a number of orifices on a pavement close to his parents' house. He approached Nicko whilst prudently keeping his distance from the prone form. It was plain that Nicko was in crisis. Brian called an ambulance whilst keeping a watchful eye on his stricken but still dangerous charge. Nicko was detained under the Mental Health Act and then years later discharged into supported accommodation. His expression of simpering bewilderment was characteristic of those who had been chemically coshed, but even in his befogged state Nicko had never forgotten Brian's reluctant Samaritanism.

'All right, Nicko?'

'Not bad, Brian. I'm waiting for my carer. We're going Christmas shopping. I'm buying my mam a cardie.'

'That's nice. Looking forward to Christmas?'

'I'm having pork for my dinner this year. I don't like turkey. It's too dry.'

'Wise choice.'

Nicko returned his gaze to the coffee in front of him, gibbering softly to an invisible companion. He exuded the vulnerability of a newborn infant and probably in need of similar nurturing. It was hard to equate this ponderous man-child with the blood-drunk monster who had turmoiled his way through the lives of those who entered his orbit. He was no longer the alpha raptor of the urban wastes as his authentic self had been erased by strong medication. Brian had meditated upon the ethics of imposing such a curative, but when he recalled the horrors Nicko had visited upon others he also wondered if he himself had done the right thing, whether the morally correct course of action would have been to walk away and leave Nicko to die. The only solace Brian could draw was that medication had defused this dirty bomb in a beanie hat. He was now as harmless as any other recipient of community care; and just as embattled by circumstance.

Brian drained the contents of his glass, grabbed his briefcase and strode into the numbing early afternoon cold. It was not yet one o'clock but the sky was darkening to a Gothic gloom, an apt backdrop to his appointment with fear. He swept through the automatic doors of the bank, alighted at the reception desk and was then deliberately ignored for a full five minutes by a gum-chewing blonde in a two-piece suit and cravat. Brian was

119

debating whether to leave when she silently pointed a carmine fingernail to a flight of stairs. As she was probably au fait with Brian's current plight he could almost understand why she deemed it pointless to waste civility on him. People in daily close proximity to large sums of money must have little time for those with none at all. Penury inferred a moral debility that could be contagious. He wouldn't have been surprised if she had worn a surgical mask to avoid cross infection.

The upstairs lounge was decorated in comforting pastel shades, a subliminal message to customers that they were cloistered in a place of safety. The decor did nothing to efface Brian's apprehension, nor did the sensuous female voice wafting around the room from the PA system, breathily intimating that there had never been a better time for homeowners to secure a loan. An array of coop-like offices against one wall afforded the financial advisors and their clients just enough space to confer in private. After a moment or two Brian was hailed by a substantial woman wearing a shirt and slacks from which her maternal embonpoint and large behind strained for release. Brian checked his watch and was pleasantly surprised to note that the meeting would be conducted at exactly the appointed time. If the expected disappointment came then at least it would arrive punctually, and he could return to the pressing business of getting miserably drunk.

She held a sheaf of papers, and with a toss of her chestnut mane beckoned him to follow her into an office. Brian learned that her name was Liz and her job was to offer solutions. He wasn't the first or the last to find himself in difficulties. The bank was ready to assist all of its customers whenever possible. In fact, she whispered conspiratorially, compared to the travails of many people she'd dealt with, Brian's problems were a mere bagatelle.

He wasn't about to lose his home for instance, unlike other customers to whom she'd had to offer a sympathetic tissue as a sop to their justifiable misery.

'So what exactly are we dealing with here, Brian?'

'Well I've got a massive overdraft. Since I split from my partner I'm living alone and finding it a bit of a stretch. I'm forever incurring bank charges because I'm always over my overdraft limit. I'm left short every week and it's just getting worse. I'm in way over my head so I thought maybe I could borrow to clear my overdraft, and on top of that borrow a bit more to sort out my direct debits. I could make a fresh start. If the loan period could be over a good few years to keep the monthly payments low, that'd be brilliant.'

Liz bobbed her head, her yep-yep-yepping signalling her agreement with Brian's suggestion. Evidently, this was, "Very doable". It would be a simple case of restructuring a debt that was merely a drop in a very large and toxic ocean. She would discuss this with her line manager and return in about ten minutes, but in the meantime Brian should help himself to coffee. She swept from the office like a bosomy cyclone, her demeanour of easy professionalism suggesting that closure was imminent. A brisk, sensible person was about to offer a brisk sensible solution to his problems. When they had concluded their business, Brian could get on with the rest of his weekend untroubled by such trivial concerns as deciding upon the most expeditious method of killing himself.

Whilst Liz was out of the office he immediately began making plans. When he was certain that all of his debts had been cleared he would open a separate account reserved purely for household expenses. He would shop around for cheaper deals to lower his utility bills. His car would be restored to a roadworthiness consistent with existing law. By gradations he would decrease his alcohol intake. He would eat more healthily. He might take up jogging. He might not take up jogging. He resolved to be kinder to those around him, although as he didn't know many people then the salutary effects of such a commitment would be negligible. He would try to live better than he did before. He would grow old with dignity. He might even marry Pat if their first Christmas together went well.

Liz came back into the office, shook her mane as though she'd been for a canter across frozen moorland, snorted and sat heavily behind the desk. Her large blue eyes dilated and she smiled broadly with undisguised pleasure. Brian felt the first stirrings of an erection. He wanted to shrive himself before her, cover her feet with slobbering kisses and perhaps request her hand in marriage. He was certain of their compatibility, whereas his relationship with Pat was at a more equivocal stage.

'Well, Brian. We can definitely do something for you.'

'That's fantastic news.'

'We're more than willing to restructure your overdraft to allow you to borrow all you need to make that fresh start you're after.'

'Great.'

'All you'll need to do is pay off your existing overdraft first and we're in business.'

Suddenly the room became airless and unbearably hot. Brian became a sub-aqueous creature, a merman snatched from the depths with a hook in his mouth and cringing before the death blow. Again he had been thwarted, wrong-footed by this fat useless cow with her catchpenny spiel. He was again the sap, the patsy, the butt of another cruel joke to be laughed at behindhand. The gloom outside grew even darker.

'You've got to be fucking kidding me.'

'I'd really appreciate it if you didn't use that sort of language. But you don't sound too happy by the bank's offer. Why is that?'

'Why would it matter?'

'I've been tasked with creating a database to quantify levels of customer satisfaction. We're grading positive outcomes using a scale from one to ten. This will then feed into a national database using information collected from all of our branches. Your input would be very useful.'

'How about this. I've lost half a day's pay to be told that I'm in exactly the same shit as I was before I walked in here.'

'But we're more than willing to restructure the terms of your overdraft if your existing overdraft is serviced first.'

'You know and I know that my overdraft is the very thing that can't be serviced because of the bank charges I keep running up. Because you greedy fuckers keep piling them on. Working for this outfit you must know what it's like to be in over your head, only in your case you had the fucking taxpayers to bail you out.'

'Now language like that doesn't really help us at all, does it?

'Taxpayers. People like me. Which we did. We gave you exactly the same bailout I'm asking for now.'

'I'm sorry we couldn't be of more help, but get the overdraft down—

'How can I get the fucking thing down if you bastards charge me thirty-odd quid if I go a penny overdrawn? How does that make any fucking sense to you?'

'I think you're being rather hostile. Your attitude isn't helpful when I'm trying to offer doable solutions.'

'Oh DO fuck off. And have a nice fucking Christmas.'

Brian left the office door open as he made his departure, his contemptuous glare at the gum-chewing blonde ignored as she continued filing her nails. He wondered if she had known beforehand the outcome to his appointment with Liz and had spent the last fifteen minutes enjoying his misplaced optimism. He debated whether to march back into the pub across the road to get drunk, but reminded himself of the increased vigilance of the police at this time of year. Their assiduity in securing the convictions of drink-drivers at Christmas was matchless, certainly when compared to their usual clear-up rates of crime. As the fates were already against him then a drink-driving conviction would be the crowning humiliation. He trudged towards his car parked in front of a small arcade containing a craft shop, a gaming outlet, two charity shops and a loan company. Brian halted in front of the loan company, peered in and entered.

The reception area was deserted but the place seemed open for business. Brian hovered, uncertain as to why he was in there. A small, perspiring man appeared from the lavatory, wiping his hands on the seat of his trousers. He greeted Brian with an overfamiliarity that rekindled his wrath. Whoever Brian was, he was not this huckster's pal. The man extended a clammy hand, introduced himself as Barry and demanded to know what he could do Brian for. Brian studied Barry's round florid face, blotched with flocculent wisps of red hair that hadn't quite got the hang of cohering into a beard.

Brian was muted by confusion. He had no idea why he had entered this office nor why he was being addressed by Barry. Perhaps the mere proximity of money had ignited a certain voyeurism, an ugly desire to gaze at the object of his longing without the satisfaction of consummation. There was something very wrong when a middle-aged man found the presence of money a fetishized experience. This was a psychopathy yet to be recognised by leading authorities in the field of paraphilias. A man sees a pile of banknotes and becomes aroused. Inexplicable, and bearing all the hallmarks of a deviance requiring clinical intervention. Unless of course the middle-aged man in question was a hedge fund manager. In which case it would be perfectly understandable.

'Let me ask you a question, pal. Have you got a full-time job?'

'I'm a social worker.'

'Fuck me. I'd lock the kids in a cupboard if you called round our house. Have you got a bank account?'

'I've just been to the bank.'

'Sorted. How much do you want to borrow then pal? A grand? Two grand?'

'A thousand quid would be okay. When would I get the money if I take out the loan?'

'If we get the paperwork done in the next ten minutes it'll be in your account before four o'clock this afternoon.'

'You're having me on.'

'See me giggling, pal? I'm going to need proof of income and proof of identity. How're you fixed?'

'I've got my last three payslips in this briefcase and my driving licence. Will that do?'

'Sunshine supernova, pal. Come on. Let's give that missus of yours a Christmas she won't forget. Get her a bit of jewellery. You're guaranteed a gob-job on Boxing Day if you give her a charm bracelet.'

'I'll bear that in mind.'

Brian meekly followed Barry into a compact office rancid

with the afterstench of takeaway lunches and cheap deodorant. Perspiring copiously, Barry dragged a sheaf of official-looking forms from a desk drawer, reached for the biro behind his ear and silently proffered an outstretched palm into which he expected a bank card and a driving licence to be emplaced. Brian scrambled to produce the required documents and duly deposited them. Barry winked and continued to scribble as quickly as his tight little fist would allow. Brian stared at the world through the small window at the back of the office. It was now almost completely dark and apocalyptic rain smashed against the pane. After fifteen minutes Barry leaned back in his chair and inhaled heavily, signalling the conclusion of his clerical business. He then intoned that he was obliged to relate the terms and conditions of the loan, the interest rate imposed and the date of the first withdrawal of the direct debit. Brian nodded, hoping that his alert expression concealed his utter incomprehension of the contract into which he was about to enter.

Barry spat a volley of words from his mouth whilst his eyes roamed around the rank confines of his office. Brian nodded at inappropriate intervals and averred that he had no further questions. He admired the unaffected honesty of Barry's usury. It was free of the humbuggery and customer service hokum of Liz and harpies like her. He recalled a comedian once observing that a bank was the place to which you went for a loan, providing that you could prove you didn't need it. Barry and people like him were the very people you went to if you were in desperate need of a loan and they didn't patronise you either. There was a knowingness to Barry, a visceral understanding that his customers were in the direst of straits. Brian imagined Barry as the lieutenant of an underground movement, a financial marquis skulking in the sewers under finance houses, an enemy of the high rollers who had pissed misery on the world. Barry and his cohorts offered succour to the downtrodden whilst planting improvised explosive devices of unsecured loans to inflict carnage on the plutocracy. Or more probably, Barry was just another parasite feeding on his cringing carcass.

'Right, pal. Here's my card. Check your account any time after four. If the cash isn't in by then give me a ring and I'll get on the blower to give someone at HQ a fucking.'

'Thanks for your help.'

'Any time, pal. Have a nice Christmas.'

Brian gingerly shook Barry's outstretched paw, hoping that the moneylender hadn't been abusing himself in the lavatory prior to their meeting. The contents of Barry's hard drive were unlikely to inspire nobler feelings. As he tramped towards his car Brian was again suffused with a sense of detachment. He was drunk on turpitude, light-headed with adrenalin. After lingering by the car he retraced his steps into the town centre. He wouldn't need the car as he was now jobless, and events in the bank suggested recourse to the tobacco tin at some time over the weekend. His situation was unsalvageable so he might as well surrender and spend the rest of the weekend doing whatever he liked. When the loan he'd acquired arrived in his account he would be very much in pocket. If this wasn't worth celebrating then nothing was. He would be dining out this afternoon and taking a taxi home.

Recalling that he had gifted Elouise his morning newspaper, Brian drifted into an off-licence-cum-newsagent. The narrow store was compacted with weather-beaten pensioners swaddled in layers of woollens, breathing hard and vying for the shop assistant's attention. All of them were straining to purchase lottery tickets for the weekend. Brian was jostled, trodden on and

127

crushed between a broken-veined besom and her lumpen husband as he waited to purchase newspapers held in a soggy hand. Such was his discomfiture that he was almost moved to lecture the mass of shuffling, sweating ancients that any hope of improving their lives with a lottery win was futile. They should instead join him in just giving up and liberate themselves from their insane optimism. They'd also save themselves a fiver. But when he gazed into the clouded eyes of these aspirants to millionaire-hood, Brian knew that his exhortations would fall on deaf ears. This was the irrational hope of the damned, the drowning clutching at empty air. He finally managed to purchase the newspapers and a bottle of cheap navy rum as a gift for his host later that evening. The oldsters continued to queue in droves.

Low indigo cloud discharged a payload of sleet as Brian entered the bistro. Cold light from the ceiling irradiated pristine white tables. Smooth jazz oozed from the in-house sound system. Other than a couple at the far end of the restaurant, Brian was the only customer. He sat down and browsed the obituary columns of the newspapers. He was disappointed to learn that no one famous had died that week. He stared into the dark, rain-punished street until a young and very pretty blonde in a white blouson smiled and enquired if he wished to take lunch. Brian gently nodded and then almost sheepishly asked if he could take a large whisky with a dash of soda before dining. The smile of the waitress grew broader as she trilled her assent.

Brian reflected that one of the few consolations of middle age was the ability to gaze at young women without the merest whiff of salacity. Far from being an object of sexual interest, he presumed her to be the daughter of a man his own age. Had he elected to have children she might have been a contemporary of his own offspring, talking together about college and boys. He had always found the notion of a liaison with someone much younger quite unfathomable. One might as well suggest a harmonious congruence between a doe and an aging crocodile. As the afterglow of the whisky warmed him, Brian leaned back and closed his eyes. Another large whisky, some food and a glass of wine would banish the last of his hangover. As it was only two thirty, he would have plenty of time to take several more drinks before paying his usual Friday evening visit to his parents and then on to chez Splatch. He luxuriated in the ravelled calm of the bistro. Such was his equanimity that grazing on the litany of bad news in the newspapers was almost a pleasure. Nothing mattered now other than the sating of civilised appetites.

His eyes settled on the thirty-something couple across the restaurant. They both stared unblinkingly into the screens of smartphones, oblivious to each other and their surroundings. Their fingers moved almost imperceptibly, palpating the instrument as though trying to detect hidden tumours in the body of the machine. They wore scarves tied in that curious knot favoured by hipsters but had removed their expensive cagoules. Occasionally one of them would halt their palpations, grin, and then continue with their prodding's on the keyboard. They embodied the new age, adults infantilised by a device that Brian considered to be this generation's Rubik's cube. In recent months he had noticed that whenever people walked into any new environment they instinctively patted their pockets to ensure they were equipped with a telephone. They could be entering a room noisy with animated conversation but all of them displayed the same clutch reflex. Brian thought them to be in fear of being earthbound, surrounded by imperfect reality instead of the comforts of cyberspace. It seemed that people were being slowly Facebooked into imbecility; but, as with every other fad from

'The Twist' to children playing jackstones, it would probably die away at some point.

Gazing at the couple he reflected that perhaps it was the fate of all those in long-term relationships to eventually relegate the other half to something as ignorable as a piece of furniture. Over there is a television, over there is a standard lamp, and that over there is my husband. Perhaps familiarity breeds not contempt but something more ignoble, a perception of one's partner as an item of property. And, as with most items of property, the owner eventually tires of the current model and wishes to usher in something newer, possibly with upgraded functionality and a more attractive fascia. Helen had always averred her innocence of dalliances with other men prior to their sundering, but perhaps betrayal would have been preferable to being regarded as simply obsolete.

By the time he had finished his second whisky Brian was suffused with a serenity so all-consuming he could have cheerfully dropped off to sleep. He gently berated himself for not whiling away half an hour in the second-hand bookshop nearby. He and Helen had spent many pleasant interludes in there chatting with the amiable and obviously dotty owner whilst scouring the shelves for something dog-eared and interesting. He considered it a civic duty to support small businesses standing defiant in the face of high street behemoths and Internet trading empires. Then he remembered that as he might die before the weekend was out, buying a book he wouldn't finish would be a waste of money. Had he exercised a similar fiscal prudence in the preceding months then perhaps he might have avoided his impending suicide. Hindsight is the most pointless of all human attributes.

He took a half-carafe of house white wine with a chicken

fajita, followed by a coffee and a large brandy. The waitress, whom he now regarded with a paternal eye, hovered around him like an eager-to-please hummingbird. He was conscious that her solicitude towards him was that shown by the young towards the older. Perhaps Brian resembled her father and expected him to display the same social maladroitness as her parent. He resolved to leave her a large tip when able to rouse himself sufficiently to walk to the exit unaided. Outside, shoppers contorted themselves into the shape of question marks in response to the foulness of the weather. Umbrellas were scant protection against the skewering wind and all of the passers-by looked like the recipients of very bad news.

As he dodged motability scooters and trudgers hauling their Christmas shopping, he was stirred from his alcohol-induced torpor by the consciousness of his imminent unbeing. This could well be the last time he would look upon the centre of his home town with its beggars, dreadful buskers, window-gawpers and wailing infants. He was afforded the perspective of a visitor taking a dispassionate view of somewhere unfamiliar. He concluded that it possessed little in the way of interesting landmarks or points of historical interest. In its defence, however, it was an excellent location for a suicide. Perhaps that particular plus point should feature on the town's website.

As the availability of taxis was always at a premium in the festive season, Brian was thankful that a cab was idling by the rank. He climbed into the back seat and waited for the driver to request his destination. The toadish driver remained silent, dragging on a roll-up with menacing slowness. The radio was attuned to an MOR station playing the hits of yesteryear to afternoon nostalgists. Brian was momentarily concerned that the driver had experienced some form of seizure. When he had ascertained that the driver was still breathing he requested to be dropped outside The Long Pig. The driver gave no outward signs he had heard Brian until his tobacco-toasted voice posited a question.

'D'you know this one?'

'Erm… it's familiar. From the seventies?'

'No. 1982. Shoot that Poison Arrow Through My Heart.'

'Right.'

'This was me and the wife's song. We had the first dance at our wedding to this one. She kiffed it a good few years ago, like.'

'Sorry to hear that. Was it cancer or something?'

'No. Her boyfriend killed her. She took my motor out for them to have a shag in. When he'd finished he got her bladdered off her tits. When she fell asleep he ran a pipe from the exhaust with her still sat in the car. Then he fucked off to Spain. I was in bed, me. I hadn't a clue. They thought I'd done it till they caught him.'

'Bloody hell. That's awful.'

'It was my car I was really pissed off about. They fucking ruined it, the pair of bastards.'

'Right.'

'So I got shut of it and bought this one. Where did you say you were going?'

'Least.'

'Jesus. I wouldn't be going in that Long Pig this afternoon. They've had Father Christmas in there handing out presents to the kids. Our base controller said the bobbies have made four arrests. Blood everywhere. It's that time of year, innit? I turn sixty next week, me.'

As the car grumbled through the rain, the wattled amphibian regaled Brian with episodes being propositioned by drunken

132

nubiles in lieu of payment of the cab fare. He was a gentleman, however, and gallantly refused their shameless offers of physical satisfaction. Instead, he sternly advised them to go to bed promptly upon their arrival home. He was a man who embraced old-fashioned values and recoiled at taking advantage of hyper-sexualised women on the outside of a surfeit of the hard stuff, although they were all right dirty bitches and would benefit from having their knickers pulled down and given a good smack on the arse. He was unopposed to meting out the punishment himself if these fallen women benefited from such chastisement, but the world was too politically correct these days for such a bracing admonition. Brian shrank in his seat, his post-prandial serenity fading as he envisioned this repugnant oddball's reclusion. A bachelor flat surrounded by vile erotica, old tabloid newspapers, empty soup tins and twilit squalor. There was a pointlessness to this man's life matched only by his own. At least for Brian the horror would soon be over.

He alighted outside The Long Pig and scuttered into the convenience store, ignoring the crowd of cheering spectators encircling two massive women tearing at each other with the ferocity of pit bulls. He lingered by the wine selection, chose a bottle of red and a bottle of rose and then submitted himself to the baleful ministrations of Kelly-Leanne.

'Are them two still scrapping out there?'

'Erm… if you mean two women, then yes.'

'The really fat one's my mam. She doesn't half show me up.'

'Well, God gave us our relatives. Thank God we can choose our friends, eh?'

'Are you taking the piss?'

'No. Sorry. It's just a saying.'

Brian quailed as Kelly-Leanne immobilised him with a

reptilian stare. If the fistic prowess of her mother was any yardstick then he could be in serious trouble. He practically ran from the convenience store. Nat King Cole exhorted shoppers to have themselves a merry little Christmas as chaos reigned outside The Long Pig. Drinkers were arrayed around the gladiatrices, clutching bottles and glasses and cheering as the conflict became bloodier. In Least, Christmas had officially arrived. He dropped off the bottles of rum and wine at home and slipped the catch on the front door to ensure he could re-enter the house without another struggle with the lock. He surmised that his visit to his parents would be brief but not without incident when he apprised them of the termination of his employment.

He entered his parents' home, hallooed his arrival and was immediately berated by his mother for making so much bleedin' noise whilst she was trying to nap. The living room was as sultry as a Spanish summer and the volume of the television loud enough to rouse the dead, common features of a household containing older people unaware of their increasing deafness and circulatory problems. As was usual on Fridays she enquired whether Brian wished to stay for his tea. Brian demurred, reporting that he was unable to linger as he was expected elsewhere later that evening. Whilst reporting the details of an eventful day to his plainly disinterested mother, his father arrived home. Derek was wet, irritable and hungry following a visit to a former colleague in an intensive care unit. Brian then reported to his parents that he'd been dismissed from his post.

Derek was unconvinced by Brian's protests that his sacking was the consequence of governmental austerity measures. He shook his head and smiled wryly, tacitly conveying his opinion that as usual it was all Brian's fault. How could Brian blame David Cameron for being given the white fiver? Other people had remained in a job, therefore, the only reasonable conclusion was that his son was again the author of his own destruction.

Brian shook his head in mournful disbelief at his father's unwisdom and advised him to read a literate newspaper once in a while. Analyses of the chancellor's ambitions for the nation were rarely discussed in the racing pages. Paget senior merely wondered when Brian was going to visit the job centre. Derek would accompany him as he was such a half-soaked sod he would either lose his way en route or neglect to claim his full entitlement. Brian departed without bidding farewell to either of them. As he made his way towards the front door he heard his father bawling.

'You've done it again you, you dozy bugger. You'll have your mother in the bleeding loony bin before you're finished. She's on enough tablets as it is.'

Despite the cold and implacable rain, Brian arrived home hot with rage at his mother's ennui and his father's derision. It was understandable that his parents preferred to live in 1978, as they found today's Britain incomprehensible. In common with many people their age they cleaved to the comforting nostrums of hard work bringing its own reward, that there were clear divisions between the deserving and undeserving poor, and all of the country's ills were directly attributable to immigrants, paedophiles, homosexual television presenters, rap artists, drug abusers and the homeless. Their instinctive deference towards their supposed betters also precluded the possibility of questioning the status quo. They refused to acknowledge the nightmare of job insecurity, a collapse in living standards and a wage freeze that threatened to last until the middle of the century. Their infuriating complacency was complemented by a convenient amnesia. Most of their adult lives were lived in an age of near full employment and improvements in living standards underpinned by bellicose trades unions. By comparison, modern Britain resembled the Regency. A nation of colossal disparities in income, bosses vulgarised by greed, increasingly poor mental health and malnutrition a go-go. Brian bitterly reflected that if youth is wasted on the young, so reasoned argument is wasted on the old.

A note on which red ink had morphed into rivulets of illegibility suggested that Splatch had again been in the vicinity and more pressing in his demands that they convene at his flat. It was impossible to telephone him as Splatch had refused to own either a mobile phone or subscribe to a landline. Given his previous history perhaps that was just as well.

Stephen Peter Latchford was the most enigmatic, prodigiously gifted and utterly dissipated human being that Brian, or indeed anyone else, had ever met. He was *sui generis*, a one-off who had spawned a host of imitators. Despite Brian's invariably futile counselling, Splatch had remained defiantly himself in spite of a multitude of self-inflicted depredations. The popular music cognoscenti had long dismissed him a flame-out, a fuck-up whose pale light had burned all too briefly before being extinguished by alcohol, drugs and general depravity. In classic rock magazines Splatch was occasionally given respectful mentions, but these days they were epitaphs for a fallen hero rather than adulatory retrospectives. Brian remained mildly wonderstruck that a legend such as Splatch hailed from his unremarkable home town. The popular music pantheon was usually from the big cities of London or Birmingham, not anonymous post-industrial towns in the North-West. Even more amazing to him was that when young, he and Splatch had been the fastest of friends until their paths had diverged sharply in later life. Splatch became an internationally renowned rock luminary, regarded as the voice of his generation and feted in the arts pages of the serious press. Brian would work shifts in a factory.

At the age of eleven, Brian and Splatch befriended one other simply because no one else would. Brian's farouche demeanour did nothing to endear him to his classmates, and even at that age Splatch exercised discrimination in his choice of companions. Each was regarded as odd, but whilst Brian inspired sniggers and derision, Splatch was regarded with the fascination reserved for an exotic but poisonous insect. Laconic, unblinking, unsmiling, loose-limbed and athletically built, Splatch seemed to be someone whom it would be unwise to allow too close. He could be either a genius or a madman. As it transpired he was an irresistible combination of both.

As though born to remind other people of their own mediocrity, Splatch displayed his array of gifts with an infuriating sangfroid. His academic excellence eclipsed the stolid efforts of his classmates, and his tutors predicted a place at Cambridge. Brian remained resolutely average, confounded by academic disciplines requiring the application of logic. He could no more understand the point of numbers than he could the point of mole rats, although in Brian's defence he received little in the way of encouragement. To Derek and Jean, secondary education was merely a hiatus, somewhere to go and something to do before the serious business of earning a wage began. Apart from anything else, they'd left school before the age of fifteen and they'd made out all right. Brian would probably do the same if the silly bugger shaped himself instead walking about with his head up his arse all the bleedin' while.

In addition to his academic prowess, Splatch was also endowed with an enviable athleticism. He broke existing records for distance running and long jump, but his long stride and powerful engine were the least of his gifts. On the rare occasions he was sufficiently interested to participate, Splatch captained both the school football and rugby league teams to previously undreamt success in inter-school competitions, languidly leading his teams from the back and garnering interest from a host of professional clubs. He was unmoved by requests from scouts to meet with his parents, preferring instead to stare evilly at unshaven men in soaking macs who littered the touchline whenever he deigned to make an appearance. Brian, gifted with an ability to defy universal laws of locomotion by actually decreasing his speed of travel if he broke into a run, would observe his unusual friend from a distance before shaking his head at the pointlessness of contact sports.

Splatch's parents were dazzling creatures who never swore, pronounced their aitches, wore suits to work, drank wine and encouraged Brian to visit as often as he liked. The convivial ambience of Splatch's home was in stark contrast to that of Brian's, where all visitors were viewed with suspicion and encouraged to keep their coats on. Brian was also unnerved by the equanimity of the Splatch household. They all seemed to get on with one another, whereas at home there was always at least one minor skirmish going on. Either between himself and his sister, Elaine, between him and his parents or between Elaine and everyone else. To further inflame Brian's envy, as an only child Splatch was showered with largesse granted to other children only in their dreams. Brian's only regular sources of income were a sum of one pound pocket money and two pounds he earned from an evening newspaper round. By comparison Splatch seemed to be Midas incarnate. Each time he rummaged in his trouser pocket his hand emerged clutching at least one pound

138

note, more usually two or three. At a relatively early age Brian was made acutely aware of the self-confidence wealth confers upon the gilded few. The Grosvenor family seemed impoverished when compared to the Family Splatch.

Reflective of his natural curiosity and precocious mental powers, Splatch was omnivorous in his musical tastes but dismissive of the youth tribalism of the seventies, a period in which skinheads, mods, soul boys, hippies, trench coat wearing prog-rockers and metal-heads vied with each another to be the most objectionable to their exasperated parents. Splatch had carefully cherry-picked the best of any given genre. If the music appealed to him then no further immersion in the culture was necessary. His hair remained collar length and his sartorial style understated. In his opinion work boots, leather jackets, feather cuts and patchouli oil were adornments fit only for the rabble. His conservative style only served to amplify his disquieting individualism.

Splatch explored strands of popular culture not usually to the taste of pubertal adolescents. He greedily consumed the novels of The Beats, the poetry of The Movement and the strange and jagged electric music of the American underground. Brian was reluctantly catechised by repeated plays of The New York Dolls, Iggy Pop and Lou Reed. The two boys also absorbed progressive rock, a genre evolving popular music away from its roots in the American South. Splatch listened to records with the rapt, silent attention of a tiger stalking its prey. He ingested every note, every pause and every key change. Brian tapped his foot and took an occasional swig from a can of lukewarm stout provided by Splatch's attractive although heavily medicated mother. He pretended to be as enraptured as his friend by sounds that really didn't make much sense to him, but by dint of their rejection of the bromides of mainstream pop he and Splatch were now an indivisible gang of two.

They slouched around school corridors, disporting albums with lurid polychromatic sleeves depicting Tolkienesque landscapes and scantily-clad women astride fire-breathing hydra. They were contemptuous of everything and impervious to the derision of others. Responding to the jibes of their classmates with two-fingered gesticulations or the occasional jabbing of Splatch's lit cigarette into the faces of those who ventured too close, they continued their absorption of pop culture relatively undisturbed. And then one day, having satisfied himself that he was sufficiently informed about popular music to be good at it, Splatch decreed that he and Brian would form a band. Of course, Brian didn't fancy this at all.

With the hauteur epitomising his social caste, Splatch immediately nominated himself as lead guitarist and creative director. Brian would be the fulcrum of the band, providing a solid foundation for the rest of the group on rhythm guitar. Brian was happy to be nominated as a functionary as even at that age he was aware of a deficit of personal magnetism. Splatch also decreed that they would soon be augmented by a drummer, a bassist and a keyboard player. Within five minutes the band was fully fledged, a tight and cohesive unit ready to rouse the world from its torpid complacency. All that was needed now was a name, additional personnel, musical instruments and expertise on their chosen instruments. It was the last four elements that would probably provoke certain difficulties but none that were insuperable. Brian blenched with foreboding. His mind's ear was already being bombarded by jibes at his pretensions to being a musician of any stripe, never mind an electric guitar player.

Our Brian's getting dafter by the bloody minute. He's

walking around thinking he's Alvin bloody Stardust. He'll be wearing flares next. Dressing like one of them bloody puffs off *Top Of The Pops*. I'm sure he's the rent-man's, him. He can't be one of mine.

Each Saturday morning the two boys would trawl the record shops. Brian would be flush with the wages from his paper round whilst Splatch would be simply flush. They riffled though racks of album covers arrayed in alphabetical order with a discerning eye, their scholarly appreciation of the artists underpinned by avid reading of the weekly music press. On occasions a particularly arresting record sleeve, usually featuring a pair of pneumatic breasts, would transfix them and they would request a listening booth in which to hear a snippet. They were almost invariably disappointed by the turgid mush of redneck boogie or tissues of melancholia whined by an English literature graduate with an unrequited love for someone called Pippa, but they remained sanguine in the face of such vagaries. They were on a learning curve and the occasional misstep was inevitable. Then, on a humid May morning, Splatch decreed that they should forego their usual itinerary and instead head straight for the pavilion-like quarters of the town's musical instrument retailer. For both of the boys this would prove to be a watershed moment, albeit for very different reasons.

The ground floor of the instrument retailers was given over to the respectable world of classical music. Strings, woodwind, brass and grand pianos were assayed in reverential silence by serious adults and their equally serious children; but all the good stuff was in the basement. Splatch and Brian descended the staircase to the basement with the bubbling excitement of toddlers entering Santa's grotto, although Brian couldn't help noticing that the stale air in this dimly-lit tabernacle was an unedifying mix of wood polish, unwashed feet and male armpit. The boys gazed upwards in awe at the weapons of first resort hanging on the walls, cooing at the humbucking pickups and sunburnt finishes.

After an interval of ten minutes Splatch addressed the lugubrious, moustachioed long-hair behind the sales counter who was absently picking his nose. He pointed to an impossibly expensive guitar built in the United States and demanded to try it out. The long-hair started as though Splatch had roused him from sedation. Brian detected in him the same tremulous uncertainty he'd witnessed in others when encountering this other-worldly adolescent for the first time. After returning Splatch's glare, the long-hair shrugged, gave a curt nod of assent and slouched from behind the counter. He casually inserted a guitar lead into an amplifier, unhooked the cherry-red double-cutaway from its mooring and handed the instrument to Splatch. The long-hair's folded arms and sceptical gaze inferred that he considered this disturbing boy to be just another pubertal wannabe whose risible incompetence would now be exposed. Brian silently prayed that his friend would acquit himself well enough to avoid humiliation. He needn't have worried.

Splatch seated himself comfortably and then casually knocked out several familiar chord progressions with the drop-dead skill of a seasoned practitioner. Pausing for a positive reaction from his audience he then continued with several blues scales punctuated by triads. Unusually for a novice, whatever he played made musical sense. The long-hair nodded his approbation and returned to his perch behind the counter to continue picking his nose. Splatch smiled and lowered his head in an exaggerated display of modesty. Brian remained silent, piqued by his friend's withholding of his clandestine endeavours on the guitar. Splatch sensed his friend's irritation and held out a hand for Brian to shake.

'You didn't tell me you were having a go at playing the guitar.'

'You didn't ask.'

'Who's been teaching you then?'

'No one. I found a couple of old tutor books a few weeks ago and borrowed a guitar from a mate of my mum. She sings folk songs and plays a Spanish guitar. She's fucking terrible. The exercises in the books are piss-easy once you've done them a few times.'

'Are they?'

'Oh yeah. An absolute doddle. I can't see what all the fuss is about. Once you get cracking on this you'll be like Jimmy Page in six months.'

'Ooh. That'll be all right then.'

Splatch returned to noodling on the guitar, his face a rictus of abstraction. The instrument on his lap flattered him like a well-cut suit, imbuing him with a quiet gravitas. Although understandably ignorant of the significance of this moment, Brian and the nose-picking long-hair were the first to glimpse the man Splatch would become; the talented, ridiculously photogenic but self-destructive adult who would mesmerise a generation before tail-spinning into degradation. Brian became bored and went to have a look at the drum kits. He liked shiny things.

Drum kits appeared to Brian as arachnids made of chrome, wood and skin. He wandered over to the coal-black kit squatting in an underlit corner and ran his hand over the skin of the snare drum, silently marvelling at its coarse-smooth texture. He tapped out a simple tattoo with his forefingers and was surprised at how little force was required to produce a respectable volume. He speculated that beating the bejesus out of the skins with sticks would be an exhilarating experience, but concluded that playing the drums was not for him. The drum kit's portability alone would pose untold logistical challenges. He supposed that the renowned mental instability of drummers was directly attributable to onerous task of assembling, disassembling, transporting and reassembling the kit. It would be akin to moving house every night, something that would drive most sensible people insane. Then he received a brutal punch in the shoulder. In shock, he turned to face his aggressor. Brian quailed in agony as the long-hair viciously twisted his ear.

'Right you, you little cunt. What's his name and where does he live?'

'Who?'

'Your fucking mate, that's who. He's fucked off with that guitar without paying for it and I want him had up for it. You're not going anywhere until you tell us his fucking name. Come on, cunty. Tell us.'

Pain quickly metastatised into bewilderment as Brian's eyes darted around the basement. Brian quickly discerned the absence of both Splatch and the very expensive cherry-red cutaway. This was serious, very serious, and every freeze-frame that flashed through his mind depicted him being in the worst of trouble. His stomach was full of crawling things and he was seized by an urge to urinate. The long-hair wrenched at his ear even more savagely, eliciting howls of protest and anguish. This was horrifying, but for the first time in his in life Brian began to think on his feet. Heightened excruciation ignited dormant cognitive skills and the Zen-like serenity referred to by athletes as The Zone. He quickly calculated that as there were no other witnesses to the crime, then

144

only he would be able to identify the perpetrator. He decided to relegate Splatch to the status of a mere acquaintance and confess only to that which his inquisitor could have learned himself.

'I don't know him proper. I only know him to say hello to. We bumped into each other in that record shop near Woollies. He said did I fancy coming in here so I said yeah.'

'What's his fucking name then?'

'Splatch. He said his name was Splatch.'

'Don't try and be clever you, you little cunt. I want his proper fucking name.'

'That's all know him as. I didn't know he was on the rob, honest.'

The long-hair released his grip on Brian's now scarlet ear, took a backward step and appraised his cringing captive through red-rimmed eyes. The boy's terror and confusion seemed genuine enough, and the long-hair surmised that any accomplice with even a glimmer of common sense would have also fled. The stain on the front of his jeans suggested that the dirty little bleeder may have pissed himself, a tangible symbol of his terror and perhaps evidence of his innocence in this affair. The boy was either completely guiltless, or a fantastic liar, or just really shite at nicking stuff. At this point none of these possibilities could be discounted. The long-hair lit a cigarette and then pointed a yellowed forefinger at Brian, gravely informing him that he was calling the pigs and if he so much as farted he'd pull his fucking lungs through his nose. Brian nodded vigorously whilst mentally steeling himself for the ordeal to come.

Within ten minutes a huge lantern-jawed policeman lumbered into the basement. He aimed a chilling stare at Brian who dallied by the drum kit rubbing his ear, and then strolled towards the counter. The long-hair took out a pack of cigarettes and the two men smoked companionably whilst conferring in low voices. Brian fidgeted inside the pocket of his jeans, vainly attempting to relocate his genitals away from the uncomfortably wet patch in which they nestled. After what seemed an eternity the policeman tamped his cigarette and ambled over to where Brian stood to attention.

'Now then you, you little fucker. What've you been up to?'

'Nothing, mister.'

'Nothing, SIR.'

'Nothing, sir.'

'Sure about that?'

'Yeah. I don't know that lad from Adam. I didn't know he was going to do what he did, honest.'

'Whereabouts do you live?'

'Least.'

The policeman nodded deliberately before smashing his massive open palm against the side of Brian's head. Brian reeled, staggered and then collapsed in a heap at the policeman's feet. As he gazed upwards, he saw not one but three glowering officers of the law. He decided to address the one in the middle.

'What did you do that for? I've not done nowt, me.'

'You're from Least. You're all thieving fuckers from round there aren't you?'

'I'm not. I've not done nothing, me. What did you clout me for?'

'You said you'd done nothing didn't you?'

'Yeah.'

'That was just in in case you DO do summat. Now get up off that floor. You're making it dirty.'

Brian rose slowly to his feet, flinching in expectation of another blow. The policeman removed a notebook from the

146

pocket of his tunic and demanded Brian's full name and address. And it had better be his proper name and address, because if it wasn't he'd be getting a good hiding from four dibble and then sent to an approved school. Brian smartly acquiesced and then enquired if the officer would be informing his parents of this morning's to-doings. The policeman's rubbery features recomposed themselves into a calculating sneer and the rolls of fat under his blue collar undulated in fleshy waves. He took another cigarette offered by the long-hair who hovered at his shoulder, lit up and regarded Brian through an eldritch haze of cigarette smoke.

'I'll tell you what. I won't tell your mam and dad if you do summat for me.'

'What's that then?'

'Never come in here again. Ever. In your bleeding life. Have you got me? And when you get home, for Christ's sake change your bleeding underpants. You smell like a pub bog. Now go on. Fuck off home and never come in here again.'

The long-hair grabbed Brian by the collar of his budgie jacket, hauled him up the staircase, across the ground floor and then threw him into the sunlit street. Brian squinted as his eyes readjusted to the lemony early afternoon light. He stared wide-eyed at passers-by and was astonished to be completely ignored by them. Given that he was now an unwitting accomplice to a crime, he was expecting censure from townspeople who would march him home to face the boiling wrath of his parents. Instead, he was merely a boy in a street smelling of urine.

Brian walked the three miles from the town centre to his home, stopping only in a public park to divest himself of his reeking underwear. He was certain that the policeman had already betrayed him to his parents and was terrified of the

147

consequent firestorm. He rehearsed a tenuously plausible alibi whilst gloomily speculating that his mother had already learned of that morning's imbroglio from the louring dibble. As chastiser-in-chief of the Paget menage she would probably invite Brian into the garden and break a washing prop over his back as punishment. His mother was unfamiliar with the concept of the presumption of innocence and retribution was usually swift and injurious.

He hadn't yet decided whether to be angry with Splatch, although he was dismayed by his friend's reticence regarding both his prowess on the guitar and his intentions in the musical instrument retailers. He knew Splatch to be someone full of surprises, but that morning was one revelatory experience he could have done without. His body felt physically heavier from the weight of fear he carried. He opened the front gate, entered the house by the kitchen door and then closed his eyes in anticipation of his mother's lacerating disapprobation. He opened them again to find he was in the midst of just another eventless Saturday afternoon.

Mrs Paget was barely discernible through a haze of steam issuing from a twin-tub washing machine. A cigarette hung from her quivering lips as she received another electric shock from the twin-tub. The machine administered bolts of pain whenever her hands made contact with its exposed metal surfaces. Her skin was ashen with fatigue and her prematurely greying hair had been shocked into the perpendicular. She squinted at the nebulous figure advancing towards her and, having satisfied herself that it was only her son, continued her life-or-death struggle with the twin-tub. Brian eased past her, careful to avoid slipping over on the kitchen lino on which puddles of detergent-scented water had gathered. He glanced into the living room in which his sister

148

Elaine was playing with Tracey, a girl who lived two streets away. The television set was switched on but soundless. The sport of kings held no attraction for the ten year olds who chivvied and poked at an assortment of dolls on the carpet. Brian's father would be in the club after his Saturday morning overtime, taking a pull on his third pint, playing a hand of dominoes and bemoaning his losing streak at the bookies.

Brian padded upstairs and stood on the landing for a moment, savouring the silence of bedrooms free of people and activity. He entered his cramped bedroom, removed his clothes, and, when completely naked, abandoned himself to post-traumatic euphoria. His arms flailed, his legs kicked at invisible assailants and his torso whirled as the relief of avoiding both arrest and a severe hiding from his mother overtook him. After a minute or so he came to a breathless standstill and took stock. He was innocent of complicity in a serious crime, free of the attentions of the police and, best of all, physically intact. All that remained for him to do was to rid himself of the odour of bodily waste and normality would be restored, except for the saddening loss of a pair of nylon Y-fronts. A conversation with Splatch regarding that morning's events could wait whilst he recovered his equilibrium.

On Monday morning, Splatch hailed Brian at the school gates and together they trooped into an alcove behind the bicycle sheds. As they shared a cigarette from a pack Splatch had liberated from his mother's handbag, Brian noted a disturbing light in Splatch's eyes; he radiated an unspooled rapture only usually observed in religious and political extremists. When Brian enquired if his parents had been contacted by the police Splatch shook his head slowly whilst affixing his friend with a maniacal grin. Brian then breathlessly imparted the myriad

149

horrors he'd endured at the hands of the long-hair and the dibble. He also declaimed his exasperation at his friend for thinking he could get away stealing such a big-ticket item without serious repercussions. Splatch silenced his friend's tirade with a raised hand, grinned broadly and then slowly intoned:

'But I did, didn't I? And I've got you a guitar and an amp as well.'

'Eh? You didn't go robbing somewhere else on Sat'day did you?'

'Course I didn't. I've only got two arms haven't I? My aunty Violet runs a catalogue. They do a Jap Les Paul copy and a practice amp for sixty quid the pair.'

'Where am I going to get sixty bastard quid from? My dad's car cost less than that.'

'You don't have to. I've got them for you. They're at my house. Come and have a look at them tonight.'

'Where've YOU got sixty bastard quid from?'

'Never you mind.'

That evening, Brian's misgivings regarding the legality of Splatch's latest acquisitions were forgotten as his friend handed him the glistening Les Paul copy. Brian gazed in awed silence at the black laminated body, the slender neck and the controls that went all the way up to eight. Brian had spent hours poring over photographs of the guitar heroes of the day, salivating over action shots with instruments that looked exactly like the one in his hand. It was impossible for any adolescent male not to feel somehow validated by this thing of beauty. Physical clumsiness, ungovernable erections, unsightly spots, body odour, nervous tics and social solecisms would be erased by the mastery of this heavenly conjunction of wood, steel and electronica. All Brian had to do now was to achieve competence in its operation. This

150

was to prove rather more challenging for him than his light-fingered friend.

Splatch had informed his credulous parents of his burgeoning musical prowess and demanded that they contract the services of two renowned guitar tutors in the area. He assured them that the cost of his tuition would be reimbursed shortly after he had earned a million quid from the royalties of his first album. As it was inconceivable to them Splatch would be anything other than a coruscating success at everything he did, they complied without demur. Splatch apprised Brian that he too would receive tuition, albeit delivered by Splatch himself. Splatch would be taught by professionals and relay his learning to Brian whilst percolating out the irrelevant bits. There was little point in learning a Bach prelude when all that was required were a few power chords and a flourish of bent single notes. Brian nodded meekly, already nauseous with the fear of failure. He had no doubts regarding the brilliance of his friend but serious misgivings of whether even mediocrity was within his own gift. It wasn't.

In the ensuing weeks and months Brian's ineptitude would become depressingly evident, although Splatch was never less than supportive. He conciliated with Brian's seeming dyspraxia when trying to accurately place his digits on the fretboard, reassuring Brian that the incisions on his fingertips were merely a temporary indisposal. Splatch also spent innumerable hours slowly and deliberately counting out loud to assist Brian in absorbing the principles of tempo. Despite his persistence, the simple but essential skill of counting in multiples of four confounded Brian. Splatch gently concluded that as a musician Brian's internal clock was probably attuned to the chronology of another universe. Or to be brutally candid, he just couldn't

151

fucking count.

Brian's shame and despair was compounded by the exponential increase of his friend's effortless virtuosity. Splatch read music as though it was his first language, whereas for Brian the dots, dotted dots, dashes and fermatas were as indecipherable as hieroglyphs. When Splatch played a simple classical piece or an improvisation constructed from a scale, it all made irrefutable melodious sense. If music is the medium by which the inexpressible in words is articulated, then Splatch spoke in perfectly modulated sentences with excellent diction. Brian's efforts resembled the howls of an intellectually retarded chimpanzee being eaten by a leopard. The inequitable allocation of natural gifts was never more evident than when they convened each Friday night at Splatch's home for what they rather grandly termed a jam session. For Brian it was a form of auto-da-fé but he continued doggedly on, spurred by his friend's indefatigable encouragement.

After seven months of pain, humiliation and the incessant carping of his family, in tandem with an immoderate consumption of stout and gin purloined from the Splatch family cocktail cabinet, the tyro rock stars were able to execute a twelve-bar blues progression and a clutch of numbers by The Kinks and early Who in perfect unison. The middle eights and corresponding key changes still needed attention but this was tangible progress, a condign reward for all their hard work and unbearable hangovers. Following a particularly successful session Splatch was so transported by the result of their endeavours that he excused himself to self-administer hand relief. During this hiatus, Brian experimented with a melange of sweet martini, gin, stout and Tizer. He found both the bouquet and the aftershock of the cocktail very much to his taste, akin to an airburst in his brain. After which he was abundantly and violently sick in the garden.

Onanism and alcohol misuse notwithstanding, the two boys were pleased with their progress; but in the spring of 1976 Splatch's acute antennae were sensing a sea change in popular music. Punk rock was gestating in the south of England and slowly but irresistibly gravitating northwards. Splatch was determined to nail his colours to the punk mast. Inclusiveness was the defining tenet of punk rock. Anyone could pick up a musical instrument, be furious about absolutely everything and thus ordained as an authentic member of Britain's disaffected youth. In almost every case attitude and a copious supply of amphetamines trumped musicianship, to the extent that competence on one's chosen instrument was viewed as a totem of bourgeois complacency. The bracing concision and directness of punk suited Splatch's purposes perfectly. As a musician Brian was still tottering like a toddler who had become newly aware of his own feet and chary of walking. By contrast, Splatch, nascently virtuosic and utterly convinced of his own abilities, had already written ten songs and was ready to take on the world and its wife with a terrifying fixity of purpose.

Brian's parents had avoided the installation of a telephone as they figured that it would only encourage people to ring them up. Chez Splatch possessed two telephones, including one in the master bedroom. Since turning fifteen, Splatch had spent an inordinate amount of time on the telephone, primarily because he had been discovered by girls. Being the product of a middle-class household, his charitable instincts were piqued by the supplications of pubescent females pleading that he unburden them of their virginity. After magnanimously liberating them from the yoke of chastity he then chivalrously eschewed any

153

further contact with them. His parents were gratified by the almost constant stream of telephone calls as this suggested that their taciturn son was extending his social circle beyond the equally taciturn and grimly proletarian Brian. Predictably, Brian didn't fare nearly so well in achieving his procreative ambitions. If the Paget household did possess a telephone then there would have been little in the way of calls from girls agog to learn if Brian was free to converse and perhaps meet with them later. It was logical then for the telephone number of chez Splatch to feature in an advertisement the boys had devised for requesting the services of new band members. On a torn sheet of foolscap paper, spattered with blood-red ink to affirm their punk credentials, they scrawled a terse missive in block capitals:

DRUMMIST AND BASSER NEEDED FOR PUNK BAND THE VINEGAR STROKES. MUST BE YOUNG, LOUD AND SNOTTY. OWN GEAR AND VAN A MUST. NO TIMEWASTERS. NO PETS. MUM ALLERGIC.

As they were *personae non gratae* in the musical instrument retailers Splatch dragooned a classmate into pinning the advertisement onto the noticeboard in the basement of the store. His reward for the errand was a copy of *Penthouse* and ten menthol cigarettes. When the emissary returned with the news that he had accomplished his mission, Splatch awaited the plethora of telephone calls that would surely follow. In the event he received only two. Whilst practicing scales in his bedroom his mother instructed him to answer a call in the master bedroom. He was perturbed by the breathless ardency of a boy who sounded roughly his own age.

Right pal. Listen to this. I don't give a fuck what you fucking think. I don't give a fuck what you fucking drink. Everything's boring everything stinks. I wish you'd straighten your face. Good that, innit?

'Right. What is it?'

'It's my song is that. I'm telling you now pal, that's going straight to number one. It's punk rock's first proper love song.'

'Is it?'

'Oh aye. First one ever is that. It'll be number one in a few weeks, no Belle Vue Ranger.'

'What's it called?'

'"We Shouldn't Fall Out". Hang on a minute, I'm phoning from a phone box. I'll put another bob in.'

'Right. Can you play drums or the bass?'

'Can I fuckers like. I'm the poet of the blank generation, me. I'll leave all the farting about on guitars to you lot.'

'Fair enough. But we only need a bass player and a drummer at the minute. If we need a poet I'll give you a shout.'

'Right-oh pal. And don't forget. We shouldn't fall out.'

'I won't. Thanks for ringing.'

Following this call the telephone remained obstinately silent. The usually self-collected Splatch was despondent to the point of disbanding The Vinegar Strokes, until one evening he was interrupted by his father in the course of divesting a sixth-former of her underwear. His father averted his eyes, blustered polite inanities at the prone figure on his son's bed and then pointed to the master bedroom.

'Take the call in our room, Stephen. Someone called Tick-Tock apparently. Mum's at night school tonight. Sociology or something. Does your father golf at all, dear? I can put a word in for him at my club. Aren't trades unions ghastly?'

'Splatch padded into his parent's bedroom and to take the

155

call. He was surprised and gratified to learn that Tick-Tock was in very much in earnest.'

'Is th'all reet man?'

'Pardon?'

'I said is th'all reet. Is tha fookin' deaf?'

'Sorry.'

'Nah listen. Me and t' bass player, Muttley, we're already playing us own stuff. We're into t'satanic heavy rock lahk, but Muttley reckons that if you lads want to have a bash wi' us we've no problems wi' that. We don't know much about this punk lark but it sounds dead easy. Muttley's dad has a garage he does repair jobs in, so we can reurse in thee-er. I leave my drum kit set up in thee-er and there's a couple of combos as well.'

'What are combos?'

'Combo amps, you dozy pig. You just bring your axe and then plug it in. No mither that way is thi'? We've got a PA as well. A lad in our band looks after it forrus. He's an electrician dahn't pit so he knows what he's doing, lahk.'

'Brilliant. But I'll tell you now that we're not very experienced. Brian's learned a few chords, I've written a few songs and we're just starting out really. Would you and Muttley be happy with that?'

'It's nowt to us is this. Our other band has done loads of gigs. We've done three Sunday dinner times at the miner's welfare and we did Muttley's sister's twenty-first before t'disco started. That went really well did that. Free butties and free ale all night. Her boyfriend was a bastard nuisance though. He kept asking us to play some Motown. I said to him, we're called Turds Of Lucifer, not The Four bastard Tops. That shut him up. What motor are you driving?'

'I can't drive. I'm nearly sixteen. Brian's the same age.'

'Eh? Fookin' 'ell, is that all y'are? I'm twenty me. Never mind. I'll pick y'up next Wednesday neet. Give us your address and keep your eye out for a nurse.'

'What's her name?'

'What you on about? A nurse. Cars what they take dead bodies in t'cemetary for burying.'

'A hearse. Got you.'

Muttley's dad sorted me out wi' it. Dirt cheap it was. Fookin' drinks petrol, mind.'

'Right you are.'

The following Wednesday a hearse drew up outside the Splatch residence at the appointed time, scandalising the neighbours and panicking Splatch's parents. The excited though apprehensive boys clambered into the cavernous back seat clutching their instruments. Splatch also carried a satchel containing rough sketches of songs he'd composed. The satchel was to be his constant companion in the proceeding turbulent years and become a feature of many anecdotes illustrating his legendary eccentricity. The hearse jounced along the East Lancashire Road and then onto lanes barely wide enough to accommodate single-lane traffic. They pulled into what appeared to be a farm converted into a vehicular graveyard. Blasted and brutalised cars deficient of wheels, windscreens and doors were parked in every available space outside a forbidding barn. A Bedford van, its back doors opening onto an arrangement of rickety tables and chairs, served as a dining area. The whale song of an electric bass guitar being tuned issued from the barn. Once more Brian glimpsed an unhinged rapture in Splatch's eyes. Whilst gazing at this vista of disorder his usual pessimism resurfaced. They were miles from anywhere, with no means to contact their parents and would be lucky to get out alive and *virgo*

157

intacta.

They walked towards the barn and returned the casual wave of Muttley, an abnormally tall ectomorph in sunglasses who was vainly attempting to keep his bass in tune whilst taking draughts from a bottle of cider. As a rehearsal space the building was discouraging, resembling a conceptualist art installation. Stagnant water dripped through holes in the asbestos roofing. Car seats salvaged from insurance write-offs served as lounge chairs for customers and craftsmen alike, and the boom of the bass resonated in breeze-block walls adorned with the viscera of car engines. The centrepiece was Tick-Tock's drum kit shrouded in filthy canvas sheets. Outside the light was fading and birdsong had devolved to silence. Brian's respiratory system went into overdrive. He was overwhelmed by the urge to flee from a situation for which he was plainly unready; but then Splatch took charge.

Splatch sauntered over to Muttley, offered his hand in greeting and then removed a ream of foolscap paper from his satchel. He briefly conferred with him over the sheet of foolscap and then directed the bassist to adjust the volume control on his amplifier. Muttley meekly did as he was bidden until Splatch gave an affirmative thumbs up. He then approached Tick-Tock, whose expression was one of grudging respect tinged with scepticism. Splatch bent low, gave Tick-Tock a sheet of foolscap and then directed Tick-Tock to play a drum pattern he'd devised. Tick-Tock nodded, tentatively beat out the pattern and then gave Splatch an enquiring glance. Splatch shook his head and requested he be given the drumsticks. After demonstrating exactly what Tick-Tock should play, he handed the sticks back and then ordered Muttley to play the bass line he'd prescribed. After one minute of Muttley repeating the bass pattern he then signalled Tick-Tock to join in. The rhythm section concentrated on their allotted parts whilst Splatch grabbed Brian's instrument, quickly tuned it by ear and then plugged it into a combination amplifier. Splatch then bawled out orders over the noise of the rhythm section. Brian was to strum a single chord, count one elephant, two elephant, three elephant and then strum the same chord again. Brian nodded, strapped on his instrument and complied with the directive as competently as his frayed nerves allowed. As the trio continued to play Splatch retreated ten yards, faced the band and listened with eyes closed and arms folded. He then adjusted the volume levels on the amplifiers and signalled to Tick-Tock to slow the tempo. Having satisfied himself that the band was almost completely consonant with his direction he extricated his guitar from a bin liner and plugged into an amplifier. He affixed his gaze on Tick-Tock whilst singing the first verse of a self-penned tune called 'World Gone Septic'. Splatch's voice, naturally sonorous and capable of gliding over three octaves, ascended upwards into the leaking rafters of the repair shop. By dint of their regular jam sessions Brian was sufficiently inured to his friend's vocals to ignore this distraction. He doggedly stuck to counting elephants and strummed his single chord on cue.

The reaction of the rhythm section was marked. Muttley shot Tick-Tock a quizzical glance whilst Tick-Tock's slack, bestubbled jaw dropped further in awe as Splatch's ethereal vocals and filigree guitar runs rebounded from the walls. Some years later Tick-Tock would famously remark that hearing Splatch for the first time was like listening to a smack-addicted choir boy. This aperçu proved to be piercingly accurate.

In the months following their first rehearsal, The Vinegar Strokes set to work with the industry of young men in a hurry.

159

All of Splatch's tunes were reworked to showcase the de facto leader's vocals and startlingly melodic guitar work. They incorporated a couple of cover versions of Velvet Underground and Stooges songs and finished off with a barnstorming take on Buzzcock's 'Boredom'. With each practice session they became louder, tighter, faster and, in Brian's case, drunker. He had developed a taste for the stout brewed by Muttley's father, a concoction with the appearance and bouquet of untreated sewage.

When each rehearsal was concluded, the band seated themselves outside the decrepit Bedford van serving as their green room. Muttley had advised caution when imbibing the stout as after a particularly raucous christening party his aunty Margaret had discovered herself to be pregnant, but clueless as to the identity of the father. There were in fact several candidates, alas none of whom was her husband. Brian ignored Muttley's warnings and on numerous occasions had to be poured from the back seat of the hearse and onto the pavement outside chez Paget. It was only by dint of his mother refusing to tear her gaze away from the television and his father being at the social club that he avoided brutal retribution for his debased behaviour.

In his turn, Splatch was gratified to learn that Tick-Tock was a natural networker with contacts in the unlikeliest of pubs, clubs and social centres. Convinced that the band was ready to perform before a live audience Tick-Tock had bearded the steward of the miners' welfare, pleading with him to allow his new band to perform a Sunday lunchtime gig. Whilst the band would play for free they also wished to advertise their imminent appearance by affixing a poster to the club noticeboard, adjacent to the fixture list for the women's crown green bowls and the fishing section's next match at Leigh. The dolorous steward muttered that he'd have to ask the committee, unless of course the band elected to pay their subs and became members of the club. In which case, Tick-Tock could hang a picture up of his mam shagging a pig as far as he was concerned.

The date was confirmed and a suitably punkish flyer created in lurid felt-tip pen adorned the noticeboard. At the gig was a gaggle of tentative youths clad in what they assumed to be punk attire, a clutch of hippies and an aghast quartet of miners whose game of dominoes was ruined by some rag-arsed bastards making a noise like a fookin' air raid. It proved to be a less than auspicious debut, resulting in thrown bottles and fights on the dancefloor. The hippies were ejected on the grounds that the committee had yet to approve the admission of blokes swanning about looking like bloody girls, but Splatch and his lieutenants held the audience sufficiently rapt for a full twenty-five minutes.

The audience, including the mild drinking, Woodbine-smoking pitmen, were engaged by both the gaunt good looks of the leader and the strong melodies of the ensemble. The club steward was less enamoured by the band's *oeuvre* and as a punitive measure withheld the pie and peas usually offered to turns who played Sunday lunchtimes. The club cleaner was enjoying her annual caravan holiday in Llandudno and the steward was forced to dispose of the post-gig detritus himself. Northern punks had yet to grasp that the target of their expectorations should have been the people onstage rather than the parquet flooring of the concert room. This turn wouldn't be playing in his club again.

Brian was overwhelmed by the experience. For the first time in his life he had been the focus of other people's attention and, worse than that, had enjoyed it. At the end of the final number the exhilaration was such that he could no longer stand erect with

161

any confidence and breaking into tears was a very real possibility. As the hearse turned onto the single-lane blacktop leading to the band's headquarters, Brian struggled to overmaster all-consuming urges to either weep, vomit, masturbate or run a marathon. He endured the gamut of emotions usually associated with romantic love, the sense of awakening in a better world in which nothing was impossible and his very existence a valuable currency to others. This was in stark contrast to the sangfroid displayed by his bandmates. Their shrug-shouldered dismissal of what was to them just another gig troubled Brian. He had experienced an epiphany whilst they seemed to have already forgotten this life-changing experience and were looking forward to a drink. Even Splatch seemed to be in an emotional neutral gear, cool and dispassionate, and Brian sensed that he was already making mental notes upon how to improve the band's presentational skills. Brian felt very alone then.

Casting furtive glances at his unsmiling companions, Brian intuited that if he continued along this trajectory then at some point the limelight would wither him. Narcissism was not the same as ability, and when he compared himself to his supremely calm associates he knew he simply didn't have the right stuff. He was just a trier, a dilettante dazzled by a whiff of recognition, a talentless egotist whose natural province was the periphery. These young men seemed like they belonged on stage whereas Brian knew he should be hanging around by the cloakroom. He was convulsed by disappointment, a natural reaction when confronted with the incontestable truth that one was not much cop at something one enjoyed. He had, however, spared himself the hubris and despair experienced by thousands of musos who in their youth had shot for the moon, missed, and were then condemned to spend decades being eaten away by bitterness. The hardest lessons are almost invariably the most instructive.

Following the maiden gig, Tick-Tock rigorously applied himself to hustling more opportunities for the band to perform. The band's rehearsals increased, thus providing Brian with more opportunities to be hopelessly blotto on the man-killing stout. New songs poured out of Splatch in a welter of creativity, sometimes even during a break in rehearsals. The others would sit at the table by the Bedford van whilst Splatch walked the perimeter fence of the compound, muttering to himself and jotting down ideas in an exercise book. When he returned, his troubled expression suggested he'd experienced an ephemeral trauma of which he had only scant recall. The band's repertoire expanded to the point that Tick-Tock was able to approach local promoters proclaiming that his band could play for a full fifty minutes and provide an encore if required. The length of the band's set was unusual in a period when punk bands playing for twelve minutes was equivalent to the London Symphony Orchestra performing The *Ring* Cycle.

The Vinegar Strokes supported bands up from London in fetid clubs in Liverpool and Manchattan, winning small though encouraging notices in the disproportionately influential music press. However, the weeknight rehearsals and gigs at weekends began to erode Brian's sanity. At school he appeared ghoulish, vacant-eyed and ready to collapse at any moment. His performance in mock examinations was more disappointing than even his despairing tutors had expected. By contrast, the omnicompetent Splatch was seemingly impervious to the ravages of late nights and early mornings. He thrived on a regimen of minimal nutriment, alcohol, cannabis and casual sex. Brian was splintered by exhaustion and he wasn't even having sex, casual or otherwise. Anxieties regarding his plummeting libido would be such that he would force himself to masturbate, striving to assure himself that at least one part of his anatomy was still functional. On numberless occasions he was sound asleep before the defining moment.

It was fortunate then that Brian's father had secured a position for his son as a general labourer and trainee machine operator in the factory. Derek regularly drank with Archie, the shop convenor, and during a game of solo whist made cryptic references to someone who might be interested in a job. The shop convenor nodded sagely and counselled Derek to consider the lad employed. If the management had any problems with it he'd have the whole factory on strike within the week. Brian had joined the blue collar multitudes before he'd even left school, thus handily rendering his abysmal showing in his final exams irrelevant, but this rite of passage to adulthood also carried a tariff; childish things would now have to be put away, but at least he might get some decent sleep and a satisfying conclusion to hand relief.

When Brian broke the news of his retirement from the band Tick-Tock and Muttley were their usual phlegmatic selves, but Splatch was desolated. He made numerous attempts to change Brian's mind, but was mollified by Brian's lacerating self-appraisal regarding his abilities. Brian averred that Splatch himself would eventually feel constrained as his glittering talent sought bigger stages. He for one didn't wish to be an encumbrance. Brian's forecast proved remarkably prescient, but Splatch was inconsolable. He voiced his fears that Brian's withdrawal would prompt a permanent scission and their friendship would dissolve. Brian assured him that they would continue as they always had. Unbeknown to either of them this conversation presaged the fracture of a previously inviolable bond. The young are doomed to live only in the present, assuming

164

that their world and the people in it would remain unchanged for all time. Two boys on the cusp of adulthood were to learn that the opposite is usually the case.

The summer of 1980 was a watershed year for Brian and Splatch. Having reached the age of majority Brian was entitled to earn wages as a shift worker. The extra income afforded him the opportunity to learn to drive, to purchase an impressive hi-fi, to increase his record collection, to drink a great deal more and purchase a more expensive guitar to ham-fistedly assault. Splatch spent the summer waiting to attend university to study law. He slept at unusual hours of the day, smoked a great deal of cannabis, experimented with lysergic acid, wrote songs, learned some rudimentary piano and indulged in casual sex with bedazzled although later indignant young women who arrived briefly in his orbit. A trainee solicitor had threatened legal action when she discovered herself to be the incubator of the fruit of Splatch's loins. Splatch strove courageously on, his aspiration to be the most famous person on the planet unsullied by such tedious extraneities as parenthood.

The Vinegar Strokes had been restored to a quartet eight months previously by the recruitment of a dextrous though captious rhythm guitar player called Adey Moi. Querulous, fame-ravenous and envious of Splatch's status as the epicentre of the band, he regularly ignited the fury of the usually stoic and laconic back line. Initially Muttley would indulge Adey's self-delusive bletherings and would observe that he was just three drops short of a piss. Tick-Tock was less accommodating of Adey's irruptions and would threaten to break off one of his arms and beat him to death with it if he didn't shut his fookin' din. When it appeared that the rancorous exchanges might degenerate into violence, Splatch needed only to affix Adey with his destroyerof-worlds stare and the gadfly would be cowed into obedient silence. Adey was enough of a pragmatist to understand that creative tension has its limits and might well result in hospitalisation. He was also painfully aware of who their small but partisan following came to watch. And it wasn't him.

Unbeknown to the band, the hip young gunslingers of Britain's leading popular music publication were casting their eyes northwards. It was obvious even to the most tin-eared that The Vinegar Strokes were an outfit to be reckoned with. Splatch's debauched aristocratic mien and instinctive understanding of the mechanics of rock music were irrefutable evidence of potential greatness. The magazine despatched a rodentine staff writer to report upon developments in a province in which empty factories, football violence and appalling weather were the only notable points of interest.

Club Aargh! was a small though lively venue situated in a suburb of Manchattan and frequented by a scowl of punks, pillheads, boozehounds and sociopaths. The Vinegar Strokes had finagled a support slot to a band from the Midlands, whose renown was premised upon several gushing reviews penned by a staff writer of Britain's leading popular music publication. Prior to his arrival at the gig, the journalist had promised the headline act another favourable notice in exchange for a hotel room, an assignation with the bass player's sister and a plentiful supply of drugs. The headliners were confident that the journalist's effusions would guarantee the success of their debut album and stardom was a copper-bottomed certainty. Alas, this band's only entry into the annals of pop history was the ignominy of being the last band to which The Vinegar Strokes would be a support act.

The passage of two years had contrived a transformation in

the physical and sartorial appearance of The Vinegar Strokes. Muttley and Tick-Tock no longer disported denim jackets adorned with the insignias of hard rock bands and their Zapata moustaches had been reaped. Clad in black from head to toe, bristle-haired and as gaunt as shadows, they seemed as impervious to light as anthracite. Adey Moi had opted for brighter colours, topping his white jeans and matelot's shirt with a beret worn at a raffish angle and held in place with Sellotape. His eye make-up had provoked some derision from his bandmates but Adey had ignored their dispraise. Undeterred by his physical resemblance to a small but muscular scrum half, Adey had espoused androgyny with a gusto that bordered on the disturbing. By contrast Splatch dressed as he always did, his drab lineaments possessing no other function than to conceal his false modesty. Months later, a hack from one of the quality newspapers coined the term, "Maoist peasant chic" to describe Splatch's garb, although the average peasant might have bridled at being compared with someone so obviously careless about his appearance.

The Vinegar Strokes were late in appearing on stage that evening as another acrimonious contretemps between Adey and Tick-Tock had delayed their start time. When they finally arrived onto a small platform supported by beer crates they were adrenalised, grim-faced and intent upon the infliction of widespread collateral damage. The usually hostile audience was stunned by a ferocious enfilade of post-punk rock, Adey's rock star posturing notwithstanding. This gig confirmed The Vinegar Strokes as greatest band to emerge from the North-West of England. Brian missed the gig as he was working a twelve-hour night shift but was cock-a-hoop when he read the screed of rhapsodic verbiage composed by the journalist at the gig. In that

167

week's edition of Britain's most influential music paper, Splatch and his confrères were virtually canonised, but unfortunately there was no mention whatsoever of the headline band. The journalist declared that he had seen, "The future of British music. Take shelter". After penning the review, the staff writer had prudently avoided the intimidating phone calls from the headliners he had so treacherously betrayed. He implored his editor to intercede on his behalf but was ordered to expedite the matter alone. The editor himself had fielded a call from the bass player's sister. She wasn't too pleased either.

Events took a dizzying turn in the next few months. A photographer from the magazine whose encomium had catapulted the band to the attention of the cognoscenti was despatched northwards. His remit was to photograph The Vinegar Strokes in their natural habitat and to capture the flavour of the B-road sinkhole from which they hailed. Tick-Tock met the photographer at the railway station and transported him by hearse to the band's headquarters. The photographer, a sad-eyed moustachioed bean-pole with a runny nose, was initially discouraged by the band's preferred location and enquired if they preferred more hospitable surroundings. They were unanimous that the photoshoot would be conducted among the cadavers of crushed and violated motor vehicles or not at all. The photographer was dismayed by the challenge of portraying this collective of young savages in a complimentary light but, after a couple of glasses of Muttley senior's stout and several potent joints, he applied himself to the task.

The photographer envisaged presenting them as serious young men at large in the blighted metal-scape of a nation in decline. Depicting Muttley and Tick-Tock as grim was easy as they never smiled anyway, but Adey's look-at-me bumptiousness was distracting as he jostled for prominence in the group portraits. Splatch sorrowfully shook his head whilst Tick-Tock searched for a tyre-jack with which to sodomise Adey if he didn't fookin' behave 'imself.

The newly-sedated photographer began to enjoy himself immensely. This was the first time he'd encountered northerners in the wild and concluded that they were stranger than some of the creatures he'd seen in Chessington Zoo. Against a backdrop of twisted metal and breezeblock chiaroscuro he exhorted the band to glare menacingly at the camera. Then to glare menacingly but also slightly distracted. Then to glare menacingly, yet slightly distracted and also somewhat downcast. Then to glare menacingly, slightly distracted, somewhat downcast but touched by a scintilla of optimism. Adey did his utmost to oblige. The expressions of the other three remained unchanged.

Tiring of this charade Splatch announced he was going for a walk by the perimeter fence. He mumbled a warning that he expected to find his rhythm guitarist still alive on his return and sloped off whilst everyone else retired to the Bedford van. The photographer's rheumy eyes followed Splatch as he ambled aimlessly along the fence. The pale setting sun was egg-sliced by barbed wire and the gaunt figure of the bandleader was backlit by an autumnal half-light. This was a *coup de théâtre* gifted by Nature. The photographer rose with as much agility as his inebriated frame would allow and hailed Splatch, who turned slowly and affixed him with a cool and hostile gaze. The photographer pressed the shutter. This was the image that would adorn the walls of countless halls of residence, teenage bedrooms and bedsits for almost a decade. The royalties derived from reproductions of the photo ensured a very comfortable retirement

169

for the snapper, whilst the financial return for the snapee amounted to precisely zero. Splatch's haphazard approach to the commercial aspects of show business was already in evidence.

Despite the growing ferment around the band, there were a number of outstanding issues to be addressed. Tick-Tock was fielding calls from agencies anxious to showcase them in more prestigious venues, whilst television producers had signalled their interest in featuring them on late night arts programmes. In common with his bandmates, Tick-Tock was both bemused and intimidated by this upturn in their fortunes. He was ill-equipped to deal with the business of managing an increasingly popular rock band and demanded that someone do summat about it and fookin' sharpish. Splatch was as bereft of ideas as anyone else. He had assumed that all he had to do was to be wonderful and everything else would pretty much take care of itself. The only person they knew with any managerial experience was Muttley senior, the owner of the garage serving as their headquarters. To compound their dilemma, they were also aware that irrespective of how many new admirers they garnered they had no recorded product to offer. No manager, no recording contract, no album in the record shops and no clue as to how to remedy these demerits. But the cavalry was on its way in the formidable form of Lavinia Jacquette.

Lavinia was the progeny of a minor but moneyed aristocratic family whose antecedents had amassed a fortune from mining interests in Australia. Her family owned several properties around the globe and a dazzling yacht berthed in Villa Moura, aboard which they entertained gossip columnists, arms dealers and international kleptocrats. Lavinia had excelled at the all-girls private school to which her parents had despatched her; but her innate contumacy, coupled with extensive reading of Marxist theory, had resulted in her expulsion prior to the sixth form. Her tutors had predicted great things for this singular young woman, but unsure as to what they were. A career in Whitehall and the BBC was now out of the question, although a seat in Parliament would be easily within her gift. Her fierce intelligence, Churchillian rhetorical powers and white-hot ire at everything from monopoly capitalism to the cost of champagne for the unemployed marked Lavinia as someone to be reckoned with. Her scandalised parents were unequipped to deal with her brandy-drenched raillery against the values that had sustained their family for generations, and Lavinia was resistant to being groomed for the duties reflective of her social caste. Her penchant for wearing hobnailed boots had also led to the indefinite postponement of her coming-out party.

Clandestine meetings between her parents and the family physician had contrived a stratagem to cloister their beautiful but obviously unspooled daughter in a sanatorium in Switzerland; but unbeknown to her parents, Lavinia had despatched a review of an album recorded by a family friend to Britain's most influential music publication. Her acidulous excoriation of the disc, featuring references to the works of Orwell, E P Thompson, PJ Proby, Chomsky and Old Mother Reilly, bore the stampings of a prodigiously gifted scribe. Upon reading the review the family friend self-destructed by drinking bleach and Lavinia was questioned by the police. The police had pondered the possibility of arraigning her on the charge of manslaughter by journalistic asperity but this was peremptorily dismissed by the family solicitor. Following a positive response to her review Lavinia was offered the staff position recently vacated by a writer who had succumbed to puncture wounds inflicted by the irate sister of a bass player. Her relieved parents wished her well in her new career and immediately fled the country.

This fierce, raven-haired, impressively intelligent hedonist, endued with an erudition and mordant literary style belying her youth, quickly became the toast of London's demi-monde. Her superhuman ability to produce compelling copy whilst hopelessly drunk, narcotised or both had editors from Fleet Street prostrating themselves at her meticulously pedicured feet. Lavinia freelanced for a raft of current affairs and arts magazines, demanding and receiving huge fees for pieces that were little more than exquisitely crafted snippets of bibulous vituperation. As the philosopher princess of Britain's youth, her perspectives upon themes as disparate as Keith Joseph's misanthropy to Saint-Saën's propensity for cross-dressing guaranteed a spike in sales for any organ fortunate enough to meet her extortionate financial demands.

Although Lavinia enthusiastically subscribed to Proudhon's dictum that property is theft, by the time she was twenty-three she had acquired two large properties in London, two cars she was unable to drive due to never having learned, an enviable current account and a sexual appetite for handsome male rock musicians with conveniently low IQs. Her Stakhanovite work-rate and the sales of her first novel, a *Bildungsroman* chronicling the travails of an orphaned ingénue and her rise to the very pinnacle of Fleet Street, had realised very gratifying financial returns. But although garlanded with the fear and respect of her peers, larded with critical approbation and showered with financial reward, there was a gaping lacuna in Lavinia's life. She craved one good brave cause, or indeed several good brave causes. Inordinately proud of her radical credentials she was determined to impose her socialist, feminist, anti-racist, internationalist worldview upon a nation immolated by New

172

Conservatism.

On numerous occasions Lavinia had mused that the medium of language simply wasn't big enough to disseminate her message of hope to the masses and she had ruminated upon new modes of expression. She had considered composing a mime opera to delineate her loathing of the Western military-industrial complex, but had rightly figured that a score and libretto consisting of eighty minutes of silence would not play well with the cognoscenti. Politics held no allure for her. She had disdained association with the hard left following a number of meetings with Marxist-Leninist groups. In Lavinia's eyes they were timorous milquetoasts looking for something to do until a lectureship presented itself. But upon eyeing the snaps of The Vinegar Strokes taken by the lugubrious photographer, she knew she had found her muse. Here was the authentic progeny of the industrial north, flinty young men standing defiant in a society convulsed by establishment oppression and police brutality. She also fancied the pants off Splatch and resolved to sleep with him as soon as the opportunity presented itself. To the band proper she would serve as votary, procuress and advocate. Lavinia was quite prepared to kill people to ensure that her charges were a global phenomenon.

The initial meeting between the band and their new apologist was inauspicious. Lavinia had beckoned the band to London and organised tickets for the Saturday morning train to Euston. With their usual practicality, Muttley and Tick-Tock had ensured that the band were sufficiently victualled for the journey by preparing a breakfast of cold steak pies, cold chips, twenty-four cans of brown ale and a bottle of whisky. London was new and unknown terrain and it was only sensible to prepare a contingency when venturing any further south than Crewe.

173

However, such was their excitement that they foolishly neglected to eat. By the time the train departed the Midlands, three-quarters of the band were thoroughly irrigated and with nothing on their stomachs to slow the dispersion of alcohol into their bloodstreams. Splatch ignored the others and stared out of the window, languorously thumbing through the morning newspapers whilst his lieutenants became progressively more boisterous. Adey Moi was convinced that he would meet someone off the telly in London, because it was an indisputable fact that all famous people lived in The Smoke. They might even happen upon the nationally revered Jimmy Savile and introduce themselves as a band upon whom Jim should keep an avuncular eye. He might even fix a television appearance for them as he seemed the stripe of man interested in young people.

The rhythm section was more circumspect in its appraisal of The Great Wen. Muttley solemnly recounted that his father had visited London to watch the rugby league cup final. He was appalled to discover that not a single pub in the entire city sold mild, thus impelling him to drink beer with neither a foaming head nor a discernible taste. His father had also reported that Londoners espoused the disgusting habit of ingesting pickled eggs whilst drinking in their favourite hostelries. Such dubious practices aroused suspicions regarding the sanity of the inhabitants and, if terrible beer and pickled eggs were typical examples of metropolitan fare, then they could all easily starve to death. Tick-Tock averred that he wasn't putting a single fookin' thing in his cakehole unless Adey had eaten some of it first.

They alighted at Euston and trudged towards the exits. An abnormally tall punk with a lime-green Mohican haircut and a watch-chain pendant from his pierced nose gave a thumbs up to the quartet and signalled them to follow him. They clambered into a spacious saloon car, taking care not to spill brown ale on the gleaming upholstery. As the driver exceeded the designated speed limit, London deliquesced before the band's unblinking eyes. Tick-Tock and Muttley were cowed into fearful silence by the mammoth scale of the city and its teeming population; they had no idea that there were so many people in the world. Adey wriggled animatedly in the front seat, gesticulating wildly at passers-by he thought he recognised from off the telly. Splatch occasionally riffled through the contents of his satchel whilst gazing through a rear side window with an unreadable expression. One would have been forgiven for thinking that he was en route to either an awards ceremony or major invasive surgery.

The car turned into a street of unremarkable mews houses. Tick-Tock nodded appreciatively, reassured by their resemblance to the terraced homes of his neighbourhood, but his solace was short-lived. A front door opened into a long vestibule with burnished parquet flooring. The magnolia walls were adorned with monochrome photographs of musicians, novelists, playwrights and political figures, the identities of whom Tick-Tock was shamefully unaware. There was also a pencil sketch of a dishevelled Yorkshire terrier whom the band later learned answered to the name of Pisser. Tick-Tock chastised himself for his ignorance, correctly speculating that they must be people of significance. Perhaps even the dog had attained a renown of which he was wholly unconscious.

The band trooped into a long, high-ceilinged reception room accoutred with a grand piano, a small bar, an acoustic guitar, an easel, a large artist's sketch pad, several couches and a hi-fi that must have cost the equivalent of half a year's salary. Lavinia,

175

dressed in thigh-length black velvet boots and a simple though stylish purple dress, smiled vampirically through sable lips. One hand held a large glass of something red whilst the other was perched on a slim hip. She raised her impeccably plucked eyebrows and nodded towards the bar on which an array of canapés awaited the attention of the band. Three-quarters of the quartet gaped in wonder at their surroundings, but Splatch narrowed his eyes and stared with unfeigned hostility at his hostess. It was left to Muttley to break the tombal silence.

'Is th'all reet cocker?'

'Pardon?'

'Is th'all reet? Have you got any glasses for the ale we've brought wi' us?'

'Anything you wish. *Mi casa su casa me amore.*'

'Oui. Does that mean I'm all right to go behind that counter over thee-ur for some glasses lahk?'

'Oh God. This is wonderful. You're more primitive than even I could have hoped for. Please. Help yourself to anything.'

'Ta. D'you sup tinned ale yourself love? We've still got a few left, lahk.'

'I'd rather have my labia chewed by Pisser than drink that ghastly shit.'

'Righto. Shout up if you change your mind.'

'All of you get a drink. We have a lot to get through.'

Lavinia approached the easel and opened the sketch pad at a blank page. She took a blue felt tip and scrawled the word "manumission" on the pad. She swept her intense gaze over every member of the band in expectation of knowing nods and ironic smiles. The band completely ignored her and continued to imbibe whilst Splatch strode across the room to pick up the acoustic guitar. Lavinia inhaled deeply and then peremptorily

176

clapped her hands to command the band's attention. After taking an admirably long pull at her glass she delineated her battle plan.

In her severest bluestocking voice she counselled the band that she should now be regarded as the fifth member. In matters of business and finance she would always hold the casting vote. As to the matter of quality control and the subsequent release of recorded product, her voice would be as equally influential in deciding which material was to be released. Lavinia considered her ear for a song to be matchless and the band would do well to accommodate her opinion. And, oh yes. They were to completely revise the wholly inequitable relationship between a band and its employer. Hitherto, bands were enslaved by multi-millionaire record company moguls who ruthlessly creamed off the lion's share of profits. Bands were slow to realise any financial rewards from their artistic endeavours. Groups who had garnered an international reputation were earning little more than the average librarian. She challenged the band to answer this very simple question. Why should a record label owner, who had made no material contribution to the product, dictate the conditions of employment and income to those whose genius had contrived such glittering success? Muttley offered exactly the response Lavinia wished to hear.

'Not a fookin' scooby cocker.'

Lavinia nodded solemnly before delivering her stratagem to revise this inequitable state of affairs. As the appointed representative of The Vinegar Strokes she, in tandem with her very expert legal advisor, would negotiate with all major record companies. Each record company would be offered the opportunity to hear her list of demands. If any company failed to abide by the stringent conditions she had laid down then that company would then be immediately disbarred from further negotiations. The record company with whom the band would sign would be decided by a process of elimination. The band would exercise complete artistic control and refuse all communications with the media unless explicitly authorised by Lavinia herself.

The full cost of promotion, instrumentation, amplification, security, concession stands and back-office staff for live performances would be met by the record company, meaning that the band would need no recourse to purchasing equipment and hiring staff on their own behalf. Monies earned from live performances would directly enter the coffers of the band. Most importantly, this contract extended only to the production of one album and a maximum of two single releases. Should the band elect to record a follow-up then the negotiation process would begin from scratch. Lavinia was confident that all record companies would subsequently be only too ready to open discussions following the success of the band's debut album. The workers would finally assume control over the means of production. But there was a caveat. There would be no royalties from the sales of any recorded product. Although this might seem unfair, her accountant had counselled her upon the very real possibility of an unknown band generating miniscule sales. Live appearances, however, in tandem with merchandising and a handsome advance, would guarantee returns impossible to refuse.

Lavinia's stipulation that recorded product would not generate any royalty payments to the band was not entirely correct, but at this juncture Lavinia thought it prudent to be economical with the truth. She was gratified to note that the band appeared to care not one jot about royalties nor indeed anything else. Following her rhetorical flight, Lavinia gave a slight,

178

modest bow and readied herself to field questions she was certain her audience would posit. Tick-Tock's query was one for which she was unprepared.

'Fook me. You're not back'ards in coomin' forwards you, are yo'? And where's your toilet? I'm choking for a shite, me.'

Lavinia shook her head in despair and silently pointed towards the vestibule. When Tick-Tock had absented himself she concentrated her glower at the remaining members of her audience. Muttley seemed oblivious, Adey Moi looked ready to burst whilst Splatch had retuned the guitar to play the instrument bottleneck style, using a disposable lighter as a slide. But even as he played a simple blues it became apparent that he'd been paying attention.

Were they to give up their day jobs? If so, how would they support themselves? What percentage of the band's income would Lavinia arrogate to herself? What size of advance would the band expect to receive for signing with a label? Could they continue to live at home or be expected to relocate to London?

Lavinia visibly brightened at her prospective new lover's questioning and resolved to violate him in ways scarcely imaginable before the weekend was out. Her responses were the acme of concision. When on tour, the band would be paid a large monthly salary and also a percentage of the emoluments from ticket sales and merchandise. These sums would be in addition to their advance from the record company. All of them, excepting Splatch, could continue to reside in the North if they so wished. As the de facto leader and songwriter he might be needed to meet with record company executives and the press. Negotiations with record companies would begin the following week. She refused to countenance any resistance to her pre-conditions and forecast that the band would be astonished by the size of the advance acquired on their behalf. The advance would be allocated equally between all parties, including herself. Her accountants would ensure very favourable terms of taxation to ensure that the band retained as much of the advance as possible. And now, if they had any further questions, would the band mind waiting until she had replenished her glass and allowed Pisser to relieve himself in the small back yard. There were no further questions.

The band clustered around Splatch, anxious to learn his perspective upon the offer made by this enigmatic woman. Their leader's scepticism was palpable in his downbeat demeanour, but he suggested that if the band was serious about building a career then Lavinia's proposals should be given consideration. After all, they were hardly inundated by applications to manage them. His one caveat was that they should withhold the submission of their notice to their employers until Lavinia produced more concrete evidence of her ambitions. Like money. They concurred with slow nods of their heads and even Adey's berserk exuberance was tempered by Splatch's circumspection.

'Let's give her a fortnight. See what happens.'

'Are you stoppin' down 'ere then? She reckoned you'll have to. I don't see why, lahk.'

'It'll be okay. College doesn't start for another three weeks. If this falls through then I haven't lost anything. There's a guitar and a piano here. I don't need anything else.'

'Shall I ring your mam and dad? Tell 'em you're staying in this shithole for a few days?'

'Nah. I'll ring them myself. It's better coming from me.'

'Will you be shagging her later on then?'

'I should think so.'

'Righto. We'll be off then. I can't wait to get home, me. I wouldn't wipe my arse with this fookin' London I wouldn't.'

'Why don't we go and see some of the sights before we go? Parliament? Carnaby Street and that?'

'Fookin' shut it, you.'

Splatch rang his anxious but solicitous parents to apprise them of his absence for the rest of the weekend. As it transpired, it would be another thirty years before he returned to reside in his home town.

When the rest of the band had departed for Euston, Lavinia and Splatch drank several glasses of wine, smoked one or two joints, desultorily chatted about appointments Lavinia had organised, divested each other of clothes and then engaged in sexual congress as bestial, sanguinary and elementally violent as any coupling witnessed in an African nature reserve. Teeth were driven into protesting flesh, talons sank into buttocks, glasses were smashed, howls of anguish ricocheted from the walls, guitar strings snapped, heads were forced onto genitalia and fingers probed the most private of orifices. The room was rancid with perfumed sweat, musk, salt tang and sour breath. After a while, when it appeared that Splatch's usually creditable powers of recovery were beginning to fail him, Lavinia produced a bag of white powder. Splatch stared quizzically as Lavinia furiously masturbated him to a fully erect state and then applied the powder to the zone of interest. Splatch raised his eyebrows, gazing firstly at Lavinia and then at his penis. It resembled nothing so much as a veal cutlet.

'What's this you've put on it?'

'What? You mean you don't know what it is?'

'No.'

'Oh my dear, dear boy. Prepare yourself for the evening of your life.'

Although Lavinia was a woman who usually recoiled from

an admission of error, in an off-the-record exchange she owned that perhaps she may have been at least a component in Splatch's subsequent descent into the squalid subterrene of addiction. Her defence of introducing Splatch to cocaine and myriad other pharmaceutical products was that one could no more identify a potential addict any more than one could identify a child abuser. Prudently she forbore from mentioning her own problem with addiction, her narcotic of choice being Splatch himself. That weekend augured the burgeoning of a relationship initially sexual and monetary in nature, but within a year would floresce into something deeper. A relationship of such intensity usually led to the solemnization of the union in a house of worship, but then neither Splatch nor Lavinia were usual people.

Monday afternoon saw the beginning of five days of discussions with record company executives, but on Monday morning Splatch was feeling less than chipper. The amphetamine sulphate he'd ingested the previous day had contrived a gargantuan thirst for red wine but little appetite for sleep. He had been in the arms of Morpheus for a mere thirty minutes when Lavinia almost pierced his ribcage with the heel of a stiletto shoe whilst imperiously demanding that he shake a leg. Splatch stared befuddled at the ceiling then tottered to the lavatory as quickly as his splintered senses would allow. He then evacuated the crimson-hued contents of his stomach, dolorously wailing that he'd discharged at least one vital organ into the lavatory bowl. Lavinia was unmoved by his maunderings and ordered him to the shower. She had taken the liberty of ordering him a wardrobe for the coming conferences and there was an outfit on her bed. Her driver would be picking them up at two o'clock and she required him to be clean, sentient, sartorially elegant, androgynously toothsome and above all silent. Splatch loured at her through

182

bloodshot eyes, bared carmine teeth and stumbled back to the bathroom to void his juddering bowels.

The meetings conducted in the first four days were unproductive. Powerful industry figures gawped in disbelief as Lavinia proposed unprecedented conditions to the signature of a band of whom hardly anyone was aware. One meeting was curtailed so swiftly that Splatch had no time to finish a cigarette before he and Lavinia were heading for the exit. Each evening the legalist visited the couple to discuss yet more stratagems to realise their vaulted ambitions for the band. Splatch listened attentively whilst idly picking out tunes on the piano, but added nothing to the dialogue. He was already resigned to the improbability of Lavinia securing a deal but at least there was plenty of free drink and drugs around. At this juncture his inaugural term at university seemed unavoidable. Friday was to change all that.

Clifford Dane exulted in his notoriety in show business circles. The Great Dane was a grotesque massif of flesh, halitosis and malevolence. It was rumoured that even his own reflection found him detestable. His default settings were intimidation, bullying and gratuitous violence. Dane had lumbered his way into the music industry by providing security for middlingly popular acts on the British college circuit. He and his small team of ex-prisoners ensured that the sensibilities of emotionally fragile artists were unbesmirched by adoring fans seeking a close encounter with their heroes. A deployment of monkey wrenches and steel toe-capped boots were the de rigueur deterrents. Even female fans suffered retributive harm unless an intervention by a romantically inclined band member guaranteed their safety. Dane's crew were chillingly competent at their chosen discipline. As demand for their services grew, Dane and his pot-bellied psychotics garnered reputations for murderous efficiency. Visiting American bands playing larger halls began to insist Dane and company provide their bespoke and quease-inducing protection package. Dane expanded his company to accommodate the uptick in business whilst also increasing his fees. Bands who expatiated upon the themes of peace and love would unheedingly trudge by a stoned but harmless beardie being eviscerated by a gaggle of Dane's bullyboys. Even peace and love has its limits, particularly when a rather grubby-looking hippie was attempting ingress to the post-gig bacchanal.

Dane insinuated himself into influential circles and became both protector of and father-confessor to three of the biggest rock acts in the world. He had calculated that far from being unmaterialistic free spirits sowing their message of global harmony, they were in fact paragons of greed. These bands bemoaned the iron grip imposed upon the purse-strings by their managers and yearned to liberate themselves from The Man. Clifford Dane sensed an opportunity.

A one-day festival headlined by one of the three biggest acts in the world was notable only for the number of punters hospitalised by Dane and his staff's foul ministrations. Dane casually enquired of the headline act that if in the unlikely event that they were liberated from their current manager, would they be amenable to joining a small roster of artists managed by Dane himself. He could guarantee infinitely more favourable returns and gave assurances that their every caprice would be swiftly consummated. This was sweeter music to the ears of the band than anything they had actually composed, but given the constraints of their current contract they were pessimistic at the prospect of their release from vassalage. Dane was more upbeat.

Prior to his casual overtures, Dane and his acolytes had dropped by the home of the band's manager. Following a brief exchange of how's-the-missus pleasantries, Dane's phalanx of psychopaths placed three black bin liners over the manager's head and inserted a double-barrelled shotgun into his mouth. The agenda and outcomes of this discussion were made plain to the terrified manager, who was by now perilously close to soiling himself. Either Dane was offered the opportunity to buy out the band's contract for ten pounds sterling or the manager's skull would be blown into the bin liners and deposited in a container bound for New York. The release document was signed without demur. Dane gently insisted that the outcome of this meeting remain confidential until he had spoken to the press. The erstwhile manager nodded his assent prior to losing consciousness.

News, however disquieting, tends to travel speedily in the entertainment business. It wasn't too long before Dane was approached by the other two integers of the rock triumvirate desirous of more favourable returns on their labours. Dane assured them that negotiations with the band's representatives would be swiftly and successfully expedited, as indeed they were, although Dane's dubious interpretation of established business practices inspired only disgust in industry circles. This mattered little to him. The mewlings of other moguls were as flea bites to a mammoth and dissenting voices were quickly terrified into silence.

A happy adjunct to Dane's robust intercessions was the immediate termination of all of his new stable's contracts with their record companies. They were dropped like disease-ridden rags by companies anxious to dissociate themselves from all things Dane. The three biggest bands in the world were now without the means to release any recorded product, meaning that albums usually generating a million sales on the day of their release remained unrecorded. Conciliating with the artists, Dane charitably offered to sign them to his own record label entitled Bad Things Happen Inc. The resultant revenue from record sales, merchandise and stadium tours cemented Dane's position as the most powerful, most affluent and easily the most despicable music magnate in the world. He was the undisputed industry heavyweight in every sense of the word.

In the car heading towards the Mayfair offices of Bad Things Happen Inc., Splatch continued to grizzle his displeasure at being woken with so little regard for either the time of day or his pitiful physical health. Lavinia sensed that his peeves were merely a mask behind which to conceal his apprehension at meeting the man who could either launch his band into the big time or break every bone in his tremulous body. By contrast Lavinia was the soul of insouciance, proffering companiable chugs to Splatch's shoulder as he languished in a trough of desolation. He was in a strange town, with an even stranger companion, and isolated from everything and everyone familiar to him. Hopelessly out of his depth, he wished for nothing more than to be ambling towards his favourite pub for a meeting with Brian. If this was rock stardom then a career in the legal profession seemed infinitely more attractive. At least he would be able to experience feeling in his face and limbs.

Splatch traipsed sullenly behind Lavinia as she demanded to be shown to Dane's office by the silently resentful receptionist. They mounted a flight of carpeted stairs and were directed into a windowless space large enough to accommodate a light aircraft. A leather lounge suite was arranged around a coffee table at one end of the room. At the other was a well-stocked bar behind which lurked the most intimidating creature Splatch had ever seen. It resembled a macabre experiment in evolution that Nature had failed to complete and then simply forgotten about. Splatch closed his eyes and grappled with an urge to vomit, correctly assuming that the strange odour in the room was issuing from the vision of horror behind the bar. The Great Dane reeked of decline and depravity, and it was a truth universally acknowledged that anyone who wore Wayfarer sunglasses indoors was to be avoided in confined spaces. Dane's gorblimey bronchial rasp was almost incomprehensible to someone whose ears were attuned to the glottal stops and long flat vowels of the north. He was an abomination greater than even Splatch had imagined.

'Does it drink, Lavinia? It doesn't look fackin' old enough to drink. V'you facked it yet? And when are you gonna give my bands some coverage in the papers you horrible cant? Woss wrong wiv ya?'

Lavinia's seraphic smile was a distillation of all of the contempt in which she held her interrogator. She arranged herself carefully on a chair, pointed Splatch to the couch and nodded her affirmation at the bottle of ludicrously expensive champagne Dane was brandishing. Dane joined the couple and abutted himself closely against Splatch, who blanched and quivered in Dane's odorous proximity. Lavinia placed a contract on the coffee table and launched into her now well-rehearsed schtick. Such was his amused incredulity that Dane almost suffered a trans-ischaemic infarction. He snorted like a harpooned whale as Lavinia carefully outlined her exacting demands. She then waited for Dane's mirth to subside, held up a forefinger, reached into her handbag and fished out a ream of monochrome photographs.

'Clifford. Please. For what I'm about to show you I require your fullest attention.'

187

'What? Your tits? Do me a facking favour.'

'I think you'll find the following images a little more to your taste than my tits, as magnificent as they are. My legal advisor has suggested I mention The Children and Young Persons Act 1933 for reasons best known to himself. Here. Have a look at these.'

Dane's breathing grew more stertorous and Splatch grew ever more terrified as Lavinia casually leafed through a trove of the unspeakable. One photo depicted Dane lying prone on a threadbare carpet with his head underneath a glass coffee table, his tongue protruding from his mouth as though in expectation of a communion host. On the other side of the glass hovered the pale bare buttocks of naked boy who was squeezing out a sizeable stool onto the coffee table. The intention of the open-mouthed supplicant was obvious. In another snap a tousled blonde male starveling defecated into a frying pan. This image segued into another of Dane chewing with relish on a doorstep sandwich, the contents of which were as ineffable as they were abhorrent. The *ne plus ultra* of the collection was a depiction of Dane lying hideously nude on a huge divan whilst being licked, pinched, nuzzled and smooched by a cache of pre-pubescent males. Splatch recoiled in horror whilst Lavinia remained perfectly composed, smiling indulgently at this farrago of depravity. Dane's groan was as portentous as a church knell.

'I will cut your facking eyes and then fack this miserable streak of piss to death.'

'Now, Clifford. Let's not be too hasty. Though I should suggest that you exercise a little more discrimination in your choice of guests at these soirees. Some of them would be too happy to point an accusatory finger in your direction if it gets them off the hook. And not even you would do in a sitting MP.

Now. Here's the thing. If Stephen and I aren't out of here in ten minutes, with this contract signed, unharmed and in full command of our faculties, I've instructed certain parties to drop off copies of these photos to a newspaper owned by someone who doesn't hold you in the highest regard. An Australian, perchance?'

'You wouldn't facking dare.'

'You now have nine minutes. So? Sign this contract and your excremental secret will remain just that. Fail to sign the contract and the ramifications are incalculable. The British public can be rather judgemental about this sort of thing can they not?'

Dane affixed Lavinia with a terrifying glare whilst noisily swallowing gobfuls of champagne straight from the bottle. Splatch averted his eyes and knew it was time to act. Despite his dissipation he calculated that he could easily beat Dane in a footrace to the door, through the entrance, down the street and up the M6 if it meant being spared the humiliations that this affront to humankind might visit upon him. As for Lavinia, she could look out for herself. In the previous six days he had come to realise that the world Lavinia inhabited was very dangerous. Her idea of a working lunch might well result in him being raped, murdered and then fished out of the Thames. Evasive action was an imperative, but Lavinia had already anticipated his flight plan.

'Don't move, Stephen. We're at endgame here. Eight minutes, Clifford. Eight minutes to your name being synonymous with your dietary preference.'

Dane sighed heavily, ran his wild-animal eyes over the contract and then with the solemn deliberation of a hanging judge scrawled his signature on the dotted line. Lavinia nodded her satisfaction and directed Splatch to the door.

'The car will be outside, Stephen. I'll join you in a few

minutes.'

Splatch sprang from the couch and exited the building. The punk with the lime-green Mohican gave his usual thumbs up as Splatch clambered into the back seat.

'Orrite?'

'No.'

'Smoke this then.'

'What is it?'

'S'orrite, that's what it is.'

After three long pulls on the spliff Splatch's equilibrium began to return. Lavinia joined him in the back seat, patted his knee and directed the driver to return them home.

'There. That wasn't so bad was it?'

'I want to go home. Now.'

'Don't be ridiculous, Stephen. Apart from anything else we're going up north tomorrow. You and the boys will need to rehearse for the tour in November. I want you as tight as possible before you play your first gig in Glasgow.'

'Glasgow? We've never played in Scotland before. No one's heard of us up there.'

'Don't worry about that. By the time I've finished, you'll be regarded as the second coming. You just make sure the boys are ready. I'm looking forward to hearing you this weekend.'

'Why are you coming?'

'Well who's going to pay for our hotel? You?'

'I'll be staying at home like I normally do.'

'My dear boy. Musicians do NOT live with their parents. Not unless they've been otherwise instructed by the courts. Now. We're going for something to eat, something to drink, and then we're going to bed.'

'Great. I'm still knackered.'

190

'Are you this obtuse all the time, Stephen?'

'Oh no. You're not on. I can't. I think you've broken it.'

'Well please ensure that it's in good working order by six o'clock this evening. Blackmail and extortion are wonderful aphrodisiacs. Apart from anything else we should be celebrating. I've just made you a very wealthy young man.'

'I'm going to be sick again.'

'Oh don't be such a baby, Stephen.'

The autumn saw The Vinegar Strokes rehearse with the unsmiling intensity of a crack commando troop preparing for close urban warfare, although in truth they had been ready for the bigger stages for some time. With Adey Moi playing some incendiary rhythm guitar they were a finely-honed machine. Never a performer to suffer misgivings about his abilities, Splatch became ever more in command of his powers of invention. Lavinia was fulsome in her praise of the band's slavish application, whilst they in their turn were bedazzled by the prospect being awarded over two hundred thousand pounds each early in the coming year. Each Friday evening Splatch and Lavinia took a reservation in the swishest hotel in Manchattan before hailing a taxi to the band's headquarters. Daytime was devoted to rehearsals whilst evenings were spent in the company of the band and their girlfriends.

Muttley was affianced to Cath, an affable straightforward girl he had known since secondary school and who worked in a pie shop. Tick-Tock endured a turbulent relationship with a forthright dental receptionist called Sheila. Sheila frequently declared her intention to get shut of the silly bleeder if didn't save enough for a deposit for a house and start acting his bleedin' age. With his usual sangfroid Tick-Tock would ignore her importunities whilst demanding that she give his bleedin' napper

191

some bastard peace for a bastard change. Sheila would then punch him squarely in the mouth. Her father had boxed at the Tokyo Olympics and had expertly tutored his daughter in the fistic arts from an early age. But irrespective of her almost constant disparagement, Sheila would rearrange the features of anyone who so much as breathed an adverse comment about her partner. Tick-Tock adored her, although his adulation was tempered by an understandable caution if Sheila's dander was on the rise.

Adey's latest *affaire du coeur* was of similarly abridged stature but seemingly his polar opposite in temperament. She exuded a benevolent reserve rimed with a certain chilliness, hovering by Adey's side as he gibbered and flittered like a crazed macaque. Muttley's opinion of her was surprisingly uncharitable. He averred that she seemed a bit pointless, hanging about with that dozy fucker like a chip waiting for vinegar. Her presence barely registered with Splatch whilst Tick-Tock struggled to remember her name. For her part, Lavinia kept her own counsel. Being a seasoned main-chancer herself she could recognise a fellow traveller a mile away and sensed an agenda. In the long term this mute and complaisant enigma might prove to be a source of rancour and division. One had to suspect the motives of anyone who could abide Adey for as long as she could without trying to nail him to the nearest wall. Lavinia resolved to keep an eye on her and if necessary arrange her disappearance. She had already covertly arrogated to herself the sum of two hundred thousand pounds courtesy of Bad Things Happen Inc. and there was the prospect of more sizeable emoluments in the coming year. At this crucial pass, Adey's welfare was paramount if Lavinia's aspirations to multimillionairehood and the coronation of Splatch as the prince of post-punk rock were to be realised.

192

This aphasic bint would soon learn who the witch queen of this outfit really was.

Regarding herself as something of a social anthropologist, Lavinia applied herself to studying her protégés in their natural habitat. On Saturday nights the band and their girlfriends would frequent the fetid pubs and clubs of the dingy backwater they called home. If his shift pattern allowed, Brian would join them, although he was predictably unencumbered by a love interest. The band smashed down pints of brown and bitter whilst the ladies quaffed lager and lime chased down with rum and blackcurrant. They smoked cheap cigarettes in the street with casual acquaintances and took the rise out of each other in an argot Lavinia could barely understand. They huddled around pub juke boxes and catcalled hatchet-faced doormen, but at a safe remove to avoid violent retribution. Every evening concluded with a visit to their favourite chip shop for a disgusting repast of chips, pie and peas which they ate whilst sitting on rain-sodden pavements, oblivious to the traffic passing within inches of their toes.

Lavinia was both endeared and desolated by this freemasonry of innocents. They reminded her of the provincial boys of 1914, flat-capped ingenus looking forward to the adventure of war but unaware of the horrors awaiting them at the front. Their impending descent into stardom was her doing and they were now the catspaws of those whose sole intent was self-enrichment. She herself was now one of those parasites, her cherished radicalism now so much dust. Although she had no real talent for shame, when observing their guileless sodality at close quarters her self-contempt became almost unbearable. She had given no thought to their well-being following the dissolution of the band that she herself would engineer. She was also aware that her relationship with Splatch was doomed. In a relatively brief period she had grown to love Splatch with an ardency of which she never thought herself capable, but life confers greater agonies than rejection by one's soulmate. Love, like life itself, is transitory and almost invariably disappoints. But money? Money never disappoints.

In the months leading up to the first gig of the tour Lavinia networked and schmoozed with breathless assiduity. She had shrewdly forbore from disclosing her association with the band as this may have queered her pitch to the fauxhemians whose approbation she sought. Dane's monastic silence was guaranteed as he was in no position to expose her duplicity. In a respected though little-read current affairs magazine she eulogised the band's proletarian authenticity, dilating upon her exclusive attendance at a group rehearsal and her astonishment at their unalloyed brilliance. She predicted stardom for the enigmatic frontman and his confederates and urged her devoted readership to seek them out at the earliest opportunity. Soirees held at her home, from which Splatch and Pisser were disbarred, were occasions notable for the expensive wines, the quality of narcotics and the range of influential luminaries from the worlds of the arts and media. Lavinia was regarded as a bellwether for changing cultural trends and the glitterati who regularly convened at her home for debauches were afraid to miss out. Favourable coverage appeared in the quality dailies as the band's exposure in rock magazines increased. All requests for interviews with the band were curtly refused, their silence only adding to their mystique. As a consequence the band was valorised by sentinels of popular culture who hadn't even heard them play.

Dane was apoplectic when he discovered that Lavinia had even refused to release an itinerary of the band's upcoming tour.

She had decreed that when the band was playing in any town or city, the only notice attendees would be given was an advertisement in the local press. The advertisement would feature four severe white block capitals against a black background: VSOT. Lavinia was confident that together with the hyperbolic press coverage, sell-out houses were guaranteed. Dane was helpless in the face of Lavinia's irrepressible hubris. He envisaged both a crippling loss on his investment and a stain upon his previously pristine reputation as the music industry's alpha power-broker. Each night he lay in bed devising macabre ends to his crow-haired nemesis, and each gorier than the last.

The band were busy attending to more prosaic matters, particularly the problem of being allowed sufficient time away from work to undertake a thirty-five date tour. Splatch deferred his law degree until the following year whilst casually informing his parents that reimbursement for his guitar tuition would soon be forthcoming. Tick-Tock approached his general practitioner and bartered a sick note for six weeks in return for Tick-Tock wallpapering the physician's hall and landing. Muttley's father was adamant that the cheeky streak of piss would not be granted such a protracted absence from the garage, but relented when Muttley promised to work for a month without pay upon his return. Muttley senior was unaware of the small fortune his son would soon be awarded and equally unaware that their working relationship would be sharply revised in the coming year.

Adey simply quit his position as a storeman in a local factory, declaring to anyone who would listen that he was off to be a rock star and they should keep their eye out for him on the telly. As was the tradition when bidding farewell to a colleague moving on to better things, his workmates stripped him naked, pinned him to the floor, and then a middle-aged divorcee with castellated teeth arrived from the personnel department to dispassionately masturbate him to a humiliating climax. Whilst she tugged furiously at Adey's unruly member his workmates jeered and launched occasional kicks at the pitiful figure who writhed screaming beneath them. They then paint-rolled his torso and genitals with stencilling ink before marching him firstly around the factory floor and then into the works canteen. Adey's banshee howls echoed from the ceiling as his soon to be erstwhile workmates flicked lit cigarette ends at his genitals and doused him with cold tea. The female canteen staff didn't raise so much as an eyebrow. Over the years they had become inured to this debasing farewell ceremony. One of them enquired if Adey was stopping for a bacon butty. Adey momentarily wrested himself from the grip of his assailants and leapt upon a table, his quivering nudity the very essence of pathos. He pointed accusatory fingers at his tormentors and fulminated that he was going to be a fucking millionaire whilst these fucking losers pissed away their fucking lives in this fucking shithole and if it was left to him they'd they all die of fucking cancer. The diners were stung into shocked and recriminatory silence. This was a social solecism that could not pass unremarked. One of the ladies behind the service counter brayed:

'Oh Adey love. Now that's no way to carry on is it? Your mam would swing for you if she heard you talking like that. They were only having a laugh.'

The band's first gig in Glasgow was a triumph. The VSOT logo, published just one week prior to the gig in Scotland's biggest selling daily, ensured an immediate sell-out; such was the ravening of punks, curious students and starfuckers to be present at an, "I was there", moment. Over a thousand ticketless fans hung around, some offering punters entering the venue four times

196

the face value of their tickets. A tout was badly beaten but he gamely hung on to his cache as no one was going to thwart his ambition of making a small fortune for just one evening of casual extortion. The tout was in Lavinia's employ and the mark-up she had insisted upon assured him of two hundred pounds. Several times more than that was to be deposited in the coffers of the band.

When The Vinegar Strokes took the stage they were greeted with a raucous ovation, the near-hysterical audience ignoring the orders of the security staff to take their seats. As the band moved through the gears the crowd reciprocated by mutating into a single, screaming, undulating organism that the bouncers were powerless to overmaster. At least three slabs of Scottish beef bedecked in tuxedos were escorted away from the venue in an ambulance. The press rhapsodised upon the arrival of a new force in popular music whilst violent disturbances following the gig were featured on the following night's television news bulletins. A mere two hours' exposure to the wider world ensured that The Vinegar Strokes were already embedded in the nation's consciousness.

They were grave and unsmiling when they returned to their hotel after the gig. They sat in contemplative silence in the hotel bar, drinking pints of heavy whilst ignoring offers of free drugs, free entrance to nightclubs or interviews with the scrum of newshounds convened in the hotel lobby. They had underestimated Lavinia's adroitness for igniting a conflagration in the overlit minds of media types and were disturbed by the irruption of violence. If this was what the rest of the tour was going to be like they might well be torn limb from limb. For Lavinia, the gig announced the arrival of a phenomenon whose legend she would sedulously cultivate in the coming year. For

Clifford Dane and Bad Things Happen Inc. the gig presaged the arrival of pound notes. Many, many fackin' pahnd notes. The band moved southward, their stagecraft improving with every appearance. Following a gig in Birmingham, Splatch was moved to remark that they might be competent enough to meet even the exacting standards of Manchattan audiences. Adey declared them to be the best band in the world, an assertion that cost him a dead leg from Muttley.

The Vinegar Strokes was not a group to engage in the usual high jinks indulged in by young men with too much time on their hands. Splatch and Lavinia retired to their hotel room no later than midnight, whilst Adey went for a run to work off a surfeit of energy. With their usual practicality Muttley and Tick-Tock would calmly fold up the bathroom towels, bed linen and pillowcases in their hotel rooms and then sleep on the floor. The bed linen and towels would then be stored in the equipment vans, later to be either given away to family members or sold in their local pub. Muttley's mam was always moaning that she was always short of towels. All complimentary toiletries found in the ensuite bathrooms were to be harvested and given as gifts to their respective partners. Far from jettisoning television sets from hotel windows, Tick-Tock and Muttley appropriated the televisions from each band member's room and stored them in the vans along with the bed linen. Tick-Tock had brokered an arrangement with a TV repairman who drank in the miners' welfare to take the televisions off their hands for a tenner a set. As he was earning just sick pay and the monies Lavinia gave him for expenses, then he needed every penny he could muster. For his part Muttley was mulling over popping the question to Cath. If she assented to their betrothal, the largesse earned from selling the televisions would help in the purchase of an engagement ring.

Muttley and Tick-Tock were strangers to extravagance, a trait that would serve them well in the coming years.

Following a sweaty, triumphal gig in Bristol the band returned to their hotel exhausted but content with their exertions. Even Adey was determined to retire early, but Tick-Tock and Muttley had other ideas. They lingered in the hotel bar stewarded by a sullen and sardonic hotel employee who constantly and theatrically consulted his watch. Whilst exercising an admirable restraint in their own intake, the rhythm section plied the barman with whisky until the unfortunate curmudgeon collapsed to the floor. Muttley and Tick-Tock then removed all of the bottled spirits and snacks from behind the bar, loaded them into cardboard boxes and then proceeded to amble past the nonplussed concierge on their way to the equipment vans. As they were departing for Manchattan early in the morning, and mindful that Brian would be attending tomorrow evening's gig, they wished to present their former bandmate with gifts. Visiting strange climes and failing to bring back souvenirs was the height of discourtesy. They nodded to each other in satisfaction as they surveyed the bar denuded of strong waters before serving themselves a restorative couple of pints. At one point they debated whether to appropriate the one-armed bandit, but as they'd already stolen enough bed linen to swaddle a moderately large council estate they concluded that the road crew might take against this. Doubtless the barman would have some explaining to do, but by that time the band would be on their own midding. This was their best night's work thus far.

The night before Christmas Eve the band took Manchattan by the scruff to riotous acclaim. The after-party that ensued in the bar of the Midland Hotel was courtesy of Lavinia. She had momentarily relaxed the martial discipline she had imposed upon her charges and believed that they'd earned a reward. Conscious of the imminent orgy of gluttony and sloth propagated by the forces of reaction to sedate the slobbering masses into obedience, or Christmas as it was more usually known, Lavinia had decreed that partners would be welcome both to the gig and the shindig afterwards. A convivial crowd convened shortly after midnight and proceeded to beleaguer the unfortunate hotel staff. In the early hours of Christmas Eve morning, Sheila berated Tick-Tock for tekkin' no bleedin' notice of her all bleedin' night, and then proceeded to pulverise him with a Gideon bible. Unmoved by his antagonist's assault with holy writ, Tick-Tock produced a roll of duct tape with which he deftly bound Sheila's flailing limbs and then taped her to a chair. With a flourish he then tore off a broad strip of tape with which to silence the now immobile and wrathful Sheila. Her eyes irradiated a promise of vile retribution as Tick-Tock inserted a straw into a bottle of cider and placed it in her bound hands.

'Nah then. If yo' don't shut yer fookin' cakehole yer'll be stuck lahk that till fookin' Boxing Neet.'

Sheila's muffled interlocutions intimated a horrible demise for someone not unadjacent to where she was sitting. Tick-Tock raised an admonitory finger, advised her to think on, and then taunted her with the crisps he consumed with exaggerated relish.

'I'll tell yo' what Sheila. They're fookin' beltin', these. D'you want one? Oh bloody 'ell. Y' can't, can yo? Shame, that. I'll have t'eat 'em all instead.'

Brian and Splatch sat in animated conclave whilst Adey enjoyed revelatory fellatio in the ladies' washroom from his silent partner. As calmly as his fevered blood allowed, Muttley requested Cath's hand in marriage. Her elegant response was to exhort him to stop talking out of his skinny arse and ease up on

200

the bloody ale because it was making him daft. Cath had an early start at the pie shop in the morning but this didn't prevent her from overindulging in champagne, a beverage she thought the exclusive preserve of the Royal Family and people off the telly. She decided that the libation was very much to her taste and instructed Muttley to steal a few bottles for Christmas lunch the following day. Muttley solemnly nodded. Nothing was too much trouble for his beloved. Lavinia later decanted Cath into a taxi to ensure she arrived at work punctually, if not completely conscious. Cath wasn't looking forward to her shift as she'd been assigned the preparation of cheese pasties, the bouquet of which always made her gag.

Shortly after three in the morning Lavinia called the room to order. With a catch in her voice she announced that the band's New Year's Eve concert in London was to be broadcast on live television. Mindful of the seismic impact this gig could generate she would allow them to enjoy Christmas Day with their families, if that were at all humanly possible, but on Boxing Day all festivities would cease as they would be in rehearsal at the band's headquarters. Excuses for absence would be unacceptable. Neither were there to be any celebrations to welcome in the New Year as, on January second, the band would be in the studio to record their debut album. It would be completed by no later than January seventh to coincide with the storm of interest created by their recent public appearances. On January ninth they would all find themselves considerably richer than when the New Year began. Lavinia promised that 1982 would be the year that their lives would change forever. The band nodded and then returned to their drinking. Lavinia eyed them severely and then retired to her room.

Her new campaign would demand even greater subterfuge

but her sanguinity remained undimmed. Thus far it was all going very much to plan and it was now time to enter the next phase of her strategy. She would ensure that for the next five years Splatch would be the dark prince of rock music and she would be the wealthiest media hag in living memory. It would be worth the Judas kiss she would deliver, in spite of Splatch's certain disapprobation.

On New Year's Day the national press eulogised The Vinegar Strokes' poised and imperious televised performance. Even the staider quality publications offered sniffy but unqualified approval of the band's unignorable power. One rather over-caffeinated hack expatiated upon Splatch's singular stage presence, his louring but fragile demeanour suggestive of a modern-day Hamlet wrestling with personal demons and the agonies of indecision. Muttley thought the cheeky fucker was comparing his bandleader to a tobacco product.

The following morning they went into the studio. To the amazement of the producer appointed to oversee the recording session, the band briskly despatched six numbers and an extended version of 'Doctor Crime', the song Lavinia had chosen as their maiden single release. They concluded the recording of the album by lunchtime the following day and then disappeared to the pub. The producer and team of engineers shook their heads in wry amazement at the band's clinicism. In all of their professional careers they had never encountered a band with such an appetite for work. There hadn't been a second take of any song throughout the whole day and a half and the album needed nothing in the way of overdubs. In her severest baritone Lavinia apprised the producer that she expected a similar application to the task in hand from the recording crew themselves. Clifford Dane wasn't the kind of man to be kept waiting. They nodded their tremulous assent and worked until three o'clock the following afternoon. They were aware of Dane's reputation and also very fond of their kneecaps.

The Great Dane himself was fervid with the possibility of the album topping the charts upon the day of its release. He rasped a diktat that the biggest party in the history of show business should be thrown. Lavinia could invite the legions of hacks who genuflected before her whilst he could dragoon everyone from film stars to minor royalty into attending the bash. Lavinia shook her head. An essential component of the group's appeal was their rigorous austerity. They were untainted by the folderol of rock stardom and very much a workingman's band. A simple press release would be sufficient to command sales of over a million in the first twenty-four hours. In any case, spending over ten thousand quid on a bash for a band only weeks away from extinction would be wasteful in the extreme. Dane was enraptured by Lavinia's flint-heartedness and general turpitude. She was as incorrigibly venal as himself. In another life perhaps she and Dane might have been firmest of allies, but in this life there was still to be a reckoning. Forgiveness was for other, lesser people. Her liquidation was already in train but wouldn't happen whilst there was still fruit on the money tree to be shaken down.

The steward of the miners' welfare was impervious to Tick-Tock's pleas for usage of the function room as a venue for the album launch. On the date requested, the room was reserved for the mums 'n' tums exercise class followed by pensioners' indoor bowls. The feral mothers who attended the exercise class would quite happily disembowel the steward if their session was cancelled. Neither was he bleedin' daft enough to cancel the pensioners' bowls. They'd have him up in front of the bastard

203

committee and given the heave-ho in less time than it took for a good shit. Neither had he forgotten the band's last appearance at the club or the reservoir of phlegm discharged onto the dance floor. He wasn't having them dirty bastards in his club at any price. Tick-Tock's offer of a free telly was reluctantly declined. He could shove his telly up his arse. Sideways.

Surprisingly, it was Brian who remedied the situation. Following his early shifts at the factory he'd begun to frequent a quiet inn some three miles away from Least. On paydays he would take his lunch at the pub, the bill of fare being plain but appetising. Although he rarely exchanged more than a nod with the elderly imbibers who pored over the *Daily Telegraph*, he had become a regular and welcome patron. This pub was a far cry from his usual haunts and considerably less perilous. Not a single one of the customers appeared to be poor, covertly armed or enduring a borderline personality disorder.

On a particularly foul, foggy January afternoon, Brian mumbled to the landlady that his former band was on the look-out for a venue to host the launch of their debut album. With the egregious exception of Adey they were averse to ostentation and would be happy with somewhere low-key selling potable beer. The landlady reported that her function room was small but there was a working bar and furnishings to seat around fifty people. She escorted Brian upstairs into a dimly-lit space with a small stage at one end. The landlady disclosed that the only people to use the room with any regularity were The Boars Pursuivants, an all-male fraternity dedicated to Morris dancing, accapella harmonising, the ingestion of worrying volumes of alcohol, the vilification of the socialist enemy within, and raising money for such worthy causes as sending a quadriplegic on holiday or the purchase of a memorial plaque commemorating a late-lamented

Boar. Brian nodded his satisfaction and resolved to inform the band of the room's availability immediately upon sobering up.

The party was a homespun affair. It began as soon as the landlady's sister lifted the towels from the pumps. Cath provided a cake iced with a pink guitar, some paper plates and plastic cutlery. She had also discreetly appropriated a cache of that morning's unsold pies and pasties via a bin liner hidden in her parka. These comestibles were gratefully received by Muttley and Tick-Tock who gorged on them like starving dingoes. Rather than squander money on the services of a disc jockey, Brian had brought along his hi-fi and a box of albums in his father's car. A heated negotiation and a tip of two quid had persuaded Derek to transport his son and his impedimenta to the do. Derek was determined to absent himself as quickly as possible from this motley collective of nancy boys and druggies, but upon learning that the bar was free to all attendees he lingered to expedite the consumption of six pints and two large whiskies in a mere forty minutes. He then offered a brief valedictory nod and then drove back to Least. Whatever the circumstances, free ale was not to be demurred.

Muttley had invited his colleagues from the garage. They arrived directly from work and were still dressed in their grimy boots and overalls. Whilst entering the function room, they swore and scratched furiously at their crotches and spat driblets of hand-rolling tobacco to the carpet. Ignoring everyone else in the room, they mustered around a small table and proceeded to smash down innumerable pints of mild with whisky chasers, snarling at one another whilst playing hand after hand of three-card brag. The sole journalist invited to the gathering stared curiously at the quartet of grease monkeys until one of them stood, pointed and glared at the journalist with homicidal intent. The mechanic enquired if the nosy fucker wanted to either tek a fookin' picture or have his bastard teeth knocked down his bastard throat. The journalist blenched and beetled back towards the protective presence of Lavinia. His mother's caveats concerning the truculence and barbarism of Northerners appeared to be dismayingly correct. Splatch and Brian alternated as disc jockeys, pulling albums from a cuboid plastic case and discussing their various merits. Their mutual affection seemed as inviolable as ever. Adey talked to anyone who would listen whilst Lavinia and her legal advisor stood at the bar, surveying the attendees with increasing satisfaction. If the band continued to drink with such careless abandon this would be a productive day for both of them.

As the early dusk congealed into evening, the party was enlivened by the arrival of Sheila and a number of her colleagues from the dental practice. Adey's partner had also arrived but with considerably less noise. Although not in the least edified by either The Vinegar Strokes or rock music in general, the interest of Sheila's companions had been piqued by the prospect of a free bar and the possibility of an audience with Splatch. Having remained indoors on New Year's Eve to get uproariously blotto and to watch Sheila's beau perform on television, all three of the big-haired, raw-boned ladies were transfixed by the interstellar glare of the bandleader and had drawn lots to determine who would be the first to explore the contents of his underwear. Intuiting their intentions Lavinia's antennae had twitched, and for the rest of the evening they were always within her eyeshot. Their lubricious squawks and attention-seeking antics nettled her, but she simmered rather than boiled. There were more urgent matters to attend to. A telephone call from an elated Dane had apprised her of album sales of over two million. The royalty payments she would receive in the coming months would exceed even her inflated expectations.

After seven hours of continuous drinking, the carousers bathed in an afterglow of drowsy contentment. Even Sheila's friends were becalmed, their libidinous energies having been dissipated by a surfeit of Cuba libres and the admonishing stares issuing from the posh cow at the bar. The band sat around a table saying little to one another but smiling a great deal and lazily tapping their feet to Brian's latest selection on the turntable. Muttley declared that he was hungry again but he wasn't in the mood for any foreign cak. A Chinese with prawn crackers and extra fried rice would be just the job. Lavinia instructed the craven journalist to take everyone's order and then nodded meaningfully at the legal advisor.

The legalist strode over to the band and brandished four white envelopes. He distributed one to each of the band and casually informed them that they needed to sign the enclosed document as proof of receipt of their monies. From his handkerchief pocket he produced a pen and then waited until the band had studied their cheques. All of them were awestruck into silence except Adey, who yelped like an abused gerbil and then quickly scribbled on the dotted line of the otherwise blank sheet of A4. Muttley wrenched the pen from Adey's hand and did likewise before passing the biro on to Splatch. Tick-Tock used his own biro. Lavinia nodded soberly and crossed the floor to where The Vinegar Strokes were using the cheques to fan their grinning faces.

'Happy?'

'I think I've just shot me load. Don't tell Sheila for Christ's sake. She'll think I've been interfering with meself again. She checks me underpants for stains y'know.'

'Well done all of you. And you'll be pleased to know that you're number one in the album charts. How does that feel?'

'Are we going to America? Everyone goes to America don't they?'

'We'll talk about that, Adey. The food's on its way.'

His silent partner smiled as Adey executed a crude war-dance, his jaws clamped around his cheque whilst guttural moans escaped from his salivating lips. Muttley sniffed, ambled over to Cath and offered his cheque for her scrutiny. Her expression was one of aghast surprise commingled with a gormless grin. Muttley nodded beatifically and suggested that the two of them could stretch to a weekend away in a caravan at Towyn. Cath vigorously nodded her assent and said she'd try and get Saturday off. Sheila and Tick-Tock immediately began a furious quarrel concerning whether he should purchase either a terraced property or a new drum kit and a replacement hearse, a spat culminating in Tick-Tock sustaining an injury to his right foot from an emphatically depressed stiletto heel.

Splatch trotted over to the small stage, grinned and waved his cheque in Brian's direction. Whilst studying the infeasible number of zeroes on the cheque Brian became aware of the appetitive gaze of the landlady's sister behind the bar. It was inconceivable to Brian that he rather than Splatch would be the object of any female interest and immediately wondered if he'd done something to upset her. He found himself locked in the tractor beam of the woman's stare, powerless to avert his own. Splatch followed his friend's gaze and then offered Brian a quizzical grin. This was the lady with whom one week later Brian would break his sexual duck.

Some fifteen years older than Brian and unhappily married to the brutish chief grunter of the Boars Pursuivants, she believed that she had finally found her Milk Tray Man. As the party sputtered to a close she slipped her telephone number into Brian's hand with an injunction to keep the following Saturday night free. Throughout the proceeding days, she was driven mad by the prospect of her new sexual partner making repeated incursions upon a body already succumbing to the pitilessness of gravity and lateral expansion. She would be cherished by a youth keen to avail himself of the pleasures of a generously proportioned woman versed in the arts of physical love. She would be bedewed by kisses, shock waved by a thousand ecstasies and then accede to long withheld desires. Unfortunately for her, she had chosen Brian as her swain. He wasn't too well up on this sort of thing.

In a mildewed hotel on the outskirts of Widnes, their shadows made nebulous by the gloom of a forty-watt bulb, the two lovers coupled in shameful silence. During the course of the encounter Brian's interest was piqued by the strange disparities and even stranger similarities between male and female bodies. The blue-veined bosom he palpated with professorial curiosity felt like bags filled with something almost, but not quite, water. Her rear and flanks were larger than his but constructed from less malleable flesh. He also detected a signifier of masculinity in the faint shadow of a moustache on her upper lip. In the cradle of her armpit that he grazed with a forefinger there was a hint of stubble. Their odours were not dissimilar. A sour, fear-drenched tang commingled with the aftertaste of cheap toiletries. He also became unaccountably depressed upon climaxing, the opposite outcome to the rapture he'd been anticipating. A bloke at work had portentously reported that the French found the orgasm so overwhelming they'd dubbed it "Le petit mort". Brian's overriding emotion approximated to "Just had my pushbike nicked". Whilst they joylessly coupled, the landlady's sister stared at the ceiling and wondered what was missing on the telly. The lovers left the hotel before ten that evening and trudged in silence to their vehicles. They avoided a farewell embrace and even eye contact as they returned to their indifferent lives.

Bedazzled by their largess and languorous from inactivity, The Vinegar Strokes had ignored the envelopes arriving at their respective homes following the launch party. The bloodless legalese of a document contained in the envelopes was scarcely fathomable, but Adey understood enough to realise its import. He immediately telephoned Muttley who was back at work at the garage. The document to which they had all been unwitting signatories proscribed any further association with one another for the purposes of performance and recording. Unauthorised usage of the band's name for any commercial purposes would be subject to a legal challenge. Muttley couched the situation in rather more prosaic terms: Lavinia had shagged them all up the arse and they might be doing some jail if they defied her. He telephoned Tick-Tock, who instructed his bandmates to meet him at the miners' welfare that evening. Meanwhile they should try and locate Splatch, who they assumed to be back in London. This was impossible. None of them had had the presence of mind to take either his telephone number or his address. Fruitless calls to Brian and then to directory enquiries yielded nothing. But Splatch was closer to home than any of them realised.

After reading of the document in the bar of the Midland Hotel, Splatch inveighed against Lavinia with such bile that it left her almost completely undone. Her carapace of affected ennui was smithereened and she was uncertain if would ever recover. She was used to being the vilifier not the vilified and she cringed before her lover's shrivelling contempt. When his powers of toxic oration were exhausted, Splatch shook his head and warned

210

her not be in the hotel when he returned. He strode to a bar across the street, ordered a large whisky and soda, called Brian's home to request he take a taxi to Manchattan and then returned to the hotel.

They drank slowly and deliberately in the hotel bar, ruminating upon the fallout from Lavinia's treachery. When Splatch had signed the otherwise blank document, he personally had not only agreed to the dissolution of the band but to also deliver at least one solo album to Bad Things Happen Inc., the prospect of which was both daunting and possibly infeasible. He had tailored his songs to the ensemble sound of The Vinegar Strokes, using the band's instrumentation as a visual artist might use his palette. If deprived of the medium in which to realise his ideas he might very well flounder. For his part Brian was nonplussed by the constraints imposed by a mere signature. Just one careless sweep of a pen could prevent lawful assembly and the blameless activity of playing in a band. He thought that this only happened in the Soviet Union and his former secondary school. There was nothing else for it. To process this new turn of events with the powers of concentration it deserved, they both needed to be irredeemably drunk for the next two days. Brian excused himself to call in sick at work and then returned to the bar to order two very large whiskies and a bag of crisps. They would need sustenance for what was going to be a very long day's journey into night.

Splatch returned to London one week later, having secured the rental of a two-bedroomed property close to Lavinia's home. As she was still notionally his manager then they had no option but to meet and discuss plans for his obligatory solo project. He trudged around the corner to Lavinia's residence. Their initial encounter was typical of two former lovers riven by acrimony; a silent reproach commingled with regret and a lingering sexual tension. Splatch's demeanour was curt, defensive and utterly humourless. Lavinia was equally terse and business-like, outlining Dane's expectations whilst eyeing her client for the merest glimmer of their old empathy. She might as well have wished for a lottery jackpot, such was Splatch's impassivity. She then ushered him into the reception room once serving as the theatre of their first sexual combat. Upon hearing Splatch's sharp intake of breath Lavinia knew she had done the right thing.

The room had been converted into a musician's atelier. The stately grand piano remained but there was also a bank of expensive synthesisers, a battery of percussion, acoustic and electric basses, two electric guitars, an acoustic guitar, several amplifiers and four reel-to-reel tape decks equipped with state of the art microphones. As he walked slowly around the room brushing his fingers against the instruments Lavinia divined that Splatch was already in compositional mode.

'I'm leaving for the States in the morning. I'm on assignment for three weeks. Come whenever you like. My driver's always in. He only has to feed Pisser when I'm away so he'll have nothing better to do other than to look after you.'

Splatch nodded, his expression of unhinged rapture interring a mind already in ferment.

'Right. I'll start next week. I'm going home first to say good-bye to the band. It wouldn't be right not to. I'll tell them you said hello. They'll be sorry to hear you're not dead.'

Lavinia averted her eyes and nodded.

'Let yourself out when you're ready.'

The band convened in the miners' welfare for one final pub crawl. Splatch was relieved but slightly disappointed by their philosophical approach to Lavinia's duplicity. He expected fury and defiance, but instead they were stoic and reflective. Muttley declared that it'd all been a good laugh and he'd bought the majority shareholding in his father's garage. In the future he would marry Cath and open a chain of used car outlets across the British mainland. He and Tick-Tock would also reform Turds of Lucifer as being in a band seemed to keep them out of trouble most of the time. Tick-Tock had already purchased two pubs, having sensed a sea change in the habits of the drinking public. For some inexplicable reason men and women now wished to go out together as a couple, hankering after inns offering food and an ambience more befitting a restaurant. Cath had already been dragooned into running the kitchen until professional chefs could be contracted. She was ready to provide the best pie and peas money could buy. In the coming decades Tick-Tock would enrich himself by the creation of a chain of gastropubs before retiring to Benidorm, but Sheila's opinion of him remained resolutely jaundiced. Whenever she was cajoled into discussing her husband's success she would be irresistibly drawn to a phrase containing the words arse and elbow.

Adey's egotism remained unchecked by the dissolution of the band. He was ready to pursue a career as frontman for a synth-heavy New Romantic outfit called Weimar Republik. He would grubstake and manage the band until a major record label inevitably came knocking. Muttley gravely shook his head and advised Adey that he was better off buying a house, a new motor and putting a bit by for a rainy day. Tick-Tock nodded sagely and tactfully enjoined the dozy fucker to take his face for a shit. Adey remained sanguine in the face of such negativism as he had already set a course for the stars.

Several attempts at success would prove both abortive and costly for Adey. He would become penniless, separated from his silent partner and homeless. He gratefully accepted an entry-level position in the office of an estate agency offered by a fan of his former band, but despite his travails he remained convinced that success was only another gig away. It wasn't. Adey lived with his parents until they both succumbed to cancer, whereupon he assumed the tenancy of their council property. He developed a serious alcohol problem leading to pancreatitis and a relatively early death. Not a single member of The Vinegar Strokes was aware of his precipitous decline into depression, isolation and cheap vodka only five years after their separation.

As with many creatives short on ideas, Splatch spent the first week of his return to London simply noodling. He extruded some interesting discordances from the synthesisers, toyed with the percussion and struggled with the coffin-like heft of the upright bass, but he remained a stranger to cogent thought. At one o'clock each afternoon he strode into Lavinia's library, chose a book and then slouched off to the pub. The punk with the lime-green Mohican was a spectral presence in the house, drifting from room to room in a narcotised fog. He had secured a job of assaying the quality of drugs peddled by a local dealer and was obviously revelling in his consultancy role. One afternoon he suggested that they may as well go to the pub together as Pisser had been toileted, the weather was fine and he had ingested some spiffing cocaine. Splatch shrugged, nodded and demanded a taste of the merchandise. The punk with the lime-green Mohican was happy to oblige.

As Splatch was still largely unfamiliar with his new locality he allowed his companion to guide him to an establishment reeking of menace. It was crammed with lairy wheezers who resembled the supporting cast in a Kray Twins biopic. The punk with the lime-green Mohican nodded affably at the punters crushed at the bar and ordered a round of lagers. Splatch's attention was arrested by the unmistakeable sound of a cymbal being worried by a drumstick. He raised his eyes skywards, trying to locate the source of the metallic soughing. He then heard a trumpet tweeze out a lean and angular blues, the plangent tone of the brass distorted by what seemed to be a wah-wah pedal. Surely that was impossible. He edged his way through the crush at the bar until he found a staircase. He mounted the stairs and opened a door at the end of the landing.

Not a single member of Maderchod acknowledged his entrance whilst they raced through a piece modulating through three key changes. Splatch sat at a table, transfixed by an aggressive duologue between the trumpeter and a keyboard player and underpinned by the bellicose swing of the rhythm section. The band completed the piece and then eyed the newcomer with disdain. Splatch remained silent but nodded appreciatively at the keyboard player. The drummer counted the band into the next piece. Splatch sat motionless, absorbing the sound through his pores. He failed to notice the drink in front of him as his eyes were tightly closed. Splatch's synapses sparked and crackled. This was the polyphonic perversity to which he'd always aspired but had always eluded him. It didn't now.

'How often do you fellows rehearse?'

'If we haven't got a gig, every day. So every day. The landlord allows us to use it for free if we buy a drink.'

'Would you mind if I came up tomorrow?'

'Come whenever you like. We know who you are. Maybe the big-time rock star might buy us a drink. We've never got any money.'

'Happy to oblige. See you tomorrow.'

For five consecutive lunchtimes Maderchod sprinted

215

through a melange of be-bop, third stream jazz and funk modes with generous spaces afforded for improvisation. Splatch noted that the musicians weren't simply playing their allotted parts. Rather, the chord progressions and melodies were merely a template upon which to etch their own interpretation. The bass player rarely removed his gaze from the pianist, quizzically raising his eyebrows to acknowledge a subtle change of emphasis in the voicing of a chord. The drummer seemed to be constantly listening to the others, informing the pulse with an elasticity rarely heard in rock music. Splatch was fascinated and unsettled by the constantly shifting rhythms and wondered how the band managed to remain in time. Following a rehearsal that continued into the early evening he shared a drink with Maderchod and respectfully enquired if he was able to bring along his instrument to sit in one day. The tenor sax player, a laconic black American called Loz, replied:

'Sure. Ain't no problem. But y'all know you're gonna fuck up, right?'

'Of course. But I'm here to learn. Fucking up is the only way to learn anything.'

'You damn straight, motherfucker. Every motherfucker should be ready to fuck up. Even Bird fucked up sometimes.'

'Who's Bird? Is that one of you fellows?'

'Aw fuck you, you sorry-assed no-playing motherfucker.'

'Steady on there, mate. It was only a question. You ever had a saxophone suppository? If you don't want one I'd advise against talking to me like that again.'

As Loz predicted, Splatch did indeed fuck up. He was unused to the keys in which the band played, their collective virtuosity and the conversational interplay of their improvisations. For Splatch it was like attending a party at which he didn't know anyone. Midway through one piece Loz could no longer bear the howling dissonance issuing from Splatch's amplifier and tore out of the room. The bass player studied the floor whilst the drummer stared in bewilderment. Splatch nodded calmly and began to pack his instrument away. For the first time in his adult life he had been an unqualified failure.

'Hang on a minute.'

Splatch turned and noted an amused but benign gleam in the eye of the pianist.

'It isn't that you can't play this stuff. You just don't understand it. Give me your address. I'll call round and see you.'

'Great. What's your name?'

'Colin. I already know yours. Who doesn't?'

In the following months Colin would regularly arrive at Splatch's apartment with manuscript paper, cassette tapes, albums and tutor manuals. The pianist was touched by his student's humility and was handsomely rewarded for his tutelage. Splatch digested the music of the be-boppers, wrestled with advanced harmonic theory, memorised a selection of important standard tunes and spent hours listening to the work of such seminal figures as Ellington, Miles, Parker, Lester Young and Louis Armstrong. He began to sit in on the lunchtime sessions with Maderchod, making modest but telling contributions. He even won a nod of approval from Loz. Colin also exposed his student to the music of classicists such as Schoenberg, Debussy, Satie and Stravinsky. He figured that his student would comfortably assimilate the concept of the past eternally informing the present and warmed to Splatch's breathless enquiries into the birth of the Minimalist movement. He was also concerned by Splatch's visible disintegration.

Colin was unaware of the regular consignment of

amphetamine Splatch received daily from Lavinia's factotum. The upper afforded him the ability to go without sleep for days and to apply himself to virtually constant practice of exercises set by his tutor. If he wasn't playing piano or the guitar, the red-eyed rakehell would pace his atelier for hours at a time, pensively smoking weed with the hi-fi at maximum volume. In this period of self-imposed purdah Splatch and Lavinia rarely encountered one another, but when they did she was horrified by his ghoulish appearance. He was tail-spinning into either psychosis or death, the commercial repercussions of which were unthinkable. This was a situation requiring special measures.

Lavinia instructed her factotum to surreptitiously lace Splatch's cannabis with heroin. This most powerful of narcotics might lead to sleep, thereby deferring permanent injury to a brain without an off switch. Dane was beginning to ask questions about the availability of new product, therefore it was imperative that Splatch recovered at least a glimmer of his old facility. There was over half a million pounds of Dane's seed money sitting in Lavinia's account to which she had become sentimentally attached.

The punk with the lime-green Mohican surreptitiously administered the opiate with a regularity guaranteeing the recipient's addiction, but at least the resultant torpor palliated Splatch's burgeoning lunacy. He was transformed from being a bolt of lightning ionising the atmosphere around him to a pale, languorous shadow. Lavinia's gofer became his valet, gently reminding his blissed-out charge to shower and eat. Splatch either mutely complied or sat in silence to continue roaming the terrain of his dislocated mind. The wasted auto-didact traversed tundra, deserts and urban jungles whilst remaining motionless on the couch. When Splatch finally understood the depth of his

218

dependence, far from being angry at Lavinia's subterfuge he was imperturbability personified. He enjoyed heroin as a gourmet enjoyed good food. It afforded him a temporary respite from the burdens of good looks, talent and wealth beyond the imagining of most people. Heroin helped.

In November of 1983 he informed Lavinia that he was going into the studio with Colin and Nameless, Maderchod's double bass player. A relieved Lavinia tremulously enquired how many new compositions he had ready to record. Splatch replied that he had none whatsoever, but each day he had been documenting what little he could recall of the macabre dreams he'd been recently experiencing. His oneiromancy would be the inspiration for a series of improvisations that would eventually transmute into his next recorded work. Lavinia excused herself, tottered to the bathroom and copiously vomited.

Convinced that the bleatings of a fuddled junkie would be about as welcome to the record-buying public as a venereal disease, Lavinia cursed herself for placing too much faith in her charge's abilities. Splatch would crash and burn, Dane would demand the return of his seed money and her bank balance would suffer a severe reversal of fortune. This was a catastrophe, but then again perhaps not completely unsalvageable. Splatch's name now carried a respectable commercial cachet following his work with The Vinegar Strokes. His army of admirers might purchase his bletherings out of curiosity before dismissing them as self-indulgent trash. Perhaps the returns would be enough to reimburse Dane with his investment, but Lavinia wasn't holding her breath. She expected to begin pitching the new album to Dane in April of the following year. As it transpired, Splatch didn't emerge from the studio until the June of 1984. When he did he came armed with a work unlike anything his usual audience or

219

indeed anyone else had previously encountered.

We Have Been Observing Your Planet For Some Time was a melange of soundscapes evoking visions of rain-washed shipyards, fetid canals, pointless suicides and senseless wars. Mantric vocal phrases whispered portents of an impending doom. A double bass fed through an echo chamber rumbled whilst a soprano saxophone screamed horribly over news despatches from Northern Ireland, the conflict in the Falkland Isles and intifadas in the Middle East. Multi-tracked dialogue and orgasmic moaning excerpted from American porn movies increased in volume whilst a string quartet played a serenata. Splatch had single-handedly invented the genre of uneasy listening, a sombre aural mosaic of a dystopia collapsing to entropy.

Lavinia hated it. It was the worst stripe of vanity project as it flattered neither the creator nor the listener. Not one of its eighty minutes was remotely danceable and she wondered just how this travesty could be pitched to the public. She decided to conduct a litmus test. Given enough licence, the pseudoscenti could elevate even the most banal daubings, scribblings and caterwaul to the status of Art with a capital A. Journalists of Lavinia's acquaintance could interpret an attack of gastroenteritis as symbolic of inner creative conflict. Splatch's kaleidoscope of hateful noise might just be the emperor's new clothes they would all be clamouring to wear.

Whilst hosting another of her soirées, without preamble she depressed the start button on the tape deck and studied the invitees' response to Splatch's sonic drear. All conversation ceased as the guests stared quizzically at one another. Despair and hopelessness hung in the air like toxic particulates. Invisible beards were stroked. Some of the guests became fascinated by their shoes and others studied the waning autumn light immigrating through the windows. A woman unafraid of exposing her finer feelings allowed a single tear to roll down her cheek. After forty minutes of unrelieved foreboding Lavinia stopped the tape whilst the gloominati went into conclave.

'What WAS that?'

'You tell me, Jez.'

'It's challenging. Significant.'

'It has resonance. It resonates.'

'Like a postcard from the future.'

'A touchstone.'

'I can hear elements of the twelve-tone diatonic row.'

'I can hear Otto Dix.'

'Was that a doorbell I heard?'

'I think it was a glockenspiel.'

'What? In the hall? Who put that there?'

Lavinia sensed an opportunity. Splatch had clawed at their souls and drawn blood. Her mind's eye was already reading the effusions penned in every serious periodical and newspaper in the country. This album would not be just another pop record, it would be an Event. One of those albums essential to own and at least pretend to understand. A failure to comprehend its significance would be social death to those who affected to champion the innovative and left-field. This would be the perfect fashion accessory for the supposedly hip, a piece of indefensible dreck about which no one would dare to express an adverse opinion for fear of appearing unzeitgeisty. All she had to do was to kindle public awareness of the album's qualities via her confidantes in the press and then approach Dane to broker its release. Dane proved to be something of a challenge.

'It's dogshit. What'm I supposed to do wiv it? You fink Noel fackin' Edmonds is gonna play this? Radio fackin' One? Top of the fackin' Pops? Even John fackin' Peel wouldn't touch it, and he'll play any old shit. Fack it. I want my fackin' money back. Now.'

'As indeed you shall Clifford. But hear me out. There's already been a lot of positive coverage in the media, thanks largely to me. My plan is to release it with four different sleeves designed by four different contemporary artists. This won't be just another double album. It'll be a piece of collectible art. The beauty of this is that the punters will want to own all four of the album covers, meaning that they'll have to buy the album four times. Can you imagine selling the same dreadful shit four times over to the same purchaser? Clifford. It's the crime of the century and we're about to pull it off.'

'But there isn't a single fackin' song on it.'

'Precisely. No songs, and more to the point no lyrics. This means that people on the continent don't have to learn any. It'll be the first pan-European album.'

'The what?'

'Do try and keep up, Clifford. Don't you see? This record buys Bad Things Happen Inc. artistic credibility. This record is the key to the one place you've never been before. A place called legitimacy. You might cop a knighthood out of all this. Services to the arts, all that guff.'

'You're out of your fackin' mind.'

'Release this and everyone else will be out of your league. You need to trust me on this.'

Dane smiled his bear-trap smile.

'You'd better be right about this you barmy bitch. For all sorts of reasons.'

'Arise, Sir Clifford.'

The production of the album took a whole year but, in the interim, Lavinia busied herself assessing the work of painters and photographers whose work might dovetail with the portentousness of Splatch's *oeuvre*. Splatch himself played no further part in marketing the record, happy to spend his latest two hundred grand on drugs, drink, books, records, foreign holidays and jamming with Maderchod. Occasionally he telephoned Brian and sent him the charts for a couple of pieces he expected his friend to have mastered by the next time they met. Brian found jazz guitar chords as challenging as an assault on K2, but with his usual doleful pertinacity he struggled on. He joined Splatch in a holiday to Benidorm and the happy, drunken pair busked Hot Club de France numbers in the old town. The ad hoc duo received not a single peseta for their labours but nevertheless thoroughly enjoyed themselves. Brian was delighted to be back in the company of his old friend and was indifferent to the unsavoury-looking characters with whom Splatch would disappear. Splatch was a rock star after all and much in demand. Pints of something called sangria were very much to Brian's taste and a pleasant change from brown and bitter.

Prior to the album's release Lavinia took out full-page advertisements in all three major music publications giving several interviews to a press pack curious to learn the whereabouts of the auteur. Lavinia gravely reported that Splatch was unavailable as he was at a secret location working upon part two of a trilogy in a similar vein to the current release. He had requested that she act as his sole intermediary and she was honour-bound to accede to his need for privacy. Splatch's reluctance to court the press served to further burnish his image as un *homme serieux*. The press slobbered over the album, the grandiloquent reviews guaranteeing colossal sales both at home and in Europe.

Dane was staggered by the public's reaction and nonplussed by the plaudits he himself received for supporting the release of such a groundbreaking opus. He quickly brokered a deal with an American publishing company and the record went platinum in the United States. Scholarly essays upon the work appeared in periodicals. Arts pundits for the national broadcasting service solemnly intoned their adoration of this "new form". Politicians seeking the twenty-something vote declared their admiration of the album, citing it as a plaintive howl of indignation from the most important voice of British youth. The most important voice of British youth himself could have hardly cared less. Clean needles were his primary priority as AIDS began to mete out its singular cruelty. 1986 was a tough year for those who lived on the periphery.

Within two years of the album's release Lavinia had achieved multimillionairehood via eye-watering royalty payments and syndication of her journalism in publications worldwide. Her marriage to an eminent surgeon was trumpeted as the most important social event of the year and cemented her status as the second most influential woman in the country. Meanwhile, the first most influential woman in the country had instructed her security services to keep an eye on Splatch as a person of interest. In his turn the person of interest moved to Berlin for the purposes of supporting his habit.

In the following years the file collated by the security services chronicled unflattering evidence of Splatch's rather off-beam leisure pursuits. His profligate drug usage in the seediest of locations, regular association with known criminals, pansexual adventurism and general degeneracy obliged the most influential woman in Britain to alert her flock to the threat posed by this demonic, drug-addled sexual omnivore. Perhaps to deflect attention from the more erotically involuted within her own government, the most influential woman in Britain had declared a moral crusade against those who flouted British values with such impunity. Splatch was in her crosshairs.

Following a campaign spearheaded by Britain's most popular newspaper to, "Clean up our country" Splatch was viewed as malignity incarnate. Whilst notoriety and an appetite for the louche has rarely derogated from the popularity of the average rock star, videotaped evidence of sexual activity with females some two years below the age of consent might give even the most ardent devotee pause for reflection. Mutton-chopped shire Tories demanded the reintroduction of the death penalty for this escapee from the underworld. Leading members of the established church called for an embargo upon any further sales of his repellent *oeuvre*. Brian's father was, as ever, more succinct in his appraisal of the brouhaha scandalising the nation.

'That dirty bastard wants stringing up. I don't want to see you hangin' about with him any more, Brian. I'll set our bloody dog on him if he comes up our path.'

'We haven't got a dog. Mam's always getting bit by them.'

'Shut it you, cleverarse. You know what I'm on about. Dirty bugger, he's nowt else.'

Clifford Dane read the runes, concluded that Splatch was commercially a busted flush and that his relationship with both Splatch and his hellion of a manager would serve no further purpose. Indeed, in the long term, Lavinia and her portfolio of his illicit sexual activities might prove injurious to his now enviable reputation as a patron of British arts. Frontier justice was the only logical solution to the possibility of Lavinia fouling the nest. He despatched two of his most trusted lieutenants to Lavinia's summer home in Alcudia. No traces of either the chatelaine or the master of the house were ever recovered.

Towards the end of a weekday night shift, Brian received an instruction to take an urgent telephone call at the factory gatehouse. Immediately fearing for the safety of a family member, he flew to the gatehouse and breathlessly presented himself to Stan, the night watchman and first aid man. Stan silently pointed to the telephone before continuing to engross himself in a wordfinder quiz and a doorstep cheese sandwich. Brian held the receiver to his ear in expectation of terrible news.

'Ah. There you are Brian. Have I caught you at a busy time?'

'Splatch? Where the fuckin' hell are you? They're going mad over here.'

'So I gather. All a bit hysterical isn't it? As in hysterically funny.'

'Woah, Splatch. Hang on a minute. There's people looking to lynch you. Nutters looking for blood. It's not safe for me here, never mind you. The bastard papers have already been on to Muttley and Tick-Tock to get some dirt on you but they've told 'em to fuck off.'

'Good boys. So what do you think Brian? I was thinking about coming back to England but I thought I'd see what you thought about it first.'

'Just stop the fuck where you are, Splatch. Stop out of the bastard road until all this goes away. Where are you by the way?'

'Not a place for a nice young man like you, Brian. Too many foreigners.'

'Just be bleedin' careful Splatch. That's all I'm asking.'

The telephone was the last conversation they would hold for over two decades. Over the next twenty years there were unsubstantiated sightings of Splatch in disparate regions of the world. On a ranch in Mexico. In a nightclub in Douala. Aboard a fishing smack off the coast of Indonesia. A correspondent to the letters page of Britain's most influential music publication reported that he had spotted Splatch busking on the streets of Rotterdam with a deranged harmonica player called Stink Floyd. He seemed to be out there somewhere, but the general consensus was that Splatch would at some point would be found dead in a skip. With the passage of time Splatch was relegated to the status of a footnote, forgotten by the world save for a few dogged anoraks penning adulatory elegies on websites dedicated to their hero. And then one May evening in 2010, Brian received an email containing a telephone number prefixed by a UK dialling code. Under usual circumstances Brian would have immediately deleted the message but, as he was on the outside of some very acceptable red wine and feeling rather sportive, he replied.

Tell me who you are and what you want.

The following evening the same message arrived in his in-box. He raised his eyebrows quizzically at Helen and then telephoned the number.

'Who's this?'

'Are you Brian?'

'Yeah.'

'Hang on a minute, pal. We've got someone here you might know.'

There was a brief pause and then Brian heard a voice he thought he might never hear again.

'Ah. Brian. How are we?'

'Oh fuck. It can't be. Where the fuck are you?'

'Hull apparently. Is it raining where you are? It is here.'

Splatch had secured a passport using the pseudonym of Darren Pendlebury, returned to England, acquired a new insurance number and was living in a squat in Hull. Although it was impossible for either of them to precis twenty years of existence in a brief telephone call, each offered the gist of their current circumstances. Brian was now a social worker and co-habiting with the love of his life in one of the more affluent suburbs of their home town. Splatch was living quite close to the university with three other narcotically-inclined lotus eaters. He had, however, crossed swords with purveyors of the oriental and was in something of a pickle. In other words, if he didn't get out of Hull toot sweet he'd be floating in the Humber. He enquired if Brian was able to offer any assistance with relocation to the North-West. Both of his parents were now dead and they'd neglected to bequeath Splatch the family seat in the event of their passing. Securing some form of safe and habitable accommodation was essential.

'Jesus, Splatch. I had no idea. What happened to them?'

'Mum killed herself. She was always a bit loopy anyway. Dad leaving her must have sent her over the edge I think.'

'What happened to your dad?'

'A heart attack while banging the secretary he left Mum for. Even I could see that coming. You know what personnel officers are like. Heavy lunches, leggy office temps and a busy social life. The police said that there were no suspicious circumstances. That was kind of them. I'm a forty-eight-year-old orphan of no fixed abode. Worse than that, I'm living in fucking Yorkshire. Whatever will become of me, Brian?'

'Gimme your address. I'll be over on Saturday. Be ready to move out.'

'Good man. I'll try to stay alive until you come. And can you bring me a coat?

Brian was shocked by Splatch's dereliction. At first he failed to recognise his old friend, tentatively enquiring of the toothless wraith who opened the door if a Stephen Latchford lived at the address. When this vision of decay stuck out his hand in greeting, Brian recoiled before pointing Splatch to the car. Splatch evidently travelled light as his only luggage was a grubby holdall and his trademark satchel. The cherry-red double cutaway was conspicuous by its absence.

The initial meeting between Splatch and Helen was unpropitious. It was loathe at first sight. The odium Helen harboured for Splatch was so authentic it could have borne a hallmark. His phantom presence sullied her home, and his sordidity was an affront to the values of her social caste. Whilst Splatch was in the spare bedroom and doubtless doing something illegal and self-destructive, Helen would glare malevolently at Brian and make it plain that the responsibility of finding this eerie hobo a home fell to him. Should he fail then Brian himself would find himself looking for somewhere to live. Either Splatch went or they both went. Unusually for Brian he didn't procrastinate, although his expeditiousness didn't prevent the sundering of he and Helen less than a couple of years later.

He quickly made an appointment with his general practitioner, a capable and pragmatic clinician refreshingly free of the preachiness that makes people from good homes so tiresome. The physician nodded vigorously as Brian explained that he was acting as an informal advocate for an acquaintance experiencing a multiplicity of health and personal problems. Brian would ensure that Splatch was registered with the benefits and housing agencies but to advance his friend's application for state assistance it was essential to be registered as a patient by a general practice. The doctor readily agreed, but following his examination of someone he thought he recognised but couldn't quite place, he insisted that Mr Pilkington be referred to the community drugs team as a matter of priority. Brian did as he was instructed but assumed that Splatch would no more engage with rehabilitation services than throw himself from a tall building. In the event, Splatch was compliant with his drug treatment program in order to acquire a supply of methadone he then sold on to those with appetites similar to his own. He also acquired a set of gleaming though ill-fitting dentures. When he affixed them in his mouth and smiled, his face resembled a Mexican death mask. Helen considered calling upon the services of an exorcist to sanify her home of Splatch's diabolical presence.

Brian conspired with the general practitioner to produce a letter supporting Splatch's application for housing. They prudently omitted the applicant's predilection for the illicit and stupefying, focusing instead upon Splatch's undoubted academic prowess and his intention to enter further education when he had secured a place to call home. To lend further weight to the application Brian was careful to emphasise that his client was already in receipt of housing benefit, therefore a transfer to his new property could be transacted with minimal administrative legwork. Within six weeks of returning to his home town Splatch was awarded the keys to a flat on the top floor of a local authority apartment building. A tiny bedroom, an even smaller living room and a galley kitchen were deemed sufficient for his housing needs.

Brian was gratified to discover that ingress to the building was available only via a lobby and controlled by a locking system activated by the tenant's telephone. As Splatch had already made connections with vendors of the illegal, the building's security might deter the visits of his creditors when law-abiding citizens were abed. Helen utilised her contacts in the charitable sector to acquire a single bed, bed linen, a crumpled lounge suite, a primitive stove, a table, storage shelving and a small television for the new occupant. Brian donated an old but serviceable compact disc player, some clothes, an iron and the address of a local laundry service. He also completed an application for Disability Living Allowance on his friend's behalf, confident that any assessor would take one look at Splatch and confirm his eligibility. Put bluntly, Splatch could frighten rats.

Muttley and Tick-Tock were apprised of the homecoming of their former leader and quickly convened a meeting in one of Tick-Tock's gastropubs. They too were shocked and saddened by Splatch's debasement and immediately offered sizeable sums of money to help arrest his decline. Splatch graciously waived their offer, but meekly enquired if they could purchase some instrumentation on his behalf. Such high value purchases were currently beyond his means and without a guitar to hand he felt rather unmoored. Muttley and Tick-Tick readily complied, but Brian also sensed a reluctance to rekindle their relationship with the man who had changed their lives forever. They were now middle-aged, rimed at the temples, as large and comfortable as favourite armchairs. With their expensively acquired bellies and age-appropriate loafers they exuded contentment. These days their overarching concerns were grandchildren, long holidays and autumn years untroubled by failing health and erectile dysfunction. The past should remain just that and nostalgia was only for those disappointed by the present. Brian correctly intuited that neither he nor Splatch would be seeing them again when their meeting had concluded, but they made good on their promise to purchase the requisite instrumentation.

The next couple of years saw Splatch settle into his new environs with relative ease. He indulged in bouts of petty thievery to support his predilection for narcotics but managed to maintain a legitimate, and trouble-free occupancy of his small but secure apartment. In the recent past Brian had also recourse to seek out new accommodation arrangements, albeit for very different reasons.

Brian decanted from the taxi outside Splatch's apartment building, deposited his guitar case on the pavement and depressed a button on the keypad. A crepitant croak issued from the loudspeaker adjacent to the keypad.

'Where have you been? It's well past eight.'

'It's Christmas, Splatch. You can't get a taxi at this time of year. It's all the fucking office parties.'

'The gun laws need changing. It's our civic duty to shoot people who only drink once a year. What have you brought?'

'Rum.'

'Proceed.'

Brian ascended four concrete stairwells, his ears attuned to the yells and murmurs of the isolated and desperate. The block was a holding pen for those considered not yet ready to assume a tenancy in one of the town's forbidding social housing estates. The occupants were deemed at risk of self-harm, self-neglect or abuse from those who prey on the vulnerable. Splatch had been assigned a case worker whose remit was to develop his daily living skills to the point that he could manage a tenancy independently. He hadn't seen her for over a year.

As the door to the apartment was ajar, Brian entered without knocking. He was astonished by the sight of a pristine racing bicycle leaning against the wall outside the bathroom.

'Nice bike, Splatch.'

'Oh, that. I'm selling it tomorrow.'

'Why? It's a great-looking machine.'

'It isn't mine.'

'Right.'

Brian entered what passed for the lounge. Two cold light illuminators used for viewing radiographs hung from the ceiling, bathing the room in an antiseptic light. Splatch appeared even more spectral than usual and the battered safety helmet he was wearing did nothing to flatter him. He was also naked save for a pair of truly horrifying boxer shorts. Brian learned that Splatch had earlier been invited by a new neighbour for an Italian meal. His host, together with another man, offered lavish helpings of beef and tomato pasta accompanied by bottles of Valpolicella. The only stipulation of his attendance at the repast was that he should join his hosts in being completely naked whilst at table. Not being in a position to demur the offer of a free meal, Splatch had happily complied with this peculiar request and, had Brian not been visiting, he would have remained to make free with the abundant supply of wine. Brian frowned his disapproval.

'Well at least you're eating. But d'you know anything about this bloke? Him and his mate could be nutters. Rapists or whatever. You could have been gang-bummed. I'd be careful around blokes who want to eat their tea with nowt on if I were you.'

'In this world there are no strangers, Brian. There are only enemies you haven't made yet. I've also eaten five bars of Kendal mint cake. Excellent fuel when the weather's like this.'

Splatch held out a skeletal hand into which Brian placed a bottle of dark rum. Splatch nodded his approval, unscrewed the top of the bottle and immediately drained a third of its contents down his throat. He then pointed to Brian's guitar and demanded he tune the instrument. Instead, Brian went to the kitchen area to root around for a receptacle sufficiently free of effluvia from

233

which to drink. No one could accuse Splatch of being pernickity. There were municipal dumps more sanitary than this environment. Brian settled on a mug extolling the blandishments of Lanzarote, but whether Splatch had actually visited the island he knew not. It was more likely that Splatch had either found or stolen the vessel. After washing the mug under the cold tap he poured himself some red wine whilst Splatch constructed a joint the size of a corona cigar. Splatch inhaled heavily from the joint whilst Brian sucked pensively on a cigarette.

Splatch had never offered Brian narcotics of any kind, opining that his friend was psychologically ill-equipped to deal with the *Sturm und Drang* of drugs. On numerous occasions Splatch had expatiated upon the theme of narcotics being the enemy of melancholics like Brian. He was simply too much of a worrier. With the passage of time Brian had admitted to the veracity of his friend's counsel. In a professional capacity he'd dealt with many men and women who had been detained in secure mental health facilities as a result of their predilection for the psychotropic. The recurrent themes in conversations with these broken people were anguish, insomnia and untameable paranoia. Brian well understood their torment. A keening desperation and the horror of being at large in an increasingly incomprehensible world constituted a normal day for him. Cigarettes and alcohol had always been more than enough to be getting on with.

Splatch reached for his guitar and tuned it by ear. Brian fished his own instrument from its fashionably battered case and did likewise. They plugged in and then drank in tranquil silence before Splatch handed Brian a sheet upon which was scrawled a series of chord changes.

'I wrote this yesterday. It's an instrumental called 'I'm

234

Coming For Your Children'.

'Any particular reason it's called that?'

'I shout it at people when I'm busking. Give me a steady four with a slight whump on the one and three. I stole it from Ellington but there's a few weird chords in there as well. If you're not sure about them, shout up.'

'Will do.'

They ran through the chord changes three or four times until, finally, Brian began to contrive sounds from his instrument approximating music. Splatch nodded his approbation and raised a horny thumb, his wrinkled face suffused by a still beguiling smile. Despite his dissipation Splatch's ragged charisma could still prove magnetic to members of both his own and the opposite sex. He leaned back and relit his now extinguished joint whilst Brian recharged his mug. For the next few hours they relaxed into one another, taking time between numbers to reminisce about strange escapades and even stranger acquaintances. The rancour and introspection usually informing the exchanges of men in the final chapters of their lives were refreshingly absent. Splatch's natural insouciance in the teeth of seemingly insuperable problems had conferred upon him a state of grace only usually found in the saintly, and he was far from saintly. Brian had never really had too much to lose anyway so his current circumstances were hardly a national tragedy. All that mattered was now. The music, the memories, the booze, the cigarettes, the laughter and their immutable unity. Splatch related his latest weak joke, a play on words a child would disdain as unsophisticated. He collapsed into wheezy cackling at the punchline whilst Brian shook his head in affected sorrow. Brian solemnly imparted the news that he'd had so little action on the sexual front that he was considering offering his genitalia to a local charity shop. Splatch offered to acquaint him with a lady who, although of uncertain temperament, might look favourably upon Brian as potential bed mate. Brian diplomatically demurred. If she had coupled with Splatch then she might well be carrying rabies and would certainly benefit from a comprehensive health check.

After playing several more numbers, interspersed with a short break to afford Splatch the opportunity to throw up in the kitchen sink, Brian visited the tiny bathroom. Capsules voided of their contents, blades of disposable razors, used tissues and cigarette butts were strewn across the bathroom cabinet. A pointillist pattern of dark blood stained the toilet bowl; Brian reflected that in a rational world his friend should be dead but he seemed unkillable, a cloistered relict cloistered from the world and living under a pall of artificial light. Brian tried to imagine the nuisance Splatch would make of himself when, in his incorrigible dotage, he was finally consigned to a care home. Pawing lasciviously at the staff, stealing medication from other residents, parading naked in the front garden, gleefully jerking off in full view of passers-by and inflaming the fury of policemen charged with rescuing him from the hard shoulder of the M56. Brian smiled ruefully and shook his head. If nothing else was worth staying alive for, witnessing Splatch's future shenanigans just might be. His friend had enthralled, confounded and scandalised the decent majority throughout the whole of his adulthood. Taking a different approach to life at the age of fifty would be an illogicality.

Brian returned to the living room and picked up his guitar. Splatch called for a reprise of his new composition and then drained the lees of the bottle of rum. As Brian was now more familiar with his part he was able to devote greater attention to Splatch's playing. As always, it was a numinous joy. Passages of his extemporisations were beyond the realms of the abstract. It seemed he was finding notes and phrases of which only he was aware. Among the cognoscenti, it was a cherished tenet that the hallmark of a great musician was someone who never played the same piece, in the same way, twice. Splatch never played the same piece, in the same way, once. He was both a pioneer and an innovator, an alchemist of sound, a fearless improviser and a man to whom countless lickspittle imitators owed their catchpenny fame. But as entrancing as Splatch's six-stringed arias were, Brian was discomfited by the prospect of having to broach the issue of his friend's copiously bleeding rear end. Splatch suddenly raised his hand to call a halt to the proceedings.

'What's wrong with you?'

'Eh? Nothing. Why? Am I playing this wrong?'

'No. It's near fucking perfect. That's the problem. What happened today?'

'Nothing.

'You're lying. Have you lost your job?'

'How d'you know that? You haven't rung my mam and dad have you?'

'No. It's because you seem almost happy. You're not supposed to be happy. Your face usually looks like an unwiped arse. What's wrong with you?'

'Can I ask you something? There's someone who's been on my mind for a bit.'

'Who? One of your clients or whatever they're called?'

'Yeah. I think he wants to kill himself and I can't think of a good reason why he shouldn't. Have you ever thought about doing that?'

'Suicide? Christ, no. There are too many people I haven't pissed off yet. Why?'

'No reason.'

'Speak. Prevarication is a very unattractive quality.'

'I just wondered what you thought about it, that's all.'

'And someone talking about killing himself is the reason you're so happy is it?'

'Of course it isn't. But I've got to find a good reason for him to stay alive.'

Splatch leaned forward and affixed Brian with a blood-freezing stare.

'Take the average hospital. Right now there's a baby fighting for his life. On another ward there's an eighty year old being kept alive artificially and praying for a death that won't come. One wants a shot at life while the other wants it over with. In a decent world they could do a swap. She dies, he lives. But they can't. Why? Because it's a dogshit world. So my advice to you is that if you're thinking of killing yourself, don't. You've got to play this out. If only for that baby who won't get his shot at life in the first place.'

'It isn't me I'm on about.'

'Yes it is. Now listen. I've been asked by a bloke if I'd be interested in doing a few numbers at his daughter's wedding. A few standards, a few Sinatra tunes. Finish off with a bit of Ellington. It'll just be background music. No one listens anyway. All people do at these things is talk over the band and stuff their fucking faces. A typical jazz gig really. We do forty-five minutes, half-inch some food, take sixty quid off the father of the bride and then go and get blitzed. Dead easy. I reckon there's a market for this. It's stealing money without any comebacks. That'll be a first for me.'

'I dunno, Splatch. Isn't there anyone else you can use? I just get too nervous.'

'Fortune favours the fucking stupid Brian. Feel the fear and... that's about it really. I want you over here on Sunday. A good rehearsal, do the gig next Saturday and then go and get falling-down drunk. That'll be our Christmas party. I brook no objections. Apart from anything else I need the money. I'm being pestered by unruly youths. The money from the gig and selling that bike will keep them off my back. Now call a taxi and fuck off home. I'm expecting visitors.'

'Splatch?'

'Yep?'

'Are you er... having problems with your erm...'

'My arse? Most definitely. He isn't in a taxi yet. Sunday. Eleven o'clock. Bring rum.'

After eleven fruitless calls to three different taxi companies Brian gloomily reconciled himself to trudging the five deathless miles home. He entered the silent street and shivered reflexively in the unusually mild air. At twenty past midnight the town was a necropolis. The older Friday night carousers were now at home, gorging messily on takeaways, spatting with their spouses, channel-surfing and avoiding sexual congress. Twenty-somethings were caged in bestiaries masquerading as nightclubs, scantily clad despite the season, slathered in hair gel, downing shots and swearing vengeance upon the cheeky bastard who had given them a dirty look. School-age boys were drinking vodka in public parks, smoking their parents' cannabis, chuntering about sex and terrible parenting.

A herd of empurpled cumulus scuttered across a starless sky. The only sounds were Brian's laboured breathing, his heels clicking against the pavement and the insistent staccato of rain hitting tarmac.

Whether from fatigue or the alcohol he'd ingested, Brian

was surprisingly even-tempered. His evening with Splatch seemed to have provided sufficient diversion to efface his soul-sickness. Given the turbulence and disappointments of the day, if he hadn't visited his friend he might have killed himself already. He was now purely intent upon getting home, getting warmer, having a nightcap with Wes Montgomery and collapsing into bed. He also admitted to himself that he was intrigued and amused by Splatch's latest flim-flam. God alone knew what the bride would make of a member of the undead fetching up at what was supposedly the happiest day of her life. He predicted an exchange of strong words between the newlywed and her father. To Brian's left there was the unmistakable thud and after-rattle of a door being viciously kicked, followed by a wrathful male roar. There was movement in the darkened pathway leading to the entrance of an unkempt semi-detached house. Brian quickened his step.

An instant later a cyclone of short legs, beefy arms and unmoored mind swept past him on the inside of the kerb. Brian scented whisky in the slipstream of a figure dressed only in jeans and T-shirt, muttering imprecations whilst jabbing a forefinger at an invisible adversary. Bringing up the rear was a woman whom Brian guessed was no older than thirty. A blonde bob framed a delicate face streaked with rivulets of mascara. She was naked save for a sheer nightgown, her bare white legs so thin they resembled switches. She was shoeless but padded doggedly on, screaming insults and entreaties at the figure who turned and bawled a single-vowelled obscenity at her. Brian crossed the narrow road, stared straight ahead and feigned obliviousness to the unseemly tableau playing out on the opposite side. In the season of peace and goodwill such public discordances were not uncommon and it was prudent to keep one's distance.

240

The diminutive blonde exhorted the compact, equally youngish man to, 'Get back in the bleedin' house, Dale. You're a fookin' clown, you. This is what happens when you get fookin' pissed.'

Dale bared his teeth, growled and yelled at her to, 'Just fook off and leave us alone you, you fookin' twat.' Brian tried to remain impassive but his heartbeat accelerated and adrenaline coursed through his veins. This wasn't going to go well for the woman if she persisted in harrying her plainly unhinged partner. The figure in front picked up the pace as the blonde continued to hurl insults at his retreating back. And then, with a turn of speed that would be admirable in less fraught circumstances, she lifted the hem of her nightdress and sprinted towards her fugitive spouse and grasped a hank of his hair in her tiny fist. A primal howl of anguish ricocheted from dark and silent houses as the man fought to free himself. He then caught her full in the face with a forearm smash and resumed walking without a backward glance. The woman buckled soundlessly, grazing her head on a low wall.

Oh Jesus, no. No, no, fucking no. Twat-farting, arsing bollocks. All I want to do is to get home. Why these two fucking arse-twatters? Why twatting now?

Brian ran across the road as quickly as the weight of his guitar case would allow and knelt before the woman who leaned against the wall, her legs akimbo and her head in her chest. Brian quickly concluded that she may have sustained a concussion or possibly worse. She flinched and inhaled sharply as Brian gently held her jaw. Attempting to focus upon Brian with suspicious eyes, she exhaled fumes of stale wine. It was obvious that she was in immediate need of medical attention.

'Can you tell me your name?'

'Debbie.'

'Okay Debbie. Now I'm going to hold some fingers up. D'you want to tell me how many fingers I'm holding up?'

'No I don't. Fook off.'

'Debbie. Listen to me. You might be concussed and your jaw might be cracked. I'm going to call for an ambulance and get you looked at, okay?'

'I'm not goin' fookin' nowhere in no fookin' ambulance. Just fook off and leave us alone.'

'Sorry Debbie. Can't do that. Now then. Can you wiggle your fingers and toes for me?'

'You're off your fookin' cake, you.'

There was a peremptory tap on Brian's shoulder. He turned, looked upwards and gazed into the face of Dale. Considering the events of the previous two minutes Dale's expression was strangely impassive. Brian didn't detect even a scintilla of remorse in the man's florid features. Realising at once that he was disadvantaged by his position on the ground Brian stood to his full height. The man stepped closer to him.

'What you doin', pal?'

'I've come to see if I can do anything. She looks in a pretty bad way.'

'Are you a copper or summat?'

'No.'

'Then what the fook has it got to do wi' you how she is?'

'I'd do this for anyone. This is what normal people do.'

'Are you tekking the piss?'

'I'm not taking anything. But if I were you I'd call her an ambulance. That jaw needs looking at and she's took a bang to the head.'

'Have you called an ambulance?'

'Not yet, no.'

The man nodded slowly as though digesting a profound piece of philosophical insight. He then took a step backwards and booted Brian squarely and forcibly in the midriff. Brian staggered backwards and fell to the ground, deracinated and ready to soil himself. As he attempted to right himself on the pavement Brian heard a female voice screaming, 'You don't want to be fookin' doin' that to 'im Dale.'

When Brian finally came to, he foggily recalled the impact of the guitar case slamming into the side of his head. His skull was sore. Nastily, throbbingly sore. He leaned against the low wall and checked his scalp. There was no blood. He checked his watch. It was almost one o'clock. Both the couple and his guitar case were gone. It began to rain heavily.

It was a surprise when the tears came. There were no prefatory sobs, no declamatory howls, no wringing of hands. He rummaged in his pockets for a cigarette, lit up, inhaled, exhaled, and his tears commingled with the rain. The fact of his tears was as surprising as the unbidden assault. After a minute he heaved himself erect to stumble the last few miles home. Whilst trudging through the rain Brian resolved to check the contents of the tobacco tin. If he'd harboured any lingering doubts about absenting himself from the world he had none whatsoever now. He'd spent fifty years on this planet and it didn't seem to want him. He didn't belong here. He never had. The prospect of carrying on living out this wretched life on this wretched earth surrounded by these wretched people not only enfeebled him but irritated like a stone in the shoe. He was angry and bored at even the thought of it. Sunday would be his last day on earth and Splatch would have to find another partner for the wedding gig.

SATURDAY

Gritty-eyed and grumbly, Brian awoke and stared at the yellowed lounge ceiling. He heaved himself from the couch and immediately palpated his head. There was a sizeable lump but much less painful than he'd expected. It was nothing more than a dull throb similar to that suffered after a half-bottle of cheap whisky. His tongue tentatively waggled a newly loosened molar, but the dislodged tooth wasn't in the least painful. His stomach felt tender to the touch but he was ambulatory and relatively sentient. He stretched his arms to the ceiling, groaned horribly, and then noticed with pained surprise that he was still wearing the suit he'd worn to work the previous morning. After shucking off his jacket and removing his tie he opened the curtains.

The milky December light suggested that it was around nine in the morning. He needed coffee, a shower and a change of clothes. Passing by the beat-box on his way to the bathroom he turned on the radio. The white chocolate female voice on the weekly magazine programme fully oriented him to time and place. Gratified by the absence of blood in his urine he returned to the kitchen and put the kettle on. He popped a couple of painkillers to further dull the pain inflicted by the psycho-wassailer's assault and glanced around the kitchen. His Saturday mornings were usually devoted to shopping, domestic chores and ironing clothes in preparation for the coming week, but now there was no week to prepare for. Now there were no more weeks, or months or years. Time was something else he wouldn't have to do. This was liberating but disconcerting. The lacuna left by the

244

absence of domestic drudgery had to be filled somehow, if only to use up the time until Saturday properly began. The planning and structuring of this day assumed a significance he hadn't reckoned upon, particularly as he was still in funds.

He resolved to go to the ATM but not before he'd swallowed at least two more cups of coffee. He also resisted a desire to turn on the laptop and enter the flesh labyrinth. Brian chastised himself for almost surrendering to an inexplicable impulse. The after-effects of a brutal physical attack should not, under any circumstances, inflame one's libido. If a kick in the stomach and a blow to the head conduced tumescence then his redaction from human life was both timely and deserved. It was bad enough having two former members of the Bullingdon Club at the helm of the nation without him adding to the general *fin du monde* depravity.

At eleven thirty he threw on a coat and trudged towards the ATM close to the convenience store. He cast an apprehensive eye at the clutch of bleared, shivering tipplers already convened outside The Long Pig, one of whom was smashing his balled fist against the entrance and demanding ingress. They were clad in football shirts, suggesting that an important match was in prospect. Even Brian could recognise the colours of Manchattan worn by the quarrelsome congregants outside the pub. The drone of a police helicopter surveilling the area for skirmishes between rival fans was already audible. Even Curly, Larry and Mo were up and around this side of midday. This game must surely be an event of national importance if those three were at large.

These bovine, unblinking and invariably silent siblings were well known to the police and social services. Each of them suffered some form of learning disability or mental disorder in tandem with aberrant and anti-social behaviours. Larry's jail term

245

for offences of indecent exposure had been commuted to probation following psychiatric reports, much to the chagrin of the children's parents. These dishevelled disparates shared a three-bedroomed dwelling with their mother, who herself was no stranger to the custody suite when in her cups. Squad cars were regularly observed outside their property but there were occasions when the family was entirely blameless for tumultuous goings-on in nocturnal hours. During one memorable weekend they were subjected firstly to the attentions of a mob howling their demands that they leave town, followed by a terrifying episode of fire-raising. This peculiar clan endured the contempt of Least with the stoicism of martyrs, but took care to never venture out alone. Brian had also heard lurid, although probably apocryphal rumours regarding the relationship between the three men and their mother. Least's skewed ethical code would deem incest just cause for bloody retribution. It promised to be an interesting afternoon in The Pig.

In the convenience store Brian's inability to choose even his last meal on the planet dispirited him. Helen would have swept through the aisles and purchased the requisite victuals before Brian had even selected a newspaper. He ambled the aisles uncertainly, picking various items from the shelves and then forlornly replacing them. He couldn't even remember if he actually enjoyed many of the foodstuffs on offer. Since he and Helen had parted, food was merely fuel as opposed to a pleasurable epicurean experience. Most days he was happy with anything that could be inserted between two slices of bread or, better yet, simply pulled from its packaging and crammed into his mouth. The only certainty was that tomorrow, cooking would be out of the question. Brian believed cooking to be a pastime pursued only by men who despise books, music, their families and reflective thinking. His main course would be the very acme of practicality, consisting of several bottles of wine accompanying something microwaveable. Anything nutritious was to be avoided. Rocket salad tasted of nothing but air and he'd had quite enough of that when with Helen.

After what seemed like a period of double maths Brian selected his valedictory meal. For dessert he opted for lemon cheesecake and vodka. For the self-annihalator the sedative qualities of vodka were self-evident, whilst the cheesecake would be a memento mori of the halcyon years with Helen. Cheesecake had always been her favourite dessert and also handily reduced to half price.

Brian rounded off his shopping expedition with the purchase of two cheap cigars and an extra newspaper. It was good to lash out occasionally as suicide tended to limit the opportunities for frivolous purchases thereafter. He elected to smoke one of the cigars some time that day and save the other for tomorrow, his last afternoon alive. He'd blow glaucous jets of smoke towards the ceiling whilst slowly metamorphosing into hospital waste.

After making his way home and storing his shopping Brian glanced through the window, checked his watch and was gratified to note that it was still dry outside and the pubs were open. He deliberated whether to take a taxi to the more affluent suburbs but elected to walk instead. He threw on his heaviest coat, grasped his umbrella and newspapers and headed out. The air was cold and moist as he tramped from the grimly urban to more verdant locales. He was surprised by his indifference towards his surroundings, especially as this would be the last time he'd ever see them. He had read that those aware of their imminent demise experienced a world transfigured, spending their final days searing images of familiar places and people onto their retinas.

Brian was more enthused by the absence of rain.

The pub was hard by a Gothic church so old it had borne witness to the English Civil War. He entered via a sturdy oak door and glanced around for a suitable table. He savoured the hushed calm, the fragrance of scented candles and the blessed absences of television screens and lager drinkers. He ordered a large whisky with a brown ale chaser and noted a chirrup of mature ladies clad in anoraks hunkered in one corner. Brian hazarded them to be a rambling group who convened every weekend, striding purposefully hither and yon before taking a convivial lunch and the opportunity to chunter about their husband's new job, the achievements of their adult children and the ghastliness of their new neighbours. Expensively coiffed hair, crease-resistant skin, designer windcheaters, dainty walking shoes and a general lustre stamped them as solidly middle class, the very template from which Helen had been created.

Comfortably off, well insured and never without a paper hankie, these women were confident of their place in the world. Least women of a similar age seemed older and sallower, much less kempt and either morbidly obese or unhealthily emaciated, fulminating their rage in expletive-riddled tirades. The fragranced coven in the corner spoke in low but perfectly enunciated tones, all aitches pronounced and esses delicately sibilated. Disinhibition of any stripe would doubtless be condemned as conduct unbecoming. Infidelity, drunkenness, tattoos, graphic novels, all-inclusive package holidays and other indecorums were the constituency of the unmannerly and culture-phobic, but if challenged all of these women would vehemently repudiate their fear and disdain of the lower orders. Helen would never miss an opportunity to declare her egalitarian credentials, sometimes citing Brian as a living exemplar of her principled opposition to social divisions. Brian always forbore from mentioning her aversion to diplomacy as it would have been pointless in any case. He smiled grimly as he recalled their first encounter.

He had been unsure what to do with himself that Wednesday night. The previous night he'd inadvertently left the driver's side window open after parking on the factory car park. The following morning when he eased his exhausted body into the car his nether regions were immediately steeped in rain-sodden velour. This was not the most encouraging start to his three days off. Upon his arrival home he showered and then immediately retired to bed to avoid his father. Derek rose for work irritable and flatulent thirty minutes after Brian's arrival home and always demanded a bulletin of the latest to-doings in the factory; none of which interested Brian in the slightest.

After his final night shift Brian usually rose early and strolled to the working-men's club affiliated to the factory. There was always a gaggle of similarly torpid night shifters who convened for a game of snooker or a hand of five-card brag for a five pence ante. On midweek afternoons there was little else to do other than drink, watch the racing on the telly and then call at the chip shop on the way home. On his few weekends off he sometimes joined his workmates in the hunt for a one-night stand in the town's teeming nightclubs, but this was rarely to his taste. He hated the plodding, bass-heavy dance music, the dreadful beer and the too-close proximity of strangers. He was also handicapped by shyness, his innate introversion unhelpful in snaring sexual quarry. If any female signalled her romantic interest he became tongue-tied, flustered and ultimately superfluous. On the very few occasions he'd been invited back to someone's home she either wanted to vent her spleen about her previous boyfriend or to discuss the failure of her disappointing marriage. These trysts usually concluded with Brian being advised to take a taxi home before his companion dissolved into disconsolate tears. As an isolate by nature, and not particularly popular with his workmates, Brian preferred the quietude of the underlit, sparsely-patronised workingmen's club. He'd exchange genial nods with the retirees who constituted the daily domino school, sniff the odours of beer and cue chalk and lend an ear to the witter of the television high above the bar.

He had risen shortly after midday, quickly swallowed a cup of coffee and then ambled to the club. He ordered a brown and bitter and drifted into the billiards room. It was in almost complete darkness except for the light illuming the table and the sun filtering through narrow windows. Eric Diggle and Goldfinger were playing out a tense finish to their third and final frame. Brian nodded to the two men and inscribed his initials on a blackboard confirming his intention to play the winner of this titanic struggle.

'Yorrite cocker?'

'Not bad Eric. You?'

'Kin' knackered pal. The wife wouldn't let me go to bed this morning. I had to go shopping with 'er at nine o'fuckin' clock. Traipsing round that bastard supermarket dead on my bastard feet. I've gone past my sleep now. You're up early. You shit the bed or summat?'

'I got a few hours in. More than you by the sounds of it.'

'She's no pity, she's not. I've only had three pints since I come in here. I can't sup ale when I'm cream crackered, me.'

Goldfinger, who had acquired this soubriquet to reflect his propensity for very vigorous and very public rectal digging, derisively shook his head at Eric's whimperings.

'Tek no fuckin' notice of him, Brian. He always needs summat to bastard moan about.'

'Get fucked you. I'm bollocksed and that's all there is to it. I'll still win this one though. You're playing me next Brian, not this dozy fucker.'

'Right. Should I hang on or go back in the bar?'

'Stop where y'are. This won't tek a minute.'

Eric bent low over the table and hit the white ball smoothly with a practised backspin. The white gently nudged the black towards the left mid-corner pocket but without sufficient force to consummate the pot. The white ball slowed, leaving Goldfinger with the easiest of shots.

'Ooh, you fuckin' jam-strangling bastard.'

'Fuckin' blind bastard you're nowt else. Watch and learn, Brian.'

Goldfinger comfortably despatched the black ball and then performed a soft-shoe shuffle. Eric made to hit him with his cue before heading to bar. Brian stepped forward to the table and retrieved the balls from the pockets to reset them for the next game. Outside it was becoming brighter and the bonnets of the few vehicles scattered around the club forecourt glistened in the increasingly warm sun. This was perfect weather for a pub crawl but Brian doubted he had the stamina to undertake eight hours of aimless drinking. Valuable sleep had inevitably been lost in the course of four night shifts and if he fell asleep in a pub he'd never hear the last of it. His father had already bequeathed him the appellation Dozyarse and this had stuck like a louse to a mongrel. He was chary of providing more fodder for the locker-room wags.

Brian broke off, scattering the reds across the baize. Goldfinger bent low to the table, thickets of brown nasal hair bristling as he focused upon his first shot. The beer was taking hold and uniting the gamesmen in a woozy sodality. Eric took a long pull at his pint of mild, rolled a cigarette, sighed and then pensively picked his nose. Between visits to the table Goldfinger chivvied his sphincter with a bony middle digit. Brian concentrated on extending his score beyond a solitary red. He wasn't much cop at snooker but enjoyed the calm of the billiards room and sedate pace of the game.

As Brian knew nothing about football, rugby league, boxing or horse racing the conversation turned to matters at work. Eric bemoaned the discomfort he endured when wearing the ear defenders and goggles recently issued by the management. The acid-resistant rubber boots he was now forced to wear drew his feet so badly that his wife insisted he shower and powder his feet before sexual congress would be vouchsafed. Eric had querulously objected that preliminary ablutions derogated from the spontaneity of the act but his wife remained unmoved. She wasn't going anywhere near them smelly feet. Eric wondered if he should talk to the shop steward about taking out a grievance against the company for ruining what was previously a perfectly mediocre sex life.

Goldfinger nodded sagely as though intimately acquainted with the vagaries of married life and exacting standards of personal hygiene. To the most casual observer it was plain that he was not. Goldfinger exuded an ineffable odour, a primal stink intermixed with stale tobacco and baked beans. His clothes appeared to have been stolen from the putrescent corpse of a dead tramp, but his strangely-configured physique militated against the wearing of more stylish attire. Looking older than his forty-four years, Goldfinger was functionally illiterate and wholly reliant upon others to decrypt written communications.

Nevertheless, his collection of pornography was so large and diverse it could have easily occupied an entire floor of The British Library. He was a connoisseur of the mortifying and gynaecological years before such a predilection would be diagnosed as a mental disorder. No one departed his two bedroomed flat without feeling morally debased and mentally addled. He also expended a great many of his meal breaks engaged in self-abuse in the gentlemen's lavatory in the factory, vocalising his journey to ecstasy in the fashion of someone cheering on an Olympic sprinter. But whilst Goldfinger was catastrophe incarnate he was not without finer, deeper feelings. For the first time in his life he was in love and desperate to give tongue to his tendresse for Janine, the recently appointed secretary of the factory's managing director. He leaned upon his billiards cue in the manner of a Biblical prophet exhorting the godless multitudes to return to the path of righteousness.

'Have you noticed that when she walks, one arse cheek goes up and the other one goes down? And then the arse cheek that's down goes up, and the arse cheek that's up goes down? Amazing that, innit? My arse don't do that. Well I don't think it does anyroad. I've tried watchin' it but I can't turn my head round far enough.'

Eric sighed, shook his head and pointed a reproving finger. He'd been forced to listen to Goldfinger's rhapsodies upon the theme of Janine for the whole of last night's shift and reluctant to hear any more.

'If you don't stop rabbiting on about her I'm going to knock your bastard teeth down your bastard throat. Now bastard shut it and play the fuckin' game. You'll have it fuckin' dark if you carry on. And will you stop pickin' at your fuckin' arse?'

'What do you think, Brian? She's fuckin' gorgeous in't she?

'I've never took that much notice of her to be honest. She's never took any notice of me mind.'

'I'd use her shit for toothpaste, me.'

'Ooh. Right.'

'I'd lick the fart-stains off her knickers I would, Brian.'

'Fuckin' hell Goldfinger—'

'Will the pair of you get on with this fuckin' game?'

'Well if you like her that much why don't you ask her out?'

Goldfinger's eyes narrowed as he trained a menacing stare on his opponent.

'How d'you mean?'

'Well… you know. Go for a drink or whatever. She can only say no can't she?'

'You are one dirty bastard you, Brian Paget.'

'Eh?'

'She's courting strong in't she? How would you like it if someone kept trying to nick your chips off your plate? You wouldn't like it would you? You're bang out order, you.'

'Well I didn't know she was courting strong did I?'

'I'm having a word with your dad, me. You need to see a fuckin' doctor you do.'

'Eric? Will you get a grip of this barmy fucker?'

Eric had dropped off to sleep. Brian ceded the game on the blue ball and departed the billiards room as the volume of Eric's snoring approached the decibelic. The Claw, an electrician assigned to Brian's shift, beckoned him as he purchased another pint. The Claw was looking for players to join him in a hand of five card brag. Brian enjoyed the game as it was reliant purely upon luck rather than any discernible skill. He and two other men carelessly threw some spare change onto the card table. As one hand concluded and another began the players swapped epithets,

254

anecdotes, gossip, and news of former workmates who were gravely ill or had passed away. One of the players declared that he was struggling with the quick crossword in his tabloid newspaper and requested assistance from the others at the table. Brian glanced at the crossword and immediately noted that the quizzer had inserted the answer "gass" to the four letter clue "fossil fuel". When Brian gently suggested that that "coal" may be a better fit, the quizzer immediately took umbrage. He snarled a denunciation of Brian's limited intellect and demanded to know the name of the special school he'd attended. Claw's eyes rolled heavenward before shaking his head mournfully and declaring that they were both wrong. The answer was obviously "wood", but thick fuckers like them two wouldn't know that. Claw's lofty determination sparked a furious debate upon the legitimacy of wood as a fossil. Bored by the pointlessness of the altercation Brian focused his attention on the television above the bar.

In common with everyone else he knew, Brian was militantly apolitical. Politics were the preserve of politicians as Sundays were the preserve of hangovers, car boot sales and family rows were for the rest of the populace. He hadn't been old enough to vote in 1979 and hadn't bothered since. The two men in sober suits being interviewed on television were apparently the architects of the transformation of the Labour party. Their determination to throw the Tories out of office was eclipsed only by their commitment to renewal. The renewal of what Brian was unsure, but they seemed sincere enough. The Scottish bloke looked a bit frightening whilst the other one resembled a well-meaning but ineffectual supply teacher. They couldn't do any worse than the current crop and, as with all politicians, they would be forgotten as soon as they were out of office. In Brian's view politicians were like cyclones. They entered one's life for a short period, created havoc, and then disappeared forever. He wondered if the pie shop was still open.

Following his fourth pint Brian's eyes began to feel gritty, a sure signifier that he needed a nap. He strolled slowly home. Mam was still at work, Elaine was staying over at Dave's flat and his father wouldn't be home until six that evening. He wearily mounted the stairs to his bedroom, took out his signed copy of *We Have Been Observing Your Planet For Some Time* and dropped the stylus onto the first side. He then lay on the bed, stared at the ceiling and wondered where in the world his old friend was right now.

When he awoke it was dusk and his parents were having a row. Derek was haranguing his wife for storing his snooker cue in the shed where it might fall prey to damp and woodlice. Between drags on her thirtieth cigarette of that day his mother calmly apprised her husband that if he didn't shut his mithering bleedin' cakehole that stick would be going where the sun never bleedin' shone. Brian sighed, checked his watch and waited for his father to slam the front door behind him as he hurried to the club. Upon his father's departure he rose, showered and dressed. From his bedroom window he gazed at the coral sky and wondered what to do next. His priority was to get out of the house, but these days the only entertainment in local pubs was televised football. It seemed that people were watching football around the clock, even those who had evinced no previous interest in the game. He elected to catch a bus into town. Rock blues was not usually his cup of tea but there was sure to be a band playing at the Tarred and Feathered. Before he headed for the bus stop Brian poked his head around the living room door. His mother stared open-mouthed at the television whilst biting into a coffee cream.

'I'm nipping out for a pint in town, Mam.'

'Right.'

'I've got my key.'

'Make sure you have. If you haven't, don't bother coming home.'

'Right.'

The Tarred and Feathered was the epicentre of what passed for counterculture in Brian's home town, providing a haven for those who enjoyed guitar-based rock music, denim shirts and hair longer than that of a member of The British National Party. On the rare occasions he'd frequented the establishment, Brian was convinced that its interior decor was a replica of Castle Gormenghast. The ugly flock wallpaper begriming the walls was aged by nicotine, sweat and beer breath. The biro scrawlings of three generations of hirsute rockers historicised the punters' laudations of blues combos, progressive rock ensembles and heavy metal superstars. There were also lewd cartoons of young ladies in various states of undress who were generally considered by the male clientele to be dead fit and well up for it. Doubtless some of these Sharons and Anne-Maries would now be in their mid-fifties and past their enviable prime. The toilets were beyond crapulent, the lighting was funereal and it was unlikely that the heavy scarlet drapes covering the ancient windows had ever been laundered. Brian supposed that the licensee had waived the pub's refurbishment at the behest of his regulars, who were as dishevelled and oddly smelling as the pub itself. The Tarred and Feathered remained a cherished institution, however. It was a local joke that if the town was razed to the ground following a nuclear attack the Tarred And Feathered would assuredly remain standing. It was also likely that no one would notice the damage.

Brian alighted at the bus stop and trudged into the pub. He

lit a cigarette and eyed the "What's On" poster at the entrance to the small concert room. The evening's entertainment was a "Hard-rockin' bloozy power trio from Northwich".

Whilst waiting to be served at the bar he evaluated the high quality and ludicrous cost of the band's PA system. He could never understand why groups playing to an audience averaging seven people sported enough amplification to induce auditory nerve damage in a crowd at the Reading Festival. Other than a bearded oldster in a wheelchair, dressed in a kaftan and whose hands shook when he raised a pint to his toothless mouth, Brian was the only attendee. The burly, beer-bellied band members were in conclave with their sullen leather-clad girlfriends, smoking furiously whilst poring over the set list. Their repertoire would probably consist of numbers lamenting the lonesomeness of the Delta, catfish in the fishin' hole, blood on the killing floor and the hard lives led by men who lived by the Mississippi. The band themselves looked like they had never ventured any further south than Stoke-On-Trent. Brian resolved to give an ear to one or two numbers but if they were overly loud then he was out of there.

During the course of a deathless minor pentatonic guitar solo Brian's flight or fight instinct alerted him to an unseen presence. He swivelled round and was transfixed by the inquisitorial gaze of a woman who stood to his right with two other females. Brian returned his attention to the band, checking his watch as he did so. If the band broke into 'Route 66' then this would be a cliché too far and he would be taking the bus home. Conscious that he was still being stared at he turned to face the woman again, nodded stiffly in her direction and then continued to focus his attention on the small stage. A porcelain hand alighted on his.

'Excuse me. What kind of music is this?'

Brian almost had a cardiac infarction, such was his shock at this unexpected intrusion. He hoped that she wasn't collecting for charity or inviting him to a religious meeting. She looked the type.

'Eh?'

'This music. I'm not familiar with it. What is it?'

'Well. It's the blues innit? Muddy Waters, Wolf, Elmore James and that. They call it three chords and the truth. In this lot's case it's three chords and a load of bloody feedback. Any more of this and I'm off.'

'Oh. Don't you like it?'

'I can take it or leave it. An old mate of mine got me into Robert Johnson, Blind Lemon and Charlie Patton. That's more my kind of thing.'

'You come here a lot then.'

'Nah. I don't bother with the place normally. The ale's crap as well. D'you come in here?'

'My first time. One of our colleagues is leaving us so we thought we'd go for something to eat then try a few pubs. They're very loud aren't they?'

'Too bloody loud. There's no need for it. There's only five of us in. Their girlfriends as well like, but they've got no option have they? If this lot played in sign language they'd still be too bloody loud.'

'Oh. Do you sign?'

'Sign what?'

'Are you able to perform sign language? That's a real advantage in my profession.'

'Sign language? Me? You're kidding aren't you? I struggle to speak proper English me, never mind owt else.'

The woman smiled wryly and studied her shoes. She was of

medium height, dark-haired and slender. Dressed in a mackintosh, a white shirt, a black midi skirt, black stockings and brogues, she was smart but fetchingly casual. Whilst not conventionally pretty her face was interesting, her dark unblinking eyes compelling Brian's attention. Her light voice was informed with a pleasing dulcity and free of a local accent. Brian's amatory inclinations had been stirred, but his instinctive pessimism overrode any romantic feelings. She was probably just idling away ten minutes or so before her boyfriend arrived who would then take umbrage at finding her conversing with a strange man. Brian had no wish to be embroiled in a possibly perilous standoff with an irate suitor. It was best to revert to his usual mode of silent hostility and indifference. When the woman offered her hand by way of an introduction Brian stared straight ahead in mute rebuttal of her overture. From the corner of his eye he noted her dejection and confusion. She would soon bugger off back to her mates and leave him alone. He then gasped as a sharp poke in his lower ribs deflated him. The large dark eyes of his assailant bore intensely into his.

'What d'you do that for?'

'I thought you couldn't hear me.'

'Well I can't over this lot can I? What d'you want?'

'What's your name?'

'Brian.'

There was a pause. Brian eyed her fearfully, speculating that she might punch him in the face. Anyone who tried to puncture a lung by way of a formal introduction was capable of anything.

'Don't you want to know mine?'

'Not really no.'

'It's Helen. Do you have a telephone number?'

'Oh aye. We've had a phone in our house for a good while

now.'

'Can I have it?'

'What for?'

Helen's eyebrows arched slightly and her gaze became unignorable. Brian shrugged resignedly and hailed the tattooed besom behind the bar. He requested the usage of a pen, tore open a beermat, scribbled his number on the exposed white interior of the beermat and handed it to Helen.

'There y'are. Will that do you?'

Helen nodded slowly and then turned away to rejoin her companions. They departed before the end of the band's fourth number. Brian sighed and by closing time had dismissed his encounter with the insistent woman from his mind. He found a seat on top deck of the last smoke-filled bus home and then fell into bed for ten dreamless hours.

A few weeks later, Brian, Eric and Goldfinger were trudging towards the social club following the end of a shift heralding their first full weekend off in a month. The early shift on Fridays prior to a weekend off usually prefigured forty hours of going out on the pull, long lie-ins and varying degrees of drunkenness. Sozzlement was curtailed only by the final pint of the Sunday lunchtime session as the boulevardiers girded themselves for another working week. Eric was taking the missus out for a Chinese that night whilst Goldfinger was taking the train to visit a strip club in Manchattan. He was determined to see some proper tits and didn't care if he was thrown out of the club for interfering with himself. Brian was suffering a cold and was resigned to spending his days off in bed with analgesics and cheap brandy. Eric had warned him to walk two steps behind he and Goldfinger to avoid catching his lurgy, a fiat with which Brian dutifully complied. It was bad form to infect a workmate with what might

261

be influenza on a long weekend off. He wouldn't hear the last of it if Eric came into work on Monday with a streaming nose.

Brian hovered by the entrance to the club. He cleaved to the ridiculous notion that viruses were as susceptible to the effects of alcohol as their hosts, therefore it was only logical that if he was blind drunk then the spiteful microbes would also be half seas over, thus diminishing their potential for mischief. Not even an obdurate and malicious flu bug could withstand the inundation of a half-bottle of whisky chased down with Irish stout, but Brian realised that if he didn't go home then he might well collapse. He raised a pallid hand to his companions, purchased medication and brandy from the local convenience store and drank several fortified teas whilst listening to the Cannonball Adderley Quintet. Brian's failure to be reinvigorated by either 'Love For Sale' or alcohol confirmed his fears that he really was unwell. He swallowed two flu-caps and then slithered into bed.

When he awoke the following lunchtime Brian felt considerably brighter, although still frail and rank with sweat. He stumbled downstairs and put the kettle on whilst acknowledging his mother with a curt nod. Jean was ironing, watching the television and smoking. She regarded her son with a disapproving eye and enquired if he was going to walk around like that all bloody day. He looked like no bugger owned him. Brian grunted and muttered that he still wasn't well and would be shortly going back to bed. He enlivened his tea with a liberal measure of brandy, swallowed two more flu-caps and enquired of the whereabouts of his father.

'Where the bloody hell d'you think he is? And someone phoned up for you last night when you were in your pit. She sounded right posh an' all.'

'Yeah? Who was it?'

'Some woman.'

'What was her name?'

'I never bloody asked. I put the phone down on her. I thought she was trying to sell us summat. Now make yourself useful and make me a brew.'

'Right.'

Four brandy-laced teas later, Brian was ready to retire once more. He lay awake for half an hour, struggling to focus upon the pages of a science fiction novel before relapsing into unconsciousness. He awoke in the early hours of Sunday feeling better than at any time in the previous three days. He rose, crept past his parents' bedroom, briefly lent an ear to their repertoire of snores, farts and eructations and nodded beatifically. The house would be his for a few blissful hours until his mother rose for work at five a.m. He prepared a coffee with brandy and swallowed two analgesics before fishing out his Sony Walkman from a kitchen drawer. He listened intently to an album of Rachmaninoff piano duets he'd borrowed from the town's library. The filigree tinkling of the two pianos sounded like ice crystals forming, at once profoundly moving whilst not completely comprehensible. Brian had imagined that all Russians resembled the stone-faced members of the Politburo who clapped like clockwork monkeys at the nuclear armoury paraded annually before them in Red Square. The fragility and complexity of Rachmaninoff's compositions suggested that these strange people were gifted with an unsuspected sensitivity, although the erasure of the Berlin Wall six years previously had dismayed him. Its dismantling was seen by many as a cause for celebration, but Brian considered the wall's removal as merely another addition to the planetary tumult. At least nuclear warfare was avertable if more rational heads finally took charge over there. On hearing the first stirrings of his mother he returned to bed.

Brian awoke around eleven o'clock, stretched and smiled at the realisation that the malaise that had ruined his time off was finally expunged. He padded downstairs into the kitchen where his father was louring at the back pages of a salacious Sunday tabloid. Neither acknowledged the other as Brian busied himself making a cup of tea. Derek eventually broke the silence.

'What're you up to today Dozyarse?'

'Not much. What time's Mam finishing?'

'About two. When she comes in tell her I've had to go to the club. There's a coachload of bowlers coming over from the Isle of Man next Saturday so the green's got to be up to snuff. Are you going the club after?'

'I've not thought yet. I might do. I'm on late turn tomorrow so there's no rush for getting up in the morning.'

Derek briskly folded his paper, reached for his coat and left for the club. Brian sat at the kitchen table pondering what to do with the rest of Sunday. Then the telephone rang.

'Is that Brian?'

'Yep.'

'Oh hi, Brian.'

Brain was nonplussed. He didn't know anyone who used that overly familiar greeting. He immediately thought that the caller was trying to sell him a conservatory, the current must-have for aspirational property owners. Brian wasn't aspirational in any sense and her intrusion into this benevolent Sunday morning would be given short shrift.

'What do you want?'

'It's Helen.'

'I'm none the bloody wiser.'

264

'From the pub. With the loud band. Remember?'

Brian winced, closed his eyes and spluttered a profuse apology for his curtness. He explained that although feeling much better following a bout of illness, he hadn't been in the mood for any unsolicited calls. To his relief Helen briskly dismissed his mea culpa and enquired if he was free for Sunday lunch later. Brian's eyes widened.

Lunch? Not dinner? Oh Jesus. She's posh. She sounds like Splatch's old girlfriend. I hope this one's not as off her fucking head as she was.

He tentatively agreed and enquired where she would like to meet, assuming she would choose a gastropub in which all of the main courses featured processed peas. She instead suggested a newly opened family-owned trattoria in one the more opulent purlieus of the town and handily close to where she lived. The people were friendly, one didn't need to book and the wine list was palatable if a little unexciting.

Brian stared at the telephone receiver in incomprehension. He had no idea that wine had a duty to excite and the only Italian food he'd ever tasted was frozen pizza. As for Italians generally, his only encounter with the Latinate demos was via the films of Martin Scorsese. If Scorsese's cinematic portrayal of Italians was accurate they may as well have hailed from Least. They enjoyed horrific violence, calorific meals, ladies with huge and pendulous breasts, cocaine and the Catholic church. Worse than of all that was their predilection for opera. Opera was superseded only by death-metal in its supreme daftness.

Brian's instinctual aversion to the untried and unfamiliar was stirred. His lack of *savoir faire* virtually guaranteed humiliation. Least men never frequented restaurants unless they were dangerously drunk, it was well past midnight, and the bill of fare was ludicrously cheap. The turbaned owners of such establishments would insist upon all meals being purchased prior to being served as a precaution against the flight of the customers without paying. Helen's choice of eatery sounded posh, and posh usually translated as expensive. He was certain to be disappointed by the restaurant and be disappointing company for his companion. He'd be much better off going to the working men's club, the milieu in which he felt most secure. He strained every mental sinew to conjure an alibi of even tenuous plausibility to extricate himself from this engagement. He'd already squandered his ace card by declaring himself fit for an afternoon out, but perhaps his mother was in bed recovering from a fall sustained only an hour ago. His father had been abducted and murdered by Middle Eastern terrorists. He was terrified of big tits. He sighed and capitulated to the inevitable as not a single excuse he could contrive seemed remotely plausible. He glumly assented to a rendezvous in a pub close to the restaurant and was determined to hate every minute of this farrago.

Helen arrived slightly late. Whilst she greeted Brian warmly, he detected a slight moue of distaste when he lit a cigarette. Brian mentally scored a demerit against her. If she disdained the inhalation of the most readily accessible calmative for the chronically anxious then this occasion would definitely be a one-off. They sat together in a corner of the busy pub, straining to hear one another over the jukebox. She enquired how he was feeling following his bout of illness and her solicitude seemed unfeigned. Brian professed to feeling much better and timorously volunteered that this afternoon would be his first experience of Italian cuisine. Helen's eyebrows arched in surprise but she reassured Brian that he was certain to enjoy the paisan ambience and the authenticity of the food. Brian vigorously nodded his agreement without having understood a single word she'd said.

When they entered the restaurant, the couple was met with such effusiveness by the staff that Brian wondered if Helen was related to them. After warmly shaking his hand a waiter guided him by the elbow to a table. Brian was so disconcerted by the waiter's ministrations that he forgot to sit down, staring blankly at the waiter as though awaiting further instructions. Helen was much more at ease as the attendants buzzed around them. The rangy Italian owner of the establishment ambled over to greet Helen and introduce himself to her dining partner. He enquired if Brian might enjoy an aperitif before ordering food. Nonplussed, Brian shook his head in bewilderment until Helen helpfully suggested a whisky. Brian nodded eagerly. Whisky was a word he was definitely acquainted with.

Helen's wide unblinking eyes scanned the menu whilst Brian scoped out his new surroundings. Although the place was almost full, the volume of chatter was barely audible. Brian was struck by the impeccable behaviour of the children dining with their parents. Their placidity and perfect table manners were slightly unnerving, reminding him of the children in *The Midwich Cuckoos*. These children were definitely not from Least. If they were the waiters would be seeking asylum in the kitchen. The ambience was almost reverential, an eating house as a temple of worship. As he absorbed the modernist artworks and black and white photos of Italian-American crooners, Brian shook his head in wonder. He wasn't quite sure where he was but he knew he liked it.

He was so abstracted by his new surroundings that he visibly started when Helen blithely demanded to know if he was carnivorous. Brian had to think about this as he was unsure whether the consumption of meat was acceptable in establishments as grand as this. He tentatively offered a preference for chicken, but if that was unavailable then he'd be content with whatever she was having. In truth, such was his delight at his new environs he would have been quite happy with a Spam fritter. Helen hailed a waiter hovering by another table.

As Helen ordered the food Brian marvelled at how posh people were able to sound both ill-natured and urbane at the same time. To his ears she sounded rather peremptory, but the waiter fawned over her every perfectly enunciated word. A sommelier whose gait was so smooth he seemed to walk on air arrived with a bottle of wine. With a priestly gravitas he swept the bottle before Helen's discriminating eye and then swiftly removed the cork. He raised a querying eyebrow at Brian who quickly indicated that Helen should taste the wine first. He was excited enough without the fruit of the vine further amplifying his elation. Brian was not an oenophile. As far as he was concerned any wine got him blind drunk and didn't make him gaseous was a vintage year. He couldn't even pronounce the name on the label of the bottle from which the waiter was filling his glass, never mind offer any authoritative assessment of its contents. Helen raised her glass in salutation and Brian did the same, although with markedly less elan. He felt he should say something but was gripped by the aphasia of the socially maladroit. Fortunately for him Helen was the soul of volubility.

During the course of a long and immensely enjoyable afternoon, culminating in several desserts and myriad fortified coffees, Brian learned that Helen had eschewed the academic route taken by her parents, both of whom were university lecturers and published authors. They had gently insisted that Helen train as a doctor lest her academic brilliance might be squandered in less demanding disciplines. However, in a rare instance of defiance, she had chosen a different stripe of public service. Whilst omitting to divulge her impressive array of qualifications she began her career on the bottom rung for a charity assisting the street homeless. She then expanded her already considerable repertoire of skills by volunteering for the Citizen's Advice Bureau as a case worker. Mummy and Daddy were initially dismayed, but as she ascended to a regional directorship of the largest social housing group in the country they had to admit the rightness of her decision.

Helen declared herself happy to be constantly busy. On any given day she would be dealing with the management of hostels and women's refuges, working with mental health charities and assisting local authorities in accommodating difficult-to-place tenants. She was even called upon by people in central government to brainstorm new strategies for social housing provision. Her slender physique belied her appetite for a full plate. She enjoyed a wide variety of interests, particularly reading literary novels. She had no time for thick-lit, the genre that diarised the love lives, friendships, fall-outs and weight-loss campaigns of vacuous self-absorbed women. She was also a regular attendee at art galleries and the theatre, and although not particularly musical she had recently joined a local operatic society. She also managed to slip to the gym twice a week, having discovered that physical fitness was aid to mental alertness.

Brian was exhausted by simply listening to her. He wondered if she found time to sleep. He also wondered whether her limitless *joie de vivre* was pharmaceutically fuelled, as with his absent friend Splatch. No one could cram so much into a day unless completely out of their gourd or battery-operated. Brian was almost apologetic as he listed his gamut of interests. He worked shifts in a factory, he lived with his parents, he possessed a record collection, he'd recently bought a TV and DVD player for his bedroom and owned a couple of guitars. He also enjoyed drinking. And sleeping. And little else.

Helen's smile was inscrutable but her expression was affectionate and indulgent. As he gazed into her large eyes Brian sensed that a decision had been made to which he was not yet privy. Helen checked her watch, gravely nodded to herself and muttered that she had a very early start in the morning. Brian nodded vigorously and hoped he hadn't detained her for too long. Helen declared that she had thoroughly enjoyed the afternoon and wondered if he would be free at the same time next week. Brian averred that he certainly would. Helen held out her hand and Brian shook it warmly.

'Great. I'll call you next weekend. If for any reason you can't make it, just give me a call. I'll give you my office number.'

'Oh I'll be around all right. I finish lates on Saturday night then I'm off till Tuesday.'

'See you Sunday then.'

Brian watched her leave, enervated by an incomprehensible yearning. Something he wanted very badly was no longer here but he couldn't pinpoint what it was. It was identifiable only by its absence. He then became aware of the sommelier gazing at him in aghast wonder, as though he'd just pulled a Ford Fiesta from his backside. Brian intuited that the sommelier was wondering how the luminous Helen could submit herself to dine with someone so obviously banal and lacking in couth. Brian had to concede that the waiter had a point, but he treated himself to a triumphant grin. Some pigs do fly after all. He tentatively raised his hand and took out his wallet. The sommelier glided over to him and made a dismissive gesture with his hand.

'You no pie. De lady she pie.'

'Eh? Honestly? Bloody hell. That's all right innit? Thanks pal. Here. Get yourself a pint when you knock off.'

Brian pressed a five pound note into the sommelier's hand and made for the exit. He found a telephone box and directed a taxi to the pub in which he and Helen had met earlier. He entered the pub and sat quietly nursing a half. He was filled to satiety, unusually buoyant, and as excited about another meeting with Helen as a child on Christmas Eve. He arrived home and glissaded through the front door as smoothly as the sommelier earlier that day. He was stunned to learn that it was almost eight o'clock and the travails of work would now need to be considered. His mother was in the living room, barely visible through a pall of cigarette smoke.

'Where the bloody hell have you been till this time?'

'Nowhere, Mam. Just out.'

'I thought you were poorly. You're never too poorly to sup ale though are you? You're worse than your bloody father, you. What're you on tomorrow?'

'I'm on late turn. Where is he?'

'Where the bloody hell d'you think he is?

'I'll see you in the morning.'

'Not unless you're up at the same time as me. Which I bloody doubt.'

'Right.'

Brian retired to bed and slept better than he could remember.

In the proceeding couple of years Brian led two discrete and very different lives. Whilst he continued to live with his parents and work at the factory, Helen introduced him to a milieu of which he had been previous ignorant. In the theatres of Manchattan he was transfixed by flesh and blood people in hushed auditoria who held his attention like armed aggressors.

271

He leaned forward in his seat to catch every utterance, enthralled by the inventiveness of the staging, the atmospherics and the unspoken communion between the watchers and the watched. Unlike in television and film the interlocutors spoke at length and in meaningful, sometimes very moving dialogue. This was in thrilling contrast to a few gnomic mutterings followed by the glimpse of a concealed weapon, as seen on the telly. Theatre seemed more real and more visceral than anything mediated via a screen, despite being merely another exercise in artifice. Theatrical drama seemed to explore what it is to be imperfectly human, whereas in the cinema and on the telly people just did stuff. He was particularly taken by the plays of Tennessee Williams and quickly identified with the damaged and bibulous protagonists who came to an unhappy ending. Blanche Dubois could easily be working behind the counter of his local pie shop.

Helen smiled enigmatically as Brian breathlessly anatomised the latest piece they'd seen. At this early stage of their relationship he had yet to develop the studied insouciance of the cognoscenti, the bearded poseurs who stand at theatre bars snarking about how little they cared for the characters or the subplot. That was to come later. Whilst attending the theatre, Brian also couldn't help noticing the absence of people like him. It seemed that Helen's social caste had ring-fenced this form of entertainment purely for their own pleasure. This struck him as rather unfair. When he subsequently read interviews with theatre people they were always at pains to point out that theatre was for all, not merely for the financially well-endowed. Brian wondered if they'd ever taken a shufti at their paying customers.

As their relationship evolved Helen became ever more insistent that Brian meet with her small circle of friends. As he was instinctively averse to meeting strangers Brian prevaricated until a brittleness in Helen's soft voice inferred that this was a compulsory, rather than invitatory engagement. To his relief he discovered that they were all very much like Helen. They were polite and earnest, but like Helen veined with a hauteur that revealed itself particularly when politics was the conversational meat. Brian bore silent witness to their shrill denunciations of the current Conservative government. They declared it self-evident that such a morally bankrupt executive would be removed from office at the next election and jolly well not before time. Plutocrats and the old boy networks would be quaking in their boots at the prospect of higher taxation to fund failing public services.

Although his understanding of politics could be written on a fag paper, even Brian was aware that the current lot in Downing Street was the party of posh people and Labour was supposed to represent grubby no-accounts like him. He was confused by his companion's opposition to a government he assumed to be promoting her best interests. At this point Brian was unaware that Helen's intimates also occupied lucrative managerial posts in the public and charitable sectors, therefore the loosening of the strings of the public purse would doubtless result in an enhanced income for these strident proponents of a fairer society. Enlightened self-interest was not yet a concept with which Brian was familiar.

After several months of assignations that by mutual consent had elided into dates, the eternally problematic issue of sexual congress inevitably arose. One blustery winter weekend Helen quietly suggested that instead of going out she and Brian should spend the evening at her home. They could telephone out for food and perhaps listen to some music. Brian was initially chary at spending an evening indoors as he'd endured six days of

273

claustration in the factory and chez Paget. Protocol dictated that a break from work was inaugurated by a night spent in the wider world, preferably in a pub. He relented when Helen's faintly menacing timbres inferred that this particular engagement was non-negotiable.

They were now more relaxed in one another's company and had shared kisses burgeoning in passion with each passing week. After some Chinese food and a surfeit of wine it seemed natural to falter towards nakedness on Helen's settee. On television Fritz Lang's *Metropolis* foretold a dire future for humankind as they awkwardly undressed. Neither of the two lovers could boast either much experience or expertise in the sexual arts. Helen had endured a strange relationship with a humanities student at university, lost her virginity with the absent-mindedness that other women lose their purse, and then after an acrimonious split devoted herself to excelling in her studies. Other than the occasional dinner date with male colleagues and the concomitant post-prandial fumble she had remained resolutely celibate. Brian's last relationship was a brief and disastrous liaison with a divorcee who worked behind the bar of a pub close to where he lived. Her outward equanimity when sober belied a terrifying volatility when drunk, which was often. Whilst she was by some measure more sexually adventurous than anyone Brian had previously encountered, when in the grip of a doleur she resembled a Tasmanian devil with toothache. The incident with the breadknife was enough for Brian to call time on this particular *affaire de coeur*.

They quickly expedited the consummation of their relationship. Post-coitus they leaned back against the couch, donned their underclothes, patted one other on the hand and then stared at the television, each hoping that the other would break

274

the taut silence. The silence was so protracted that at one point Brian considered getting up and leaving, believing Helen's uncommunicativeness to be a mute condemnation of his unsatisfactory performance. He was relieved but slightly dismayed when Helen's pealing laughter rebounded from the stippled ceiling. He tentatively enquired what was funny.

'Oh Brian. Your face when it happens to you.'

'When what happens?'

'You know. The release.'

'What about my face?'

'You look like someone having a fatal heart attack whilst staring at a winning lottery ticket. It's like it's all gone right for you then all gone wrong.'

'Do I?'

'Oh yeah.'

As their lovemaking increased in frequency their ease with one another waxed accordingly. Neither were particularly libidinous or harboured any curiosity about the wilder forms of sexual expression, but they were happy enough with their intimacies. Helen was always at pains to observe that sex was a relatively minor detail on a much larger canvas. Brian readily agreed, mainly because he regarded this as a tacit exoneration of his indifferent sexual prowess. During the course of their couplings he also learned that Helen was beset with a hitherto unsuspected prudery. This extended to refusing to entitle his pudenda by its more carnal soubriquets. Not even the relatively innocuous appellation of willie would pass her lips. The pale and unimpressive knar of flesh obtruding from his body was, according to Helen, his delivery system of life. This was later truncated to his delivery system. For his part Brian would stutter with embarrassment if he so much as attempted to utter such

275

words as tit and cunt in a sexual context. Such words were part of the lexicon of the factory and to be used nowhere else.

Brian blenched at Helen's repeated suggestions that they should spend time in the countryside. There was simply too much of the countryside and nothing of any interest in it. Fields and meadows intimidated him and the weather always seemed worse than in the tightly-woven streets of his home town. He had a prefatory glimpse of Helen's pertinacity when one dreary Saturday morning she arrived unbidden outside chez Paget. Brian peered through the living room window, mystified as to how she had acquired his home address. She waved at him and beckoned him outside. Brian studied her heavy waterproof coat and leggings and enquired why she was dressed like a trawlerman. She instructed him to don his warmest coat, thickest jeans, a hat and the most substantial footwear he owned. Where they were going training shoes would not suffice. Brian's face creased into a frown of trepidation. He wasn't going to like this.

They drove for over thirty miles, Brian becoming increasingly sweaty with the number of T-shirts worn underneath Elaine's old rugby jersey. The landscape became dauntingly scarped and white dots of sheep were pixellated against the dark greenery of the hillsides. They pulled into a makeshift car park and Helen motioned Brian to exit the car. He decanted himself onto the tarmac and gazed at mammoth grey cumulus moving at a stately clip across the sky. The air was so sharp it was like sucking an ice cube and he was jittered by the absence of urbanism. This was definitely another country, sparsely populated and not at all hospitable.

Helen stood beside him and smiled beatifically at the soundless rusticity. She then took Brian's arm and marshalled him onto the narrow road. As he was unused to walking on such

276

rough terrain, and confused by the notion of walking without any discernible destination in mind, Brian struggled to find a rhythm and tripped several times. He discovered that walking in lockstep with Helen was the safest method of ambulation. They tramped in silence for about a mile before Helen began to mumble, flittering from one disparate topic to another. After another mile or so she then launched into a sotto voce tirade that grew more splenetic with each step. Brian was alarmed by the tears streaming down Helen's face. This was not an interior monologue, more a series of dust-ups with various unseen adversaries. And very un-Helenlike.

Brian remained silent as she gripped his gloved hand tighter. Although ignorant of the workings of the human mind, it dimly occurred to him that she was self-purgating. Away from the eyes of others she was mentally unzipping, fleeing from reason, ceding self-control and expelling the toxins of self-doubt and despair. This was quietly amazing to him. He had sometimes thought she was an ergonomically designed superperson, someone against whom it would be both pointless and dispiriting to measure one's own worth. Her snotty tearfulness and anger endued her with a fragility Brian had previously considered infeasible. It was a relief to discover that she was just as tormented and confused as the rest of humankind and craved the occasional private catharsis. He also realised that she was privileging him with her tacit invitation to witness her private anguish, and confident in his unconditional discretion. He swore there and then to never disappoint her. Which of course he would. Brian just being Brian for a protracted period would disappoint anyone.

After a while Brian sensed the old Helen returning. He perceived the firmer set of her jaw, the brisker tempo of her step and a renewed awareness of her surroundings. Apropos of nothing, she queried what Brian was reading at the moment. His face, already scarlet with exertion, reddened deeper. He confessed that he wasn't reading anything of any interest. He had revisited some of his sci-fi potboilers when insomniating after night shifts, but that was about it. Helen nodded her head gravely and pointed towards a dale some three miles ahead.'

'We're stopping for lunch in a pub there.'

'Are we? Thank Christ for that.'

'Are you really not reading anything right now?'

'No.'

'This is so wrong. Your brain will turn into tapioca.'

Immediately upon their arrival at the pub Helen advised Brian not to eat too much as he'd develop a stitch in the long walk back to the car. After a pint of warmish real ale, a doorstep cheese and chutney sandwich and a restorative double whisky Brian leaned back against the velveteen bench seat to stare vacantly at the flat-capped rustics standing at the bar. So sated and content was he that he could have easily fallen asleep. Helen's intense and unsettling gaze apprised him that he'd better remain awake.

'I'm uncomfortable at the prospect of being romantically involved with a philistine.'

Brian's eyes narrowed and his voice thickened to a growl.

'I knew there was summat up. Where'd you meet him? Work was it?'

'What in God's name are you talking about?'

'This philistine bloke. Office romance was it?'

'Are you always this stupid or is it something you have to practice?'

'You're bang out of order you are. You should have told me

this before I got dressed up like Captain fucking Birdseye and come to this shithole. I don't why I bother I don't. It always ends up like this. The women I go out with are either bleeding mad or always on the lookout for summat else.'

A faint flicker of a smile played around Helen's lips.

'And where do you think philistines come from Brian?'

'Dunno. Somewhere foreign.'

'Dear God.'

Helen regarded Brian with an expression usually reserved for war-wounded children. In her severest pedagogical tones she then explained the true meaning of the epithet. Philistines need not hail from any given geographical location. They could be from anywhere as wilful ignorance recognises no borders. Such was their ubiquity that a philistine might even be found here in this pub having recently eaten a cheese sandwich. Brian nodded, chastened by Helen's veiled rebuke and rued his sweary irruption. She then grasped his hand and offered him a compact. If Brian read one decent book a week Helen would buy him a bottle of wine of his choosing. She would nominate the book Brian would read and they would discuss it in depth on their regular walks in the countryside. Brian gawped at Helen whilst contemplating this new dispensation. Not only would he have to read worthy but tedious novels bereft of either space vampires or a comprehensible plot, he would also be obliged to yomp around this hellscape of horizontal rain and animal dung on a regular basis. Helen was exacting a heavy price for his devotion. Their amour now involved sending his flabby mind to boot camp.

As the weather improved and Brian's reading grew more omnivorous, by the end of each working of each week he was agog in anticipation of tramping the moors whilst expatiating upon the text he'd absorbed in the previous week. Initially he was

279

uncertain of his opinions and wondered if Helen was condescending to his clumsy attempts at criticism. This was very far from the case. Helen nodded eagerly at his observations and averred that his aperçus were forcing her to re-evaluate books with which she thought herself well acquainted. Brian's self-esteem rose exponentially in response to Helen's laudations. Reading serious books and being taken seriously by a serious person was something he could definitely get used to, although on certain issues they were not completely consonant.

During the course of their animated dialogues he learned of Helen's rose-tinted view of the working classes. She tended to generalise "the workers" as an amorphous mass of voiceless peons, the pawns of a rapacious boss class intent upon debasing them in the name of profit. Whilst admiring her principled stance against the victimisation of the downtrodden, he couldn't help wondering if Helen had any real understanding of those she wished to deliver from servitude. All that everyone that he worked with wanted was simply more. More of everything. More money, more time off, more alcohol, more drugs, more takeaways, more telly and more sex. The only things they wanted less of was weekend overtime and unplanned pregnancies. He doubted that any of these aspirations would feature in a manifesto for social change propounded by Helen and her ilk. In the factory he was surrounded by a motley of moaners, time-servers and crotch-scratchers. Amoral creatures, free of aspiration and social conscience. People like himself in other words. A visit to Goldfinger's flat might well conduce a revisal of Helen's lionisation of the proletariat. She would probably faint dead away at the size and preponderance of delivery systems on show and probably request an appointment with a psychiatrist. He figured that he might inculcate Helen with some unedifying truths in exchange for her informal literary and political tutelage. After all, he was in pole position to issue despatches from the front, whereas the Helens of this world remained in the maproom.

Subsequent their sundering, Brian had grudgingly conceded that their weekend rambles had been the some of the most exhilarating times of his life. From the outset he had understood and accepted the essential imbalance in their relationship. He had been her project, her lump of clay and she his sculptress. Week after week she had patiently chipped away at those bits of him she had found either superfluous or repellent, modelling him into someone his previous self wouldn't have recognised and probably disdained. In the months immediately following their scission he missed her polymathic mind and unquenchable belief in the goodness of people. Helen possessed a preternatural ability to make even the most doltish feel they actually mattered; even if in the long run they didn't.

Brian's first experience of a holiday abroad with Helen proved transformative. She had passed numerous holidays in Andalucia and was resolved to acquaint Brian with a province and culture very close to her heart. A scorched, dusty pueblo with narrow thoroughfares some fifty minutes from Malaga was Brian's first experience of Spaniards who didn't speak English or offer an all-day breakfast. Overwhelmed by the inexplicable foreignness of it all he was reliant upon Helen's linguistic skills and understanding of Spanish social mores to assimilate the dark, sanguinary heart of Spain. He was daily buffeted by a series of culture shocks and abashed by his ignorance of a country still recovering from civil war and an ignoble dictatorship. Until Helen had imparted a potted history of the nation and recommended he read Orwell's *Catalonia* chronicles, he hadn't even heard of General Franco.

Each day at a table outside his favourite watering hole he studied the old men who daily convened under the shade of a solitary tree. They sat on an ancient bench and smoked, exchanged a few mutterings and then simply stared into space as the afternoon heat squeezed the breath from those foolish enough to be awake. They seemed steeped in a melancholy born of horror. Brian presumed that they were the children of war, men who had seen the worst of life much too young. Their silent watchfulness and austere demeanour moved him profoundly. These gnarled oldsters entered local restaurants with their families as though leading a garrison. All of them were straight-backed, elegantly dressed in blazers and slacks and perfectly groomed. Whilst at table their few basso profundo utterances were as the hoots of an alpha male calling his troupe to order. When the patriarch spoke, his family fell into respectful silence.

Brian's curiosity was piqued. It seemed that the Spanish found their locus of stability in the pre-eminence of a male elder, a patriarchal construct his stridently feminist partner found oppressive. Having witnessed the dehumanising effects of tyrannous men upon their families, Brian could understand Helen's repudiation of the classical family model; but in this society it seemed to work. Perhaps it was a cultural thing, part of the national psyche and difficult for modernist tropes to supplant. Brian found these vignettes of Spanish family life charming. In a world growing progressively loopier as it gyred towards the end of another century here was the perfect confluence of familial harmony and the observance of an established order. It was plain that the Spanish understood the value of rules.

One evening Helen insisted that they attend an evening of flamenco. Brian was initially chary, having woozily witnessed a performance in Benidorm some years previously. It seemed to

282

consist of a lot of clapping and flouncy dresses by which Brian was decidedly unmoved, but he did as he was told and went along anyway. Helen's expansive knowledge of the nation's culture offered meaningful insight into the true nature of the flamenco form. He learned that Andalucia had been colonised by Arabs who had introduced new forms of learning, architecture and religion into southern Europe. Flamenco was a melange of musical styles incorporating European, Romany and Arabic influences. When Helen read him translations of the poetry of Lorca he immediately made a connection between flamenco and early American blues. The similarities in subject matter and content were immediately apparent. Flamenco chronicled suffering and existential despair, thus suiting Brian's penchant for miserabilism perfectly. Polyrhythms were tapped out by the dancers underpinned by cryptic gestures and flourishes understood only by the cognoscenti. Astonishingly dextrous guitar playing propelled the dancers towards the transcendence of duende. Brian quickly divined that far from being perma-cheerful attendants of thirsty holidaymakers, the Spanish were steeped in blood and cafard. Even their places of worship depicted scenes of crucifictal agony difficult to look at for more than a moment. In that first visit to Andalucia, the fates had never seemed unkinder. If life had taken a different turn he might have been a member of a race of pessimists who also produced very good wine and played impossibly brilliant guitar. Instead he was condemned to live and work in Least, endure appalling weather, stomach his mother's cooking and his father's scorn.

In the late summer of 1996 Helen had decided that it was time that Brian finally meet her family. Her parents resided in an affluent suburb of Manchattan, having purchased the house when it was still affordable to young academics with a child to raise. It was now worth several millions. Helen's father, Richard, was as impressive and intimidating as a classical monument. Impeccably dressed, tall and with extravagant salt and pepper hair, he greeted them in florid but chillingly precise language. He slobbered a kiss upon his daughter's forehead and extended a large sculpted hand for Brian to shake. When Richard trained his fierce eyes upon him, Brian he felt as though he was being X-rayed for contraband. He could easily imagine Richard as a fifties film star playing the role of a stern English boffin determined to create an antidote to the moral squalor of the nation's youth. Grasping Brian's outstretched hand in both of hers, Helen's mother was equally exact in her utterances but seemed warmer and less serious. Although broad of hip, heavy of breast and wide in the thigh, it was obvious that she had been a great beauty in her day; and a cook par excellence if the smells drifting in from the kitchen were any yardstick.

For what would not be the first time that afternoon, Brian wondered why everyone in this family seemed to be good at everything and what the bloody hell he was doing in such august company. He also noted that Helen became almost kittenish in the presence of her impressive male parent, her arm snaking around his slim waist as they tramped through the lobby and into the corpus of the three-storey house. His sister, Elaine, was never so complaisant in her father's company. She referred to Derek as "Smellyarse" and disparaged Jean with the soubriquet "Fag Ash Lil". Brian reflected that families are as discrete in their composition as thumbprints. The only feature common to all family units were familial tensions, but he couldn't imagine even a whisper of discord in this particular menage. Helen's clan was evidently above such vulgarities as having a stand-up barney behind closed doors.

284

Richard led the couple into his study and immediately offered them both a port. Frantically grasping at a conversational touchstone Brian immediately expressed his appreciation of the hi-fi that nestled on a shelf amongst numberless books. He caught the faint glimmer of a smile on Richard's face and the two men were quickly immersed in a discussion concerning the qualities of different amplification, speakers and turntables. Brian disclosed that he had recently bought a top-of-the-range CD player but the lower bass frequencies in compact discs suffered by comparison to vinyl recordings. Richard nodded vigorously and fished out a long player containing Pablo Casal's reading of a Bach prelude. Although unfamiliar with both the piece and the cellist Brian gave a thumbs up to Richard, who acknowledged Brian's approbation with a slight, graceful nod. When Brian enquired who had written the music and who was on bass, Richard eyes widened. He then shuffled to the French window to stare into the afternoon sun and recover his equilibrium.

Dinner was a largely convivial affair, but Brian's nervousness led to his overindulgence in the array of wines made available by his hosts. Inevitably he committed a few social typos that were doubtless stored somewhere in Richard's formidable brain. When he reluctantly divulged that he worked in a factory, Richard became immediately animated and pressed Brian to describe his occupation, the working conditions, trades union representation and examples of victimisation leading to industrial unrest. Brian simply shrugged and muttered that no one was much bothered about that sort of thing. They'd taken a vote and opted for an open shop, meaning that union membership was no longer mandatory. The thing his workmates mostly rowed about was sport. Sometimes fighting would break out in the locker room if the weekend's results had proved disappointing.

Richard was visibly horrified, but enjoined Brian to describe his average working day. In a halting voice Brian outlined a typical, tedious eight or twelve hours in the factory. Richard was rapt and beat the dinner table with his knuckles at surprising interludes. Helen gazed at Brian with the proprietorial pride of an owner of an unusually intelligent primate whilst her mother gazed silently at the contents of her plate. Brian intuited that she was on his side here, probably aware that her husband could be a little overbearing when loosed upon the unwary. People who have been married for thirty-odd years tend to know a bit about each other's foibles.

In the early evening Brian shook hands with his hosts and made his way to the car. Helen lingered to bid a more fulsome farewell to her parents before climbing into the driver's seat. She gave Brian a passionate kiss and playfully squeezed his crotch.

'Ooh. What have I done to deserve that?'

'What a marvellous afternoon. They'd like to do it again in a couple of weeks, but next time go out somewhere.'

'Do they? Right. I thought I'd blotted my copybook a bit. It went okay then did it?'

'Oh yeah, it was fine. When do I meet your parents?'

'Eh? What for?'

'Brian, we've been together for ages now. You have told them about me haven't you?'

'Well. They know I'm seeing someone but that's as far as it goes. They've never even asked me your name.'

'Really? Why not?'

'I dunno. It's just the way they are.'

'Well I'm going to meet them. It's the only correct thing to do.'

'Oh Jesus…'

A few weeks later Helen drew up outside chez Paget and rapped on the front door. Brian invited her in and awkwardly vouchsafed her a peck on the cheek. It was a typical Paget family weekend afternoon. Derek was at the club and Jean was in her usual chair, smoking and chuntering imprecations at black people on the television. Brian ushered Helen into the living room. She squinted through the haze of cigarette smoke and winced at the fug hanging in the air.

'Mam? This is Helen. My friend.'

Jean sighed, craned her neck to stare suspiciously at Helen and then returned her gaze to the television. A crepitant croak issued from Jean's throat.

'Does she want a cup of tea?'

Mortified by his mother's rudeness, Brian quietly enquired if Helen required a cup of tea or would prefer to disappear to the pub. Helen defiantly shook her head and averred her desire for a quick coffee. Brian closed his eyes in resignation and retired to the kitchen. Whilst preparing the beverages he could hear Helen's desperate attempts to engage his mother in conversation. Jean remained as silent as a porcelain urinal and Brian envisioned her not even removing her eyes from the telly. Of all of the mistakes he had made during his relationship with Helen, this was surely the most egregious. He returned to the living room, gave Helen her coffee and then silently nodded his head in the direction of the front door. Helen deposited her mug on an armchair and departed for the car.

'I'll be off then Mam.'

'Have you got your key?'

'Yeah.'

'Well you think on.'

'How d'you mean?'

287

'You don't want to be knocking about with her too long.'

'Eh?'

'I've seen her type before.'

'Where? In the canteen at the bus station? I don't think you have.'

'Shut it and listen a minute. She'll be off as soon as there's summat better round the corner. She'll be like shit off a shovel and you won't see it coming, you. Dozy sod that y'are.'

'How do YOU know we're going to split up? Give over Mam.'

'Never you mind. I'm not daft. Not as daft as you are any road.'

'Right…'

They drove away from chez Paget in silence. Brian expected Helen to voice her justifiable anger at Jean's boorishness but instead she was silent and abstracted, her expression one of pained confusion. As he drove, Brian ruminated upon the meaning of Helen's encounter with his mother. Whilst Helen's silent desolation stirred his sympathies, Brian couldn't help but consider this another salutary lesson in the essential immiscibility of differing social castes. He could only give thanks to providence that his father wasn't at home as disaster would have immediately devolved to catastrophe. He was resolved to ensuring that Helen never visited the Paget family seat again.

Brian woke up one morning and was surprised to find himself co-habiting with Helen. This turn of events was neither pondered upon nor discussed by either of them. It had occurred by a process of small gradations. He began to stay over with greater frequency and inevitably required several changes of clothing. Helen helpfully emptied a couple of drawers and made

288

room for his shirts and coats in a wardrobe. After a period of several months, he became exasperated by Helen's rather primitive sound system and installed his superior hi-fi in the living room. Brian had also noted that she possessed only classical stuff by way of a record collection, therefore, it was only logical to introduce his own. She was initially chary of some of Brian's more esoteric listening choices but found herself warming slightly to Ornette Coleman and Steve Reich, or at least the bits between the mayhem that made any sense. Helen's mind was a machine constructed from the raw material of rationality. To her ears many of Brian's records were the sonic equivalent of an epileptic seizure. She invested in a pair of expensive headphones and presented them to Brian, who was beside himself with gratitude. For her part Helen was relieved that the house no longer sounded as though it was collapsing after a gas explosion.

Helen's continued membership of the local operatic society had finally born fruit. In possibly the first example of gender-blind casting she had been awarded the role of Curly McClain in a production of *Oklahoma*! This challenging role demanded a great deal from even competent singers. Helen's enthusiasm and an American accent borrowed from Foghorn Leghorn were poor compensations for her incomprehension of tempo, phrasing and pitch. She insisted that Brian accompany her on guitar as she practiced her repertoire. Brian complied, although it was far from his idea of fun. His sensibilities suffered multiple assaults as she nightly murdered selections from the Rodgers and Hammerstein catalogue penned for a more dulcet, and indeed male, vocalist. Her rendition of 'Oh What Beautiful Morning', complete with gestures across the living room towards a bright golden haze on the meadow would compel any listener back to bed until at least early afternoon.

The couple espoused a mutually satisfying domesticity. Brian was happy to wash dishes, put the hoover around and operate the washing machine. He was, however, prohibited from ironing, particularly when he'd been imbibing strong waters. Helen was an expert vegetarian cook and enjoyed the therapeutic mindlessness of concocting flavoursome dishes she'd found in one of her many cookbooks. For Helen, cooking was a creative diversion whereas for Brian it was a tedious and potentially life-threatening activity. He was to meal preparation as the average pigeon is to environmental hygiene. Having developed a palate for vegetarian food but militantly opposed to preparing it, Brian would sprawl on the settee with a whisky to hand and idly pick a few chords on the guitar whilst Helen performed feats of culinary alchemy.

On occasions they took an early dinner at one of several gastropubs in the area, particularly when Helen came home fissured by emotional distress. Brian was the very acme of solicitude as Helen inveighed against the pettifogging of junior colleagues, the flintiness of local authorities and the brutishness of law enforcement agencies. Although most of Helen's fulminations were indigestible, Brian was happy to lend an ear until there was a break in the clouds. As Helen's discomposure abated Brian's equanimity increased, although his amiability was largely due to the red wine he'd imbibed. After their meal the couple would linger to have a crack at the weekly pub quiz and the opportunity to win some raw meat. To the resourceful, every crisis presents an opportunity.

As Helen's home was a bequest from her parents, the couple was unburdened by a mortgage. Brian coughed up a hundred and twenty quid from his pay packet each week as his contribution to the meeting of bills, food and sundry expenses, a sum that Helen was more than happy with. As exacting in her approach to household management as she was to her profession, Helen deposited unexpended monies in the bank that were ring-fenced to purchase holidays abroad. Brian also contributed some extra income earned from the overtime he occasionally but reluctantly worked. To his surprise he found himself in all manner of exotic locations and at unusual times of the year. The couple bade farewell to 1996 in one of the most storied and alarmingly expensive jazz clubs in New York.

Helen continued to introduce Brian to a range of new experiences his previous self would have baulked at. He voraciously absorbed the *New Statesman*, the *Guardian* and even dallied with the *LRB*. Helen regarded him with pedagogical pride as he bearded her to explain the point of articles he'd ploughed through. The discussions over their evening meals became ever more animated, particularly as Brian's views increasingly dovetailed with Helen's own. Although unconscious of his metamorphosis, Brian had been transfigured into a member of the comfortable, complacent left-leaning middle classes. He lolled in a caul of bourgeois contentment, sharing the home of a highly intelligent woman and surrounded by books, music, unusual art prints and a well-stocked wine rack. He spent weekends in wine bars in which cocktail jazz dripped from the in-house sound system, ate in Manchattan bistros, slept through the occasional Shakespeare production and continued to read rapaciously. His personal life could have hardly been more rewarding. His working life was another matter.

Brian was gnawed by an indefinable dissatisfaction. He was daily becoming more desolated by the prospect of spending another twenty years in the factory, but the challenge of finding a more rewarding alternative seemed insuperable. The factory had sustained him through two damaging recessions and would doubtless be able to survive the next. His job might be tedious but provided a bulwark against an increasingly capricious labour market. However, he was also conscious of the glaring disparity in professional status between he and his partner. Whilst not at the very pinnacle of her profession, Brian could envisage a future in which Helen was the doyenne of her field and possibly in the lower echelons of government. Brian's aggregate vocational attainment was passing his fork lift truck test. She was certain to weary of his persistent underachievement at some point. Paralysed by his own inertia, he felt helpless to do anything other than wait until everything unravelled. He was between a rock and hard place; a very unappealing location.

The arrival of 1997 did nothing to lift the bleak mood of the factory floor. The demeanour of many of Brian's workmates had darkened following their entanglement with the Child Support Agency. There had been a huge and largely inexplicable uptick in divorce among men of his age, although all-day drinking and the arrival of satellite television may have been contributory factors. Following the creation of the CSA, with its powers to rescind legally binding divorce settlements, his bewildered colleagues shared horror stories of the exorbitant and, in all likelihood, fallacious back payments demanded by the agency. Brian was particularly moved by the plight of Vimto, a softly-spoken man of thirty-eight with a birthmark on his forehead resembling a wine-red splash that made him an unmissable target for the vinegar tongued.

One morning Brian had wandered into the locker room to discover Vimto weeping softly, his filthy digits clawing at his face. Brian wondered whether to enquire what was the matter or to leave him languishing in misery. He hovered uncertainly until

Vimto waved him to a bench and offered him a cigarette. He needed to ventilate, and, although generally regarded as a bit of a dickhead, Brian was not someone to betray a confidence or exult in the misery of a workmate.

The brickbats Vimto had endured since childhood had contributed to the development of a taciturn and defensive disposition. He was so inured to the jibes concerning his appearance from his parents, schoolmates, schoolmasters and girls he worshipped from afar that he rarely spoke unless spoken to first. He was, however, an astonishing footballer. He was fast and gifted with the evasive reflexes of a housefly. His left foot was so gorgeous it was an object of lust among the scouts of elite clubs. Although he signed for one of the giants of English football his debilitating shyness made him a poor fit for the alpha male redoubt of the professional game. He practically cowered when yelled at by puce-faced coaches. The dressing room became a torture chamber as his timid performances were viciously razzed by teammates. Utterly desolated by failure, he returned home and resumed playing for the amateur club at which he had so often dazzled.

Without an apprenticeship or other bona fides he drifted from job to job until finally alighting at the factory. His commitment to playing for the works team sealed the guarantee of a position that would leave him free for Sunday fixtures. The occasional emolument slipped into his palm by the managing director for leading the team to success more than compensated for the loss of overtime. He also fell deeply in love with the vivacious and garrulous Sheena. They were a good fit as Sheena's bubbly extroversion countervailed Vimto's natural reticence. By the time he was twenty-five he was married with two daughters and living in a modest semi purchased with the assistance of a

293

golden goodbye from his former professional club. It seemed that everything was going to turn out all right after all, but a hand injury sustained in the course of a night shift would change all that.

A meaty gash resulted in Vimto being despatched to hospital with an injunction to go home immediately after the wound had been treated. At one o'clock in the morning he arrived home to find Sheena and a teammate from the works football team rutting enthusiastically in front of the three-bar gas fire in the lounge. His teammate displayed not a scintilla of remorse, merely retrieving his clothes and quickly dressing before giving Vimto a parting wink. Far from being mortified at being caught in flagrante delicto, Sheena excoriated her husband for his intrusion. She demanded to know what the bloody hell he was playing at coming home in the middle of the bloody night. He could have woken the bloody kids up, so just for that he could bed down on the settee. Vimto meekly did as instructed and wept until the children awoke.

When the children had departed for school Vimto attended his local surgery to tearfully dilate upon this emotionally crippling turn of events. The doctor immediately issued a sick note, thus allowing Vimto to attend to his affairs. By that evening he was back living with his parents and billeted in their cramped, dingy box room. They were not at all pleased with this change in their domestic arrangements and made this plain to their traumatised son. He had failed firstly as footballer and now as a husband. They were tired of his shortcomings and his obstinate refusal to make a success of his life. His father made it transparently clear that Vimto's return would be a purely temporary arrangement, so he'd better start looking for somewhere to live as soon as possible. Vimto was homeless, friendless and denounced for his inadequacies by his odious parents. His already fragile mental well-being curdled and a debilitating depression was exacerbated by his refusal to take time off to repair his psychic wounds. His stoicism was so damagingly corrosive that he made an attempt upon his own life. Typically, he took pains to ensure that his tilt at self-destruction was enacted away from his aspersive parents. He didn't want to cause any fuss.

Unfamiliar with the volume of analgesics and alcohol required to kill himself, he drank three pints of lager, swallowed four aspirin and a couple of antidepressants. He then threw himself from a lock gate into the Manchester Ship Canal. His natural athleticism foiled his self-extinction. As soon as he plunged into the freezing, feculent water he knew that he was instinctually unable to submerge himself long enough to fill his lungs with fluid and filth. He swam a couple of breadths of the canal and emerged shivering, stinking of effluvia and daunted by the prospect of the walk home. Upon his arrival he spluttered an apology to his parents that he'd accidentally slipped off the towpath whilst taking a walk. They didn't deign to reply. He couldn't even manage something as simple as suicide without buggering it up.

Whilst continuing to live with his parents Vimto began to reassemble the tatters of his life. He renounced football forever, preferring the uncompetitive pursuits of distance running and fishing. He struck up a relationship with an older woman who was kindlier than anyone he'd ever encountered. He was also a model absent father, having negotiated parental access every other weekend and an annual caravan holiday in Wales with his daughters. Vimto thought he was doing okay until the CSA demanded forty-four thousand pounds on pain of an attachment of earnings order. Brian blew out his cheeks in astonishment. With the exception of Helen, he didn't know anyone who could even count to forty-four thousand, never mind put their hands on such a sum at short notice.

'I'm fucked, Brian. My car's not worth a carrot, I haven't got a house and I've got fifteen hundred nicker in the bank. I've never missed a single payment of my maintenance. Not one. You can ask the ex-missus that. Even she said it's not fair what they've done. I wouldn't mind but she's been married for the last four years. He's working and she's working now.'

'Surely the bastards take that into account?'

'They say it doesn't matter a fuck. The money's for the kids, not for her.'

'Jesus. Are you fuckin' royalty or summat? Whose kids from round here need forty-four fuckin' grand?'

'They don't need it as much as I do. They'll do to me what they did to The Oaf.'

'What?'

'They just took it out of his wages. No names, no pack-drill. I won't have enough money left to pay my board to my mam and dad. Oaf got left with twenty quid a week. Mind you. He's got more kids than me, the dirty bastard.'

'You seen anything of him since he left?'

'Nah. Someone said he got a job as a bouncer but it fell through. You know what he's like. Prob'ly fell in with the wrong crowd like he normally does. I don't know what I'm going to say to Diane. I'm scared she'll bin me off if I can't pay my way. I'm not a deadleg, Brian, you know that. But if you're borassic all the time why would she bother carrying on with me?'

'That's a bit premature, Vimto. Apart from anything else she's not like Sheena is she?'

'I'm fucked if I know. You don't know what anyone's like until they come up against summat like this do you?'

'S'pose not.'

When Vimto was absent from work for four days, Brian feared the worst and decided to visit his parents' home. Vimto's appalling father opened the door to curtly report that Vimto had departed two mornings ago without leaving a forwarding address. He and his missus didn't know or care of his current whereabouts. If he hadn't been into the factory, then he'd either left town or snuffed it. They weren't really bothered which. Neither Brian nor anyone else ever heard from Vimto again. He doubted that Vimto's experience as a missing person had been a happy one as he had a certain genius for victimhood. As with football, it was something he'd never really had to work at.

Vimto's desperation had haunted Brian. He was terrified of a future in which he too was psychologically broken and quarry for predatory creditors. He was also finding the company of his workmates stultifying. He was becoming progressively more irritated by their limited horizons, their dark-age sexism, their contempt for the unfamiliar and general parochialism. It was like working with a troop of baboons but less emotionally rewarding. But, hard on the heels of the general election Labour landslide in May, he was presented with an opportunity for salvation. The company had pinned up notices requesting the names of those interested in voluntary redundancy.

Whilst invigorated by the prospect of making a new start, Brian was nevertheless gripped by his usual anguish. He simply wasn't sure of his ability to make a success of life outside the factory or whether he possessed the mental strength to embrace the concomitant upheaval. If life was a game of blackjack then Brian was definitely someone to stay his hand at sixteen. If he decided to leave then failure was unthinkable as there was no returning to the womb of the factory. He needed to confer with Helen to discuss the implications of this exciting new possibility, but it transpired that he needn't have bothered. Helen was already ahead of him and her insouciance was chilling.

'Great. What is it, a year's salary? Take it. You'll never see that much money again in a very long time.'

'Yeah, but it won't last forever. What am I supposed to do for a job?'

'That's no problem. I've already spoken to a few contacts. We'll get you police checked and then you can start working in care homes and hospitals.'

'Eh? What? Nursing and that?'

'You're not qualified to be a nurse but you could be a nursing assistant or a care assistant. Get some on the job training, get familiar with the report writing and you're away.'

'What? Wiping arses? Changing old blokes' nappies? Are you tapped? I get embarrassed shaking hands with people, never mind taking them to the bog and giving them a bath.'

'You can get used to anything if you do it long enough, Brian. By the way. You're also enrolled on an access course in September.'

'Am I? And what's that when it's at home?'

'It's a foundation course in social work. Get through that and you're eligible for taking your degree. Before you know it you'll be queuing up for your cap and gown.'

'A what? Oh no. No, no, no. You're not on. I haven't tried writing an essay in twenty years and I was crap at it then, never mind now. I haven't got a cat in hell's chance. Let some other bastard take redundancy. I'm stopping where I am.'

'Listen to me, Brian. You're far from stupid, but you're in

grave danger of being one of those people capable of doing something worthwhile but end up doing nothing. And don't think that this is the end of the redundancies. This is just the start. All you'll be doing is just waiting for the axe to fall again. And when it does? You'll have no qualifications, no prospects and you'll be hitting forty. I find uselessness a very unattractive quality in a man, don't you?'

Brian stared at her in stupefaction. It seemed that she had been waiting for this opportunity and all he had to do was exactly as instructed. The thinking had already been done for him.

'Yeah but… what about all the bookwork? I don't think I'm up to it. I'm too old for it.'

'I'll give you a hand. While you were on night shift last week I wrote an essay for an A level history student. Simplicity itself. It's just a matter of reading the question and reading the set texts.'

'Well that's easy for you to say innit?'

'Of course it is. Why else would I say it?'

Brian's application for redundancy was accepted without fanfare. He was circumspect about disclosing his decision, but inevitably his father learned the news from the work's convenor. Derek was incandescent and inveighed against Brian for giving up a secure job and a works pension. It would serve him bloody right if he ended up on the bones of his dozy arse. Hobart, a bestubbled spectre who always seemed just a bad cough away from an early death, was more charitably disposed. Brian was brushing steel shavings from around a bank of lathes when Hobart mooched over, hands in pockets and puffing on a roll-up fag that seemed to have been surgically implanted into his face.

'Tek no notice of these dozy fuckers, Brian. You're doin' the right thing, pal. Get out of this shithole while you can. There's nothing down for any fucker in here now. It'll be shut in three

299

years this place.'

'Cheers Hobart. It's a bit of a gamble but you only pass this way once don't you? I might as well have a crack at it.'

'And listen to me when I'm talkin'. Your dad says you're courting strong. Is that right?'

'Did he tell you that? I didn't think he was that bothered to be honest.'

'Do yourself a favour. Get her kicked into touch and be quick about it.'

'Eh? Why?'

Hobart raised himself to his full height. Brian realised only then that Hobart had been slouching all of his adult life.

'Oh, you're all lovey-dovey right now, Brian. Right now you can't do no wrong. But I'm telling you now kidder. All that'll all stop. After a while being married is just like a job. And you've got a job. Who wants two fuckin' jobs? I fuckin' don't. And having the doings? That sex palaver? Jesus Christ. I'd rather have a good shit these days. You'll get fed up of it before she does.'

'Give over, Hobart. You and your missus have been together for years.'

'I know. And look at me, Brian. Just fuckin' look at me. She won't even make my butties up for work now. It's no life this, y'know. I've got three daughters at home. One of 'em's never off the fuckin' toilet, another one's always taking money off me, another one's pregnant and they all fuckin' hate me. This'll be you in a few years if you're not careful, I'm not kidding you. The only thing I look forward to now is taking our bastard dog on the park. He likes having a shit on the football pitch of a morning. He bit me on the bastard arm the other day, the cheeky bastard.'

No one on the shop floor thought to organise a farewell pub crawl for Brian. He departed the factory after an uneventful night shift and was alone when he threw his boots and hard hat into his locker for the last time. The sun cheered him as he drove through the deserted Saturday morning streets. Helen was already up when he walked through the front door. She presented him with a large glass of wine and suggested they go for lunch later. He smiled sleepily, sat in the living room and napped until nine o'clock. He awoke refreshed but puzzled by the flatness of his mood. He'd anticipated an intoxicating rush of elation resulting from his disenthrallment, but instead there was only a vacuum in the region of his mind once occupied by the factory. He had forgotten two decades of working life in an instant.

It was some six weeks before his police check arrived but Helen had ensured that Brian's free time was far from leisurely. She had contacted a friend in the local college and acquired the reading list for his foundation course along with some ancillary texts, sermonising that preparation was all if he was to stay ahead of the game. These dry theoretical tomes seemed to have been penned by people who held humankind in great esteem but harboured only loathing for their readership. It took a Herculean effort of will for Brian to devote any attention to the unctuous prose and ugly taxonomy. Words such as "paradigmatic" and "prosocial" held neither meaning nor resonance for him, sounding little more than the gibberings of a cocaine fiend. Reading just a single paragraph of a much-lauded academic was like being chloroformed, therefore by lunchtime his thoughts were already straying towards the pub. He was dissuaded from obeying his natural instincts by the dread prospect of Helen's nightly tutorials. Agonising interludes in which she pressed Brian to dilate upon the contents of these dreary screeds. He had however gleaned enough to understand that government-funded social care was a relatively recent development and that the country was a suppurating mess. Britain was paralysed by drug abuse, alcoholism, paedophilia, domestic violence, racism, homophobia, disablism, mental disorder and homelessness. If just some of the depravities documented in the pages of his reading matter were extant then it wasn't safe to go outside. Unnameable horrors of which he was hitherto unaware were probably being enacted within a stone's throw of his own home. He now realised that he was living in a terminally decadent society and his observational skills required much work.

His maiden post was as a care assistant in a network of facilities dotted around his home town. Brian learned that in the rush to decant patients of institutions into the community, the government had been uncharacteristically prodigal. Care providers were granted almost limitless cash to purchase handsome properties in British towns and cities. Monies to furnish the properties were also freely disbursed, meaning that the care homes in which very modestly paid care assistants plied their trade were palatial when compared to their own abodes. Brian was assigned to a huge bungalow accommodating one male and three female residents. He tentatively settled in and learned his craft from the overwhelmingly female staff. He was schooled in continence care, bathing, the operation of hoists and techniques to avoid back strains when manually transferring residents from bed to bath to wheelchair.

The shifts were long, arduous, smelly and a test of Brian's reserves of stamina. At the end of each deathless working day he would drive home slowly as his vision was impaired by fatigue. During the course of any given shift he might be bemerded, strafed by vomit, punched in the face by the male resident or attacked by the feral cat residing in the garden. This vile creature deposited the heads of dead mice on the back lawn as gifts for his hosts and clearly enjoyed recreational massacre. Brian loathed domestic animals of any stamp but reserved a special odium for this sway-backed, evil-eyed brute. He wondered whether to borrow an airgun to summarily dispatch the creature, but decided against this as some of the staff had taken an unfathomable shine to the muscular bruiser. One younger staff member regularly left meat scraps on the lawn and sometimes invited the beast into the house as a therapeutic diversion for the residents; but not everyone shared her affections for the animal. Big June, a meaty-armed mother of five who worked regular night shifts shared Brian's antipathy towards the cat. It reminded her of her much-loathed former husband and she had tired of the creature's malignity. Late one evening during handover she whispered to Brian that he should come in half an hour earlier in the morning. When all the residents were deeply asleep, she set to work with a handful of sodium valporate and a mallet. Brian was happy to throw a black bin liner containing a small, stiff cadaver into the canal before the arrival of the other staff members.

He quickly learned that this profession was the dominion of women, a gynocracy in which men were either of no account or at the very top of the chain of command. He was one of only five male members of staff in a complement of eighty. Following the payment of his first salary he also realised that the people entrusted with the care of the elderly, the mentally disordered and the learning disabled were paid less pro rata than the average barmaid. This egregious disparity was compounded by the almost insuperable obstacles to professional development. Undertaking training as a nurse or a social care worker was nigh impossible for mothers with children, despite their obvious aptitude and the college fees loan system inaugurated by the new government. In households where one or both breadwinners were

303

poorly paid, every penny counted. Unless a Gordian knot was cut, care assistants were embayed in a cul-de-sac of continence pads, sick bags, dirty linen, rectally administered diazepam and sharps boxes. Physical strength, mental fortitude, household management skills and an absence of squeamishness were essential prerequisites for this most demanding of occupations. Brian's reservoir of attributes germane to the performance of his duties was far from bottomless. He realised early on that he could never reconcile himself with the rigours of continence care and he inwardly quailed at the sight of moribund flesh.

There were compensations, however. As he was younger than many of his female colleagues he was treated with a curious mix of the maternal and the flirtatious, although the possibility of indulging in any hanky-panky was out of the question. Brian was all too aware of his physical demerits and correctly concluded that he was merely a harmless diversion from the quotidian drudgery, a comic relief for these hardy, resourceful women. They in turn reciprocated by keeping a tender eye him and constantly plying him with tea and the cakes they'd baked in their spare time.

The collegial environment of the workplace was a refreshing change from the aggression and machismo of the factory. There was little factionalism, although it was natural that certain women gravitated towards others with whom to discuss their considerable personal problems. Brian was happy to evanesce when he heard the sussurus of whispering in the kitchen. It signalled that a few had convened to discuss a singularly female problem to which Brian should not be privy. As he'd have been useless at providing any practical advice in any case, he kept one eye on the residents and the other on a dreadful afternoon soap opera he found unaccountably compelling. When his colleagues

304

emerged from the kitchen he would gauge their expressions and tailor his approaches to them accordingly. A woman who has been weeping is rarely in the mood for levity. Brian would reflect upon the heaviness of the burdens his colleagues bore with such stoicism and humour. He sometimes wondered how they managed to stay upright. Whatever stuff they were made of, it was definitely the right stuff.

As the nights began to draw in Brian became increasingly agitated by the prospect of undertaking his foundation course. He had approached his manager to declare his intention to attend the course and requested a change of shift pattern to support his foray into further education. He had secretly hoped that his company would deny his request, but Helen had called his bluff by contacting a company director. He immediately and very inconveniently avowed his unswerving support to Brian in his goal of self-actualisation. Brian fervently hoped that the bastard's fillings dropped out as deserts for condemning him to the classroom for the next nine months.

Helen presented him with a rucksack to ensure that he looked the part when entering the college. She adjusted the straps to ensure that the rucksack hung rakishly from one shoulder and declared that he looked every inch the mature student. Brian muttered that he felt like someone attending a funeral dressed as a very pissed-off clown. Before leaving the house for his first lecture he ensured he was equipped with a large flask of coffee and the day's newspaper. Having his own beverage meant that he could avoid people in the canteen and hide behind his newspaper to deter the over friendly. He wondered if the college provided a course in antisocial work. If it did, he would definitely request a transfer.

To avoid his anxiety transmuting into vomitous panic, Brian

took pains to arrive early. He stalked the draughty corridors of the fifth floor until slumping behind a desk at the very back of the deserted lecture room. Other students drifted in, their uncertainty evinced by friendly simpers in his direction. Brian grimaced his acknowledgement before returning to his newspaper. When the room was half full the lecturer bustled in and smiled benevolently upon the new intake. She insisted that they refer her to her by her first name, but if they didn't mind she would offer some ground rules. Regular attendance to class was mandatory, punctuality was a good habit to get into, discriminatory language would not be tolerated and views inconsistent with social work values might lead to expulsion from the course.

The other students nodded eagerly whilst Brian inwardly quaked. Their familiarity with what constituted social work values inferred that they had prepared for this ordeal a lot more than he had. At least his years in the factory had familiarised him with the nature and definitions of discriminatory language. The glossary of cuss words in common usage on the shop floor was probably more extensive than the entire vocabulary of some of his fellow students.

His classmates also seemed much more at ease in this oppressively genial environment, exchanging nods and smiles as they grew more comfortable. Brian would have happily thrown himself out of a window to avoid even catching someone's eye, and foresaw a thousand humiliations when the academic work began. With the exception of the only other male in the room, a thing in a denim jacket festooned with the logos of heavy metal bands and a head riveted together by facial piercings, they all seemed much smarter than him. The torment continued as the lecturer trilled that the students should introduce themselves by stating their names, their current occupation and why they wished to take the course. Brian readied himself to self-immolate.

As his fellow students imparted their personal details Brian was relieved to learn that almost all of them were care assistants. Most of the female students were also married or with a partner, and proudly disclosed the names and ages of their children. The lecturer, a robust woman of indeterminate age with a chignon and a formidable chest, thanked each of them as they volunteered rather more information than Brian was ready to ingest. At least his pullulating anxieties were becalmed by his classmates' candour and relatability. He learned that the other male in the class was called Clem, he played drums in a band, enjoyed fishing and drove a minibus for the local authority. He expressed his pleasure at driving the retards to and from day centres and expressed his determination to pursue a career in social care. The lecturer's eyebrows skyrocketed and she gently admonished Clem for usage of inappropriate language to describe the differently abled. Judging by his stunned expression, Brian intuited that Clem was both confused and piqued by the lecturer's rebuke. This would not be the last time that Clem's descriptive powers would provoke concerns.

Brian was the penultimate class member to volunteer his personal details, the slight tremor in his voice betraying his horror at being the focus of other people's attention. The lecturer paused slightly before addressing a woman who appeared to have suffered a terrible accident in her wardrobe. The strident colouring and incongruence of her clothing made her resemble a figure dreamed up by Francis Bacon after a particularly heavy night on the hooligan water. In rasping tones, this sartorial nightmare announced her earthly name as Alison but she preferred to be addressed as Blithe Hunter, which was apparently the name of her spirit guide. The lecturer enquired if she wouldn't mind being called Blithe as this might save a bit of time in the long run. Blithe graciously assented and then informed the class that she was a Reiki practitioner and would be happy to lay hands on everyone present to improve their general well-being. In addition to pawing them with her healing hands she would also chuck in a naked candlelit dance evoking the dawn of the machine age. Brian was certain he saw Clem become visibly animated at this all-too resistible offer and resolved to avoid them both when using the lifts in the college. He thought it a minor miracle that Blithe had survived so long in this socially conservative town without being burned as a witch.

Brian departed the college fatigued by the exertion of quelling multiple anxieties and reinvigorated himself by listening to Radio Four whilst driving home. Upon his arrival Helen greeted him as though he'd survived an Antarctic expedition and suggested they walk to the pub for a late dinner. Brian was happy to acquiesce and, prior to their departure, Helen did something to Brian he had always assumed she didn't enjoy. As they walked hand in hand to the pub Brian reflected that this college malarkey might not be so bad after all.

'So what are the other students like?'

'All right I s'pose. Two of them would frighten a police horse.'

'I wouldn't worry about them. The loopies rarely stay the distance. They have some weird evangelical notion about wanting to make a difference. They just make trouble for everyone else instead. They won't be around long.'

Helen's predictive powers were unerringly accurate. Blithe attended one more lecture before disappearing forever. Clem received a notice from the college advising him that an

308

unwelcome diatribe about his estranged wife had disquieted his course tutor. Referring to his erstwhile partner as a, "fookin' two-timing cunt of a slag" during a debate upon the future of the nuclear family implied that his academic ambitions may be best served by a discipline other than social care. Clem did not appeal the decision and in a brief valedictory exchange with Brian he disclosed that he was transferring to a course in leisure and tourism. He possessed a PSV driving licence and quite fancied the idea of being the coach driver of holidaymakers to Spain. If he could manage fourteen mongs every morning then a coachload of coffin dodgers would be a doddle. And the ale was cheaper over there. Whilst queasy at the prospect of Clem being responsible for a busload of senior citizens, Brian wished Clem every success in his new endeavour. He also made a mental note to keep a closer eye on the international news in future; particularly events in the Costa Del Sol.

To his surprise Brian found himself looking forward to the lectures. With Helen's assistance he developed a detailed understanding of the various arms of the welfare state, its function and its purpose in the lives of vulnerable people. The lecturer herself was both expert and engaging, enlivening her factual expositions with anecdotes taken from her career as a practitioner. Brian found her sometimes hair-raising exploits fascinating and wondered if he possessed the imperviousness to derision and distrust that the job apparently entailed.

Achieving a pass mark on the course was largely predicated upon regular attendance and the student's absorption of the course material as evinced by their contributions to class debates. There were no examinations and just a few essays. With Helen's exacting tutelage his efforts were passable if rather stolid. Expressiveness and concision in writing a language he'd spoken all his life was arduous and depressed him deeply. When in front of the computer screen, he suffered a lexical outage when attempting articulation on the page. He drew little comfort from Helen's observation that his turgid compositions were exemplars of the form. He should be proud that his efforts would induce rigor mortis in the general reader as good reportage was analogous to a meat pie. It should be flaccid, unappetising but full of substance. She confidently predicted a rewarding future for him in a new profession. Brian wondered if he and Helen had a future together.

The course seemed a curious hybrid of an informal discussion group and the almost doctrinaire instillation of progressive values. A readiness to apply doublethink was essential if a candidate was to successfully negotiate the minefield of ethical and social issues under consideration. Brian had learned from Clem's experience that every utterance should be free of content that might be construed prejudicial towards supposedly oppressed social groups. There were no bad people in the world as criminality was an inevitable by-product of the structural inequalities inherent in Western capitalism. Brian wondered if the defendants at the Nuremberg trials might have used this as a defence.

He also maintained a diplomatic silence upon the concept of relative and absolute poverty. The needs of the people he grew up among were, by and large, satisfactorily met by a combination of the licit and illicit; but the lecturer also demanded that her students consider the denial of artistic enrichment as a definitive of social deprivation. The lecturer contemned the pastimes of sport, Hollywood blockbusters and vacuous pop music as opiates devised by the elite to lull the masses into passivity. Brian thought this rather patronising. In twenty years of factory work he had never once heard anyone lament their ignorance of the works of Chekhov and Stravinsky, neither did he see anything intrinsically wrong in offering fast food to a famished mind. It was certainly better than nothing at all. She was also ignorant of the pressure to conform to socially approved norms. It wasn't to the advantage of a working-class male to declare an interest in cerebral pursuits. If he so much as washed his hands following a visit to a pub lavatory he would almost certainly be impugned as a bloody shirt-lifter and a target for vicious invective. Reading a book in full view of other people might invite real trouble. Brian concluded that the gulf between the social castes was unbridgeable. Each would always be incomprehensible to the other but one would always have the upper hand. And it wasn't hard to work out which.

The news that he had successfully completed the course with a merit conduced Brian's usual irresolution and foreboding. Full-time education was all very well but he was clueless as to how he would support himself should he elect to continue his studies. Helen's expression was one of pity commingled with exasperation as he gave tongue to his anxieties.

'If I carry on with this malarkey I won't be able to work. I've always worked. I've worked since I was sixteen. I can't not work. What do I do without work?'

Helen's responses were terse and iced with impatience. At this pivotal turn in her grand design she could do without Brian's cringing equivocation. Her wide eyes darkened further, reflecting her increasing displeasure.

'You will work. Weekends and evenings. There are hostels, children's homes, care homes and hospitals. They're always looking for relief staff to cover sickness and holidays.'

'But you'll be on your own at weekends. What will you do

311

with yourself when I'm not here?'

'Parting is such sweet sorrow.'

'I still won't earn enough though will I? What about bills? Holidays? Running the motor?'

'You take out a student loan.'

'A student loan? Who'll give me a student loan?'

'The student loan company.'

'I'll get turned down. I know I will.'

'This is the closest you've been to dying in a very long time.'

Brian's acceptance onto the degree course was a formality, principally because there was a shortfall in candidates. With Helen's less than gentle hectoring he acquired a student loan, was accepted as a nursing assistant by the NHS and also continued his role as a support worker on a sessional basis. Far from being under-employed he was overwhelmed by offers to deputise for those taking sickness or holiday leave. A telephone call from the bank advised him that his overdraft facility had been increased to five thousand pounds. When Brian querulously observed that he hadn't requested a larger overdraft, the bored young man on the other end informed him that it was there anyway and he could do what he liked with it. Brian was initially perplexed by the bank's solicitude, but then supposed it was looking to retain his business following his ennoblement as a social care professional. Brian considered this a salutary gesture of support and chided himself for reviling high street banks as sinks of avarice and self-interest. It transpired that the customer's welfare, or his at least, was of paramount concern. He debated whether to compose a letter avowing his undying fealty to this most benevolent of high street institutions.

Brian's first term at college was more pleasurable than he could have hoped for, but he was also forced to make swift revisals to his rather passe assumptions about social relations between the sexes. Excepting Vernon, a languorous boho who smoked cannabis with the regularity that Brian fumed cigarettes, he was the only male in an intake of thirty students. He found this new situation disturbing as he preferred a respectful distance between males and females in the workplace. In the factory there had been no women at all on the shop floor, a satisfactory arrangement as it precluded the fairer sex from observing the disgusting habits of his workmates. But as the first term progressed, he was gratified to learn that his female classmates could be as funny, potty-mouthed and brutally candid as some of the men he'd encountered in an industrial environment. They hailed from gritty post-industrial sprawls in which tattoo parlours did a roaring trade and the police were always kept busy. Early in the first term he and Vernon were dubbed Cannon and Ball after a gormless Northern comedy duo, soubriquets to which neither objected.

He was also shocked by the preponderance of female students involved in messy divorces by the end of the first term. These women had glimpsed an escape from stultifying marriages and were ready to realise long-suppressed personal and professional ambitions. They were walking towards the light and the useless lump of factory fodder they had married when young was now an encumbrance. By Christmas of that year two of his female classmates had moved in together. The announcement of their co-habitation prompted rapturous applause, a congratulatory card and a whip-round. These neo-sapphics declared themselves to be the happiest they had ever been, but Brian's scarcely repressible social conservatism bubbled to the surface. He tried to imagine how he would feel if one day he came home from school to find himself fatherless, living at a new

313

address, sharing a bedroom with new and unfamiliar siblings and his mother kipping down with someone he assumed to be a friend from college. He doubted that he would cope well, but then again he wasn't universally feted for his mental resilience or his sensitivity to changing sexual mores. Perhaps in the coming millennium such arrangements would be commonplace and he was out of step. Evidently it wasn't only his record collection that was stuck in the 1970s.

Vernon's personal life was, perhaps wisely, a closed book. His rakish geniality, dry humour and sometimes politically incorrect utterances made him popular with the female cohort. Even Brian detected a simmering sexual ferment between Vernon and certain members of the class. Vernon also played the ukelele, a pastime that along with lager drinking was a key signifier of frivolousness. And yet, despite his insouciance, Brian detected in Vernon an iron determination to conceal his true self. In both class debates and in conversation he preferred drollery to anything resembling a firmly held opinion. He was as impenetrable as a steel door but companionable and happy to go to the pub with whoever was going. That was usually Brian.

Brian remained irredeemably himself. The possibility of any extracurricular dalliances with him were, by common consent, inconceivable. Whilst sharing a cigarette during morning break, the most junior female class member, Belinda, declared that Brian resembled her dad but without the body odour and volcanic temper. Brian nodded beatifically whilst silently giving thanks that he hadn't sired this tactless sow. He hoped that the ecstasy tablets she had purchased from Vernon earlier were of only moderate toxicity.

Although Brian was largely free of the arrogance and sanctimony of the average undergraduate, by the end of his second year he was strafing Helen with psychobabble and theoretical models familiar only to sociologists, political scientists and other people who didn't get out much. Helen would arch her eyebrows and smile serenely as Brian took issue with Eysenck. She had also noted a marked dissipation in Brian's social gaucheries and a growth in the certitude of his views. It seemed that the imago was beginning to emerge from the chrysalis. Brian himself admitted that he wasn't quite the nervous Nelly he used to be and was reasonably satisfied with his scholastic abilities, but he confessed to struggling with the psychology module. At one point he had consulted a medical textbook to locate the whereabouts of the id, ego and superego in the human brain and was disappointed to discover that they actually didn't exist. He was drawn to the substantive rather than speculative and psychological theories seemed to be a collection of assumptions and generalisations thought up after too much to drink. In Brian's view Freud was an incorrigible pervert and Carl Rogers a wimp.

After decades on the factory floor, Brian came to regard his college years as the longest and most expensive holiday he had ever enjoyed. To begin the day at a civilised time and return home almost as fragrant as at its beginning seemed impossibly privileged. The occasional bunk-off to the pub armed with periodicals he'd filched from under the nose of the college librarians made him feel a little like how Hugh Grant must feel every day. On spring afternoons he'd sit in the college refectory and gawp at the array of vivacious young things who studiously ignored him whilst clattering along in high heels. Brian correctly assumed that they mistook him for one of the maintenance crew come to fix a radiator.

He sometimes wondered if these ingenues were aware of

how fortunate they were to have little else on their minds other than essays, sex and the flawlessness of their appearance. As carefree as puppies and convinced of their own importance, they had postponed the uncountable agonies of adulthood for at least another two years. He was all too aware of the vagaries awaiting them in the normal world and wondered if they were sufficiently robust to survive them. Just five minutes of Goldfinger's company would be enough to have them reaching for strong medication and mewling for a course of counselling. For a decent change Brian seemed to be ahead of the game. He was also conscious that at some point the student loans would have to be repaid and his ballooning overdraft serviced, but at this junction he was content to ignore his usual forebodings. His relationship with Helen was strong, he would graduate shortly, his future appeared secure and impending middle age was to be embraced rather than feared. At Helen's insistence he had even invested in a wardrobe of cheap suits. She fiercely denounced people who came to work dressed in casual wear and was determined that Brian avoided that unforgiveable social solecism. If the public was paying his salary then the least he could do was look smart for his paymasters, although Brian would be the first to admit that he was not naturally disposed to dapperness. Dressed even in Armani he could still manage to look like he was breaking it in for someone else.

Helen and Brian saw in the new millennium in a hotel on the Welsh border. The much-anticipated bug failed to disable the technology upon which everyone was increasingly dependent, and the Dome's disappointing inaugural knees-up was broadcast to the nation. The much-heralded Millennium Eve was as anti-climactic as all the preceding New Year's Eves. The hotel guests sat in the lounge checking their watches and yawning whilst a

Sinatra impressionist warbled through the highlights of the old curmudgeon's repertoire. Helen and Brian retired before eleven o'clock with champagne and nibbles, enjoyed some tipsy sex and were asleep before the witching hour.

Whilst heading home on New Year's Day, Brian enquired if Helen felt differently now as she was living in the century regarded by science-fiction writers as the future. After a moment's deliberation Helen shook her head, but reflected that this was probably a good thing. The twentieth century was steeped in gore and chaos and so perhaps this downbeat beginning presaged a new age of peace and international co-operation. Brian nodded emphatically and expressed his confidence that the next ten years would be dull for all the right reasons. On their arrival home Brian picked up the newspapers and went for lunch in the local pub whilst Helen girded herself for the working week. He sensed that she was recalibrating and needed some time alone. When he returned around six o'clock that evening she was already in bed and soundly asleep. As the start of the new term was still a week away, Brian was untroubled by thoughts of an early start and decided to make the most of it. He cracked open the bottle of expensive whisky gifted to him by Helen's parents, donned his headphones and listened to Brubeck and Broonzy until midnight. He couldn't recall being happier in all of his thirty-eight years.

In May, Brian graduated with a respectable Desmond and received his award in one of the grandest stages in Manchattan. The Paget family didn't bother to attend as this would mean taking time off work. They didn't wish to waste some of their holiday entitlement watching Brian get a piece of paper and a daft cap and gown. Despite having secured a First, Vernon was also absent from the ceremony, but his elsewhereness did nothing to derogate from the conviviality of the occasion. Even Brian was happy to pose for photographs with his fellow graduates, his camera-shyness having been effaced by liberal quantities of wine prior to his arrival at the venue. Helen smiled, chatted and shook hands with Brian's classmates, who in their turn almost curtsied in deference to Helen's rarified status in the caring profession. They were anxious to make a good impression upon someone who at some time or another might be their employer. Brian was particularly amused by Belinda's fawning over the woman with whom he shared his life. In the previous three years he had disclosed virtually nothing of his relationship with Helen, nor had he boasted of her standing within her chosen field. Belinda had already filed an application to work in Helen's organisation and was a gibbering wreck when Helen quietly reported that she would be perusing her application the following morning. Belinda spluttered her effusive thanks and then gawped at Brian in aghast incomprehension. For her this was akin to discovering that Wonder Woman was married to her window cleaner. It didn't make any sense on any level.

Brian registered with a number of agencies supplying workers to the public, private and charitable sectors. He was wholly unprepared for the demands of agency work and found the early years in his new profession exhausting. It seemed that every few months he was parachuted into a new local authority in a new town and utterly clueless as to his purpose for being there. For someone as averse to turbulence as Brian, this was tortuous. Each time he undertook a new assignment he felt like a latecomer to a melodrama in which the relationships, motivations and intentions of all the characters had already been established. He had to quickly determine those who were approachable and those who were not, discern the decent people from the backbiters, devise alibis to avoid the malcontents and also seek out the lair of the few smokers in the department. Weekly remittances to the tea and biscuit fund were essential as failure to do would invite obloquy upon those who did not.

There were times when he was so dizzied by the pace of change that he felt his head would spin off. He struggled to improve his somewhat undercooked interpersonal skills and professional confidence. At least he could ventilate his terrors to the cool and practical Helen upon his arrival home each evening. She advised him not to panic, never drink heavily on week nights, go to bed early and invest in a treadmill to walk off the tensions accumulated over the working week. All of this was excellent counsel to which Brian paid not the slightest attention. But gradually, and after much suffering, he began to acquit himself with a degree of proficiency.

He was courteous if somewhat diffident towards co-workers, steadfast under pressure and sedulously avoided the sometimes poisonous office politics. Among his employers he garnered a reputation for reliability, but his gloomy demeanour and air of detachment provoked aspersive comments from colleagues. Whilst they admired his diligence, he seemed to irradiate a mild hostility commingled with an unfathomable melancholy. When working with a learning disabilities team his arrival at the smoking corner prompted an embarrassed silence and the tamping of unfinished cigarettes. By contrast, the admin ladies had taken a shine to the quiet bloke who was always in a hurry and whose shitty car was always breaking down. They also admired his principled refusal to contribute to the purchase of a cow for an African village. They couldn't see the point of it either. In their view, the up-herself bint who had proposed this act of selflessness had more cheek than Cyril Smith's arse. She should have had a whipround to buy a bleedin' life for herself instead.

Whilst Brian grappled with vocational dilemmas, his private life continued to fructify. Helen had assembled the disparate elements of him into a coherent, if not fully functional, whole. As both were confirmed paedophobes the couple had never given any serious consideration to starting a family. Brian was utterly convinced of his own ineptness for such an undertaking, a candid self-appraisal with which Helen readily concurred. For her part Helen was militantly opposed to expending valuable energies upon something unable even to feed itself. To be cloistered indoors with a creature at only the larval stage of its development was anathema to her. Besides which, she already shared her life with someone who was hardly a paragon of self-reliance. Brian was more than enough to be getting with. They were content in their hermetic coupledom, rarely venturing out with others and needing only a small social circle to enliven their leisure time. Declaring their love for one other was rare, as their mutual affection was as self-evident as oxygen. Such was the sense of permanence to their relationship it was as though neither of them had had an amatory past. There was and had been only the two of them and this arrangement would continue in perpetuity.

The razing of the Twin Towers foreshadowed the revisal of the world order. A nondescript little man, who mispronounced the word "nuclear" and thought that Africa was a country, was tasked with helming the most powerful nation on earth. He promptly granted tax cuts to the wealthiest and then declared war on a Middle Eastern nation that, although brutally repressive, provided a bulwark against Islamic extremism. The British government also thought a pointless war was a good idea and decided to tag along with the Americans. The mandarins

320

responsible for Britain's entry into the conflict had overlooked the possibility of British Muslims being rather ticked off by the senseless killing of fellow apostles of Allah. The outrage and despair provoked by terrorist attacks in British cities by disaffected Muslims revitalised a hitherto moribund right wing intent on making Britain white again.

Britain became a different, stranger place. Orders to keep one's luggage attended at all times were barked from the tannoy systems of railway stations and airports. People with brown skins garbed in hijabs were regarded with suspicion. The nation became slowly but inexorably enveloped by a fog of acrimony towards those whose faiths and ethnicities differed to those of the natives. A smoking ban was imposed to appease a middle class determined to build a nation fit for the broadsheet-reading classes whilst disingenuously claiming the moral high ground. Brian was granted yet another increase in his overdraft and persuaded to accept a credit card. He decided to explore their purchasing powers.

For almost a decade the couple enjoyed a gilded existence. They frequently spent weekends in London, catching up with Helen's university friends and trying restaurants recommended by gourmands in lifestyle magazines. They also attended new productions in the West End whilst imbibing ridiculously priced red wine during the intervals. Their numerous holidays were movable feasts of walking tours, visits to galleries in Europe, sybaritic self-indulgence in adults-only hotels and the occasional cruise. Contrary to Helen's advice, Brian purchased a second-hand saloon car. His choice was premised purely upon the quality of the CD player rather than the efficiency of the vehicle. Keith Jarrett's American trio had rarely sounded so good on compact disc. Helen shook her head in resignation and warned him to expect many invoices for the repairs that this waste-skip on wheels would undoubtedly incur.

Brian's visits to his parents became less frequent upon their retirement. He had tired of the palpable tensions and sulphurous atmosphere following another of Derek's innumerable home improvement projects. He arrived at chez Paget one Friday evening and almost swooned when confronted by the sight a cow ingesting the back garden lawn. Brian closed his eyes, shook his head and returned to the living room in which his mother was taking a cup of tea and swallowing several tablets. She looked up and gazed at Brian in expectation of the question he was sure to ask.

'What's that doing there?'

'It's your father's.'

'Has he pinched it?'

'No. He's thinking of buying it. He's giving it a test drive sort of thing.'

'A bloody test drive? Not even he's daft enough to ride a cow on the M62.'

'You think not? Huh. Think again. It's not for riding though. It's for milk.'

'What? Milk? Like from a carton?'

'He reckons that now I'm not working I'm supping too much tea. He said that having our own cow will save us a fortune in the long run. With us being pensioners we'll have to watch the pennies.'

'Is he completely bloody mad?'

'Course he is, you dozy pig. If he's right in the head I'm Shirley bleedin' Bassey. He's thinking of having the fireplace put back in here as well. He says that Indians burn dried cow doings like we burn coal. We can turn the central heating off during the day and put cow doings on the fire instead. I've told him I have. Either that bloody cow goes or I do.'

'What did he say?'

'He's not made his mind up yet.'

A thunderhead rarely presages a flood any more than a slight engine tremor augurs an aircrash. Brian paid scant attention to news footage of anxious customers clamouring to remove their savings from a building society usually regarded as an exemplar of prudence. The news that Britain's debt now exceeded the country's earnings inspired only public incomprehension or indifference. The collapse of an American bank went unremarked upon as people went about their business blissfully unaware of the tectonic shifts under the world of high finance. The national imagination had been diverted by the prospect of Britain hosting the Olympics in the next decade, although inevitably this celebration of chemically enhanced athleticism would be held in London, as the rest of the United Kingdom didn't really matter.

Helen and Brian went to work, went home, watched television, read books, drank wine, ate out, ate in, discussed plans for the weekend and took holidays in warmer climes. Brian tested the limits of his overdraft and the raft of credit cards he'd been issued, having been reassured by the government's pronouncement that turbulence in the financial sector was a self-corrective; but as the crisis ballooned even he succumbed to the jitters beleaguering the nation. This was terrible and seemed to get worse daily. No one in government, banking or the media was able to offer a satisfactory explanation for The Great Mess. Helen muttered darkly that the government would carry the can for this hoo-hah and be booted out of office at the next election. Brian countered that the electorate wouldn't be hoodwinked into believing such an outrageous falsehood and would stick with serious men for serious times. As usual, Brian was catastrophically wide of the mark.

In collusion with the third largest political party, the austerians hobbled into Downing Street with an agenda to balance the books. The chancellor declared that if the British public could withstand five years of hardship then the nation would be back in the black. Everyone soon learned the kind of blackness to which the chancellor was referring. It seemed that the lights were going out forever. The service and small business sectors were refused bailouts by moribund banks revived by quantitative easing. Previously vibrant high streets suffered desertification. The slashing of local government funding came as a hammer blow to those who had taken the presence of libraries, play areas, community centres and Sure-Start centres for granted. The national mood was one of gloomy resignation admixed with perplexity. People scratched their heads in disbelief at the eye-popping pace of decline and were unconvinced by the prime minister's war-cry that they were all in this together; but their bewilderment was as nothing when compared to Brian's as he sensed a cooling in his relationship with Helen.

Over time their union had developed the usual hairline cracks present in any enduring relationship, as each were endowed with foibles that could grate upon the less complaisant. Helen's righteousness could sometimes elide into prating sanctimony, but Brian had learned to tune out when she spluttered her outrage at the latest social injustice reported in the media. He sometimes wished that Helen would accept that most people were horrible bastards and unburden herself of her secular saintliness. He was convinced that this would do much to improve her general wellbeing.

Brian's drinking habits, his bent for pop culture and talent for procrastination sometimes infuriated Helen, but his deadpan drollery and dubious taste in clothes still endeared. Best of all, he could still make her laugh. His railing at the malign invisible forces that toyed with his sanity as he ricocheted from one self-created mini-crisis to another could reduce her to giggling idiocy. He was also one of life's truth tellers, an inveterate bean spiller, as incapable of duplicity as he was of DIY. And whilst justifiably proud of her talents for alchemising order from chaos, she needed Brian's unfussy but unequivocal support to sustain her when she was foundering. When she arrived home, tearful and beset, Brian would remove her coat and run his finger down her nose. He would then embrace her in silence until she had collected herself. It was as though he was trying to absorb her desperations through his skin and take them as his own. It was easy for Helen to envisage spending the rest of her life with this crumpled, daft but essentially decent man. And yet.

To deny the existence of a glass ceiling for women in the workplace was as ludicrous to Helen as the consumption of dead animals. She had heard too many stories of talented female contemporaries being overlooked in favour of indifferent but decidedly male colleagues. To compound her own sense of thwartedness she was also increasingly aware of another damaging but hitherto unacknowledged bias. In recent years there had been a slow but discernible disappearance of the public realm from the regions, leading to its almost exclusive concentration in London. Whilst attending meetings and conferences in the enormolopolis, she had been struck by how much closer to the centre of things she seemed. She'd also gaped in disbelief at the rock star salaries earned by professionals who were, in her opinion, little better than drones. But for Helen monetary gain had really never been an incentive. More than anything else it had always been about getting things done and getting them done right. She had also been troubled by the number of important initiatives implemented without the consultation of colleagues residing any further north than Luton. Fait accomplis were not to Helen's taste, nor was being dismissed as a hayseed provincial. Her remoteness from the epicentre began to rankle.

Her coruscating abilities had not gone unnoticed. There had been casual overtures from a number of think tanks, offers of posts in social policy forums, and guest lectureships at several universities. A journalist for Britain's leading liberal newspaper had practically begged her to assist in the composition of another state-of-the-nation treatise. It was also rumoured that she was on the radar of a prominent politician keen to expand his team of advisors as he plotted his next election campaign. If she impressed as a SPAD, then a safe constituency seat or even a place in the shadow cabinet was within her gift. Each time Helen arrived in the capital there was a ripple amongst power mongers gagging for clean skins to brighten the murk of metropolitan public life. The Thames was her Rubicon and all she had to do was wade in; but there was a problem. Brian didn't like getting his feet wet in the place he called That Bloody London.

Throughout the whole of their relationship, Helen had been conscious of Brian's peculiar attachment to his home town. As with most of his confreres, his antecedents had immigrated to build the Ship Canal, found work in the plentiful mills and factories and then made their home in this lugubrious satellite of Manchattan. Over the course of a century large families had colonised districts within the town, and in many instances grandparents and grandchildren were separated by only a few streets. It wasn't unusual to find three generations of the same clan working in the same factory. Neighbours, workmates and drinking partners were absorbed into the family unit as de facto kin. Children who played together in the street might be partners in later life, as people rarely married out of their home turf. In a nation atomised by individualism, Brian's people still cleaved to the collective.

Perhaps they were driven by a hive mentality, an unconscious compulsion to cluster together to combat inevitable hardships. Despite the radical redrafting of his personal and professional lives, Brian was still enculturated to the mores of his home turf. In chance meetings with old acquaintances his body language changed, his accent became more pronounced, his glottal stops shorter and his responses monosyllabic. Helen couldn't fathom whether this was a reflexive response or a defence mechanism, but unlike the pseudo-plebbing of her well-heeled colleagues when scoring cocaine, it was completely unaffected. When he needed to be, Brian was an authentic copper-bottomed pleb. She would redden slightly as she recalled how ugly she found his Lancastrian burr and his liberal usage of swear words early in their relationship. Prior to meeting him she had derided the snobbishness of her fellow public school alumni, only later having to admit to an element of pot and kettle.

Helen was sufficiently pragmatic to appreciate how fortunate she was. Her exalted position within her company was unassailable, she enjoyed a lucrative income, she was in excellent health and life with Brian was serene but rarely dull. She sympathised with colleagues whose relationships were either loveless or drowning in a morass of betrayals and acrid recriminations. She had seen the faces of colleagues whom she admired as bastions of reason fall floorwards when taking a

327

personal call. They visibly disintegrated when listening in pained resignation to yet another ultimatum from a vengeful spouse or a petition from a solicitor. Her heart went out to the children whose parents were tearing at one another like fighting dogs. She had also noted with distaste the penchant for one-night stands using the increasingly indispensable smartphone. She had never worried about Brian engaging in such behaviours as his telephone was so old the callers probably spoke in Elizabethan English. His modus vivendi was alighting on something he could cope with and then sticking with it, be that a telephone, a job, or a relationship. Anything more complicated or demanding was regarded with suspicion or simply ignored.

Whilst Helen sometimes found his incuriosity unfathomable, she concluded that this was his way of keeping things manageable. But, as she continued to abjure a raft of fetching job opportunities in the Great Wen in the interests of preserving their domestic idyll, the occasional knocking in Helen's skull became more insistent. Each time she spurned an enticing new offer she became increasingly resentful of her partner's reluctance to tear himself away from the parochial. What had previously appeared to be a briskly simple approach to life began to seem merely simplistic, even timorous. It smacked of a fear of the world and its possibilities. Helen hadn't got to where she was by standing on the touchline when the game was on. To abstain from a challenge was contrary to her competitive instincts. She was primed for leading roles on bigger stages whereas Brian was happy to continue as a spear carrier. The hairline cracks began to fissure.

When she finally began to disclose that she was in demand, Brian would nod absently as though he hadn't quite heard and wasn't really interested anyway. Initially she was wryly amused that he regarded her news as a superfluity, but with every airy dismissal of an exciting new gig she grew increasingly snappish. Brian would gape at her in incomprehension as the mutterings under her breath became more acidulous and cruel. Although cravenly opposed to confrontation he would await his cue and then quietly enquire what the matter was. Her obsidian eyes spangled with ferocity whilst Brian resembled a puppy pleading for an exculpatory pat for a misdeed he hadn't known he'd committed.

Helen hated herself at these moments. She was conscious of Brian's knack for seeing everything except the obvious, a failing that made her sardonic petulance seem all the more despicable. Worse than that, she was allowing herself to be tortured by paradox. The very qualities she admired in Brian were now impediments to realising her ambitions. She bitterly reflected that if the boot was on the other foot it would be her aspirations deferred in favour of her male partner's. In this case she was a prisoner of her partner's trepidation. They had arrived at an impasse of which Brian had little understanding. He had been a member of the only social caste charged with the injunction to better itself and had escaped the fetters of his class with no little industry and application. His current circumstances would have been a pipedream to his younger self, therefore the plateau from which he now tranquilly gazed suited him perfectly. Why attempt to climb any more mountains?

Had Brian ever thought to posit this question, Helen's grim retort would be that they were scalable and awaiting their conquest. She needed to reassert control over her destiny, with or without Brian. Her father would no doubt concur that the realisation of one's potential and romantic love were sometimes incompatible. She also implicitly understood which should come

329

first. She prepared herself to confront Brian with the opportunity to go with her to London on pain of a permanent scission in their relationship. The house would be sold, she would be the primary breadwinner, Brian would eventually secure a post in the public sector and together they would make this work. But then Splatch broke surface from the subterrene.

Upon meeting the pitiable Splatch, Helen's charitable instincts fired on all cylinders. She insisted that the creature take up residence in the spare bedroom and charged Brian with brokering the support that this fallen angel needed to fuel his crash-landing into normalcy. Having worked extensively with the homeless earlier in her career, Helen regarded Splatch as just another beneficiary of her creditable skill set, yet another client to be swiftly reintroduced to the mainstream; but as she became more intimately acquainted with the unhinged cuckoo in her nest she realised that she had grossly underestimated Splatch's unusuality, his ongoing love affair with chaos and the almost shamanic power he wielded over Brian. This was more, much more, than the average bromance transposed from adolescence into middle age. There were darker elements in play.

In Splatch's company Brian regressed into sniggering juvenescence and a repellent faux obeisance. She grew quickly exasperated by their giggling reminiscences encrypted in a language only they understood. Worse than that was the smell. No amount of scented candles and air fresheners could nullify the putrescent stink of Splatch when he joined Helen and Brian for their evening meal. He would arrive at table late, barely dressed and obviously enlivened by something illicit. He would then immediately down three huge vodkas and coke whilst insisting Helen revise her choice of music as the entree to their salad and vegetarian pasta. One evening he ripped a recording of *The Four*

Seasons from the CD player and hurled it across the street, screaming at her genteel neighbours that the Italian Baroque was a crime against sentient humanity. Brian's abject refusal to admonish his friend for his vile behaviour was nothing short of contemptible. Helen's core began to melt down. She mused that there were three people in this relationship and one of them had to go. To London.

When Splatch finally moved into his own place, Helen moved with the rapidity and economy of movement of a professional assassin. Following her acceptance of a board-level position in a charitable organisation in Croydon, she called her office to inform her secretary that she wouldn't be available for the next three days. She then purchased two tickets for a gig at The Band On The Wall for a supposedly dazzling South African jazz pianist valorised by Splatch as the future of jazz. She also booked two rooms at a mid-priced hotel close to the centre of Manchattan and insisted the two men enjoy a couple of nights of bonding over a drink or twelve. She then scoured the lettings pages in the local newspaper for furnished properties in Brian's terra domum before handing over a bond and a month's rent to a dishevelled individual who disclosed that he suffered angina and was moving to Lanzarote because the fags were cheaper. After accepting the keys to the property she spent her last day away from the office transporting all of Brian's belongings to his new domicile.

When Brian arrived home later that evening he was in an expansive mood and intimated that he wouldn't be unopposed to a spot of sexual intercourse on the dining table. Helen peremptorily informed him that they were going for a ride in the car. When the car alighted outside a property in Least, Brian raised his eyebrows, utterly unaware of the hammer blow about

331

to delivered. Helen handed him the keys, opened the passenger side door and ordered him to ring her later. Brian stood on the pavement as the rain began to teem, staring at the keys in fuddlement. Helen quickly drove away as he inserted the key into the door of the nondescript two-bedroom terraced property.

He stared around. His hi-fi was shelved in one corner of the room and his collection of compact discs and paperbacks in the other. He walked into the small kitchen to discover his beatbox on a worktop. He opened the refrigerator and eyed the beers and bottles of white wine. He shook his head and trundled into the ground floor extension serving as a bathroom. In the bathroom cabinet his wet razor, deodorants and aftershave were neatly arranged and ready for use. He mounted the stairs and opened the wardrobes in the larger of the two bedrooms. They contained all of his suits and casual clothes along with a miscellany of his footwear. He then sat heavily on the bed, retrieved his telephone from his jeans pocket and called Helen. What transpired were the most devastating five minutes of his life. And then, after almost three bottles of white wine and a great many tears, he finally fell asleep on the couch in the living room.

Helen was a terrible bridge burner. After speaking to Brian she wept uncontrollably, drank four vodkas and a bottle of Merlot before vowing to reverse her decision to sell the house, relinquish the post in Croydon and invite Brian back the following week; but she knew deep within herself that her resentment of his intransigence was ineradicable and in the future she would only despise him for all the opportunities lost. Although the weeks following their separation were hell she was sufficiently resilient to ignore his repeated telephone calls. She refused to open the door when he plaintively snivelled through the letterbox pleading for reconciliation. His supplications finally came to a halt when she threatened him with police intervention following his unannounced visit to her office with a bouquet, as bereft as a lone toddler weeping in an airport atrium. Upon witnessing Brian's unwinding, Helen wondered whether to contact his doctor and express her concerns. She speculated that he was drinking himself stuporous and descending into that underlit world populated by rudderless middle-aged men who die whilst watching television at three in the morning.

Brian was like a child staring at the sky and jutting out his tongue for a snowdrop that would never come. His return to Least had not gone unnoticed by the locals and the news of his reappearance finally reached the ears of his parents.

One grim Saturday morning Brian was awoken by an insistent banging of the door knocker. He grabbed his insanitary dressing gown from the bathroom, raked his fingers through his greying mop and opened the front door. His mother gazed sadly from beneath her sodden headscarf. Her expression was a testament to vindication. Brian had buggered up again, something she'd been expecting for quite some time.

'You back round here then?'

'Yeah.'

'I thought you would be at some time or another. I'm surprised she didn't get fed up of you before now.'

'Cheers for that. D' you want a brew?'

'No. I've got frozen stuff in this bag. It'll go off if I hang about.'

'Right.'

'D' you want your tea later on? Your dad's on fish.'

'I'm all right.'

'Right-ho. D' you want your dinner tomorrow? It's Sunday. We're on beef. You can go to the club with your dad as well if

333

you want.'

'I'm not that keen on beef to be honest.'

'You used to be. Do they not eat beef then?'

'Who?'

'Them posh buggers.'

'Not usually, no. They hardly eat meat at all really.'

'Serves 'em bloody right. Your dad's got shut of the cow in't yard by the way. I'll see you tomorrow then.'

'Right…'

A month later Brian paid a visit to the house he and Helen had shared for so many years. A "SOLD" sign had been implanted in the garden and her car was no longer parked outside. He stared at the pavement for a full minute, ruminating upon how human love was essentially an exercise in masochism. He vowed there and then never to practice such a perversion again. Surprisingly, Splatch was the epitome of solicitude in this wilderness period. He rang regularly, exhorting Brian to visit with his guitar and strong alcohol. Splatch managed to staunch the bleed-out of his friend's broken mind and within a few weeks Brian had reacquired at least some of his old equanimity. He also wished to avoid visiting Splatch too regularly as some of the company he cultivated was quite deranged. One lunatic from Salford proposed stealing a van, filling it to the gills with cans of beer and then to go hunting for a colony of rare natterjack toads rumoured to be thriving near Southport. If the amphibians were caught, boiled, and the resultant fluids drunk, everyone who ingested this elixir would be off their fookin' tits for three straight weeks. Brian declined the offer. Splatch of course did not.

Brian's grip on all matters financial had always been rather shaky, but his increasingly perilous financial situation simply didn't seem to matter in this time of despond. He continued to abuse his credit cards with a profligacy that would inevitably invite a reckoning, whilst also falling behind in his obligations to utilities companies. He paid his rent on time but that was only out of fear of reprisals if he didn't cough up the cash. Right-of-centre thinkers and journalists were fond of levelling the phrase, "Robbing Peter to pay Paul" against their political opposition. Brian's modus vivendi of robbing both Peter and Paul whilst hoping his luck would change at some point would not have endeared him to the chancellor of the exchequer. In desperation, he tried his hand at the National Lottery and purchased scratchcards, aspiring to the jackpot win that would doubtless change his life for the better. He won precisely nothing. The pile of threatening correspondence on his occasional table from various agencies grew larger and his thirst for strong waters burgeoned, but at least his sense of desolation was becalmed. And tomorrow his agonies would be over.

The perfumed coven of ramblers rose to bid their tactile farewells, promising to reconvene on Boxing Day. Brian took out a newspaper. Enervated by increasing pain in his jaw, he decided upon another drink to palliate the ache and lift his flagging spirits. Outside, grey rain fell from a grey sky onto a grey world. His phone rang. He debated whether to answer it but he knew that Pam would continue calling until he responded.

'Well he's not dead yet.'

'That makes two of us.'

'What're you on about you, you dozy gobshite? And when are you coming round? And when's he going to cark it?'

'How should I know?'

'Well you're the bloody social worker, not me.'

'Not any more I ain't.'

'What're you on about?'

335

'I got the heave-ho on Friday. Someone else will be taking Arthur's case.'

'So when are you coming round to see him then?'

'I can't Pam. I'm not Arthur's case worker any more. Professional boundaries, all that guff.'

'Well that's bloody typical, that. You can't even bother your idle arse to come and see a bloke who won't be here for much longer? Bleedin' social workers. Load of wankers they're nothing else.'

'Pam—'

The line went dead. Brian sighed, returned his phone to his coat pocket, drained his glass, ordered another whisky and mused upon whether it was worth trying to call a taxi. Given the weather and his general lack of kilter, the walk home seemed as daunting as a self-administered vasectomy. Time seemed to have slowed. He felt consigned to a third place, a numinous space between heaven and earth, a dimension in which all of the clocks had stopped, the sun neither rose nor set, it had rained for all eternity but at least the pubs were open. He took another drink, called a taxi, returned home and promptly fell asleep on the sofa.

Reinvigorated after three hours of nap, Brian checked his watch and was gratified to discover that it was only eight o'clock. There was a missed call on his telephone from a number he didn't recognise. He figured that it was either a salesman or one of his creditors. Money never sleeps, not even at weekends, and certainly not in the Christmas season. Whoever it was they wouldn't be receiving a return call. Brian's last night on earth wouldn't be wasted on some creep casually enquiring about whether he'd like to discuss a declaration of bankruptcy. Whoever he was could go to hell; quickly followed by Brian himself.

He showered quickly, donned his favourite sweatshirt, checked his pockets for his keys, phone and wallet and decided upon The Long Pig as his first port of call. Whilst schlepping through the moist darkness, Splatch called.

'Where are you?'

'In transit. I'm off to The Pig.'

'Good man. Get unapologetically bladdered. Don't forget tomorrow. Bring rum.'

Brian grimaced and then grunted to himself, wondering how his old friend would take the news of his passing.

'And what's a dashing young sophisticate like you getting up to this evening?'

'I've got rid of that racing bike so I'm having a little at-home time with a couple of my associates. It promises to be an interesting night. Someone's scored a shedful of Tenuate Dospan. I didn't know you could get your hands on chalkies any more. It's making me quite nostalgic.'

'Enjoy.'

'I most certainly will. Don't forget eleven o'clock tomorrow. God knows what state I'll be in but come anyway.'

'I'll do my best.'

'Don't do your best. Do as I tell you. Life's so much simpler when that happens.'

As he approached the beer hall Brian braced himself for the sensory onslaught of The Long Pig in full hedonistic swing. Whilst passing through the glass entrance he noted Spex affixing a defibrillator to the wall. The sheets of noise, kaleidoscopic lighting and frenetic cavorting on the makeshift dance floor were like blows to the face as The Elvis Dalek Karaoke Disco provided the evening's entertainment. The coiffed and plainly Eastern European Elvis was ably assisted by a scantily clad drag artist called Donna Kebab. He/she exhorted the punters to take a turn on the karaoke in the saltiest language permissible in a public place. Brian manoeuvred himself into position at the bar. Wesley was sipping ruminatively at a pint whilst humming along to a classic by The Temptations. He winked at Brian and wished him all the best for Christmas. Brian nodded and smiled.

He lingered at the bar and gazed around. The room was a human termite mound, a welter of movement and activity. Tough lads in baseball caps were shaking hands, hugging and then threatening to kill one another in the course of a single conversation. Thickset blokes, whom Brian knew only by sight, sat in silence with their equally thickset female partners. He had no idea that these unsmiling beer monsters even had partners, such was their determination to live a single life in the context of a familial relationship. These men went to the pub as often as their spending money would allow whilst their women stayed at home to act as keepers to their unruly offspring. This familial arrangement was so out of step with modernity as to be worthy of investigation by anthropologists, but in Least these archaic family units still endured. Brian reflected that had he remained a poorly educated, socially unaware, factory-working animal, he might not be at the pass he found himself now.

Elvis Dalek held a device that transformed his voice into that of a genocidal alien that had terrified the nation's children when television was young. Brian laughed uproariously as Elvis emoted a cheesy eighties power ballad before screaming the signature, "Exterminate, exterminate" into the microphone. Zorb and another bouncer, both garbed in tight-fitting tuxedos, stared unblinkingly around the room. Bellicosity seeped from their every open pore. They were locked, loaded and desperate for an incident requiring their vicious interventions. Brian sensed that however innocuous a stand-off between unruly punters might be, these two would make the participants pay dearly for their contretemps. His telephone rang. He fished it from his pocket and frowned. It was the same telephone number as earlier. He promptly cancelled the call and eased his way to the back of the beerhall where Jimmy The Bike and Spex were seated.

As time passed, the air became foetid with the tang of violence and an almost palpable sexual tension. The dancing got dirtier, the clamour of voices more raucous, the shouted exchanges more heated. Given the tightly-wound atmosphere, this scenario would either elide into boozy good humour or degenerate into a mass brawl. Even at this remove Brian could practically hear Zorb's caveman muscularity creaking into attack mode. He resembled a bull mastiff crossed with a saltwater crocodile ready to crunch on human bone. Spex's penchant for the primitive was becoming aroused by the beserk animality of the revellers. Some faces were going to get smashed and some babies were going to get made tonight. A bearded oldster in a flat cap reeled around the dance floor, baring his colossal belly to a vampish Goth with whom he cavorted. She in turn lifted her top to bare her bosom, "LAGER" and "BITTER" tattooed on each pale, pierced breast. Zorb's co-worker moved swiftly to clip the oldster around the head and push a meaty finger into the face of the plainly terrified Goth.

Brian grinned ruefully and wondered at how Helen would perceive this vista of degeneracy and mayhem. She would probably stare in pained disgust before blaming ruthless turbo-capitalists for fomenting violence, alcoholism and promiscuity in the underclass. It would be inconceivable to her that degeneracy was in fact a lifestyle choice. The doomed have no time for the formulation of career plans and pension provisions. All that mattered was tonight, tomorrow and possibly the day after. That was more than enough to be getting on with.

Following the sound of a text alert Brian checked his ancient telephone again. On the tiny screen there was a message from the same unknown caller: *WHERE ARE YOU?* He shook his head at the effrontery of moneygrubbers and misery-mongers calling him outside of business hours, deleted the message and returned the phone to his pocket. He hadn't noticed the occupant of the seat adjacent to him until she patted him on the knee.

'Is anyone sat here? I saw it was empty so I just sat down.'

'Well there was, but I can't see him about. If I was you I'd just sit there until someone tells you to shift.'

'Right. I'll move out the road if he comes back.'

Brian was unable to parse the expression on her pretty oval face as she sipped at a large vodka and coke. From large sapphire eyes she stared at the antics of the carousers on the moiling dance floor with neither amusement nor displeasure. Unseasonably dressed in a flattering white two-piece suit and with immaculately distressed hair, she struck Brian as someone unfamiliar to Least and waiting for someone to arrive and something to happen. Her stylish dress sense and emotional aridity were at variance with everyone else in the room. Brian surmised that she was romantically involved with either a drug dealer or a local hard man and awaiting his arrival. It would be prudent to ignore her and perhaps dissociate from her completely. He drained his glass and then stood to make his way to the bar.

'Will you get me one?'

Brian turned to stare into her hypnotic eyes. She was about his age, possibly younger by a couple of years. Her skin had been toasted by regular applications of artificial UV and she was pleasingly ample in the belly and bosom. He narrowed his eyes

340

in suspicion, immediately sensing an agenda. Women like this didn't importune men as underwhelming as he; unless from a sense of mischief or malevolence. But her perfectly confected face betrayed nothing.

'Er... yep. No problem. Are you waiting for someone?'

'No. I'm here on my own. My name's Patricia but people call me Pat. What's yours?'

'Brian.'

'Right then, Brian. I'll have a large vodka and coke. You get this one and I'll get the next. Where are the toilets in here?'

'Walk past Elvis Dalek and you can't miss them.'

She removed her jacket, placed it over the back of Brian's chair and then pulled a pristine mackintosh from under her own. This she draped over the back of her own chair, taking care to lift the hem from the grubby parquet flooring. She nodded, exhaled slowly and then smiled at Brian.

'No one'll be pinching our seats now. I'll see you back here in a minute.'

'Right-ho... any crisps or anything?'

'I'm all right. I might fancy calling at the chipper later on though.'

'Fair enough.'

Brian dodged and excuse-me'd his way to the bar feeling very peculiar. An adrenaline charge coursed around his body. At the bar, Wesley raised his eyebrows at him in amused surprise whilst Brian shrugged his shoulders and shook his head in bemusement. He was as astonished as Wesley at this turn of events. On the dance floor, a now shirtless Spex danced alone, his spasmodic jerks suggestive of a tonic clonic seizure. Zorb and the other doorman kept an eye on the cavorter but maintained a respectful distance, aware that Spex was unlikely to be intimidated by strongarm tactics and probably hospitalise at least one of them. His reputation as a dangerous headbanger had blossomed subsequent to his discharge from the loony bin.

Whilst at the bar, Brian was seized by an ungovernable urge to void his bladder and signalled Wesley to keep an eye on the drinks he'd purchased. Wesley nodded, winked and squeaked that they'd be there for him upon his return. Brian braced himself to negotiate a trajectory through the pheronomal scrum of bodies. Having arrived in the gentlemen's conveniences relatively unscathed, he ignored the conclave of weed smokers in the cubicle behind him, unzipped and waited. The face of the young man next to him was impassive, but suddenly he turned to Brian and gave tongue.

'Tell you what, kidder.'

Mid-piss and feeling a pleasurable catharsis, Brian turned to face his inquisitor.

'Yeah?'

'Someone in this pub has got kidney problems.'

'How do you know that? Are you a doctor?'

'Am I fuckers like. But I'm telling you now, the piss in this trough smells like fuckin' Sugar Puffs. Whoever's been stood here before us needs to go see a fuckin' doctor. He's not well whoever he is. Prob'ly a pisshead. I bet his shit stinks like Manchester tart as well. Me dad's was like that before he carked it. That's what happens if you drink all the fuckin' time and don't eat.'

'You've missed your calling in life. You'd be a brilliant nurse.'

'You reckon? Fuck that pal. Too much shift work. I'm all right where I am, me. Laters.'

The tyro diagnostician zipped up and departed. Brian

finished up, and went back to the bar. Zorb's bull-like back obstructed his view of Wesley and the round of drinks he was desperate to take back to the table. Gently, and with no little trepidation, he tapped Zorb on the shoulder. Zorb's huge head swivelled slowly round and then lowered to meet Brian's simper with a blood-curdling grimace.

'Orrite Brian? Long time no see. I heard you'd moved back round here. How's it going pal?'

Brian nervously blinked. Coming from Zorb, even a casual pleasantry could sound like a death threat. In the best laddish voice he could muster Brian explained that he and the long-haired one had had a bit of a disagreement and decided to call it a day. Zorb nodded slowly and placed a giant hairy hand on Brian's shoulder.

'I know what you've been through, pal.'

'Do you?'

'Oh aye. Getting the white fiver happens to the best of us at some time or another. Most of the cunts are more trouble than they're worth if you ask me.'

'You've surprised me, there Zorb. I couldn't imagine you having trouble of any kind, never mind woman trouble.'

'Oh aye. That's why up until recently I was only shagging the married ones. They're less trouble and they go home after you've finished with them. Dead straightforward. I've got to behave myself now though. I'm spoken for.'

'Oh yeah? Who's the lucky lady then?'

'Tracey. She used to knock about with your Elaine. How is your Elaine by the way? Is she still a stuck-up cunt?'

'Oh yeah. She's living in the big city now. Engaged and everything.'

'Tell her I said all the best. Nice to see you back round here

343

Brian. Look after yourself kid.'

'Will do.'

When Brian returned to the table Pat seemed to be lost in reverie, but smiled when he handed her the vodka and coke. He tentatively observed that he hadn't seen her in here before and wondered if she was new to the area. Pat disclosed that she had been resident in Least for a year and was currently looking to purchase a house. The sale of her deceased parents' home had afforded her the largess to purchase a property outright in an area where house prices were comparatively low. Brian learned that she was a customer service manager for a water company and she would be the beneficiary of a handsome pension upon her retirement. Brian noted that she neither swore nor smoked, maintained an air of reserve but was candid about her ambitions. She was as self-assured as someone who had arrived for an interview for a post she knew she'd already secured. Brian was intrigued and a little fearful of her.

Pat drained her glass, enquired if Brian would like another drink and then took their glasses to the bar. Brian watched her admirable derriere disappear into the mass of boozers crowding the bar and speculated upon this enigmatic woman's agenda. He could only presume that she was feeling lonely and wished to while away a few hours with someone she had mistook to be the sanest person in The Long Pig.

His telephone rang again, the same number as earlier. Whoever this bastard was he was certainly persistent. It was almost midnight and he was still trying to pester him. He studied the number in the hope of memorising it then pocketed his telephone when Pat returned from the bar. She seemed genuinely interested in his now defunct career as a social worker and expressed her sympathies upon learning of Brian's wretched

344

schism from Helen. Then, as last orders were called, she drained her glass and placed her hand firmly on Brian's crotch.

'I think you and me should be going to the chipper, Brian.'

Brian's eyes widened. It's a truism that people who are having sex for the last time are unaware that it is indeed the last time. Given that he had an appointment with his tobacco tin tomorrow, Brian was most certainly aware that this was his final assignation and was determined to enjoy it. Pat was already through the exit door as he scrambled to don his coat and scarf. She walked in the direction of the Chinese takeaway and turned to suggest something to eat before going back to her place. Brian nodded eagerly, entered the Chinese and purchased two fish suppers. They ate and talked whilst walking, but there was no thawing of Pat's self-collectedness. Brian sensed that this encounter would be purely transactional, a satisfaction of need leading to an awkward parting in the morning. After a period of enforced celibacy this was something Brian could live with. Just watching Pat eat mushy peas made him tumescent.

Pat opened the front door of a darkened semi-detached house that smelled strongly of curry. She turned on the hall light and then invited Brian to follow her into the lounge. Sprawled on the couch was a tousled figure dressed in a soiled T-shirt, cardigan and jeans. He casually eyed *Match Of The Day* whilst dunking a sandwich of two digestive biscuits into a mug of tea. Brian could not have been more frightened and confused if the man on the sofa sported three heads.

'Y'orrite pal? D'you want a brew?'

This friendly but utterly confounding overture prompted Pat to discharge a volley of surprisingly graphic expletives at the prone figure. He completely ignored Pat and nodded amiably at Brian.

'D'you like football pal?'

'Not really. Not much of a sports fan at all if truth be known.'

'She's never bothered with it either. Have you cocker?'

Pat's tanned face began to redden as she unleashed another cannonade of insults, warning the recumbent figure that if he didn't shift his bone-idle arse off that fucking settee she'd cut his fucking dick off with the bread knife. Although usually slow off the mark and woozied by drink, Brian quickly discerned that the shabbily-dressed figure on the couch was Pat's husband. He had no idea of the differences that had sundered them or why they were unhappily co-habiting, but he knew that it was time to beat a hasty exit before things got even stranger.

'Look Pat. I'll leave you to it. It's getting a bit late.'

Pat affixed Brian with a terrifying stare.

'Don't you fucking move. We've come here to do some shagging and that's what we're going to do. You? You bone-idle twat? Get off that bleedin' settee and get up them fuckin' stairs if you want to keep your bollocks.'

'Can't I watch the end of this game? It's nearly finished.'

'Get the fuck upstairs or else.'

Pat's husband rose reluctantly from the settee, yawned expansively, stretched his arms towards the ceiling and ambled through the living room door. Pat waited until he had departed then removed her coat and jacket and went into the kitchen. Brian hovered uncertainly, wondering whether to make a dash for the front door before this situation became even seamier. His libido had plummeted and it occurred to him that should this encounter not be concluded to Pat's satisfaction he might be subject to the ministrations of a bread knife. To Brian's relief she returned with a bottle of wine and two glasses. Pat instructed him to sit on the settee still warm from her husband's body and began pouring the wine. At the sound of movement upstairs she immediately ceased pouring and listened intently, her large eyes boring into the stippled ceiling. She whispered conspiratorially to Brian.

'I think he's having a shit.'

She continued to listen intently, and then satisfied that her husband had finally retired to bed she handed Brian a glass of Chianti.

'Right then, Brian. Drop your keks and undercrackers.'

'Look, Pat. We don't have to do this.'

'Don't be daft. You can't buy the chips, walk me home and not leave here without a smile on your face. Come on. Just sit where you are and drop your keks.'

Brian sheepishly did as he was bidden. Pat removed her pants and underwear to reveal a rounded but taut belly and long browned legs. Brian became immediately interested in the proceedings again.

'Right Brian. So we don't waste any time I'm going to get myself going if you don't mind. It'll be quicker if I do it.'

'Whatever you think's best.'

'Good lad. I'll not be a minute.'

Pat closed her eyes, opened her legs and pounded furiously at her pudenda with her middle finger. Brian sat back, taking a scholarly interest in this display of female self-love. After two minutes Pat's vitreous blue eyes suddenly opened and she nodded at Brian.

'Right then matey. Ready for lift-off?'

'Well if it isn't too much trouble...'

'This won't tek a minute. You look like you're going to go off like a bottle of pop.'

Pat straddled Brian and inserted him into her, slowly rocking her body whilst sipping at her glass. Brian closed his eyes and

347

surrendered himself to the attentions of this exquisite female. She was a triumph of middle-aged beauty and seemed to have fallen from the pages of a top shelf magazine. Pat removed her shirt and brassiere and tossed them carelessly onto the carpet.

'Do you want to have a feel of my tits as well?'

'Would you mind?'

'Not a bit. It'll pass the time on a bit for you won't it?'

'Er yeah. I suppose it would really.'

He reached up and slowly caressed her firm, tanned and very kissable breasts. Pat moaned quietly and upped the tempo of their coupling. As she accelerated her jouncing Brian began to feel distinctly queasy. Whether it was the volume of alcohol he'd imbibed or the surfeit of greasy comestibles sitting uneasily on his stomach he didn't know, but he was feeling very uncomfortable. Beads of sweat appeared on his top lip, his stomach roiled and he was confronted by the appalling possibility of vomiting mid-coitus. He held Pat by the waist to slow her movements and his eyes pleaded for her to dismount, but Pat's grunts and sighs suggested that she was not to be foiled in her mission to achieve le petit mort. She closed her eyes tightly and jutted out her chin, at which point Brian disgorged the contents of his stomach all over her gravity-defying chest whilst noisily breaking wind. Pat opened her eyes and stared down in disbelief at the stinking detritus dripping over her nipples and down towards her navel.

'Oh. You. Fuckin', Dirty. Bastard. I'm going to fucking kill you.'

'Oh dear God I'm so sorry…'

'What the bleedin' hell do you think you're playing at? Is this how you get your rocks off? Upchucking on women you're shagging?'

'God no, absolutely not…'

'Fucking dirty bastard you're nowt else.'

At that point Pat's husband craned his neck from behind the living room door. His snort of disgust perfectly synopsised the ugliness of the situation. Brian's own feelings of horror and self-loathing were so profound as to be inexpressible. He couldn't even conclude his final sexual encounter without provoking revulsion and anger. Pat bawled at her husband to fetch a towel from the kitchen whilst slowly extricating herself from the penitent and very smelly Brian. Pat's husband returned with a towel, tossed it to his wife and gave Brian an appraising stare.

'Well at least he hasn't vommed on the carpet. Good job as well. It's not paid for yet.'

'Fuck the carpet. My tits stink. And he does. Dirty bastard he's nowt else.'

Pat's husband stared at Brian and shook his head in amused resignation.

'Fucking Brad Shitpit here. Serves you right, pal. Anyone who has fish, chips and peas before having a lucky bag is asking for trouble.'

'How do YOU know he's had fish, chips and peas?'

'Easy. They're all over your tits, you dozy bitch. The peas look like they're from that Chinese near The Pig. They're not bad as it happens. A bit of a waste really.'

Pat glared at her husband and ordered him from the room. Brian eased himself from the settee, corrected his dress, made his way to the front door and muttered his final apologies before commencing the trudge home. Before his departure Pat gave him a valedictory kick in the backside. Brian nodded and headed into the early hours.

SUNDAY

Upon arriving home Brian tore off his sodden clothes and stood under the shower for a full twenty minutes. He washed away the scent of vomit, the fragrance of Pat's crotch and his own stale sweat. Less easily eliminated was his mortifying shame. He donned his threadbare dressing gown, lit two candles, poured a sizeable vodka and orange juice and slumped onto the settee. Sipping slowly at his cocktail he mused upon the previous night's events and concluded that perhaps it was just as well that his sexual life was now over. How he had stumbled into such a weird ménage and events had taken such an ignominious turn he had no idea. There had been articles in the quality Sundays of couples who were together but apart, living in separate homes but spending their free time in blissful union. Pat and her husband had bucked this trend by leading separate lives whilst living together, their co-existence infused with loathing and contempt. This arrangement might be predicated upon either economic necessity or some darker interdependence, but in any event on open marriage seemed a dismal business. Had he observed Helen being impaled on another man's erect penis he would have contemplated killing himself well before now.

He stood, yawned, and then ambled over to his collection of compact discs, pining for something elegiac and dramatique. He chose *Sketches Of Spain*, mixed another screwdriver and then pondered the choice of music appropriate to the ingestion of euthanising medication. Even after almost forty years of music fandom he still hadn't tabulated a deathbed playlist. He leaned back and closed his eyes, drinking in the music with the same languor as he sipped at his cocktail. The fragility of tone and choice of notes by the trumpeter always seemed to make sense in an otherwise senseless world. Towards the end of 'Solea' he could he hear voices outside and someone attempting to open the front door. He shook his head in resignation. On the very last day of his life he was going to be burgled by one of the many nocturnal animals prowling Least in the early hours.

He leapt from the settee and peered through the blinds of the living room. If the burglars saw that he was awake then this might deter them, although this was by no means certain. He recoiled when he saw his sister Elaine vainly grappling with a key to the front door. Her fiancé stood behind her, smoking furiously and urging her to open the door before they both froze to death. Brian opened the door and was immediately slapped across the face by his sister. He reeled and then staggered backwards as Elaine and Dave pushed past him to stand in front of the flame-effect gas fire.

'Do you want to tell me why you haven't answered your phone all night?'

'What did you do that for?'

'I've been ringing and ringing. I've sent you texts. You didn't answer a single fucking one of them. Not one. Give me your phone.'

Brian handed Elaine his ancient device whilst rubbing his face. She quickly raised the call registry and pointed an accusatory finger at the telephone number that Brian had repeatedly ignored.

'There must be ten missed calls on here. Why didn't you answer them?'

'I didn't recognise the number.'

351

'It was me you fucking idiot.'

'Well I didn't know that did I? You never ring me anyway. You could have been anyone. And what's so bloody urgent that you turn up here at this time of night? And how have you got a key to my house?'

'It's Dad's.'

'What's he given it to you for?'

'He didn't. He's dead. He had a heart attack when he came in from the club. You need to come and see Mum. Now.'

Brian's eyes widened in shock and his legs buckled underneath him. He had always regarded his father as an immortal, as permanent as misery, a creature unconstrained by the straightjacket of time. This was Derek Paget, his incorrigible, unkillable father. For him to die was an illogicality; and yet he had. The fact of this made him want to vomit again.

Tears trickled slowly down Brian's silent face. Dave pulled out a pack of cigarettes and gently suggested that Brian sit down and take a minute before getting dressed. Someone's dad dying was not a cool thing to happen. Elaine checked her phone whilst Brian smoked and stared unseeing at the guttering candles. Dave whispered that Derek had gone to the working men's club and returned home around seven o'clock. On returning home he had complained to Jean that he was feeling a bit rifty and had gone to bed early. An hour later, Jean had wandered into their bedroom looking for her best slippers and was surprised that Derek's usually sterterous snoring wasn't rattling the windows. Mildly concerned by the absence of noise issuing from the bed she had stood over him and shook him gently. He had gone, but at least Jean had located her best slippers. She was glad she'd found them in the bathroom. She didn't wish to be seen in her usual scruffier pair when the ambulance arrived.

Brian dressed, extinguished the candles and trudged after Dave and Elaine. When he arrived at chez Paget, Jean was in her usual chair. She was smoking pensively but seemed calm, even beatific. She raised her eyebrows in mild disapprobation at Brian but stayed silent. Dave put the kettle on whilst Elaine checked her phone. Brian sat down heavily, dizzied and nauseous. He was trapped in the middle of a whirling cyclorama of images, memories and emotions extending from early childhood to the present and wondered whether he should go to the bathroom to void his stomach again. Dave brought him a cup of tea and hovered at a respectful distance until Elaine ordered him into the kitchen. She frowned at Brian before going upstairs to find a blanket to cover her mother's withered legs. Jean sniffed and a catarrhal cough irrupted from her chest. She regarded Brian through tired red eyes.

'Last time I saw summat like you I was on the ghost train at the fair.'

'I've felt better.'

'Your dad was hoping to go to the club for a pint with you on Christmas Day. You'll have to go on your own now.'

'Is there anything you need me to do?'

'What for?'

'For the…'

'Elaine and Dave have got it in hand. We're looking at next Friday. Dave's already talked to the steward at the club about putting butties on afterwards. Your dad wants cremation. They're always quicker than burials. His mates can get on the ale quicker afterwards.'

'How are you feeling? It must have been terrible for you.'

A shadow passed over Jean's lean, ashen features and she reached for another cigarette. Then she shook her head.

'Not really. When you get to me and your dad's age and you sort of expect it. I'm just glad he didn't end up in one of them care homes. Pissing hisself all the while and not knowing who he was. You wouldn't wish that on anyone, never mind your dad.'

'True. I've seen that sort of thing and it's not pleasant.'

They sat in silence for a full ten minutes. Brian wondered what his father might have been thinking as he lay in bed before his departure, whether he was in pain or terrified by the prospect of unbeing. He had never known his father to be afraid of anything. The possibility of Derek dying fearful and alone enfeebled him and he wished more than anything that he could have been present at his father's final moments. Elaine and Dave made their excuses and left, promising to return when they'd had some sleep. Jean yawned and lit another cigarette. Brian remained rooted to the couch, paralysed by grief. Jean nodded at him as though she understood her son's inner turmoil.

'Do you want to move back in here?'

'Move back in? Why?'

'Well it's your house.'

'How d'you make that out?'

'Your dad left it to you in his will.'

Brian sighed, raised his eyes to the ceiling, shook his head and then smiled gently at his mother. Even from beyond the grave Derek was able to foment his peculiar havoc.

'It doesn't work like that, Mam. You can't just hand over a council property to someone else, no matter how long you've lived in it. It still belongs to the council.'

'What are you on about? Me and your dad bought this place years ago.'

'Eh?'

'We bought it off the housing.'

'What? You mean the right to buy thingie back in the eighties?'

'That were it. We only paid about three thousand quid for it. It's worth a lot more than that now mind.'

Brian stared at his mother in stupefaction as she continued her cigarette. It was perfectly possible that Jean and Derek had purchased their home without his knowledge as they never discussed financial matters with either of their offspring. But this bolt from the blue provoked a number of questions. He had always assumed in the event of their passing, Elaine would be the co-beneficiary of their parents' estate. Given her obsession with self-enrichment she would not look favourably upon his sole ownership of the parental pile. Apart from anything else his mother was very much alive and in need of somewhere to live. The prospect of co-habiting with his mother for even a day was anathema to him. He wasn't in the mood to pursue the matter as it would only further amplify his melancholia. He shook his head and studied the cooling tea in his beaker. Jean drained the contents of her cup and gazed evenly at him.

'Look, you. This house is yours to do what you want with. Your dad always knew that Elaine would be all right. She's always looked after number one and she's done well for herself. Her and Dave have got more money than sense these days.'

'Well that wouldn't take very much would it? Fifteen quid would just about cover it.'

'Shut it a minute. Your dad always worried that you'd end up on the bones of your arse when you got older. I'll bet you've not got two ha'ppenies to rub together right now. Am I right?'

'Well it's fair to say that I'm in a fair amount of trouble moneywise.'

'Just like your dad always said you would be. So he left this

355

place to you. He said to me that whatever happened after he kiffed it you would always have a roof over your head and a few bob in your pocket.'

'Seriously?'

'Have you not been listening? Your dad always knew you'd never amount to much. And he was right.'

'But what about our Elaine? Surely she's entitled to half the value of the place?'

'And your dad said that she's not having it. Don't you be worrying about her. There's twelve thousand quid coming her way next week. She's happy with that. What I don't want is you going and telling her that you're getting the same. You need to keep your gob shut about it. You know what she's like when she starts.'

'Twelve bloody grand? Each? How did my dad get twenty-four bloody grand to give away?'

'How d'you think? By working all his life and being careful with his money, that's how. He was never a big spender was he? He only took me out twice a year. New Year's Eve and my birthday. If he remembered it, like.'

'Hang on a minute Mam. You need somewhere to live. This is your home you know. You own this place.'

'I'm moving in with Aunt Florrie.'

'Aunt Florrie? Prestatyn Aunt Florrie?'

'Oh aye. She's got an empty bedroom in her bungalow and she's been on her own for years. I've got mine and your dad's pensions to live on so I'm all right. There's bingo three times a week, plenty of cafes and a market every Sunday. That'll do me. I want to see the bright lights before I kick the bucket.'

'It's Prestatyn, Mam, not Las sodding Vegas.'

'Give over you. It'll see me right. You can do what want with

356

this place when I bugger off. I won't be taking much with me the week after next. It'll only tek an hour for me to shift out.'

'Good God. I can't believe I'm hearing this.'

'Believe what you bloody well like for me. Now shift yourself. I'm buggered after the night I've had. I could sleep on a bloody clothes line.'

'I bet you could. I'll come over later when you get up.'

'No rush. There's all day not touched yet. D'you want your Sunday dinner? I've got a joint in. It was for your dad. No point in wasting it. If I know you're coming I'll get some gravy on.'

'We'll see. But get some sleep if you can.'

Brian's mind was a maelstrom as he walked slowly through the small-hours darkness. At one point he wondered whether he was asleep and dreaming this staggering volte-face in his fortunes. It was all simply too much to process, too many options for him to consider, each of them caroming against the other. He felt feather-light, a diaphanous thing, something made of sound, a creature made of music. He was now a property owner, someone with collateral, someone for whom debt would now be a previous rather than present nightmare. He had agency in the world. He was a single, relatively wealthy middle-aged man who could do as he pleased. He had options.

Options. Choices. Prospects. Words that only yesterday belonged to the lexicon of another language.

Perhaps he could continue to rent his current home whilst claiming housing benefit and dole, sell his parents' house, buy a pension with most of the proceeds and then spend the remainder on holidays in places where the fags were cheap and the sun glittered on the Med. Or perhaps he could privately rent the house to a suitable tenant, use the income from the property to supplement his benefits and then join the shadow army of labourers working in the black economy.

Perhaps, perhaps…

The only certainty was that he was not going to kill himself now. Self-destruction would be a disgusting mockery of those who submitted to the void because they were out of alternatives. Brian's alternatives now seemed numberless. He began weeping again as he struggled to gain egress to his house. The faulty lock was a poignant reminder of his father's hopelessness at practical tasks. Brian realised that he would be grieving for a very long time.

Upon entering the house he strode into the kitchen and took the tobacco tin from its berth on a cupboard shelf. He stared at the contents, contemplating the enormity of what he had managed to avert by only hours. It was obvious now that despite a lifetime of corrosive jibes and general dispraise, the cantankerous old sod had loved him deeply and had plotted his son's deliverance from misery. He was a man who had never failed to surprise, and not always pleasantly; but this was his greatest trick yet. He had managed to conjure nothing less than his son's salvation whilst being dead for some seven hours. Brian shook his head in wry disbelief, wept a little more and then deposited the medication into the swing-bin. Even Splatch would be amazed by this turn of events, and he didn't amaze easily.

He peered through the blinds of the living room window. It wouldn't be light for another four hours. He was adrenalized by grief, euphoria and indecision. He knew that sleep would be impossible unless he imbibed something cool, wet and concussive. He poured a very large vodka and orange juice, chose a much-thumbed but unread novel from the bookshelf and then slumped onto the settee. He read the glowing eulogies to the novel penned by other celebrity wordsmiths and then fell soundly asleep before finishing the last of the vodka.

He was awoken by an insistent banging on the front door. Fingers of thin sunlight streamed into the living room as Brian peered groggily through the blinds into the street. A shivering figure in a puffa jacket, ripped jeans, boots and Chet Baker teeth waved at him whilst pointing at a suitcase. Brian shook his head in resignation and opened the door to The Dame Of Disorder.

'Hiya, Brian.'

'All right Tracey? And to what do I owe the pleasure?'

'I heard about your dad. Sorry pal.'

'I think it was quick and painless. That's all you could wish for isn't it?'

'Oh aye. Now are you going to leave me stood here like a chip waiting for vinegar or are you going to ask me in?'

'Sorry. Come on in. And why have you got a suitcase with you?'

'I'll tell you in a minute. You won't believe this Brian.'

'Oh I think I might…'

Tracey wheeled her suitcase into the living room and dragged chipped fingernails through her unruly curls. She smiled broadly at Brian.

'Have you got owt to drink? I could sup the piss of a nettle after the morning I've had. And I'm celebrating. My luck's changed. I'm out of this shithole for good, me.'

'Well that's worth drinking to.'

'Watch it you, you cheeky bastard.'

Tracey followed Brian into the kitchen and breathlessly related the events of the last forty-eight hours. She disclosed that two mornings previously Zorb had left early to go to Yorkshire. There was a Staffordshire pit bull pup he'd had his eye on and was determined to purchase before the breeder increased the

359

price of the mutt. When Zorb had departed for Yorkshire she had again been forced by Zorb's son to sexually abase herself. On this occasion it was an act so humiliating that her already profound shame and self-loathing couldn't be effaced by the two bottles of cheap wine she had quickly imbibed after the loathsome boy had left for school.

Barely dressed, tear-sodden and as crazy as a snake, she had staggered to the local medical centre to demand strong medication from the horrified receptionists. Two general practitioners emerged from their consulting rooms to investigate the commotion. A young female doctor then ushered Tracey into her consulting room and gently interrogated her. The doctor frowned, called a girlfriend in social services and requested she come immediately to the surgery. As Tracey related the full horror of her plight to the professionals, the social worker rang a women's refuge in Manchattan and demanded to speak to the manager of the facility. After a heated exchange between the manager and the social worker Tracey was accepted as an emergency referral. The social worker herself offered to transport Tracey to the facility over the weekend on condition that Tracey met her at a location away from her home. She had no intention of meeting either Zorb or his son unless accompanied by a police officer, and given that Zorb's son was a minor with whom Tracey was having regular sexual relations that scenario could become very messy.

'So... where's Zorb in all this? He surely must know something's up if you've packed your case this morning?'

'That bastard? He hasn't come home from last night. I was expecting that. He was working in The Pig last night.'

'I'm aware of that.'

'Well you know the script with him then, don't you? Some

slapper's come on strong to him and he's spent the night at her place. He does it regular, the dirty bastard.'

'What about his son?'

'That fat lazy fucker is still in his pit. Wait till they find out I've done one. Zorb'll go ballistic, but fuck 'em Brian. It's all about me now.'

Brian smiled broadly as Tracey sipped pensively at her neat vodka. The fates had intervened to offer them both a third act in the dismal farces that were their lives. Whilst enjoying another drink Tracey enunciated her rather over-ambitious plans for the coming year. She would knock the ale and weed on the head, acquire a flat in Manchattan, learn to drive, get a posh job and then marry a bloke who wasn't a fucking barmpot. Her stratagem seemed gloriously simple and completely unrealisable. Brian nodded and raised his glass in salute.

'I'll drink to that. It seems like we've both had good things happen to us just recently.'

'Fuck me, Brian. Your dad's just died. I don't know what you'd call bad news.'

'Ah, but what he left behind? You wouldn't believe it. I'm not joking when I tell you he saved my life.'

'Did he? Ooh. That's all right then in't it?'

'Yeah. It is.'

'So… what are you going to be doing with yourself then?'

'No idea. I only know what I'm not going to do. Something I was going to do today actually.'

'If you ask me, you need to stop wanking yourself daft in here and get yourself a proper woman. You're getting too old for all that malarkey.'

'I'll bear that in mind. What time are you being picked up?'

'In about half an hour. I said I'd be outside the garage. She said she'll give me a ring five minutes before she turns up.'

'I hope I never see you round here again Tracey.'

'You won't, Brian. This place can go and fuck itself. Cheers.'

Brian's telephone rang. He raised his eyebrows at Tracey and glanced at the number before staring at the ceiling. This was a call he'd been expecting.

'Good morning, Kali. And how are we today?'

'You're a shitbag you, Brian Paget.'

Tracey giggled and pointed accusingly at Brian. Brian shook his head, grinning as he did so.

'You don't sound too happy this morning.'

'I've lost my bloody job because of you. What did you think you were playing at?'

'All I did was tweak the assessments to make sure they were consistent with a decent minimum of care provision. I didn't sign them off. I think you'll find that that was your job.'

'Oh I know that, Brian. I know that. And the chief exec does. He rang me up yesterday. On a Saturday as well, and I'm always busy on Saturdays.'

'That must have been unpleasant.'

'Oh, it was Brian. Believe me, it was. He wants to see me Monday morning. He wants to see you as well.'

'I don't have go and see him or anyone else. Let him ring me if he wants to speak to me. I didn't sign off those care packages. I didn't do anything other than my job. It's game over for the pair of us but who cares?'

'I do, you bloody shitbag. That's my career over with. You fucked me Brian. You fucked me.'

'No I didn't, Kali. You fucked yourself. Oversight is everything. I'm sorry but that's the way it is. At least Paul gets a shot at the job now. He should have had it years ago if you ask me.'

It was Tracey's turn to raise her eyebrows as Brian suddenly

362

ended the call.

'Bloody hell Brian. She didn't sound pleased at all with you. What've you been up to?'

Brian dismissed Tracey's enquiry with a brief shake of his head. Kali and everyone else from his former life were now in the past, so distant from him that they seemed light years away. His outlook, concerns and ambitions were now focused purely upon trying to immerse himself fully into his new life and staying out of trouble. He made a mental note to visit Barry at the loan company and the horsey woman at the bank as soon as possible. Despite the impending trauma of his father's funeral, by this time next week life would be considerably more bearable. He took Tracey's empty glass from her.

'One for the long and winding road?'

'Go on then. I don't think she'll be here for another half an hour.'

Brian entered the kitchen, cued a Thelonius Monk CD on the beatbox and prepared another cocktail and another shot of vodka for Tracey. When he returned to the living room Tracey was staring in terror at the front door. He glanced quizzically at the door and then at Tracey.

'He's fuckin' out there, Brian.'

'Who is?'

'Zorb.'

'But he doesn't know you're here does he?'

Tracey sighed heavily and her features crumpled.

'This morning I told that nosey cow of a next door neighbour that I was going to call on you to pay my respects for your dad and then take myself on a coach holiday to Wales. I bet the dozy mare has told him where I was going when he came in from shagging someone. Oh fuck, Brian. This could put the mockers on everything. He's going to fucking kill me.'

Brian gave Tracey her vodka and placed his drink as

363

carefully as his trembling hand would allow on the occasional table. He put his fingers to his lips in silent entreaty to Tracey and then peered through the living room blinds. Zorb caught his eye and snarled. Brian recoiled in horror and then pointed Tracey to the back door of the house.

'Go through there. It takes you onto the backs and then onto the main road. Go that way and he won't see you. Even he won't try to do you over in front of passing traffic.'

Tracey began to shake and her dark eyes dilated to the size of hubcaps. She then quickly swallowed the vodka and began lugging her suitcase to the back door. Zorb's granite fist slammed against the front door as he roared a command to Tracey to join him on the pavement. She stared imploringly at Brian whilst he inhaled short staccato breaths and pointed her way out of the property. The thudding against the front door grew louder.

'He'll fucking kill us, Brian.'

'No he won't. But when you get out onto the main road call the police. If they know it's Zorb they'll come straight away. Get going while you still can.'

She scurried through the back door whilst Brian remained in the living room, greedily swallowing the contents of his glass. He was now pleasantly drunk and suffused with a Zen-like calm. Tracey would make her escape and call the police. Zorb would be manhandled into a squad car, the truth of his son's squalid relationship with his former partner would be investigated, Tracey might finally find some stability and Brian himself would be free to live out the rest of his life in relative tranquillity. He might even enjoy the lemon cheesecake he'd purchased the previous day. Suddenly life seemed beautifully simple. And then the front door lock that his father had so assiduously bodged fell onto the parquet flooring. Brian closed his eyes as Zorb entered the living room. Dressed in jeans and a T-shirt that barely contained his massive sweaty chest, he was even more

364

intimidating than when dressed in a tuxedo.

'Right then. Where is she?'

'Tracey? She left a while ago. Not here I'm afraid.'

Zorb assumed a prissy effeminate voice.

'Not here I'm afraid, not here I'm afraid. Well if she isn't here where the fuck is she then?'

'I don't know.'

'You fucking lying bastard.'

Zorb pushed past Brian and ascended the stairs. Brian could hear him crashing around the small bedrooms to discern if his errant partner was hiding somewhere. Zorb then returned to the living room and grabbed Brian by the throat.

'Right pal. You fucking know where she's gone and you're going to fucking well tell me.'

'And I'm telling you that I don't know.'

Zorb shook his head slowly and relinquished his grip on Brian's throat. Brian sagged in relief and slowly rubbed the area crimsoned by Zorb's death grip. Zorb stared uncomprehendingly at Brian before hulking towards the front door. He then turned on his heel and smashed Brian full in the face. The force of the impact was such that Brian's neck snapped instantly. He was dead before he collapsed to the floor. Zorb tried to rouse Brian before shaking his head in contempt at his victim's inability to absorb such a relatively harmless blow. He then re-entered the pallid morning sunshine and wished he'd brought a coat. Brian's mother hadn't been able to sleep so she had inserted a joint of beef into the oven. Brian would enjoy it with gravy, potatoes and peas when he called around later. It was nice to have someone to cook for now Derek had gone. There was no point in wasting good meat.